SCARLET RIDERS

SCARLET RIDERS

Pulp Fiction Tales of the Mounties

Edited by
Don Hutchison

Mosaic Press
Oakville, ON - Buffalo, NY

Canadian Cataloguing in Publication Data

Main entry under title:

The scarlet riders: pulp fiction tales of the mounties

ISBN 0-88962-647-2

1. Royal Canadian Mounted Police - Fiction. 2. Short stories, Canadian (English). * 3. Canadian fiction (English) - 20th century. * I. Hutchison, Don.

PS8323. M6S22 1998 C813'.010805 C98-930578-3
PR9197.35.M6S22 1998

Published by MOSAIC PRESS, P.O. Box 1032, Oakville, Ontario, L6J 5E9, Canada. Offices and warehouse at 1252 Speers Road, Units #1&2, Oakville, Ontario, L6L 5N9, Canada and Mosaic Press, 85 River Rock Drive, Suite 202, Buffalo, N.Y., 14207, USA.

Mosaic Press acknowledges the assistance of the Canada Council, the Ontario Arts Council and the Dept. of Canadian Heritage, Government of Canada, for their support of our publishing programme.

ISBN 0-88962-647-2
Printed and bound in Canada

MOSAIC PRESS, in Canada:
1252 Speers Road, Units #1&2,
Oakville, Ontario, L6L 5N9
Phone / Fax: (905) 825-2130
E-mail: cp507@freenet.toronto.on.ca

MOSAIC PRESS, in the USA:
85 River Rock Drive,
Suite 202, Buffalo, N.Y., 14207
Phone / Fax: 1-800-387-8992
E-mail: cp507@freenet.toronto.on.ca

MOSAIC PRESS in the UK and Europe:
DRAKE INTERNATIONAL SERVICES
Market House, Market Place,
Deddington, Oxford. OX15 OSF

Acknowledgments

The editor would like to express sincere appreciation to Peter Gallacher for his assistance in the preparation of this book. Thanks also to Hugh B. Cave, Don Daynard, Jamie Fraser, Peter Halasz, Lois Johnson, Neil Mechem, Will Murray, Talmage Powell, Robert Weinberg, Elwy Yost, and the Western Historical Manuscript Collection at the University of Missouri at Columbia, preservers of the Lester Dent Collection.

"Deadly Trek to Albertville" appeared in *Posse* magazine, March 1957. Revised version copyright 1998 by Talmage Powell. Reprinted by arrangement with the author.

"The Frozen Phantom" appeared in *Western Trails*, April 1933. Reprinted by arrangement with the author's literary executor, Will Murray.

"Spoilers of the Lost World" appeared in *North-West Romances*, Fall 1938. Copyright 1938 by Glen-Kel Publishing Co.

"White Water Run" appeared in *Western Story Magazine*, Feb. 14, 1942. Reprinted by arrangement with the author, Hugh B. Cave

"Red Snows appeared in *Thrilling Adventures*, February 1938. Copyright 1937 by Standard Magazines, Inc.

"The Driving Force" appeared in *Complete Northwest Magazine*, July 1938. Copyright 1938 by Northwest Publishing Company.

"Snow Ghost" appeared in *Western Trails*, May-June 1933. Reprinted by arrangement with the author's literary executor, Will Murray.

"Phantom Fangs" appeared in *North-West Romances*, Spring 1942. Copyright 1930 by Glen-Kel Publishing Co.

"The Dangerous Dan McGrew" appeared in *Ace-High Magazine*, March 2, 1931. Reprinted by arrangement with Mrs. Ryerson Johnson.

"Death Cache," previously unpublished, is printed here by special arrangement with the author's literary executor, Will Murray.

"Doom Ice" appeared in *North-West Romances*, Summer 1942. Copyright 1942 by Glen-Kel Publishing Co.

"The Valley of Wanted Men" appeared in *North-West Romances*, Spring 1940. Copyright 1940 by Glen-Kel Publishing Co.

**Scarlet Riders is dedicated
to the memory of
Ryerson "Johnny" Johnson
and
Sergeant John Flint Roy, R.C.M.P.**

Contents

Introduction: SCARLET FICTION .... Don Hutchison xi

DEADLY TREK TO ALBERTVILLE .... Talmage Powell 1

THE FROZEN PHANTOM .... Lester Dent 17

SPOILERS OF THE LOST WORLD .... Roger Daniels 41

WHITE WATER RUN .... Hugh B. Cave 85

RED SNOWS .... Harold F. Cruickshank 99

THE DRIVING FORCE .... Murray Leinster 117

SNOW GHOST .... Lester Dent 131

PHANTOM FANGS .... John Starr 159

THE DANGEROUS DAN McGREW ...... Ryerson Johnson 179

DEATH CACHE .... Lester Dent 197

DOOM ICE .... Dan O'Rourke 217

THE VALLEY OF WANTED MEN .... Frederick Nebel 235

Introduction
SCARLET FICTION

It was just over a century ago—1896 to be exact—that a man named Frank Munsey introduced a new concept in publishing—magazines of popular fiction printed on cheap paper that would be affordable to the poorest reader.

What became known as pulp magazines (so-called because of the shag-edged wood pulp paper on which they were printed) took off like a flashfire. With their vibrant-colored covers and their feverishly-paced escapist fiction, the pulps supplied daydreams for the masses for some sixty years before eventually being outgunned by paperback thrillers and television.

So successful were the pulp fiction factories that they churned out swarms of different titles between the world wars. Magazines ranged from the exploits of avengers like The Shadow and Doc Savage to detective, sport, science fiction, and aviation thrillers to such innovative exotics as *Pirate Stories, Railroad Stories,* even *Zeppelin Stories*—something for every appetite.

As author Robert Sampson once described it: "After the long days work, when the newspaper was discarded and the after-dinner silence set in (unbroken by the sound of radio or television), the adventure fiction magazine opened the walls of your well-known room. Out of the pages emerged a new world, hot with color. In that world, life was larger than the one you knew. The air bit more sweetly and the heart grew large out there.

"No longer were you another face at the mill, another farmer on the fields. You found yourself to be unique, competent in action, undaunted by the strange. You saw mountains thrusting at a foreign sky. You traveled beneath fleshy leaves along trails twisting toward strange destinations. You moved easily into the past, that black ocean."

Although the pulps are remembered chiefly for their mystery, science fiction and horror, far and away the most popular titles in their heyday were Westerns. In his book *The Pulp Western*, researcher John A. Dinan notes 184 separate magazines devoted exclusively to Western fiction—a list which he admits is incomplete.

In magazines with titles like *Blazing Western, Wild West Weekly,* and *Western Round-up*, legions of dusty Galahads blasted six-gun trails to pulpwood glory. Vast and forbidding, the landscape of the American frontier produced one of the most alluring blank canvases in popular culture. And pulp Westerns, with their visions of high adventure and idyllic romance set in that perilous dream world, gloried in the nostalgic appeal of the uncivilized—total escape from anything that might be crowding you.

As Western titles proliferated, attempts were made to diversify. Magazines with titles like *Big Chief Western, Rangeland Romances,* and *Masked Rider Western* were introduced in order to stand out from the crowd. One of the earliest of these mavericks was *North-West Stories* (later titled *North-West Romances*) produced by Fiction House publications beginning in 1925.

North-West Stories featured tales set entirely in the Canadian barrens, the Yukon, and other far north locales. The magazine's theme proved so popular that it went on to become one of the longest running titles in pulp history. Its success would eventually prompt rival publishers to produce their own versions—*Complete Northwest Novel Magazine* in 1935 and *Real Northwest* in 1937.

In their attempt to specialize the magazines' publishers seized upon a type of fiction that was already popular. The Yukon Gold Rush of 1897 had sent hordes of wealth seekers scurrying up the Yukon River and over mountain passes. In their wake writers like Jack London, Rex Beach, and Robert Service struck their own form of pay dirt with such books as *The Call of the Wild* and *The Trail of '98*. Service, a Whitehorse bank clerk, parlayed his talent for composing gold rush doggerel (*The Shooting of Dan McGrew,* etc.) into financial independence and world-wide fame as the "Bard of the Yukon" and the "Canadian Kipling." What followed was a literary avalanche of so-called "Northerns," populated by casts of picaresque traders, trappers, gold seekers, lumbermen, Indians, outlaws, and of course the flame-coated heroes of the Northwest Mounted Police.

"They always get their man." Those five words conjure up a powerful and romantic image of Canada's legendary national police force—one so appealing that the men of the Mounted became a staple image in novels, movies, poetry, theatre, opera, radio, comics, and mountains of merchandise produced throughout the world. Mountie figures appeared on pen knives, toy badges, bubble gum cards, pillow cases, cookie tins, postcards, wall paper, ceramic dolls and even cigarette ads and booze. In Britain there was a comic strip Mountie named Dick Daring and, in France, Jim Canada. It was, of course, the Americans, champions at mythologizing their own frontier history, who exploited the image to the fullest.

In the Golden Age of Hollywood scarlet-clad lawmen (usually filmed in black and white) may have even outdone Uncle Sam's G-Men as ubiquitous screen do-gooders. Movie Mounties ranged all the way from curly-topped baritones (Nelson Eddy) to vocally-challenged cartoon characters (Elmer Fudd). Most of the B-movie cowboys from Tom Mix to Buck Jones were often cast as Mounties, and such major stars as Errol Flynn, Tyrone Power, and Alan Ladd (who must have bypassed the force's height requirements) at one time or another sported the famous red tunic and dark blue riding britches.

Famed Western writer Zane Grey's contribution to the redcoat saga was his comic strip character King of the Royal Mounted, written by Grey's oldest son, Romer. Allan Lane played Sergeant King in a 1940 Saturday matinee serial which was such a hit with the popcorn crowd that he reprised the role two years later in Republic's follow-up hit *King of the Mounties*. These were but two of a host of cliff-hangers featuring men of the mounted as action folk heroes.

tion.

A contrast to Lester Dent's entertainingly improbable Mountie fictions, Murray Leinster's "The Driving Force" is a realistic portrayal of man against nature. Leinster (real name Will F. Jenkins) is best remembered as a top science fiction writer even though he wrote every conceivable type of pulp fiction, published nearly 100 books and made 1,500 magazine appearances in his lifetime. Although a Virginian by birth, Leinster's story is closest to Mountie fiction written by Canadians, in which the characters are not superhuman and in which the elements of nature are a greater menace than the miscreant being pursued.

It has been said that Canadian fiction tends to be a realistic literature which does not take kindly to heroes. Perhaps that's why so many of the improbable but entertaining Mountie stories were turned out by foreigners. The only bona fide Canadian in the *Scarlet Riders* crew is Harold F. Cruickshank, a prairie pioneer who once received the Alberta Achievement Award for his published stories of early life in that province. Cruickshank's by-line appeared in dozens of pulps from *Argosy* and *Battle Stories* to *Doc Savage* and *Wild West Weekly.* He specialized in air war stories but *Thrilling Adventures* carried his "White Phantom Wolf" series while *Ace High* featured a number of yarns set in the northern wilds starring a wolf cub protagonist named Keko. Despite Cruickshank's experiences as a genuine Canadian pioneer, "Red Snows" is a typical pulp tale of blizzard-bound Red Coat adventure.

Author attribution to our story "Phantom Fangs" represents a pulp phenomenon known as the publisher-owned "house name," used to mask the identity of other writers for various reasons. Interestingly, there really was a John Starr. His stories were rejected by the editors at Fiction House Magazines but they liked his name so much that they purchased it as a communal pseudonym.

One authentic name that should be familiar to mystery fans is that of Frederick Nebel. He was a one of the mainstays of the fabulous *Black Mask* magazine, home to such hard-boiled literary giants as Dashiell Hammett and Raymond Chandler. Nebel was a friend of Hammett's and his *Black Mask* stories featuring freewheeling private eye "Tough Dick" Donahue were almost as popular as Hammett's own Continental Op mini masterpieces. Like most full-

west, and effectively prevented annexation of Canada's western lands by the rapidly expanding United States. When pioneers arrived from the east they found peaceful prairie settlements guarded by a force of men who ruled impartially without the dubious benefits of lynch laws and six-gun justice.

Despite the fact that early Mountie exploits were every bit as heroic as their later fictionalized versions, the history of the Canadian west was perhaps *too* tame to inspire much outside attention had it not been for the great Klondike Gold Rush. It was the lure of instant riches which captured the world's imagination and inspired tens of thousands of fortune seekers to venture north by every means possible. Dawson City, which sprang up like a weed on the junction of the Klondike and Yukon rivers, became a frozen hell hole of lawbreakers, gamblers, prostitutes and common toughs who routinely flaunted Canadian law and Canadian sovereignty.

Into the fray rode Sam Steele of the North West Mounted. Working around the clock under frightful conditions, Superintendent Steele and his men fought their way through howling snow storms to set up government outposts at the Chilkoot and Whitehorse Passes. They sent known lawbreakers packing and transformed the unruly streets of Dawson City into those as safe as any in London or New York—perhaps even safer.

Inveterate troubleshooter Sam Steele was a prototype of the resourceful hero of the north who would come to be celebrated in song and story. Following world-wide attention given to the gold rush, the scarlet-coated image of the North West Mounted was too alluring to be ignored. Numerous writers, many who had never set foot in Canada, combined fact and fiction to churn out thousands of stories featuring stalwart Mounties on snowshoes or horseback endlessly pursuing outlaws portrayed with hearts as cold as frosted gun barrels.

Popular authors like James Oliver Curwood, Rex Beach, and James B. Hendryx built careers specializing in tales of the frozen frontier. Curwood, an American, was even remunerated by the Canadian government for his efforts in producing so many articles, short stories, novels and screenplays promoting the magnificence of "God's Country."

Small wonder that the insatiable pulp magazines so often fea-

MILE-A-MINUTE ACTION . . . WITH A THRILL
FOR EVERY MILE! As your favorite cartoon hero comes to life on the screen in a sensational new adventure . . . leading his famous Mounties to battle against a ruthless gang of foreign spies!
ZANE GREY'S
King OF THE ROYAL MOUNTED
Based on the newspaper cartoon sensation!
ALLAN LANE · ROBERT STRANGE
ROBERT KELLARD · LITA CONWAY
HERBERT RAWLINSON
A REPUBLIC SERIAL IN 12 CHAPTERS

tured tales of the big snow country and especially those of the chivalric Mounted Police. Pulp covers were designed like circus posters to capture the eye with urgency and brilliance. Because shrill reds and yellows were favored to predominate, scarlet-coated men of the Mounted often leaped off the covers of adventure titles like *Short Stories*, *Action Stories*, *Adventure*, and *Argosy*, and of course in such unique fare as *North-West Romances* and *Complete Northwest*.

Pulp fiction Mounties and their supporting casts were often as stereotyped as their movie counterparts. One unfortunate holdover was that of the "half-breed" who—whether Mexican, American, or argot-spouting French-Canadian—was a Hollywood scriptwriter's answer for a villain who apparently required no other motivation to explain his cussedness. In their mission to entertain, pulp fiction writers seized upon such stock characters not to belittle real people but to keep the action rolling with a minimum baggage of characterization. Were the stereotypes meant to be malicious? I think not. Pulp writers produced fiction for two reasons: to earn money and to provide their fans with pure entertainment. They were vendors of excitement, not significance.

With so many Mountie stories being published, a few pulp fictioneers began to specialize. Ryerson Johnson, a popular and prolific freelancer, was given a career kick start by the advice of a fellow writer and friend named William Byron Mowery. Often referred to as "the Zane Grey of the Canadian Northwest," Mowery was making good money selling Northerns; he suggested that Johnson should pick a field of popular interest—Canadian Mounties for instance—and build himself a name in it.

"I didn't know a mounted policeman from a uniformed doorman," Johnson once confided, "but Bill loaned me books and I got more from the library. Official Mounted Police Bulletins and a book by Washburn Pike—*The Great Canadian Barren Lands*—supplied the fundamentals. I read for a week and took notes."

Johnson's first Mountie story, "Cougar Kelly gets a Break," sold to Clayton Publisher's *World Wide Adventures* for $100—as the author put it, "two or three times the weekly wage of the magazine editors who read the story and shaped it up for publication." In quick succession he produced numerous other north country stories bearing titles like "Caribou Gold," "All Trees and Snow," "The Carcajou and the Loup Garou," and "The Eskimo Express." One of his early Mountie adventures, "The Dangerous Dan McGrew" is featured in this book.

Despite the pulp field's penchant for specialization, there never was a magazine devoted exclusively to Mountie stories only. If there had been it might have been titled *Scarlet Riders* and it might have looked just a little like this book. Featured herein are the bylines of some of the field's most popular authors, including that of Lester Dent. Under the publisher-owned house name Kenneth Robeson, Dent created and wrote some 165 adventures of that fabulous fiction icon Doc Savage, the hero of every red-blooded teenager in the Great Depression. Author, explorer, inventor, photographer, aviator, lecturer, Dent was a story-producing phenomenon who boasted that he could write, at full speed, some 65,000 words a week. In addition to his Doc Savage chores he routinely turned out western romances, air war thrillers, detective yarns and straight adventure pieces to a variety of magazines.

Thanks to the generosity of Will Murray and the University of Missouri's Lester Dent Collection we are pleased to present three of Dent's early pulp writings. Short on realism and character development but full of fist-swinging action and unbridled imagination, Dent's early efforts often presaged his work on Doc Savage. Two of the stories printed herein (one never before published) concern the exploits of a curious Mountie known only as the Silver Corporal.

Unlike Doc Savage, the Silver Corporal is short of stature but in other ways almost as superhuman. With his silver hair and silver pupils (contrasting with Doc's bronze hair, eyes, and skin) the phantom Mountie is the devil's own terror to rogues and outlaws along the frozen trails. Perhaps his blanched, wraithlike countenance suggests a southern writer's perception of the kind of man who might exist in a landscape where winter never ends and the snows never melt. Interestingly, publication of Dent's Mountie stories coincided with initial appearances of the Doc Savage novels. Pulp readers might have been treated to further exploits of the amazing Silver Corporal had Doc not commandeered his author's atten-

For the most part Hollywood's Mountie flicks were shaped as off-beat forms of the traditional Western with clean-shaven guys in boy scout hats pursuing swarthy toughs in tuques. Most were shot on quickie schedules in pine-ridged mountains a couple of hours drive east of Los Angeles. They were rife with anachronistic saloon brawls, "necktie parties," treacherous half-breeds, red-skins on the warpath, and hard-riding, fast-shooting posses in cowboy gear galloping wildly about like mad centaurs. One film critic pointed out that Saskatchewan might as well have been in Texas.

Although it has been said that Canada had no Wild West because the Mounties got there first, the truth is that before their heralded arrival Canada's frontier *was* as wild as any Wild West dime novel. Prior to the 1870s American rotgut whisky traders routinely dodged bullets along the Whoop-Up trail into British Territory where they were free to exploit native weakness for guns and firewater. In July of 1873 reports reached Ottawa of the massacre of a band of helpless Assiniboines by drunken wolfers and whisky peddlers in the Cypress Hills area of Manitoba. Fearing a massive Indian uprising, an armed force of mounted men was recruited without delay. Thus was born the North West Mounted Police, later Royal North West Mounted, and ultimately Royal Canadian Mounted Police.

What made the North West Mounted different from the U. S. cavalry was symbolized by their scarlet uniforms—designed to distinguish a civil force of lawmen from the American "Long Knives," whose militant strategies had produced little more than massacres and subsequent retaliation.

The government of Canada had gambled heavily on the ability of a group of volunteer policemen—not soldiers—to form a scarlet thread of outposts and patrols across a territory as big as Europe. From the beginning, a tradition of the force was that "only in the last resort should a peace officer resort to such a dangerous weapon as a revolver in order to effect arrest or to prevent escape by flight." In bringing law and order to the "Vast Lone Land" their assignment was not to subdue the Indians but to eliminate the depredations of unscrupulous whites.

Operating with moral rather than physical force, Mountie guts and Mountie justice tamed the wild plains, earned the respect of native tribes, policed construction of rail lines linking east with

time pulpsters, Nebel realized that he had to be prolific to earn decent money so he crafted fiction for as many types of magazines as possible. His was a common by-line on the covers of *North-West Romances.* "Valley of Wanted Men" is typical of Nebel's lengthy Mountie novelettes, each one usually and erroneously touted by the magazine's editors as "a complete Northland Novel."

Another giant of the pulp era was Hugh B. Cave, happily still with us and adding yearly to his impressive body of short stories and novels. A more careful writer than most pulp scriveners, Hugh maintained a prodigious output by dint of long hours at the typewriter, and sold to almost every type of magazine going—some 800 stories to the pulps alone and over 320 to the more prestigious "slicks."

"The fact is," Cave once explained in an interview, "we professional pulp writers simply couldn't afford to specialize. Rates were low and a writer who tried to stay alive by doing only one kind of story was in trouble." Since Mountie stories were once popular we just knew that Hugh must have written at least one of them—hence the inclusion of his excellent "White Water Run" in these pages.

Talmage Powell, author of "Deadly Trek to Albertville," began his writing career in 1943 with a cover-featured sale to *Ten Detective Aces.* He subsequently appeared 200 times in pulp magazines. With the demise of the pulps as a major form of American entertainment he wrote for the digest-sized fiction magazines and the book markets, publishing an additional 300 short stories and twenty-five books. He also scripted numerous TV series as an in-residence writer at Universal Studios in Hollywood.

As previously noted, real life Mounties are trained to keep the peace without resorting to violence—not the ideal formula for action-hungry pulp readers. That's why canny pros like Talmage Powell realized that fictional Mounties should act more like U.S. Marshals. In his entertaining "Deadly Trek to Albertville" Corporal McCall shoots it out with a band of renegade Sioux who have crossed into Canadian territory following their annihilation of four divisions of U.S. cavalry at the battle of The Little Big Horn. The incident makes for a dandy story but the truth was that when Chief Sitting Bull led 5600 of his people north of the Medicine Line to find refuge from reprisal they were met by a tiny group of scarlet riders who informed them calmly that they were free to remain in peace as long as they obeyed the Queen's laws. Sitting Bull agreed. "The grass in Canada," he said "is not stained with blood."

But it's the fiction that makes these stories fun. They are full of blood and thunder, the imaginary history of a Northwest torn asunder by the violent acts of violent characters. The Mountie pulps were no magazines for sissies. From tales of outlaw hordes and lost race primitives to phantom killers who pursued, their spring-loaded pages exploded with fantastic adventure and homicidal excitements.

Like the subjects they dealt with and the cheap pulp paper they were printed on, these are rough-hewn tales with the bark still on. They were not intended to be great literature, nor did their audience demand that they be so. Depression-weary readers asked only that a story entertain them by spiriting them away to make-believe places far removed from the four walls of everyday existence.

Fans of the "Northern" pulps could, for only a dime or a little more, venture into the trackless wastes of a time-frozen landscape where maps led to buried treasure and X always marked the spot. Mountie stories were mass produced fictions set to a rigid formula but they spoke beguilingly to the homebound reader of men and women with civilization at their backs who were never afraid and never bored. In this simplistic country of the mind life was clear cut. There were good guys and bad guys and the good guys always won. It is a large part of these stories' attraction that they take place in such a lost world of happy innocence.

Don Hutchison
Toronto
July, 1998

No Serials! All Stories Complete!
ACTION STORIES
Nov.
20c
SNOW DUST
by Howard E. Morgan
a big, dramatic Action
Novel of the North
WARNING
DANGERS
CAPT. DINGLE—WALTER J. COBURN—CHART PITT
PATRICK CASEY—A. DE HERRIES SMITH—J. PAUL JONES

FALL
20¢
North • West
STORIES
ROMANCES
JACK LONDON
ROBERT SERVICE
DEATH TO THE RED-COAT TYRANT!
THE LAW FROZE BEYOND THE WHITE BARRIER
A Novelet of the Barrens by DAN CUSHMAN

A.N.C.
North • West
STORIES OF THE WILDERNESS FRONTIER
ROMANCES
FALL
25¢
DEATH POINTS NORTH
A Novel of the Yukon greed-trails
BAIT the REDCOAT TRAP!
Gold, furs, men — she snared them all.
A Mountie Novelet
by STEWART STERLING

ELLSBERG ★ WHITE ★ KNIBBS ★ ELSTON
15¢
Adventure
AUGUS
MAN AT ARMS!
FOREIGN LEGION NOVELETTE BY
GEORGES SURDEZ
RCMP

North West
FICTION HOUSE MAGAZINES
20c
ROMANCES
FRONTIER
THE VALLEY OF WANTED MEN
by
FRED NEBEL
SOURDOUGH GIRL
by
JOHN STARR
KING
OF THE
TUNDRA
by
OWEN FINBAR
TIMBER THIEF
by
JAMES P. OLSEN

ALL STORIES COMPLETE!
COMPLETE
NORTHWEST
JULY—15¢
Magazine
TWO BIG NOVELS
DEATH GUARDS THE OUTLAW GOLD
by
C. V. TENCH
EYES OF THE NORTH
by
HARRY SINCLAIR DRAGO
THE MOUNTED GET A MAN
by
WILL ERMINE

ARGOSY
10¢
144 Pages of Fine Fiction
ARGOSY
A RED STAR MAGAZINE
MAR. 5
WEEKLY
V.E.P.
RCMP
No-Shirt McGee
in a New Novelet
RED COAT, WHITE FEATHER

TRADE MARK REG.
North·West
STORIES OF THE W
FRONT
ROMANCES
FICTION HOUSE MAGAZINES
20¢
THE WHITE SQUAW'S EMPIRE
EVEN THE MOUNTED SHUNNED THAT FROZEN PARADISE RULED BY A WOMAN'S VIOLENT HAND
A Red-Blooded Northern Novelet
by JAMES KIRKLAND
PHANTOM FANGS
by JOHN STARR
GUN-BUCKO of
RESURRECTION LODE
by OWEN FINBAR

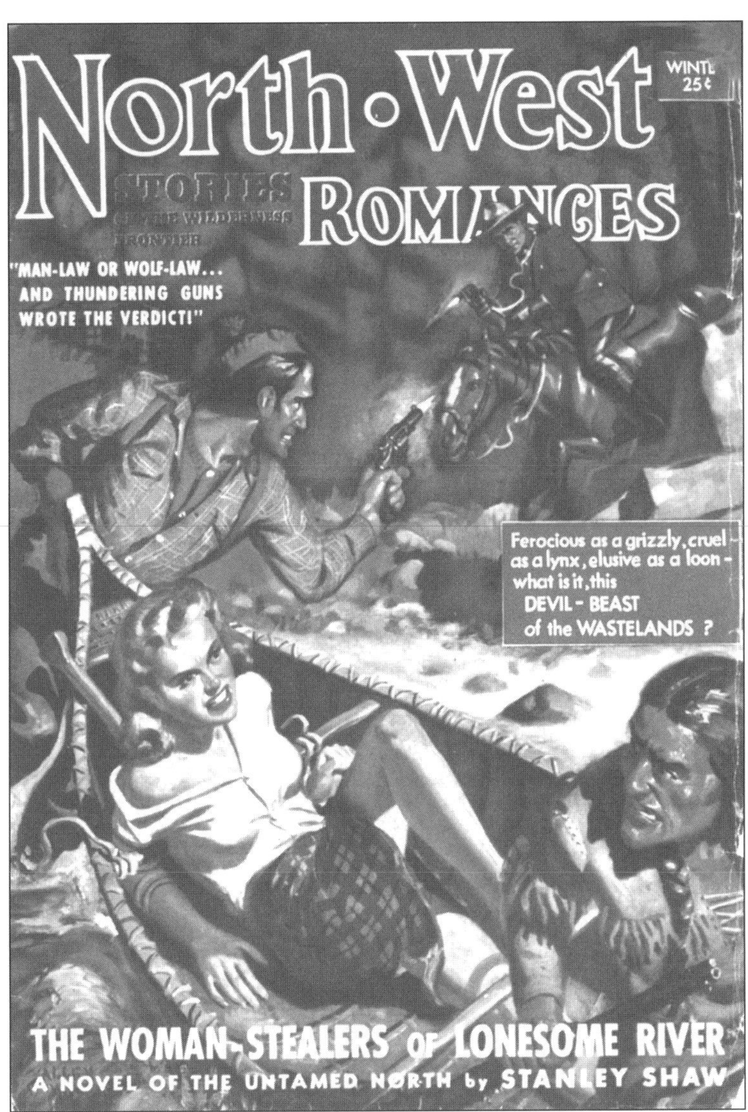
WINTE
25¢
North · West
ROMANCES
"MAN-LAW OR WOLF-LAW...
AND THUNDERING GUNS
WROTE THE VERDICT!"
Ferocious as a grizzly, cruel -
as a lynx, elusive as a loon -
what is it, this
DEVIL - BEAST
of the WASTELANDS ?
THE WOMAN-STEALERS OF LONESOME RIVER
A NOVEL OF THE UNTAMED NORTH by STANLEY SHAW

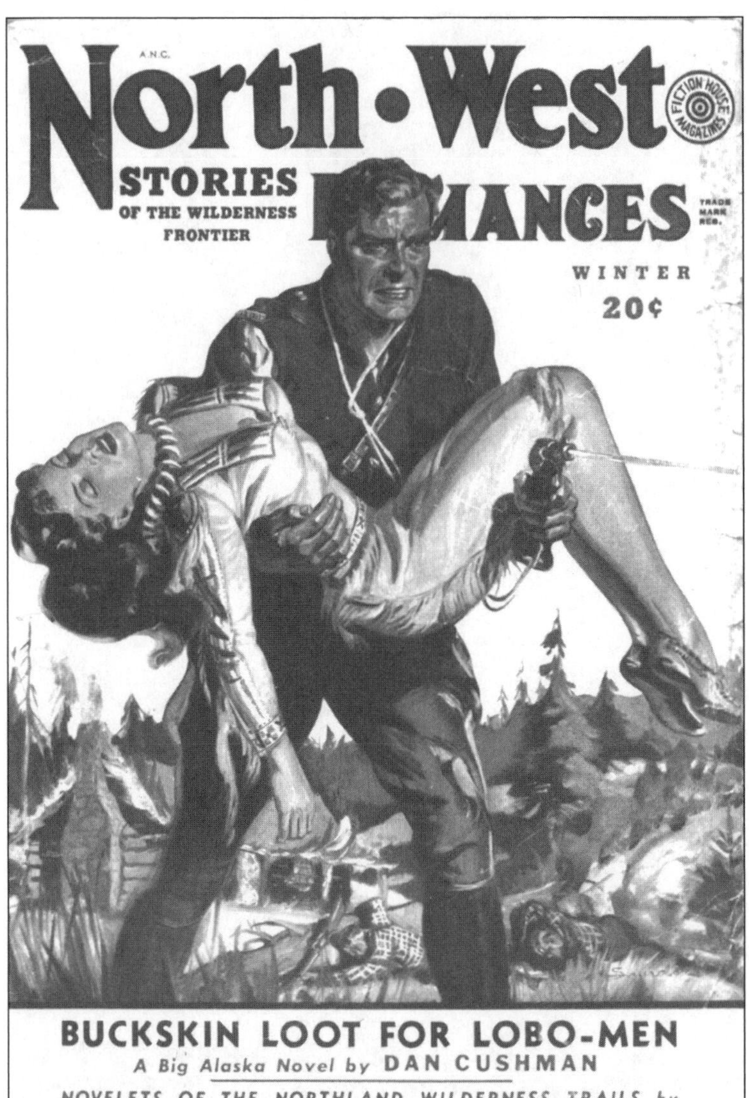
A.N.C.
North·West
STORIES
OF THE WILDERNESS
FRONTIER
ROMANCES
TRADE MARK REG.
FICTION HOUSE MAGAZINES
WINTER
20¢
BUCKSKIN LOOT FOR LOBO-MEN
A Big Alaska Novel by DAN CUSHMAN
NOVELETS OF THE NORTHLAND WILDERNESS TRAILS by
FREDERICK L. NEBEL • WILLIAM R. COX

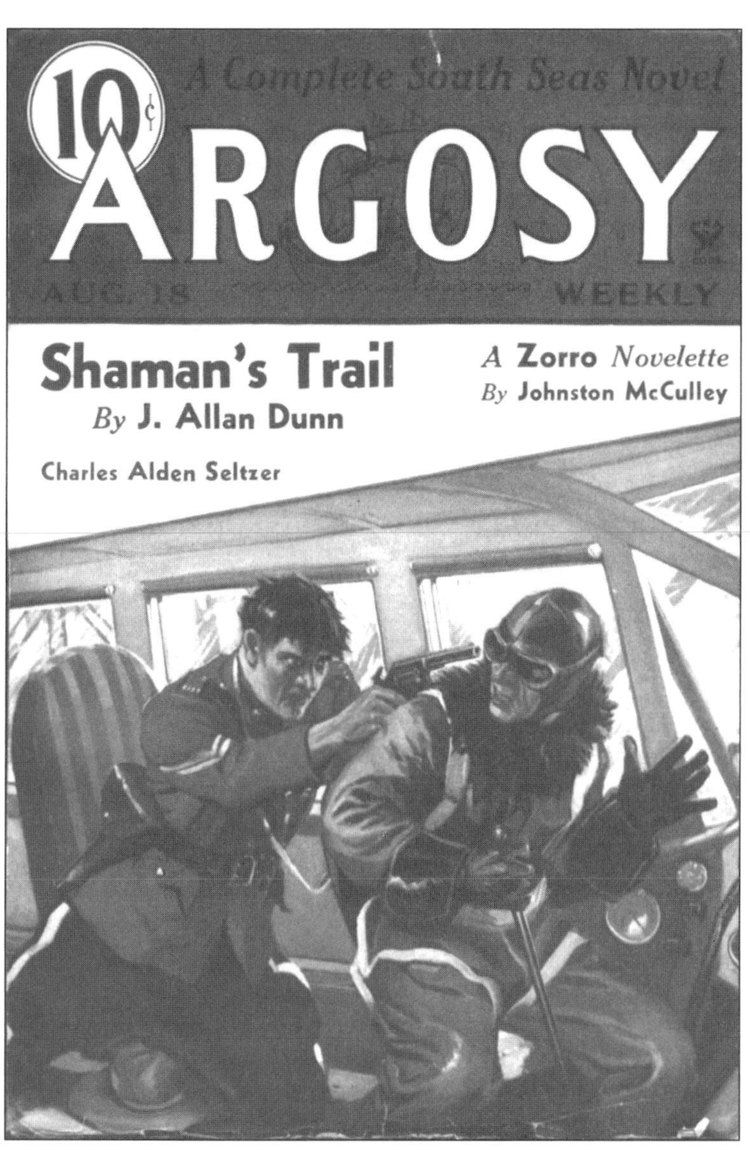
10¢
A Complete South Seas Novel
ARGOSY
AUG. 18
WEEKLY
Shaman's Trail
By J. Allan Dunn
A Zorro Novelette
By Johnston McCulley
Charles Alden Seltzer

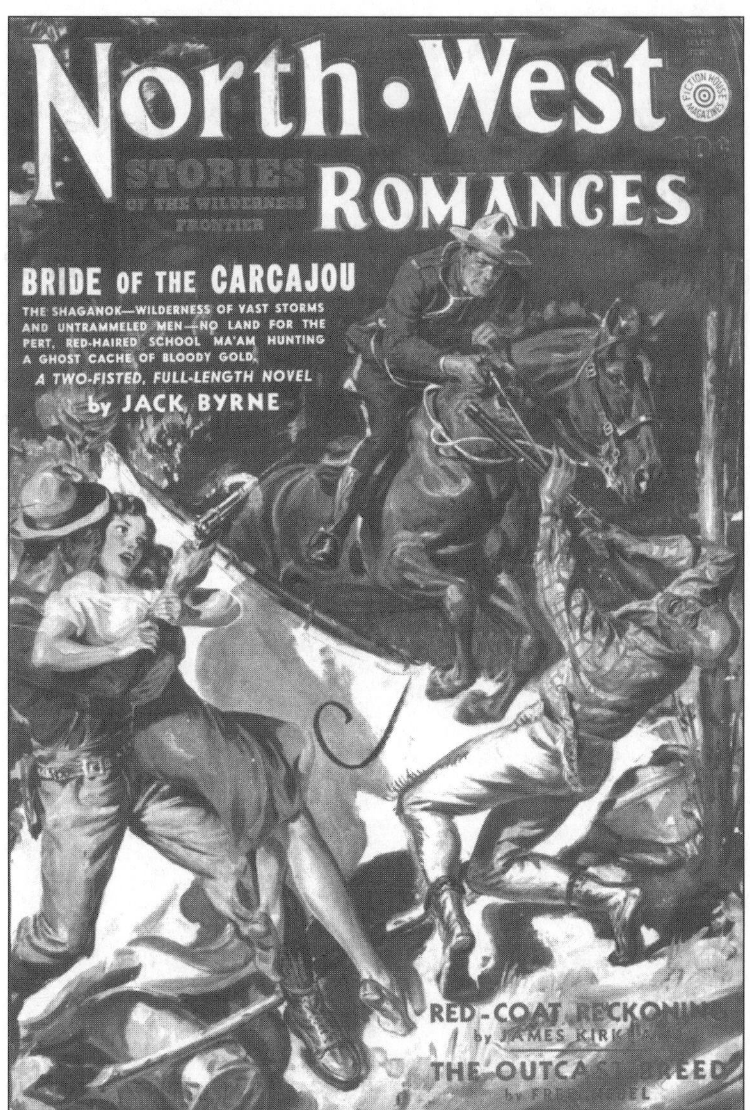
North·West
STORIES OF THE WILDERNESS FRONTIER
ROMANCES
FICTION HOUSE MAGAZINES
BRIDE OF THE CARCAJOU
THE SHAGANOK—WILDERNESS OF VAST STORMS AND UNTRAMMELED MEN—NO LAND FOR THE PERT, RED-HAIRED SCHOOL MA'AM HUNTING A GHOST CACHE OF BLOODY GOLD.
A TWO-FISTED, FULL-LENGTH NOVEL
by JACK BYRNE
RED-COAT

North·West
ROMANCES
20c
PARADISE
VALLEY
A STEAM-MADE TROPICAL OASIS HIDDEN IN THE ICE-BOUND WILDERNESS —A SAVAGE LOST RACE AND A WHITE-SKINNED, GOLDEN-HAIRED GIRL.
by
ROGER DANIELS
TUNDRA
GOLD
by
FRED NEBEL
HOBNAIL
JUSTICE
by
CHAS. NELSON
NO
LAW
BELOW
ZERO
DEATH WAS MARKED FOR THE RED-COAT WHO TREKKED THE BLOOD-SPECKED MURDER TRAIL—BUT CORPORAL McREE WAS HARD TO KILL.
A COMPLETE NORTHLAND NOVELET BY
A. de HERRIES
SMITH
FICTION HOUSE MAGAZINES

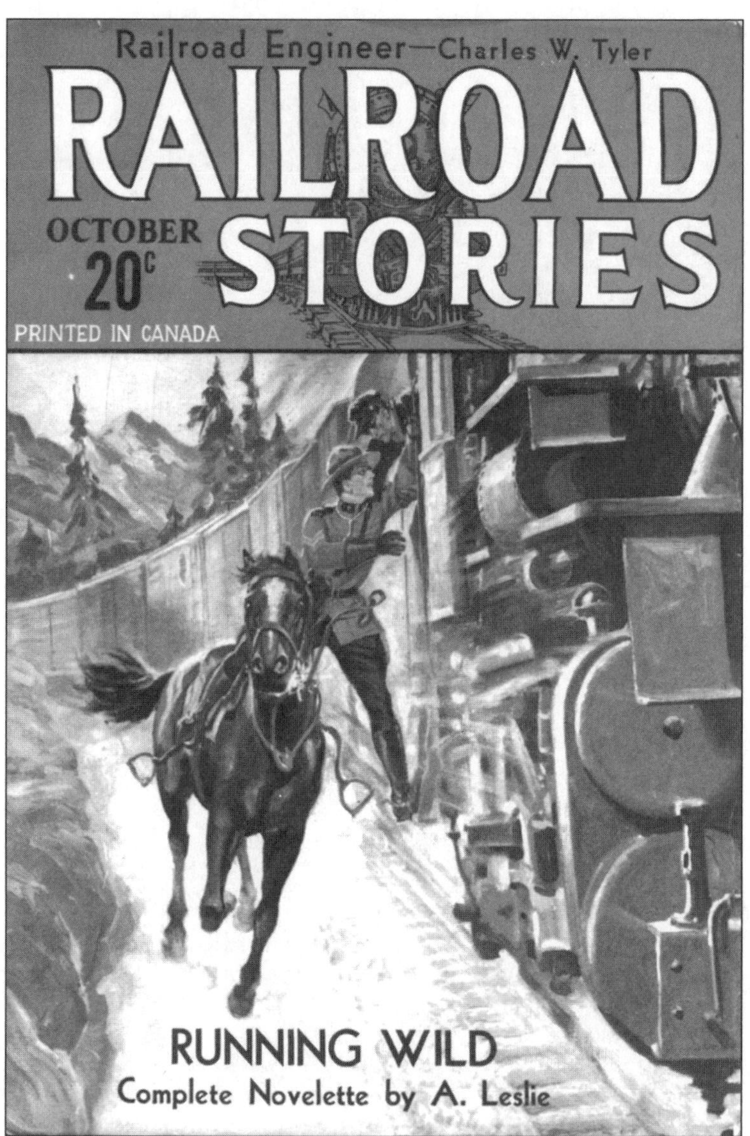
Railroad Engineer—Charles W. Tyler
RAILROAD
OCTOBER
20c
STORIES
PRINTED IN CANADA
RUNNING WILD
Complete Novelette by A. Leslie

A.N.C.
North-West
ROMANCES
TRADE
MARK
REG.
SPRING
20¢
MALEMUTE
BREED
Novel of the Dawson Trail
by DAN CUSHMAN
Robt. Service
Jack
London
North to Hellish Bondage She went . . .:
HOSTAGE OF
THE MAN-PACK
A Big Novelet by TOM BLACKBURN

DEADLY TREK TO ALBERTVILLE

By Talmage Powell

Corporal McCall's assignment appeared routine—escort the killer Kaleel back to justice in Albertville. But he reckoned without a hot-blooded lady named Valya and a pack of renegade Sioux fresh from bloody victory at Little Big Horn.

McCall arrived in Salt Lick as shadows were falling at the end of a long day in the brief Canadian summer. Astride a buckskin gelding, he was followed by a halter-reined entourage that consisted of a second saddle horse and a red-eyed pack mule.

A tall, spare man, he had dust creases on his chiseled face where sweat had dried in the growing cool of evening. Shaggy ends of jet black hair curled at the sweat band of his dusty hat.

His little parade seemed to have traveled quite a ways. The buckskin tossed its head wearily now and then as it clopped into Salt Lick, while McCall's deep blue eyes took in the village. It was something of an eyesore, squatting on its tiny territorial claim here in the beautiful vastness of the Glasworthy Valley region where nature had worked its miracles in a richness of forest, meadow, crystal-clear streams, and abundance of wildlife.

At this season Glasworthy country flaunted breath-taking vistas colored with blue crocus and wild roses. McCall was thankful Ransom Kaleel had got himself in custody at this time of year. Taking Kaleel from here to Albertville when winter blizzards swept down from arctic regions would be a job any man in his right mind would shy away from. Even in this ideal weather, McCall had no liking for the assignment. A man as mean and dangerous as Kaleel was acceptable as a traveling companion only because duty made him so.

One glance could just about take in the whole of Salt Lick, a few log-and-chink and clapboard buildings and houses hunkered alongside the stage road. It was the stagecoach passage and need of a way stop where weary travelers could get a hot meal and rest overnight that had seeded Salt Lick in the first place. As population trickled westward, Salt Lick had become a trade post for a scattering of farmers, and passers-through, homesteaders headed further west, prospectors and trappers moving on to destinations of personal fancy.

McCall drew rein before a squat log building that had a long birch shingle over the door with lettering burned into it: Office of the High Sheriff.

He grunted as he swung a travel-stiffened leg and dismounted. Reining the animals at the hitching rail he crossed the earthen sidewalk and thumbed the door latch.

No one was present in the cramped office. There was a plank desk, a couple of wooden chairs, a wooden cabinet for storage of records and official papers, a Franklin heater, a tack board on one wall displaying a polyglot of wanted posters, some of them yellowed with age.

A plank door across the room swung on its leather hinges. A big man, nearly bald, viewing the world with sleepy looking eyes in a face that passing years were beginning to soften at the edges entered from his living quarters and said, "Top of the day, stranger. What can I do for you?"

"Sheriff Jernigan?"

"Ain't his brother."

"I'm Corporal Bradford McCall, Northwest Mounted Police."

Jernigan's face lighted pleasantly. He reached out his hand, and they shook. "Pleasure to meet you. Drag up a chair."

He seated himself behind the desk. McCall one-handedly picked up a wooden chair by its back, shifted its position and sat down facing Jernigan.

While McCall fetched papers from the inner pocket of his jacket, Jernigan looked at him with interest. "Never met a Mountie before."

"Well," McCall smiled, "how do I stack up?"

"Right tolerable, I guess," Jernigan laughed. "You strike me as a man who just might herd Ransom Kaleel from here to Albertville. I ain't sorry we got an outfit like the Mounties nowadays to take over when a Kaleel has to be transported to the jurisdiction of his crime."

"He's about as bad as they come," McCall agreed. A good camaraderie had established itself between the two. "We've gathered a picture of a handsome Irishman, happy go lucky, humor twinkling in the blue eyes, a ready smile on his clean-cut face. His victims rarely suspect they're walking with Lucifer until it's too late."

The air in the office became heavily serious.

Jernigan said. "I had no idea such a man was in Salt Lick. He could have come and gone, still be on the loose."

"How'd you nail him, Sheriff?"

Jernigan shrugged. "Can't take any credit. He nailed himself. Over in Morgan's place. He was one of five men in a poker game. Biggest pot of the night, after Kaleel had been losing steadily all evening, I learned later. He thought he'd won with two pairs. Little Jeremy Bowdin turned over a four-spot hole card, gave him trips. Kaleel said, 'You touch that pot, you dirty little cheater, and I'll break that stick you call an arm.' Jeremy wouldn't know how to cheat in the first place. So he touched. And blimey...before an eye could wink, Kaleel grabbed a wrist and elbow, and smacko!, he broke that arm across the edge of the table. 'Step up, Gents,' Kaleel said, 'who's next?' He was armed with a Starr .44 in a shoulder holster for all to see when his jacket flapped open. Jeremy was rolling on the floor, moaning, and Kaleel was gathering up the money when, quiet-like, I put the business end of a pistol barrel against the base of his skull. 'High Sheriff Jernigan here, friend,' I said. 'Got no qualms about shooting an animal in the back. You freeze, then ease your hands to the top of your head, or that piece of skull between your eyeballs is going to land in the spittoon over there.' He froze, inched a look, and musta decided I meant what I said."

Jernigan shrugged. "When I had him chained in the lock-up I was nagged with the feeling I knew him. He'd never crossed my path. So I looked through wanted posters and the list of wanted men you Mounties put out. Your description fit him to a T, right down to the red scar on the side of his neck. Description said it was a reminder of a fight he'd had with a drover who was armed with a bullwhip. Wanted for murder in Albertville. So I notified your people I had him."

Jernigan shuffled through the papers McCall had laid on his desk. "Looks like everything is in order. Welcome to him, Corporal. I guess you want to leave with him come sun-up."

McCall looked at him quizzically. He had a hunch Jernigan was holding something back. "Well, now, let's see. We got some natural hazards taking this hardcase cross country. Wouldn't be the weather, this time of year. Mosquitoes right now can be pesky, but wouldn't help Kaleel. 'Course we could chance on poachers who sneak up from the Dakotas and illegally shoot our bison for the hides, having wiped out so many on their side of the border. Or might be really testy if we run up against some of the Sioux warriors who followed Sitting Bull into Canada after he killed Custer's command at Little Big Horn to the last man and brought down the full wrath of General Sheridan's forces. Some of them have separated from the main body and given us trouble when they hit an isolated homestead for food and supplies including any liquor found on the place. If I'm lucky and don't run into Sioux or poachers, Kaleel won't be all that much of a threat. He'll wear irons all the way. But I get the feeling there's more."

"Kaleel's woman," Jernigan said.

"Come again?"

"She's called Valya, and why a woman with her looks would give the likes of Kaleel a second glance is beyond me. But who knows what goes on inside a woman? She's ridden with Kaleel quite a spell. They came into Salt Lick and seemed to be well enough fixed for money, probably from a robbery somewhere, we can suspect now. They rented old Josh Loudermilk's soddy...he owns the livery, his wife had died, and he had started sleeping in the livery loft, like going back to the house spooked him. Kaleel and the girl attracted no particular notice at first, except he was a handsome devil and she was the purtiest thing ever seen in these parts. She said they had come from the east and might buy a place in this beautiful countryside. I think they were just plain tuckered from running hard from something they'd done and was just pausing to catch their second wind. Salt Lick seemed a good, quiet, safe bet. And it was, until the other night when Kaleel started spanking a whiskey baby at the start of the poker game and the real nature of the man surfaced. Was it actually a family he murdered in Albertville, McCall?"

"Like it says on the flyer," McCall nodded. "Man, wife, little boy and girl. Man had sold a big piece of land. Kaleel trailed him home and shot him for the cash. Quite coolly put bullets in the rest of the family, removing all witnesses. The boy was a tough young'un. He somehow lived long enough to drag himself to a desk his daddy had made so's the children could start the day with an hour of schooling. He wrote on his slate, 'Ransom Kaleel killed us all. He killed Papa first and took his money. He figgered us all dead, and I played possum til he was...' That's as far as he got before he slumped over the desk. No way to doubt the evidence. Boy's daddy had met Kaleel, a stranger in town, played some cards and bent an elbow with him. Had him out to the house a couple times for supper. Kaleel can come on friendly, if that's the face he chooses to wear. Three days after the murders a neighbor stopped by and found the green blow-flies gathering. Kaleel was long gone."

"The girl Valya figures to have it that way again," Jernigan said. "She's been here every day trying to see him. I got the strong notion she'd stop at nothing for the sake of her man. I deputized Red MacTavish to stand night guard, just in case she slipped around with a stick of dynamite to blow out the back wall." Jernigan stood up. "You can't get him out of Salt Lick a minute too quick to suit me. Come on, and I'll introduce you to your traveling companion."

Attached to Jernigan's office and revealed when Jernigan

pulled a curtain aside, the gaol was an eight by ten box made of logs, two small apertures in the further end admitting air and wan light. Below the ventilation slits a male figure in dirtied fringed buckskins lay on a ticking filled with straw. At the foot of the mattress was a waste pail with a wooden cover. Several feet down the wall was a water bucket, a dipper handle protruding above the rim. The room had no other furnishings.

The entry was a heavy door of hewn timber and strap iron bars, mounted criss-cross.

"You got company, Kaleel," Jernigan said through the bars. "Get off your tail."

Kaleel sat up, stretching, yawning. He rose with the suppleness of a cougar. "Top of the evening to you, Sheriff." He was a fair-sized man, a little taller, broader than average, no fat. He had an Irish ruddiness, his growth of jail-time beard reflecting a tinge of red. He drifted across the cell, feather light on his feet, his smile flashing. "You served an excellent venison stew for supper. My compliments to the cook at Morgan's place."

"Nice you enjoyed your last supper with us. This is Corporal McCall. You'll be leaving with him tomorrow morning, early."

Kaleel tilted his head for a better look through the criss-crossed iron bars. "Corporal...A Mountie, I assume. How about that, Sheriff...the Mounties have got their man."

"Just from here to Albertville," McCall said pleasantly. "The local authorities will have the chore of stretching your neck."

"You better get a good night's sleep," Kaleel said. "I won't keep you waiting. Ain't got much to pack." He shifted his alert blue eyes. "I heard my gal in your office again today, Sheriff."

"Oh, yes," Jernigan said.

"You keep me in here a hundred years, you gonna be treated to the sight of that lovely thing every day. Living ain't living for her when I ain't around, Sheriff."

"I gathered that."

"No cause to deprive her like you do. What harm if you pulled that curtain and we talked through the bars."

"I got my rules," Jernigan said. "Murderers don't rate visitors. If we was hanging you here, you'd get a farewell minute at the foot of the gallows."

"You got to respect a sheriff like this one, eh, McCall?" Something in the way Kaleel expressed it made McCall think of a man smiling before he pulls the trigger.

"I'm ready for grub," McCall said to Jernigan.

The sheriff pulled the curtain. "We'll try the stew pot at Morgan's Mansion. Welshman who owns it has got a sense of humor, naming it that. Just a short walk after we livery your livestock for the night. Originally your usual back-country tavern, one big room, plank tables and benches, a log-eating fireplace where the cook wrestled cast iron skillets, pots, Dutch ovens, sideboard holding the vittles and ale kegs. Had a loft, gents sleep at north end, ladies at south end, curtain across the middle, no traversing between ends. Then as more population spread west and stage travel increased Morgan cut the loft into cubicles and tacked on more outside. We'll get you a room and eats. Grub's better than you might expect, and his cots have got feather ticking."

"Can I get a hot bath?"

"Sure as hell Morgan tacked on a room for that too." Jernigan laughed as they started down the street leading the pair of horses and mule toward the livery stable.

"Sounds like I'm in for some royal fare," McCall smiled. "Makes for a good night's sleep."

"Yes, I'm sure. That pretty woman will lay lower than a mole in its run. She stick a knife or bullet in your ribs tonight, Kaleel's still in jail, under tighter guard than ever. Tomorrow, when the sun's well up and you and Kaleel are far clear of town, alone in open country, she'll be out there, cunning as a tigress. I'd recommend that good night's sleep, McCall..."

The morning passed without any sign of a stalking lioness on the kill for its mate. McCall was tuned to all the signs of danger, birds taking to the sky from yonder copse of trees, the echo, sensed more than heard, of a distant hoofbeat, the unnatural stillness of insect life in a meadow, the discoloration of water, however faint, in a lazily flowing brook, a mark of passage in knee-high grass.

When the sun peaked, McCall drew rein at an aspen shadowed creek. "We'll eat here."

While the horses and mule dipped their muzzles to drink,

Kaleel lifted the supply roll off the mule's back. It was an awkward task, iron cuffs on his wrists separated by only a foot of chain links. He snapped the granny knots, rolled back the edge of the tarp, and helped himself to a chicken leg and sour dough biscuit. In a cocky gesture, he motioned with the chicken leg to the hamper prepared at Morgan's Mansion.

"Be my guest, Corporal."

"Don't mind if I do." McCall said. He had a choice of cold fried chicken or bison meat roast. He chose a chicken quarter.

The creek murmured. A wild turkey gobbled off yonder. Down the creek a venturesome stag came to drink. The horses and mule grazed the green succulence. During the brief moments of rest for men and animals, McCall ate with his .44/40 repeating rifle in the crook of his arm. Kaleel hunkered with manacled arms on his knees, his eyes and expression undergoing a gradual change, darkening with worry and concern.

McCall said, "She's bugged out on you, Kaleel."

Kaleel looked at him and laughed. It was the beginning of a well of laughter. The stag bolted and ran into the woods. The gobbler shut up. Kaleel ran out of laugh, lifting his chain-joined arms to wipe his eyes.

"That's a good one, Corporal."

"Is that a fact?"

"Fact is," Kaleel's sobered gaze swept visible countryside, "something's happened to her."

"Maybe she's just letting you dangle, big man, so's you'll appreciate her all the more when she does make her move."

"May be. But don't bet on it."

"How'd a hardcase like you ever get hooked up with her?"

"It's a short story, but it would bore the hell out of you."

"So bore me."

"She got born on a hard-rock farm, of a lazy, whiney mama and a big bully daddy that drank too much mean liquor and showed his lordship by beating up on his woman and gal young'un. She was the prettiest girl you ever seen. Her mama died, and her daddy got the eye for his Valya. Might have come a time of rape, but she ran away from home. That was back east, in Quebec. She moseyed west doing any kind of temporary odd job from washing clothes to splitting shingles when her last bean was gone. She got in with some rawhiders, three or four families, following the bison, living like Indians. It was a sorry life, not much better than she'd left. She was in Manitoba territory by this time and got a job as a barmaid in Thamesgary, fair-sized timber mill town east of Albertville. I went in one night, and she served me, and our eyes met, and the world would never be the same. I went in every night for a week. On the seventh night a big lummox started putting his hands where they had no business, and when she slapped him, he guffawed like he enjoyed it and grabbed her. So I kicked his tail out of the place."

Kaleel broke off, looking inward, into his memories.

"And after you rescued the damsel in distress..." McCall prompted.

Kaleel's blue eyes darkened in a flash. "Damn you to hell, don't you put it like that, like you're making sport of it."

McCall lifted his brows. "Last thought from my mind. So after you gave her protection...?"

"I said to her, 'This is no place for you.' And she said, 'I think so too.' And I said, 'Your place is with me.' And she said, 'I think so too.' She let the barmaid apron fall to the sawdust floor, linked her arm with mine, and we walked out."

"To what?"

Kaleel shrugged. "The carefree life, my Mountie friend. No clocks, no rules, like birds."

"Falcons," McCall said, "birds of prey."

"It's the way of nature, McCall. The strong taking from the weak. You need a poke, you take a poke."

"Like from a family in Albertville."

"I didn't mean it to happen that way. I just wanted the poke, and take one of the young'uns hostage a few miles down the road until I was sure the daddy was playing cricket and sitting still until I had a long lead. The damn fool wouldn't play it fair. He reached for a gun."

"So you shot him."

"Self defense," Kaleel said.

"Then the family."

"Self defense, Corporal. They all knew my face. That boy...writing on his slate...he blew it all. Everything would have been all right if he hadn't wrote on his slate."

"How about the arm you broke at the poker table in Salt

Lick?"

"I was drinking, Corporal. I get touchy when I drink. I hadn't won hardly a pot all night. Wasn't fair. Not right. That scrawny bastard didn't deserve the biggest pot of the night. He dealt the hand. I still think he didn't come by them three of a kind in fair fashion. It would have been all right, if Jernigan hadn't been sitting behind me at a table in the corner, his back to me. I didn't know he was in the place. None of the others would have stirred a muscle. I woulda walked out, got Valya, and dusted Salt Lick."

"You seem to have been staked when you came to Salt Lick. Left a big uproar somewhere behind?"

"I guess it doesn't matter at this point if I tell you, does it?"

"Not in the slightest," McCall said.

"Well, a drummer in Perkinton got paid for a big order of dry goods. Valya and I were about down to our last. It took a pistol whipping to convince the drummer to share the wealth. Turned out he was younger brother of a big man in the region, who musta brought half the men in town on the hunt. Out for blood, I mean. Terrible time...It was days before Valya and I finally shook them and eased into Salt Lick."

"What had you planned to do after Salt Lick, Kaleel?"

"Planned? Whatever tomorrow turned up that looked exciting and profitable, Corporal."

"Kaleel, you are one crazy Irishman."

"Ain't we all. Look at yourself. Never a day to call your own. Laying your life on the line for people who wouldn't give you spit. Doing it all for a pittance."

"Oh, I get a little more than a pittance in return, Kaleel."

"Yeah, like what?"

"You wouldn't understand."

"No, I sure as hell wouldn't."

"The animals have rested. You've pushed out a gut wrinkle. Mount up."

The sun moved an hour on the downside of the sky, marking their passage. The terrain changed gradually to a stretch of open country marked by boulders, slopes of broken shale where glaciers had crawled in a primeval past.

A shadow shifted at an out-cropping half a mile away, and then another. McCall's jaw muscles bunched. He casually veered north, toward the shadows of a forest of conifers, calculating distances and speed, not yet ready to break and run, playing out the string possibility that they were renegade Sioux and would observe and decide the white men had no goods worth the price of a hot fight.

Then he saw the slim figure rising out of a stony trench. He heard the sharp intake of Kaleel's breath. He reined up and slid the rifle from its scabbard.

She ran lightly and swiftly toward them, a rifle in her hands, but gripped by the barrel with the stock thrust forward.

In homespun britches, plaid shirt, a flat-brimmed hat hanging at her nape by its chin thong, soiled by travel sweat and dust, she was nevertheless as lovely as any woman McCall had ever laid eyes on.

McCall leaned in the saddle, taking the stock of the lifted rifle in his hand.

Up close, she had black hair, violet eyes in a boldly cut, high cheek-boned face that added up to female mystery rather than feminine prettiness. She smiled. "I never thought to be using the gun as a peace offering."

She moved her eyes. "Hello, Rance. Sweet baby, I didn't intend for us to be together again like this."

"I love you, Valya," Ransom Kaleel said quietly.

Their eyes met and communed for a fraction of time. She returned her gaze to McCall. "I boned up on you in Salt Lick last evening, Corporal. Ain't often a Mountie comes to town to take away a helpless prisoner like my Rance honey. Guess you wouldn't have made it if I'd been given time to pick the time and place."

"Indians?"

"Then you've caught their sign. I had to veer off your trail when they came at me. I figured the route you'd likely take, rode hard, thinking to lose them in rough country and turn back to rejoin my Irishman. My wonderful true-blue stallion...ran until his heart burst. Shed a tear for him...thought the Indians had lost me. Walked awhile, and the red devils were coming at me again. Ran into a crevice that gave me cover. That's when you came into the picture. Right in my rifle sights, time and place just about like I'd figured. But the scene had gone wrong. I was between the devil and a hard place."

"I sure as hell don't welcome you to the hard place," McCall said, "but the Indians haven't given us much choice. How many of them?"

"Six. I'm sure they're renegade Sioux...long without a woman."

McCall's eyes and senses were noting everything as each empty second ticked. "Three of them are coming down from the rocks. Get aboard behind Kaleel. We'll abandon the slow pack mule. We can still make those trees, where we've got a chance."

In a flash, she was at Kaleel's side, looking up into his face, reaching for his extended hands, swinging up behind him.

"Move it," McCall said, wheeling his mount.

The horses had barely begun stride when a rifle shot quartered at them from the trees. Both horses were brought to rearing halt. The renegades, McCall realized, had split and cut them off from the trees in the scant minutes that had passed in Valya's surrender. Enemy at the front, enemy on right flank...no choice...take cover and keep them at carbine range until the sun sank and darkness provided whatever hope of giving them the slip.

"The broken shale," Kaleel said, speaking the thought as if right out of McCall's mind.

They wheeled and raced, ineffective bursts of rifle fire following them. The sun reflected in eye-blinding fury from the long shale slope. They slid into a shallow, canyon-like break in the stone. Hoofbeats were echoing as the Sioux on their right mounted and came from cover.

Hurtling from the saddle, McCall scrambled and belly-whopped at the rim of the depression. Three Indians were eating up ground on stolen horses. McCall's first shot lifted the one in the forefront off his bareback blanket. He was dead by the time his body hit the ground loosely, his horse rearing, whinnying, running blindly back in the direction from which it had come.

The other two pulled up, turning their mounts and moving back to safer range.

"Very nice shooting, Corporal," Kaleel said conversationally from a few feet away, where he and Valya crouched. "Now if you'll just hand me Valya's rifle, I reckon the odds will be about even, only five of them being left."

"No," McCall said.

"Looks to me like you could sure as hell use a trigger eye as sharp as your own."

"I could use more," McCall said, "but not your eye, Kaleel."

Three Sioux on horseback came out of the woods, circling to join the two among the boulders facing the whites.

"It's your only chance, McCall."

"Not quite. I'm still alive. If I hand you the gun, it raises the strong possibility of the dis-continuance of that state of existence, whatever happens to the Indians."

"I could give you my word to hand the rifle back if we..."

"Save your breath, Kaleel!"

Kaleel shifted his body slightly, as if to ease thigh muscles, looking at the spare rifle McCall had laid beside him.

"Well, my unfriendly side kick," Kaleel said, "I can see as to how you wouldn't trust me half as far as you can spit. But it ain't the only consideration...Ain't like I'd be taking candy from a baby or a poke off a dumb tenderfoot I meet in a tavern and treat to a drink...No, sirree, you'd be throwing down on me the second it looked like we had a glimmer chance of getting out of here."

"True," McCall said.

"Then why not?"

McCall briefly turned his gaze to the good looking Irishman and the slim, supple girl pressed close beside him. "Because there'd be two of you. I might just chance it if you were alone, Kaleel, but never in a million years in her presence."

Kaleel laughed, without real mirth. "Hear the way the Corporal is talking about you, sweet baby?"

"Hush," she said. "Take my hand."

"Hey, you," a Sioux voice called, "hey, you white man with the gun...we got no fight with you..."

"Catch that slur in the voice," Kaleel strained up a little. "Not just Indians. Drunken Indians, crazy people."

With hots for a woman, McCall added to himself.

As if echoing the thought, the Indian called out, "We just

be friendly with the woman, that's all. Have little party...no hurt her...give her lottsa money...we got money, from wagon moving west..."

"McCall," Kaleel said in low, even tones, "just wing that one. I want that one. Please. I want to feel his neckbone against the chain between my two hands. Just that one thing for me, McCall, and I'll thank you even if I mount the gallows."

Shadows flitted on the slope.

"They're fanning out," Valya said. "In the end they'll rush us."

"Yes," McCall said.

"You hear me, white man?" the Sioux leader yelled. "Why you no talk? You just one gun. We many. All we want is woman. We no care about you. Just leave woman and go your way...You never see us again. Woman be our squaw for while...then we give her horse and she ride to town with lottsa money...How come you no trust us with woman? You crazy? Last thing we want is hurt woman...I speak with straight tongue, white man..."

"I'm sorry, Rance," McCall barely caught Valya's softly spoken words. "I thought I might have a chance, in company with McCall. Fool's wishful thinking...when McCall killed the first one, they'd draw back, think again, go some place where the women wouldn't be in the shadow of a sharp-shooter...Now I see it's the worst thing I could have done. There's only one way of making them go away..."

Like a startled bunny, without preliminary twitch of muscle, she was suddenly a figure running up the rocky slope. Kaleel reared and lunged after her.

A drunken Indian, seeing her appearance, leaped to a boulder top and skirled a keening sound of triumph, snapping a shot in Kaleel's direction.

McCall squeezed the trigger, knocking the Indian out of sight. His companions opened up. Grit stung McCall's cheeks from ricocheting bullets.

Valya was a third of the distance toward them, black hair streaming, a sprite running on a beautiful summer day. The Indians saw Kaleel's intent as he narrowed the distance between him and Valya. A volley of fire came from the boulders. The marksmanship was bad. McCall put a bullet in one of them who moved for a better line of sight.

The shooting continued, thunder without break rolling over the landscape. Valya stumbled and pitched prone from a stray bullet or chancey shot from an Indian who didn't have full line of sight on Kaleel.

Kaleel reached her side as bullets nipped at his dirtied, slept-in fringed buckskin. He sank to his knees, bent and kissed the loveliness of her face. Then he lifted his face to the sky, a suppliant worshiping his goddess.

He lowered his head, his body shaking. He worked his hands between the shale and the small of her back, and stood with her body draped across his manacled arms.

He vented a roar of Irish triumph. "You're whipped, you pack of animals! She wanted the touch of no man but that of Ransom Kaleel. She was counting on not surviving when she sparked a fire fight. If not the fire fight she would have done it for herself, the minute you rode off with her and Ransom Kaleel was safe from you, the minute she could have snatched a dagger and turned it on herself...That's the woman you'll never have, you dogs!"

The fact that she was dead came into their comprehension. And as he stood there holding her as if he possessed something holy, Kaleel became the focus of their fire.

Olivious to the shooting, Kaleel turned and took a step in McCall's direction. McCall risked exposure, on one knee, levering the rifle in cover fire.He shot one more before the final two backed off, disappearing in the rocks, a long minute passing before the echo of fading hoofbeats came to him.

He lowered the smoking gun, a shivered racing through him, sleeve-wiping his feverish face. He saw that he was holding Valya's rifle, the chamber empty in his own.

He stood, breathing heavily, willing movement to his feet.

The bodies were about thirty yards up the slope. McCall's shadow fell across them. He wondered fleetingly how many bullets it had taken to bring the Irishman down. Later, a counting of holes in the bloodied fringed buckskin. Close to hand was the task of dead-man carry of the bodies on a horse for the remainder of the trip, draped across the horse's back, their hands and ankles lashed together belly-side.

They'd fallen snug by side, she with her head on Kaleel's shoulder, he with the ghostly remnants of a cocky hair-with-the-hide expression on his lips.

McCall stood another moment, taking off his hat and wiping the sweatband. A full moon tonight, clear skies, plenty of light for easy travel...from here on the trek was as dangerous as a Sunday canter home from church...he could deliver Ransom Kaleel in Albertville sometime after midnight..

He turned away to go and round up the horses.

THE FROZEN PHANTOM

By Lester Dent

From out of the wind-whipped snow-sheathed north came the Flame Maiden. Legend pictured her a beautiful girl with a head of flame! And legend told also of the Frozen Phantom with his ghastly Coffin of the Mad. To Constable Andy Frost this was all bunk—until he found frigid fingers clutching his throat!

Fingers had burrowed down in the snow and found Constable Andy Frost's throat. He knew that as he awakened.

Frost dashed a fist upward. The rabbit-lined sleeping bag impeded him. Snow had drifted over the bag three feet deep.

It got in his eyes. He wore a fur parka over his Royal Northwest Mounted Police tunic. It hampered his arms.

Frost was short, thick of shoulder and neck. He was built like a runt bull buffalo. His face ran too much to mouth and ears. His looks were not helped by the soot from the bottom of his tea kettle which he had smeared below his eyes the day before to guard against snow blindness.

His groping hands found the parka hood of his attacker. He dug into it and clutched a greasy face. The face owner barked gutturals of pain. It was as though a bear trap had his features.

Frost recognized the voice!

Bill-Bill Oon! His Eskimo guide from the Coronation Gulf country! Frost, between blows, wondered what had gotten into Bill-Bill. The Inuit had always been reliable, although a little superstitious. One fact was certain–it was no ordinary thing that would cause the Eskimo to attack Frost. Bill-Bill had stood in awe of Frost since the day he had seen the little, homely constable grasp a large icicle and squeeze it to a frosty powder in one iron-tendoned fist.

The flexible sole of a *muck-a-luck* smashed against Frost's head. Frost trapped the foot in his hard, beam-like arms. Bill-Bill Oon spun like a top. He sprawled in the snow.

The Inuit might have been in a steel frame, so rigidly did metal-hard hands hold him. He had an *ooloo* thrust in his belt. Frost appropriated the small half-moon skinning knife and threw it away. An *oonapik* was stabbed into the snow near by, and Frost kicked at it. The short hunting spear flipped twenty feet distant.

Bill-Bill Oon's features held a ghostly pallor. His stocky limbs trembled.

Frost frowned. The Eskimo was in the grip of a mortal terror!

"What's wrong, Bill-Bill?"

"Takuva-tongak!" moaned the Eskimo

"You saw an evil spirit!" Frost shook him. "Speak English! Why'd you try to grab me?"

The Inuit rolled his eyes. "The evil spirit give Bill-Bill warning we should go back. Bill-Bill know you only laugh. He hope grab you and take you back tied to sled."

Frost exhaled from a corner of his mouth so breath-steam would not be in front of his eyes as he peered at the guide.

"When did you see this evil spirit? What'd he look like ?"

"No man!" muttered Bill-Bill. "It woman! It Flame Maiden! A young woman, most good to look at, but with head of flame!"

Frost jerked upright. Breath expelled from his lungs, spurted a steam plume nearly to the snow-blanketed ground. He raced an alert glance about the spruce-walled clearing in which they had camped.

No living thing moved in the pale gloom of the Arctic night. Not even the dogs of their team. The huskies were asleep under the deep snow. Their sled stuck, curved end up, in a near-by drift.

"Is this Flame Maiden story the truth, Bill-Bill?"

"By the King of *Nakroom*, the great space beyond, it is!" Bill-Bill was a Christian. That was the strongest oath by which he could swear.

Frost's thoughts raced. He was near the end of his trail. Near the source of the fantastic legends of the Flame Maiden!

Constable Andy Frost had been sent to investigate the weird and terrible stories that had come out of this region for the last year. Stories of such horror that native trappers had fled their homes in the district!

The Flame Maiden appeared to travelers, whispered tales had it, and warned them to flee. To those who did not flee, ghastly things happened. Some vanished, never to be heard of again. Others were found, aimless wanderers–hopelessly insane.

The gibberings of these madmen were always the same–they had seen the Flame Maiden, then an awful monster of the night had carried them away into the sky and there destroyed their brains!

The Frozen Phantom, the strange brain-destroying demon was called. Too many men had been found in this region with deranged minds to longer regard the tales as superstitious prattle. The Mounted Police had become suspicious, curious–and here was Constable Andy Frost.

A black scowl contorted Frost's homely little face. "When'd

you see the Flame Maiden?"

"As I gathered dry wood for the fire, just after we made camp." Bill Bill pointed at the spruce which made a somber, sinister wall around them. "It is true! By all that the missionary father said was holy, it is–"

"You stay here!" Frost grunted. "I'm going to look at the tracks this Flame Maiden left! And if I don't find tracks, I'm coming back and pull off one of your arms and use it to beat some sense into you !"

"There were tracks!" A fit of terrified trembling seized the guide. "But when I followed them, they vanished as though she had leaped into the sky."

Frost nearly laughed. But the abject fright of the Eskimo kept the mirth off his lips.

"What language did she speak to you in?"

"English," mumbled the guide. "Her head–it was all a flame. Her voice was beautiful. She was the flame of death!"

Frost turned thoughtfully away. The Eskimo's manner had driven home a puzzling belief. Frost thought Bill-Bill had seen something!

The spruce pressed gloom upon Frost as he entered the thicket. The snow had been made sand-hard by the intense cold. It rasped underfoot.

Frost followed Bill-Bill's plainly discernible tracks. He carried his Ross rifle with the bolt mechanism in the slight warmth of his armpit, to be sure the fulminate in the cartridge did not freeze.

A half dozen reports like gunshots cracked angrily against his eardrums. He stiffened, then relaxed. Ice noises from the lake! It lay a quarter of a mile to his left. It was several miles in area, he had noticed from the last ridge they had crossed. It was dotted with rocky islands.

Halting suddenly, Frost stared at the snow. Here were the tracks of the Flame Maiden!

She had been real after all! In a spot where the snow had not drifted, tracks were implanted clearly. A woman's foot, undoubtedly!

Frost wet the edge of his oversize mouth, steam curling

from his tongue as he did so. He stood as though congealed by the cold.

"Aw-w-w!" he growled at last. "She's human enough, or she wouldn't leave tracks!" He followed the footprints of the Flame Maiden.

A breeze, sighing through the spruce, made a low sobbing sound. Rapping ice cracks came from the lake. The frigid wilderness seemed alive. The snow groaned a tortured dirge as he stepped on it.

Toward the lake the trail led. It entered a clearing, to the right of which lay a sheer cliff of stone some forty feet high. This was the beginning of a narrow canyon, it seemed.

Frost's nerves were taut–far more so than he would have believed possible. For, when the Flame Maiden suddenly appeared on the lip of the cliff, he all but jumped out of his parka!

After his first spasmodic start, Frost nearly shouted his relief. The girl did not have a head of flame! She simply had a tremendous wealth of brilliant red hair, which she had let down around her shoulders.

She was pretty! Even in the half darkness of the Arctic winter night, he could discern a cameo quality to her features The bulky fur garments did not entirely conceal the rather entrancing curves of her form.

Frost grinned. "You sure handed me a start, miss!"

The beautiful girl with the flaming hair did not answer. She stood motionless, silent as an apparition. Frost's spine began to feel strangely chilled. Now that he thought of it, he had not seen the girl appear. She had just materialized, as though by magic.

"Well–say something!" The runty policeman was surprised by the hollow quality of his own voice. For a long minute, no sound came from the strange feminine figure.

"You must go!" She spoke in a small, bell-like voice. "Come at once! It may not be too late to avoid the horrible fate of those who linger!"

"Cut out the play acting!" Frost had decided she was deliberately trying to frighten him as she had Bill-Bill Oon. "I'm sticking right here. Furthermore, I've got some questions to ask you."

"No!" Her voice was a frightened shriek. "No! You must

go. Go and come back! You are of the Mounted. Go and return with many men and machine guns and cannon. Only in that way can you hope to penetrate the lair of the Frozen Phantom!"

The stocky redcoat stood slack-jawed through the speech. "What are you talkin' about? Why do we need cannon?"

The red-headed girl seemed about to answer. Then, instead, she put fingers over her lips and screamed piercingly through them. Once, twice, three times, her shrieks ripped the Arctic cold.

Then she wheeled and disappeared.

Frost grunted explosively. He pitched for the low cliff. Its sheer wall defied him. He ran along it.

His mind tossed in turmoil. This beautiful girl! Was she mad like the others found wandering in this part of the north? The thought was ghastly.

It took Frost many minutes to find a spot where he could ascend the cliff. He lost other minutes locating the Flame Maiden's footprints. He followed her trail.

Down into another steep canyon, it led. The frigid wind, compressed by the sheer, blank walls of stone, was a near gale. It scooped the snow along in boiling clouds.

The tracks were already filling. And suddenly they ended!

Eyes popping in sheer disbelief, Frost stared. There was no getting around it–her trail simply stopped. He looked up. The somber sky was like a long, ragged strip of lead stretched over the crack of a canyon. Fully four hundred feet of sheer, knotty stone reared on either side!

"Somebody could've pulled her up with a rope!" Frost muttered.

Moving down the canyon a few yards, he took off his snowshoes and spiked the ends upright in a drift. He proceeded to climb the cliff. It was a torturous job. Had his muscles been less than steel, his runty frame less monkey-like and adapted to climbing, he wouldn't have accomplished it.

At the top, he made an unnerving discovery. The Flame Maiden had not been hauled to the canyon rim by anybody with a rope! The snow was more than waist deep–at times Frost was forced to lie prone and roll to keep from going in over his head.

Had anyone visited either canyon rim within hours, he would have been able to tell the fact. And no one had!

Frost peered over the edge.

"Whew!" he muttered. The cut of a canyon looked bottomless from up here. Gloom swathed the lower reaches, so deep was it.

"No sign of a shelf or a hole to be seen!" he commented. "Anyway, her tracks vanished near the center of the canyon!"

By peering steadily, he could barely see the spot where the Flame Maiden's footprints disappeared.

Stripping off an armload of spruce branches, Frost tossed them over the canyon lip, one at a time. He watched the twigs float downward like green parachutes. It took them a long time to reach bottom.

Frost swiveled a gaze about. He could see out across the lake from this high perch. The many islands hulked up darkly in the white waste. None were more than a few hundred feet across. Most were sheer of shore line, little more than gigantic stone blocks.

"Fella would need wings to get on a lot of them islands!" Frost decided. "This piece of country is plumb interestin'!"

He clambered back down the cliff-like canyon wall. He put on his snowshoes and returned to his camp.

The Eskimo guide was not there!

"Bill-Bill!" Frost called loudly. His deep voice sounded like a pair of heavy drum taps as he shouted the name.

No answer! Frost ran to the tree where they had cached their supplies to keep them away from wolverines. One man's share was gone! Bill-Bill Oon had skipped out.

"I'll bet I shake some sense into that blubber ball!" Frost gritted.

He set off in pursuit of the deserting Bill-Bill Oon—only to halt within a score of yards. There was sound to the left. A man staggered out of the spruce thicket.

"A redcoat!" the man gasped wildly. "*Dieu!* You are gift of heaven!"

The stranger was tremendously tall and so gaunt as to seem

a walking scarecrow made of bones. His eyes were dark-pupiled, red-flanked globes. His parka and *muck-a-lucks* were worn to the point of falling to pieces. The skin of his face was blue-gray where it was not covered with a coarse, blue-black beard.

When he spoke, it was out of the left side of his mouth. The entire right side of his face was apparently paralyzed.

"Who're you?" Frost had a hand inside his parka, cuddling his revolver.

The tall, disheveled man fawned like a delighted dog.

"Jules La Suede is my name," he mumbled. "*Dieu!* I am most pleased to find you. I have been wandering for weeks, barely existing on what ptarmigan I managed to kill with a club, and for a while on a caribou from which I chased wolves which had just killed it. But the next time I tried to chase away wolves, they turned on me and–"

"What became of your outfit?" Frost interposed.

The scarecrow shivered and peered furtively about.

"The Frozen Phantom, *m'sieu!*" he muttered. "The Flame Maiden appeared to me with a warning I did not heed. That night a monster, a great and horrible thing of black, pounced upon me. I managed to escape. But when I crept back to my camp, my dogs, gun and supplies were gone. *C'est tout!* That is all! I have been a half-mad wanderer since!"

Frost studied the man. A frosty look was in the little constable's eyes. "What were you doing in this country ?"

"I am a trapper, *m'sieu.* I was hunting new fur country."

Frost chewed a lip. "Do you know what this Frozen Phantom is?"

"Non, non!" The other was suddenly seized with terror. "I do not know. No one knows. A monster, a great werewolf of a–"

"Bunk!" sported Frost. His eyes narrowed. "We'll go hunt this–"

"Non!" shrieked the Frenchman. The dead half of his face gave him a repulsive aspect. *"Merci, non!* We must flee!"

Frost was bleak-eyed. Back in his head, thoughts were clicking around and becoming a chain of knowledge that led to–understanding.

Abruptly he pointed off to the right. He said, "Look !"

The scarecrow man with half his face paralyzed turned his head.

Frost swung a fist. *S-s-wap!* The blow felled the man.

As the bony man crashed his length in the snow, the redcoat sprang atop him. He tore open the fellow's parka and crammed searching fingers inside.

He brought out a big Enfield revolver.

"Unarmed, were you ?"

"*Non, non!* I meant–"

"Don't lie to me!" Frost sat on the man's chest. "It took me a minute to remember your face. I saw it on an old reward poster back at the post. Your name isn't Jules La Suede! It's Half-a-Face Pontois! You're wanted for murdering two men in a Dawson bank holdup!"

The prisoner shook his head violently. But there was an ugly light in his enflamed eyes. "You are wrong, *m'sieu!* Gladly will I accompany you to your post–"

"Sure you would–not!" Frost sneered. "I'm wonderin' why you showed up here, Half-a-Face Pontois? It's got me plumb puzzled!"

"Mon Dieu! I tell you I am not–"

"So I'm going to scout around a little," Frost said dryly. "It wouldn't surprise me a bit to find you were mixed up with this Frozen Phantom and Flame Maiden business."

Frost handcuffed the man's arms around a small spruce. He tossed his rabbit-lined sleeping bag over the fellow so he wouldn't freeze to death. Then he set out on the trail of the Eskimo guide, Bill-Bill Oon.

Snow jarred off branches and showered Frost's parka hood and spilled in clouds off his shoulders. The Eskimo's tracks kept to the open ground. They were far apart, showing Bill-Bill was running.

Frost came to a large clearing. There he Jerked up rigid. Ice seemed to clutch his spine.

Bill-Bill Oon had met some kind of a horrible fate in the clearing!

Over an area a score of feet across, snow was whipped and torn with the marks of a gigantic struggle. Frost gave those marks an incredulous stare. He could imagine no human agency which might have made them. It was as though–and he berated himself for a fool as he thought of it –some feathered monster had beaten the earth with great wings.

Frost leaped headlong across the torn snow. He found tracks.

Tracks! The runty redcoat's throat tightened. He tried to fight off the superstitious terror that wanted to seize him.

Such tracks these were! That any human agency could have made them seemed preposterous. They were circular, big as small barrel heads. In the deep indentations were narrow lines which Frost's eyes kept telling him were imprints of folded talons of gigantic size.

"C'mon out of it, guy!" Frost shook his shoulders impatiently. He made himself follow the tracks.

The weird tracks–they were spaced only a couple of feet apart–ascended a steep slope where spruces were less abundant. They crossed a ridge.

Standing on the ridge, Frost stared about.

"Well, I'll be danged!" he muttered.

On the right, he could look across to the spot at which Bill-Bill Oon had been seized. And this was the same side upon which the Flame Maiden had stood when she screamed so strangely and terribly.

Had she seen Bill-Bill Oon's fate and screamed because of the horror of what she witnessed ?

Shrugging, he went on The gloom of the spruces enveloped him. Sombre, throbbing with the knelling dirge of the wind, the place had a reek of cold death. The breeze made whispering siren voices that seemed everywhere. They breathed words, threats, pleas, into the redcoat's straining, nervous ears. And when he ignored them, the frigid snow moaned horribly underfoot.

"Andy Frost!"

The undersized constable jerked up. His name! The whispers were breathing his name. He wet his lips and shuddered Was he going insane?

"Constable Andy Frost!" This whisper was distinct!

Then Frost saw her–the Flame Maiden!

She stood to his left, almost invisible in the gloom of a spruce thicket. Off toward the Pole, the borealis fanned weird rods of tinted light in the heavens. The glow danced across the ghostly form of the Flame Maiden, making wondrous gleamings in her flaming hair.

Frost took a step forward. She did not recoil. He saw her face more distinctly . It was a nice face. But it bore–and he could hardly repress a shiver as he saw–a stamp of utter terror.

"You know my name?" Frost's voice was squeaky.

The Flame Maiden nodded. "Yes. Your guide–I heard him tell the Frozen Phantom you were Constable Andy Frost of the Mounted."

Her low belling voice had a quality of music that was muted rhythm.

"My guide!" Frost's voice was a crash of relief. "He is alive?"

He saw her slender, shapely limbs flutter like wind-punished plants as she shuddered.

"He is–alive. But it would be better–if he were not. The Frozen Phantom is putting him–in the Coffin of the Mad."

Frost's thoughts were divided– more than half of them on this entrancing bit of femininity before him. He was close enough now so that he could have touched her.

"The Frozen Phantom? What is the thing ?"

"I am allowed to warn those who come near," she choked. "That is all I can do. If they do not flee, they are seized."

Frost made an impatient gesture. "What is the Frozen–"

"I'm here to warn you!" she interposed in a frightened rush. "It may not be too late. I warned your guide. Then I came again to warn you. There on the cliff, I saw the–Frozen Phantom–stalking your guide. I knew the fate that was meant for the guide. It was so horrible I screamed. Then, fearing the Frozen Phantom, I fled."

"You are in danger ?" Frost demanded.

"I don't–think so," she said hesitatingly. "They haven't–haven't harmed me–yet."

Frost stepped to her side, took her arm She made no effort to draw away. He felt immeasurably thrilled at the throbbing firmness of her.

"You're real enough!" he grinned. "Now cut out this ghost talk! Tell me what's behind the whole–"

He swallowed the rest. The girl had pointed over his shoulder with both hands. "The Frozen Phantom!" she shrieked.

Frost gripped his Ross rifle, twisted . But even as he spun, something seemed to fill all the gloom about him with swishing sound. His arms and head and shoulders were entrapped in something which was resilient, and yet which held him with an unbelievable strength.

In the murk, Frost could hardly see what it was. It was like–and the thought was too incredible for his brain to grasp–he was wrapped in a great spider web. He tried to lift his rifle, could not.

Frost saw, flinging toward him, the Frozen Phantom!

A monster that seemed nothing but a black, tumultuous cloud! The thing was almost upon him. It was a ghastly, unreal apparition in the half-darkness.

The flame-haired girl screamed again.

A yell ripped past Frost's teeth. He dropped his rifle, fought to get at the revolver inside his parka.

Blows from the black monster began to rain on him. Terrific smashes that left frozen, ghastly numbness where they struck! He was battered down.

He took a blow on the temple. A howling blizzard of Stygian darkness seemed to gather in the distance and rush down and envelope him.

Frost's awakening was slow, fraught with exquisite tortures. He tried to move his arms. They were bound. A jarring pain burst in his side. Another! He was being kicked.

"Get up!" snarled the voice of Half a-Face Pontois.

Frost weaved to his feet. Then his eyes flashed wide with surprise.

A sizable black cloak lay near by, together with of vicious clubs, and weird, round, barrel-head-like snowshoes.

"*Oui!*" sneered Half-a-Face Pontois. "I am the Frozen Phantom!"

Four bearded men stood close. They held the red-haired Flame Maiden.

No doubt the quartette had also released Half-a-Face Pontois by shattering the cold-bristled handcuff links. The steel circlets still hung to the scarecrow man's wrists.

"You fool!" Pontois leered at Frost. "You had your chance to leave peaceably! The girl pleaded for your life. But now–we have no choice. You will be put into the Coffin of the Mad–and made insane!"

Frost gave the dead-faced man back leer for leer. He was wondering what was behind all this.

"Walk!" commanded Pontois.

Frost was propelled away. Half-a-Face gathered up his cloak-and-club rigamarole–and a square of ordinary fish netting. That net showed Frost what had trapped his arms in such mysterious fashion. Half-a-Face had merely cast it over him!

The four thugs with the red-headed girl brought up the rear.

Down into the slanting floor of a canyon they went. Frost blinked. It was the same canyon in which the girl had seemingly vanished. Ahead, he could see the spruce branches he had tossed from the canyon rim high above.

"So we're going to disappear?" he said dryly.

Half-a-Face Pontois glared at Frost. "So you figured that out? I didn't think you was smart enough to do it!"

"I dropped branches from the canyon rim," Frost advised him. "I saw one bounce in midair, and knew it had struck a fine wire stretched between the two rocky walls. It couldn't be larger than a thread, or it could be seen. You use it, and a pulley system, to haul a stouter rope across the canyon when you want to leave the hidden tunnel in the rock–"

"You got it all, didn't you?" grated Half-a-Face.

"I had to guess about the tunnel," Frost retorted. "It's mighty well hidden. I couldn't see a sign of it. But it had to be there."

Even now the fine wire high overhead was pulling a rope

across the canyon, through a concealed pulley, and back. A sort of block-and-tackle fitted with a chair ran out on the rope. The chair dropped downward. Frost was forced into it.

He was hoisted upward, then along the rope to a yard-sized hole in the sheer stone. This was closed with a stone door, so cleverly fitted that even a telescope from the canyon rim would not discern it among the many other cracks veining the vertical surface.

Two shaggy men held Frost under gun muzzles. The girl was lifted in the strange cradle that so simply explained her earlier "disappearance." Then up came Half-a-Face Pontois and the others.

"I'm so sorry–" the girl started to tell Frost.

"Shut up!" ripped one of the gang.

They went down a crude, darkened tunnel, not unlike a mine bore. Half-a-Face Pontois lighted the way with a candle. For hundreds of yards they walked.

Frost realized they were heading out under the lake floor! The tunnel was taking them to one of the little, steep-walled islands! They came out into the Arctic night at last–on the crest of a castle-like island.

The center of the rocky islet was a cup-like depression. In it were rough buildings. The structures huddled close together. The party pulled up before one of them.

Half-a-Face Pontois thrust his features into those of Frost.

"You will be placed immediately in the Coffin of the Mad!" he leered. "In only a few hours, your brain will be gone!' He snapped his fingers. "Like that! Your Eskimo guide is already in the Coffin of the Mad!"

Frost's snarl made breath steam squirt through his teeth. But before he could speak, there came an interruption.

"Drop those guns!" rapped a voice from the window of the log shack.

The window instantly magnetized all eyes. The barrel of an ancient Snider carbine projected through the aperture. Back of the weapon, a man glared grim threat.

He was white of hair, seamed of face. He had a wasted figure. An elderly man, his features were intelligent, but intense suffering, probably mental rather than physical, had put grooves around his mouth and a haunted look in his eyes.

Suddenly, with a wild leap, Frost sailed for the door of the log shack. This man was a friend, no matter who he might be. He plunged through the door.

A man, obviously one of Half-a-Face Pontois' gang, lay unconscious in the middle of the floor. The white-haired man had knocked him out.

Boom! The old Snider spoke thunder. Outside, a man screamed and dropped–a man behind whom Half-a-Face Pontois had leaped.

Then whiskered thugs poured into the door. Frost's bound hands handicapped him. He was borne down by sheer force of numbers.

The white-haired man fired again, missed, and was knocked senseless with a clubbed pistol. He fell beside the guard he seemingly had kayoed.

Half-a-Face Pontois, having kept clear of the action, came lumbering in breathing noisily from the live side of his mouth. He was dragging the girl. She clawed at him, dug at his eyes. He dodged his head from side to side and captured her hands.

"You little spitfire!" he gloated. "Tried to make a break, you and your dad! Well, I'm glad of it! I'm tired of playing along with you. I don't need to do that now, because we can do the work your old man has been doing!"

Understanding cracked in Frost's brain. This elderly man was the girl's father! Half-a-Face Pontois had been forcing him to do some sort of work, using the welfare of his daughter as a club.

"What is your name?" Frost asked.

Before Half-a-Face Pontois could prevent, the girl replied, "Loy Wynne! That is my father, Dave Wynne!"

"Why, you're the two who–" But a kick folded Frost in a gulping heap, the rest of the identification blasted off his lips.

Dave Wynne was a mining engineer. More than a year ago he and his daughter had been reported missing. But that was some hundreds of miles to the south!

Half-a-Face Pontois had kidnapped them! That was it!

"Lock up this little *singe!*" roared Half-a-Face. "When the brain of the Eskimo is destroyed, remove him. Then put this redcoat in the Coffin of the Mad!"

Frost was hauled out. A dozen yards away stood another cabin, windowless, more ramshackle. He was pitched into this. The door slammed. A bar rattled.

Frost sat up and looked around. The place was absolutely bare of weapons from dirt floor to log ceiling. It was bitterly cold. The cracks were big, unchinked.

Frost, cooling from the heat of the struggle, bent his arms against his sides and stamped his feet for warmth. He went through his clothing hastily, but found not a single article he could use for a weapon.

Laughter pealed outside. He squinted through a crack, saw a bottle of reddish liquor passing between two guards stationed near his prison.

"Damn them!" the redcoat gritted savagely. "That poor girl!"

He began to work on his wrist lashings. They were of walrus hide, stiff, tough. He freed himself at last, however. But he was little better off.

The door bar rattled abruptly One of the gang came in. He had food–a filthy mush of stuff on a tin plate.

"Your last meal as a sane man!" he leered. "Eat it! Enjoy it! For henceforth, you will dine on bark and grass and on pebbles and dirt. For you will have no brain to tell you what is fit to eat and what is not!"

Knowing he was being baited out of vile cruelty, Frost started to curse the fellow. Then he swallowed his invective A wily glitter came into his bleak eyes. He tried to keep his homely face expressionless.

"That's fine of you," he said. "Thanks."

The guard was disappointed. He made a move to throw the food out of the door, then sneered and hurled it at Frost. The stuff sprayed over the policeman and the floor.

"There you are!" leered the guard, and backed outside with the tin pan.

Frost stifled a bark of delight. He began gathering up the dirty, wet mess of food as though it were so much wealth. There was a moose hash in a mushy gruel of rice.

He balled the stuff. Then he placed it near a large crack. He made three balls, each about the size of his knotted fist.

He left them lying before the crack–in the bitter cold that swept in from outdoors. Five minutes, ten–he waited. Then he strode to the window and tested the balled food.

The soggy stuff had frozen solidly. Be now had three missiles almost as effective as half-bricks

Several times, Frost went through the windup of a baseball pitcher. Sure his throwing arm was limber, he positioned himself against the wall opposite the door. There was no time to delay, if he was to save Bill-Bill Oon.

Frost's homely face was a welted mass of taut muscle–some indication of the physical tension he was under. He knew only too well how slender his chances were.

"C'mere, one of you!" he shouted, lifting his voice.

Getting no answer, he repeated the call. He was cursed for his pains.

Frost scowled. He groped in his brain for another ruse. This one wouldn't work. He hefted the frozen food balls. Then he got an idea. He attracted the guards outside, enticing them near a crack.

"I have money," he breathed. "It was not found when I was searched. I will pay you to let me escape!"

"I'll be right in!"

Frost waited. He knew the guard, an ape-browed brute, had no idea of being bribed. The fellow merely intended to appropriate the money the others had missed.

The door bar rattled. Frost backed hastily across the room.

Behind the gaping snout of an ancient Enfield revolver, the apish guard crowded into the room. He saw Frost against the wall opposite–too far away to attack with a sudden leap. That lulled his suspicions. He turned carelessly to secure the door.

Frost had kept his hands out of sight. He produced them now, gripping his two frozen food missiles. The third was in a pocket of his scarlet tunic.

Ho lobbed one like a baseball. It caught the guard squarely in the head. It burst like a snow ball. The fellow slapped against the door, slid down it to the floor.

Frost leaped. He scooped up the dazed guard's Enfield revolver.

Clank! The Enfield barrel sounded like wood-against-wood as Frost slammed it on the man's head. The apish fellow went down. It would be an hour before he awakened, at the least.

Frost yanked open the door. The second guard was just reaching for the latch. He tried to get his gun up.

But runty Constable Frost functioned with the bewildering speed of electrical apparatus when he went into action. He lobbed another frozen food ball.

It connected with the guard's mouth. His jaws filled with dislodged teeth. He bawled. He waved his arms. Frost charged him.

The man shot, but wildly. Frost let him have another ball of frozen food between the eyes. The man's orbs were lost behind slow-shutting lids. The fellow was out on his feet. They were effective, those frozen balls. No Kerry man with a brick could have done better.

Frost grabbed another big Enfield from the fellow's slack fingers. The man wore a shabby cartridge belt, well laden with shells. Frost seized it, yanked. Leather parted and it was in his fingers. He belted the stunned man again to make the sleep semi-permanent.

With a flying plunge, Frost went around the shack. He almost speared a man on the snout of one of his two captured revolvers.

The fellow was a stocky, evil picture of fat and whiskers. He yanked back the hammer of the rifle he was carrying.

Frost stroked trigger. His Enfield roared like a brass cannon. The man of fat and whiskers lay down slowly, as though tired of it all. The bullet had coursed through his brain.

The man had come from the largest of the collection of cabins. This was no more than two score feet away. Since no one was in sight anywhere else, Frost made for it.

When he was less than two yards from the door, a man popped out of the cabin in which the girl's father, white-haired Dave Wynne, had attempted his short-lived bid for liberty. The fellow came out as though driven by explosive. He threw up a rifle. But, at that range, no rifle could have been aimed and fired in time to catch Frost.

The runty constable whipped to cover inside the large cabin. He started to whirl and take a snapshot at the rifleman. Then he stopped. His eyes widened. He forgot all about the rifleman.

"The Coffin of the Mad!" he muttered.

He did not know what he had expected, but sight of the things surprised him. It really looked like a coffin!

It was of some blackish-brown, massive mineral with a tar-like lustre. In size as well as shape, it resembled a receptacle for the dead. There was a cover, perforated with holes for breathing, secured with stout hasps.

The whole thing bore certain crudities which told Frost it had been made here in the northland! It had been mortared together roughly out of many blocks of the blackish-brown stuff.

The room held something else. Frost stared at it.

"Gold milling machinery!" he grunted.

The machinery, a small mill for crushing the rock, and mechanism for extracting the precious metal, was such as could easily be transported to this remote spot by dog team.

Stray lumps of ore lay on the packed earth floor. It was high grade stuff! The wire gold was plainly discernible.

Frost understood the whole thing now!

Half-a-Face Pontois had brought the mining engineer, Dave Wynne, to this spot and forced him to conduct the technical operation of extracting the gold from the rich ore. Beautiful Loy Wynne's welfare had been the club which had driven the mining engineer to obey.

Half-a-Face, since he was wanted for murder, could not appear openly and lay claim to this rich lode. So he had been working it secretly, and by building up the terrible legend of the Frozen Phantom and the Flame Maiden, had sought to frighten away all who ventured near.

Only one thing remained unexplained. What was the nature of the gruesome Coffin of the Mad? Frost tore at the hasps. He got the black grisly lid up.

Bill-Bill Oon lay inside. Wrists and ankles were bound. His eyes protruded. His face was purple. He looked like a man with a great fever.

Frost's heart sank. The Inuit might already be beyond help, his mind ruined. Frost peered at the strange, blackish coffin, wondering what ghastly quality it held to cause this terrible thing.

But loud yelling outside called him back to ugly reality. Half-a-Face Pontois was squawling for his men to get to work with their rifles on the Mounted Policeman.

Frost hauled the Eskimo out of the fearsome box of a coffin. He worked frantically over the man's bindings. A knot gave, then another.

Bill-Bill Oon said no word.

Frost got the bindings free.

Suddenly Bill-Bill Oon struck savagely at Frost. He raved a wild gibberish. He frothed.

Frost's heart sank. The Eskimo was beyond help! He was already insane, a gibbering idiot! With the greatest of difficulty, Frost evaded the Inuit. He dashed for the door. One of his two Enfields came up, banged.

A man–the rifleman–racing for the door, hardly stopped his headlong charge as a bullet slugged him. He ran wildly a distance of twenty feet, then became a tumbling tangle of arms and legs.

"Four down!" Frost gulped. He had no idea how many men were here. There had been eight or ten at first, he suspected.

He hit the ground outside. Digging up snow, he whirled around a corner.

The string of a violin seemed to snap in his ear as a bullet went past. The slug screamed as it ricocheted from a stone somewhere. Frost threw up a revolver, sight-nocked the man who had fired and nursed the trigger back.

He missed. But the fellow who had tried to shoot him ducked from sight.

"Loy!" Frost roared. "Miss Wynne!" He wanted to know where the girl was.

"Here!" Her voice pealed from a cabin to his left.

Frost ran for the sound. Ten feet from the door, he sailed into the air. He hit the door feet-first, a hundred and seventy pounds of bulleting force. With an explosion of rending wood the panel caved.

Frost sledded inside atop the falling panel.

White-haired Dave Wynne was there, tied to the upright

post of a built-in bunk.

Flame-haired Loy Wynne was there, also. She was flushed, disheveled. Half-a-Face Pontois had been deviling her.

Pontois himself stood wide-legged, lifting an Enfield revolver. Scratches on his face, a split in his lip, one eye badly gouged, showed the girl had so far succeeded in repulsing his advances

Half-a-Face's Enfield banged. He had hurried, and his slug split the door on which Frost coasted.

Frost pulled trigger. *Click!* Empty! He brought up his other gun. Then pretty Loy Wynne, flinging across the room, knocked aside Half-a-Face's gun just as he prepared to fire a shot that almost certainly would have finished Frost. She jabbed her fingers into the boss killer's eyes.

Frost got up off the door. He staggered to the struggling pair. He struck a blow with his empty revolver that broke Pontois' gun arm between wrist and elbow. He tried to land another blow that would have crushed the murderer's skull.

But Half-a-Face dodged He twisted free. He tried to reach the revolver which had fallen from the slackening grip of his broken arm. But he saw Frost would certainly belt him on the head before he could get it. Straightening, he ran out of the door.

Frost, seeking to follow, got tangled in the wreckage of the door and fell down.

Fighting clear of the door ruins, Frost threw his empty gun and the cartridge belt to Loy Wynne.

"Load it ! Keep it for yourself !"

He scooped up the weapon Half-a-Face Pontois had dropped. He swiveled to the door, boiled outside–a squat, homely-faced runt with the ungainly gait of a gorilla. A compact human fighting machine imbued with a recklessness the equal of which is rarely attained!

In one sense, he had gone completely amuck. He had shed every atom of caution. That he could have barricaded himself in the cabin and picked off his foes–with good luck–did not occur to him. The only thing he was seeing at the moment was the horrible, mad face of Bill-Bill Oon and the picture of pretty Loy Wynne in the hands of Half-a-Face Pontois.

Ten seconds later he bulleted between the eyes an incautious breed who thrust head and shoulders around a cabin to aim a rifle at him.

At the shot crack, Half-a-Face Pontois turned his head. Sight of the gnarled, red-coated little nemesis bounding across the snow after him seemed to lend him wings. He popped into a cabin, seized a rifle off pegs, saw it was empty and threw it down. He ran for his life. He dived out a rear door, fanned with cold air from a bullet that kissed nap off his shirt collar.

Into another cabin, he popped. He slammed the door. Frost saw this structure was long. It had the marks of a bunkhouse. He jumped feet first against the door. It tossed him back. He knew then it was too solid to smash down in a hurry. He raced around it.

A man hung half out of a window. Crimson leaked from his nostrils. He was dead.

Frost gaped. He had not shot this one!

But now he became aware of low, shuffling sounds from within the long building. They grew louder. Came a bawl of terror. Yells! Blows! Then shots! A volley of them!

Frost rammed head and shoulders in the window. Awesome was the sight that met his eyes.

Bill-Bill Oon was locked in mortal combat with Half-a-Face Pontois. Face to face, they strained across the floor. Half-a-Face Pontois had drawn a pistol. It exploded. The Eskimo jerked as the slug bedded down in his body somewhere.

Then, with a shriek, Half-a-Face was forced to drop his gun.

Bill-Bill Oon must have come directly to this cabin after Frost released him. The insane Eskimo had brought along the first thing that came to his hands–an ordinary steel crowbar.

The work of that crowbar lay spread on the floor. Three dead men!

They were piled in grotesque shapes, crushed heads staining the packed earth floor. Bill-Bill Oon must have come through this back window upon them.

Suddenly Bill-Bill discovered Frost. The insane contortion smoothed off his face to some extent, leaving it peaceful. He released Half-a-Face Pontois. He picked up his heavy crowbar. Like a big, gentle dog that has sighted its master, the poor idiot came toward Frost. He smiled vacantly. He did not know what he was doing.

Half-a-Face Pontois staggered about after being released. Then he pounced on his revolver. Bill-Bill was between Half-a-Face Pontois and Frost. Frost could not fire.

Half-a-Face Pontois shot the insane Eskimo in the back.

With a gibbering squawl, a ghastly sound that ripped through the frigid Arctic air, the Inuit whirled and sprang. Pontois' gun roared again. The bullet seemed to halt the Eskimo in midair. Then he came on. He was a violent maniac, made thus by the fiendish Coffin of the Mad! He seemed not even to feel pain. That was merciful.

His crowbar traveled a terrific arc. It brained Half-a-Face Pontois.

The Eskimo made an attempt to swing his club again, although it was not necessary. Then he seemed to go asleep on his feet. He swayed. He pitched forward across the body Pontois and the life left him.

Frost jerked his head out of the window of that cabin of death. He raced around in front, eyes alert. But a sepulchral quiet had descended upon the castle-like rock of an island.

Ice out on the lake made ghostly pop-pop-booming noises.

Flame-haired Loy Wynne and her father ran up.

"There's nine of them dead or laid up, includin' Pontois!" Frost barked. "How many's left?"

"Why–nine of them–that's the whole gang," Dave Wynne said wonderingly. "There's nobody left."

"Your Eskimo guide?" asked pretty Loy Wynne. "What about him ?"

Frost shook his head slowly. "The Coffin of the Mad got him. But he went out like a hunter of his people would be proud to go. He accounted for Half-a-Face Pontois, and three of the others."

Frost looked sharply at Dave Wynne. "That Coffin of the Mad– what makes it work like–it does. What is the thing?"

"It is made of pitchblende," Wynne explained. "It contains a rich quantity of radium. That explains its grisly operation. Radium in close proximity to the human brain is capable of doing great damage. All doctors are aware of that."

"But where–"

"Where did Half-a-Face Pontois get it? He merely stole it from a concern which is producing radium far south of here. I think he worked for the company and stole bits of rich ore until he had enough to make the Coffin of the Mad."

Frost shuddered, visioning again that awful, sleek black coffin. The Coffin of the Mad.

That nightmare faded, giving way to a picture that was real and infinitely more pleasurable. A picture of a flame-haired girl with haunting eyes. The Flame Maiden !

And from the look in the Flame Maiden's eyes, Constable Frost of the Mounted rather had a hunch he would have that picture with him for a long time.

SPOILERS OF THE LOST WORLD

By Roger Daniels

A valley of life in a land of frozen death. A golden-haired goddess in an Eden of a savage, lost race. Through screaming blizzards Corporal Peters sought them—his only sign-posts a madman's ravings and a skeleton's long-stilled boast!

"Mon Pere! *Le bon Dieu...*" Out of the night and the North, Alcide Jacquard burst into the cabin of Gordon, the missionary, on the lonely reaches of the lower Mackenzie.

For half the long Arctic night Gordon had been waiting for Jacquard's return, a vigil now of nearly three months, but he had looked for no such pitiful end-of-the-trail appearance as this.

It was seven months since the Geological Survey, for which Jacquard had acted as guide, had given up its search for prehistoric deposits and had passed back through the river trading posts bound for home. But Jacquard had not come with them. The leader of the expedition had said something about "hare-brained."

That was no new tale to Gordon. There were many who had hinted that Alcide was a half-wit, for all that he knew the

trackless ice fields and tundra as a cat at night knows a neighborly alley.

Gordon did not forget the time when he lay helpless with a broken leg and the signs of tetanus beginning to show. It was Jacquard who had fought his way through a week-old blizzard to Fort Murray and had brought back Peters, acting Post surgeon. Peters, too, was one of the few who had a liking for Jacquard and credited the guide with more wisdom than many of the half-breed's weird notions would countenance in others.

So when the flaming red and green and gold curtain of the Aurora Borealis sent its great folds rolling across the northern sky to proclaim the coming of the Arctic night Gordon prepared to wait it out for Jacquard.

Always before the half-breed had come to the little cabin with a smile that showed his even white teeth. Now, he lay where he had fallen, an inert heap of numbed flesh and fur, on the floor of the cabin.

Gordon sprang from the table, where he had been reading, to lift the unconscious figure in his strong arms and bear it to the rude bunk in the corner. Jacquard was like a dead man.

Gordon virtually tore the parka from him and with his clasp knife hacked away the frozen boot lacings.

When he put his hand to the heel of a boot to pull it off the knowledge that comes to a man who has lived long in the North told him that the foot was frozen. So he went to work again with the knife, cutting away the boot.

Several hours passed before Jacquard opened his eyes; breathless, almost frantic hours for Gordon. His medical training consisted of a thoroughgoing first aid. He had rubbed the half-breed's frozen feet and hands with snow. He had swathed him in heated blankets. But Jacquard needed more than first aid. When finally he did open his eyes it was to give the missionary another shock.

"Blind, mon Pere," he whispered, putting a bandaged hand to his face. "Two, t'ree day since everyt'ing she go red."

"Good Lord!" Gordon bent over the bunk to stare helplessly into the unseeing eyes. "How under heaven did you get here, Alcide?"

"How the leetle mole she find his way, eh, mon Pere? *Le bon Dieu*, he geev the mole no eye. How she find his way? By gar! Alcide he crawl here by his nose just lak the leetle mole she crawl!"

Jacquard's arm fell and he slipped back in the blankets. Gordon clenched his fists and turned to walk up and down the small room.

Suffering was not a new thing to him, nor was death. But after his long wait, to have Alcide come back to him broken by the Arctic weighed down on him until he could have cried out to high heaven in his anguish. Instead he knelt in prayer, and his prayer was that the end of suffering might come quickly. He was still on his knees before the bunk when he felt the half-breed move. Jacquard raised himself painfully to an elbow. His blank eyes turned vacantly toward the missionary.

Mebbe, mon Pere don' ask Alcide why he come back, eh?"

Gordon tried to answer and choked.

"Why Alcide don' care one damn if he lose dogs, eh? Why he don' care one damn if he lose t'ousan' dog, eh?"

It was a living horror to have to stand and stare into those unseeing eyes. Gordon heard what the half-breed said like a man under the grip of a terrible nightmare. Every word came to him as in a dream and he was powerless to answer, powerless even to move. He prayed dumbly that the agony of the man before him might be his own, yet knowing that the prayer was futile. All he could do was to stand there helpless and alone. The cruel torture of the journey back to civilization had driven Alcide mad.

As if the man on the bunk had read his thoughts Gordon

heard him whisper:

"Mebbe, mon Pere, he t'ink Alcide he go, w'at you call him? Off his nut, eh? By gar!" The half-breed showed his teeth in a leering grin. Then he leaned forward and went on almost in a mad frenzy.

"All his life Alcide he look for somet'ing. Mebbe, mon Pere, he ask w'at it is Alcide he find? Eh? Mebbe mon Pere he lak to know himself w'at she is?" A maudlin laugh rang through the room.

Gordon shuddered. The fear and loneliness he had felt looming up around him descended with a menacing suddenness as he sensed the cunning with which Jacquard was trying in his mad way to cloak his insane dream.

"Come, come, Alcide, you're all right now, lie quiet." He tried to put assurance into the words, but his voice sounded hollow.

The half-breed, if he heard, gave no sign. He merely grinned.

"How you lak be king, eh, mon Pere? She is fine to be king! Have beautiful wife, eh? Two, t'ree, mebbe ten wife! She is fine job, eh, mon Pere? You t'ink Alcide mean squaw. *Mais oui*, thees woman she is white. White, mon Pere, lak when gold she is white ! And eyes, mon Pere! Thees woman she has eyes so blue lak the sky! Alcide he go crazee, w'at you t'ink?"

Jacquard sank down. Gordon pulled the covers up over him and then went back to his table. All he could do was wait, he knew that. He knew also that the real task before him was to keep his own mind clear of this mad dream that had taken possession of the half-breed's brain. One maniac in a cabin above the Arctic circle was enough.

But there was something strangely insidious in the dream and in Alcide's manner of telling it. He tried to read, but instead of the printed words, those poor blank eyes kept staring at him from the page. He shut the book with a slam. The next moment he repented of his nerves. Jacquard was stirring again.

"Mon Pere, he don't t'ink there really ees king, eh? He wonder how she come there ees king? He t'ink Alcide he tell? Mon Pere, he don' t'ink thees king she has ivoree w'at you call throne? He don' t'ink there ees ivoree room ten times so big as thees shack. Mebbe, mon Pere, Alcide he come back so he could file claim !"

Again the half-breed was quiet and this time the missionary took good care not to disturb him. There was less mockery in the tone of the last speech and to Gordon it seemed that, even in his madness, Alcide was struggling to convince himself that something he had dreamed was really true.

As a young man Gordon had known the Barbary Coast. He knew the "white flower" dreams of the opium smokers. He had seen the subtle poppy work just such wreckage of the mind of a man the privations of the Arctic had evidently wrought with Jacquard. And the half-breed's dream was much like an opium vagary.

Of course there was no connection with the two, but the other helped him to get hold of himself. He had tended many a drug-soaked wreck. Why should a man driven insane by exposure put his own nerves on edge?

He tried to shake off the feeling of loneliness. Ever since the Geological Survey party had gone through he had waited with the knowledge that Alcide would come back. He knew they had gone looking for fossils. The half-breed might have gained his ivory notion from them.

A well-known explorer had claimed to have found a race of white Eskimos. When madness takes hold of the mind fantasies quickly become facts. There was enough of actual fact to have given Alcide the beginning of his dream. Then had come the loss of reason and the dream had spread its bounds.

So Gordon tried to think it out for the sake of keeping his own mind clear. Without knowing it he dropped off to sleep. He awoke with Jacquard's cry echoing through the room.

"Mon Pere! . . . *Le bon Dieu!* "

Gordon sprang to the door. Half way there he was wide awake. It was that first cry of Alcide's which had rung in his ears. And now in his haste he had knocked back his chair with a thud.

The figure on the bunk stirred and Gordon tip-toed softly over. But the sightless eyes were closed. Only a low moan came from the sleeper. The missionary bent over him and noticed that the half-breed scarcely breathed. The moaning ceased. Then an expression of pain that turned suddenly to a smile passed over Jacquard's tired face.

"Alcide." Gordon spoke low.

But the half-breed did not hear. Even as the missionary spoke his name a purple shadow came like a sudden flush to Jacquard's cheeks. Gordon had seen the shadow of death before. His prayer that suffering might end quickly had been answered.

A sob that was half grief and half thankfulness caught in his throat as he dropped to his knees beside the dead.

II

Gordon picked up the little cylinder of white bone and held it on the palm of his hand, idly balancing it, as a man does when he guesses the weight of an object. He, too, was judging its weight but not in terms of pounds and ounces. The ivory talisman impressed him as an extraordinary proof of the frailty of man. That Jacquard of all men should have succumbed to its subtle mystery!

It was with the sense that he held in his hand the chief cause of the half-breed's death that he reached up and placed it back on the hewn log above the fireplace which served as a shelf.

It was folly to think that trivial things like this could possess supernatural powers exerting an uncanny influence over the possessor. There were precious stones which had gained notoriety because of such tales woven about them. Gordon did not believe in such things but nevertheless he was glad when he no longer held the cylinder in his hand.

The Far North is superstitious. Many strange tales had come to his ears during the years of his mission work. Among the French-Canadian trappers the *loup garou*, or werewolf, was a common source of conversation. Gordon knew how easily such tales gained credence. He still recalled with a shudder his own sudden meeting with the albino wolf. How its pinkish eyes had glared at him from the undergrowth. Then the ghost-like movement as it loped off into the gloom. It had been just at dawn.

Such animals were freaks of nature, nothing more, but a freak met under unpropitious conditions is a hard thing to shake from one's mind. All that day every snow-covered bush he passed had sent a chill through his body. Even the dogs had snarled most of the way home. So does the weird and unknown haunt the mind of man and break down the courage of dumb brutes. In spite of himself his eyes roved to the ledge above the fireplace and sought out the ivory cylinder.

A cold sweat stood on his forehead at the thought that he, too, might even now be coming under its unknown spell.

"How you lak be king, eh, mon Pere?" The mad words still rang through the room.

And what was it Alcide had said about a woman "white lak gold she is white"?

Gordon was too old a hand at loneliness to know that if his present state of mind kept up he would be crazier than Jacquard was when he burst open the door of the cabin. He bundled himself in his parka and with an ax went out to cut a grave through the snow and ice.

The exercise did him good and he was in a glow all over when he came back into the cabin an hour later. But it was no easy task to lay away the body of a friend in the cold tundra. He hunted through his dunnage bag for some bits of candle. Alcide would sleep better out there in the cold if a candle had burned at his bier.

A search of the half-breed's parka revealed a crucifix. Who was he to question the faith of any man? Besides it did him good to think of the spiritual side of the half-breed's life. In another age and time Alcide might have been swashbuckler and lover by turn.

There is nothing soft in life above the Arctic Circle. But there were things which Gordon knew had been dear to the halfbreed in life. It was proper that they should be held dear to him in death.

He had waited months for Alcide. There was no reason why he should not sit a few hours longer in the little cabin by the side of his friend now that there was an end of waiting. To his tired mind it seemed restful just to sit there and watch the candles flicker. Man was like that. A candle flickering in a blustering world. Some kept the flame of life burning bright to the very end. In some lives the flame never seemed to go out but continued to burn brightly even after death.

And here was a man, true to the law of give and take, ready with an arm to help the weak, yet the flame of life was gone before half the course had run. All that remained now were a few flickering tallow candles.

Gordon was glad when morning came. At least he called it morning. He had sat twelve full hours beside the dead. Outside the winter night gave no gleam. He was a shadow bearing another shadow when he made his way to the grave he had dug with the ax. When that task was finished he turned to the ax again and ripped up a section of the floor. A cross would mark the place where Alcide lay.

When at last he came back and everything had been done–not another blessed thing to fill his mind–he sank down at his table and wept. Then it was that thoughts of the ivory cylinder took hold of him again.

He got up and brought it from the mantelpiece. Here was the thing responsible for Alcide's death. Where had it come from? Until he found it in the pocket of the half-breed's parka he had dismissed everything Jacquard had said as the mutterings of insanity. But ivory had been the burden of Alcide's wild tale. A whole room of ivory, "ten times so beeg as thees shack," were the half-breed's own words. He had spoken of an ivory throne, and the white woman–ivory was white–this cylinder was back of it all.

It was about seven inches in diameter and an inch to an inch and a quarter thick. Around the edge of it ran a series of hieroglyphics or pictographs. They were so small Gordon could not decide to which type of primitive writing the symbols belonged. Across the upper face of the cylinder was a design that he took to be an attempt at real picture making. The artist, whoever he might have been, had scratched mountains and valleys on the white surface.

But the more Gordon studied it, the deeper grew the feeling, that the real significance of the cylinder ran deeper than the meaning of the figures scratched on its surface. The ones around the edge were much older than the design on the face. Further than that he could make no conjecture. He was puzzling over it when he fell asleep. When he awoke again it was to begin where he had left off.

So gradually the spell of the ivory cylinder took hold of him. The North and the long night vanished. Alcide came back and together they worked over the secret. There was a claim to be filed. He was to be king. It was in the land where golden women lived. There were ivory thrones, whole rooms of ivory.

Gordon laughed. He laughed again at the echo.

"How the leetle mole she find his way, eh?"

It was nice that Alcide had come back to talk to him. It was like Alcide to do that. But Gordon had known from the beginning that the little half-breed would come back. And in the spring they were going to the land of ivory–he and Jacquard–Jacquard whom he had buried out there in the snow.

III

News of men and events in the world outside filters slowly into the North. It comes to the dwellers of the tundra above the spruce line through the medium of month-old papers, in frequent letters and the like that are brought by the river steamers in summer and dog-teams when the rivers close.

So it was that into the R. N. W. M. P. post at Fort Murray word came telling that the red-bearded missionary in the lonely cabin on the delta of the Mackenzie had gone mad. And with the news came other rumors linked with superstition. Evil spirits were abroad in the land. Alcide Jacquard was not only dead but buried, and the wolves had howled over his grave. Worse than death hovered about the cabin on the lower Mackenzie.

"Constable Peters will proceed at once to the old Fort Retribution post and bring back James Gordon, reported insane."

Very formal, matter of fact and to the point ran the orders of the Mounted. That was all they had to answer to both news and rumor; "Get the man."

Much that is full of glamour has been written and told about the wearers of the Scarlet Tunics of the North. Much more that has nothing to do with glamour is the workaday rule of their lives. *Maintiens le droit* is a motto of service not of words. "According to the Code" is a phrase that accepts facts as facts. Glamour is something to be found in books.

Within half an hour after he received the order from In spector Curtot, Constable Peters swung into the North at the rear of a well-stocked sledge behind a team of eleven picked dogs. Fang, a husky he had reared from a puppy, was in the lead trace.

Peters was soldier and surgeon both. He was built, like every member of the Mounted is built, for action. Just under six feet, weighing close to two hundred, smooth shaven, clean cut, and with a jaw that did not need a lot of words to show he meant business.

Heads and hands were skilled in the knowledge and use of scalpel and bandage. But that could not hold him. His heart craved the open. In the North he found the place where heart and head and hands could meet on equal ground.

Three winters had slipped by since his first trip to the old post in which Gordon had made his home. That first trip Peters had made in a blizzard that the North remembered and he was new to the country. But Alcide Jacquard had been his guide on that occasion. Now Jacquard was dead and he was alone.

It was on the tenth day after leaving Fort Murray that Peters came in sight of Gordon's shack. The broad reaches of the Mackenzie delta wind through a flat country and it took him nearly three hours to get within hailing distance after he first sighted the place.

There was no answer to his halloo. Peters had not really expected one, but still it gave him a doubt. Gordon might have gone off or died. He'd know in another minute or two. There was no answer to his knock either as he pushed open the door. Gordon sat on a corner of his bunk, gazing at the floor where the planks had been ripped up, his hands folded together between his knees. Peters walked across the cabin and laid his hand on the missionary's shoulder without speaking. Gordon did not move.

Peters had seen the cross marking Alcide's grave as he approached the shack. That accounted for the planks missing from the floor. It was just about as he thought; Gordon's mind had gone out to Alcide.

"Poor devil. Well, we've got to get him out of here, that's certain. Hullo!"

His eye roving around the room caught sight of the ivory cylinder above the fireplace. He walked over and picking it up examined it closely before the fire. He turned to Gordon and saw that the missionary was watching him. He put the cylinder back on the mantle.

"Ivoree!"

Peters was looking at Gordon and saw the missionary's lips move. But it was Jacquard's voice that he heard. For the moment it startled him.

Gordon smiled, but it was a smile devoid of all sense of reason, just the blank grin of a man who has lost his mind.

"Mebbe I come back file claim, eh, mon Pere ?"

Peters nodded. He knew now why Gordon had gone mad. But that told him nothing concerning Jacquard's death. "Ivoree," and this last about filing a claim. He knew Gordon was repeating things the half-breed had said. There was mystery enough, no doubt about that. The carved bone might be a real clue. He picked it up.

"Ivoree !" This time he was not startled.

"*Mais, oui,* "Peters answered, imitating as nearly as he could the patois of Jacquard. "She is w'at you call heem, vair nice ivoree, eh?"

The smile left Gordon's face. He clasped his hands and turned to look again at the place where the boards were torn up from the floor.

Peters took the cylinder to the table, lit the lamp and studied the markings. It was the design on the face of the cylinder that held his attention. He got out his knife and scraped the dirt out of the lines. The bone showed whiter underneath. Next he examined the dirt he had scraped out. So Jacquard had come back to file a claim.

Peters wondered how much of this ivory there was and where Jacquard had come across it. As a curio it might be valuable. The markings around the edge evidently told the story of some forgotten race. The design on the face was a map and Jacquard or someone else had carved it quite recently. But petrified bone, even though it be of the finest tusk ivory, was useless. The silica deposit that caused its petrification had robbed it of its beauty. The texture that ivory has, had gone. Another mystery had been boiled down to plain facts. If any anthropologist wanted to go digging around in the Arctic tundra, he was welcome.

"Mais, oui, thees woman she is white. White, mon Pere, lak when gold she is white."

"What !" Peters swung around.

Gordon was grinning again.

"Mon Pere, he t'ink Alcide he tell." The mad missionary threw back his head in a maudlin laugh.

Peters relaxed. So ivory wasn't the whole tale after all. A woman like gold! Well, that was enough to have turned Alcide or any other mortal man a little off. But the job now at hand was to get this other poor wreck back to Fort Murray. He slipped the cylinder into the inside pocket of his parka.

It was on the third day down to the Fort that Peters suddenly had his hands full. They had swung from the fringe of spruce that clung to the shore of the Mackenzie and were heading for the river trail when Gordon half-rolled, half sprang from the sledge. Peters threw all his weight against the gee pole, yelled to Fang and brought the dog team to a halt. But not until Gordon had jumped to his feet and was tearing along over the ice hummocks toward the black water of the rapids.

The river made a roaring drop for nearly half a mile and even the icy grip of winter could not hold the turbulent water in check. The spray drove through the air like particles of pointed steel. All winter long it had been doing that until the black water was held in by a miniature range of ice mountains, sharp, jagged hummocks that made going uncertain and a fall dangerous.

The mad missionary was unmindful of the ice; that rumble of dark water fascinated him. For nearly a mile as they followed the shore line through the spruce his eyes had never left it. Now in his mad haste he stumbled and fell. He was up again and off.

The fall had given Peters a few previous yards and he redoubled his efforts. He, too, was unmindful of the rough going.

Up one ice hummock, down and over the next, with every leap he gained. The roaring grew louder; the cut of the frozen spray blinded him.

The last hummocks were smooth as glass. Already Gordon was climbing over them. Peters went headlong then. There was no time to feel for a footing in the ice humps. He threw himself over them, fell in a heap, rolled, was up again and dived over the next hummock.

Even then he would have lost, had not Gordon paused momentarily at the top of the last ridge, fascinated by the roaring turmoil below. Peters closed on him knowing full well the almost superhuman strength insanity brings. Down they went together, thrashing back and forth at the very edge of the rapids.

Peters locked his arms around the missionary and hung on for dear life. He was nearly exhausted from the long chase over the ice; his face was grim. Either they would both go down into that seething torrent below or he would take Gordon back to Fort Murray.

The missionary strained against his arms until he thought the muscles of his shoulders would give way. Each second, and they passed like hours, he felt Gordon's strength grow while his own diminished. Still he held on, gritted his teeth at the tearing pain in his arms and with his head tried to bore upward against the missionary's jaw. Even in his madness Gordon sensed this new move; his fingers closed on Peters' throat.

Like the tongue of some insatiable fiend the water of the rapids whirled up over the ice. The icy lash of it took Peters' breath. He gasped. That viselike grip was choking the life from him. Sight left his eyes, the leering face of the madman was no longer grinning down at him. Then came a vision and with it that intuition that has saved many a clever man in a crisis.

"Mon Pere !" he gasped. "W'at . . . you. . . t'ink . . . thees . . . woman . . she . . ees . . . white . . . Iak. . . ivoree . . . she . . ."

The cruel fingers relaxed their grip. Peters slipped from the missionary's hold, sank in an exhausted heap and lay there for several minutes unable to move. In his ears rang the noise of the torrent. He had lost. He would not take his man back to

Fort Murray. But it was good just to lie there and be able to breathe.

Then he opened his eyes. There at his feet sat Gordon gazing blankly at the black water. He had sat that way on the bunk in his cabin when Peters first found him. The water no longer held a fascination for his tired brain. His whole being had gone out to Alcide Jacquard. Peters knew that it was his utterance in the patois of the little half-breed that had saved the lives of them both.

But the vision which had prompted that utterance! In that terrible moment when the world had grown dark before his eyes the golden woman had come to him. True, he had spoken the words of Jacquard–but the vision he had seen was his own. Peters, the skeptic, shook his head. It was fallacy for a man to allow his mind to run to such things.

Yet, here was Gordon sitting quietly at his feet. Back there over the ice hummocks Fangs and the dog team were waiting.

He would still get his man to Fort Murray.

IV

It was ten days after the struggle at the edge of the rapids that Peters mushed into Fort Murray. Ten terrible days they had been. Half a dozen times Gordon had broken away from the sledge. Half a dozen dead-in-earnest fights had Peters had on his hands to subdue the missionary, bring him back to the sledge, bundle him up against the cold and renew the journey.

Yet, when Peters made his report to Inspector Curtot it was the formal report of the Mounted. He had reached old Fort Retribution without difficulty, confirmed the rumor that Alcide Jacquard was dead, had seen the cross marking his grave, had found James Gordon in his present condition and had brought him back.

That was all. Not a word of the life and death fights at the rapids. It was one of the hardest jobs Peters had ever had in his life, but he reported it as though it were only a routine matter of the day's work.

Then he saluted, went to his quarters turned in and slept nearly twice around the clock. When he awoke hardly a trace of the ordeal he had been through remained. His mind was clear and the only thought he had for Gordon was one of deep pity. Peters was not one to let such things dwell on his mind. He had done his duty, no man could do more.

One thing he could not shake from his mind, nor did he desire to do so, was Jacquard's hint concerning the golden woman and the vision he himself had had of her. He was still skeptical about it. It might have been nothing more than an hallucination, yet the vividness of the vision was not in any way related to any dream he had ever had. It had saved his life, he was certain of that.

In recent years there had been great discoveries in the realm of the unconscious mind–but the unexplored regions of the unconscious were vast. Peters had delved into psychology. So his thoughts ran the gamut from skepticism to belief and back again. Nothing was uncanny. Even hallucinations did not just happen. There was a reason for everything under the sun. Even golden women did not come out of thin air.

Cunning practical Alcide Jacquard was not sent to his death by a wild dream. He had found something and that petrified cylinder with its queer markings was the key. Peters went to his parka, took the cylinder from the pocket, toyed with it for a few minutes, then reached for his hat. He was going to see Inspector Curtot.

"Humph!" grunted Curtot, after he had examined the strange markings. "Not going in for archeology, Peters?"

"Maybe, maybe not," Peter answered. "The truth of the matter is that I don't think we've heard the last of Alcide Jacquard."

"Spirits, Peters?" The Inspector's eyes twinkled.

Peters laughed. "Not quite. But you know the mind of the average trapper and as for natives–" he made a sweeping gesture sure. "None of your trappers is ever going to believe that Jacquard died only of exposure and, in that, I'll agree with them. But–"

"So it is spirits after all!" Curtot interrupted. "Take it easy, Peters. You've had a trying trip. You've done a real job. Spring'll be along in a couple of months now. You've got a deserved leave of absence coming to you and I mean to see that you get it. I'm going down to Ottawa and you're coming along."

"But, Inspector Curtot, I'm serious. I was never more in earnest in my life."

"Which is the proper way to be. So am I and you need a rest."

Peters hesitated. When he had come to the Inspector's office there was no plan in his mind. This talk of a leave of absence had changed the color of things. Funny he hadn't thought of that.

"Could I have it now, Inspector ?" he asked. "I mean the leave."

Curtot slapped his knee. "You mean will I give you permission to hunt for the spook of Alcide Jacquard. Peters, I tell you, man, you're tired out. This thing'll get you the way it seems to have gotten this poor devil of a missionary."

Peters laughed. "Really, I am serious and I think you know me well enough to put me down as the last person in the world to go off on a spook hunt. What I meant was that I agreed with the trappers. I know there is something back of Jacquard's death. I don't know what it is. I know the natives will talk. I feel that it will be bad business to let them start building superstitions. Such things once started, make mighty fine cover for a real murder. Not that they are planned that way. But the thing is in the wind. Someone is found dead and then before you get a chance to find a real clue, superstition has the whole affair so clouded you can't make head or tail or it, even if you had Sherlock Holmes with his magnifying glass and galoshes. I'm perfectly fit, I wouldn't have thought of asking for leave until you suggested it, Inspector. All I've got is the clue there on the table and something that you might call 'spirits' that has happened to me."

Inspector Curtot's face grew serious.

"When would you start?"

"Tomorrow. The dogs need another day's rest. "

"Peters," Inspector Curtot extended his hand, "I wish you luck."

V

There is an adage to the effect that to overcome trouble look for it. So Peters went North looking for trouble. He had two months, which was a mighty short space of time for the country he was traversing.

After the sun begins his return journey from the Southern Hemisphere is the time of all kinds and conditions of weather. It runs the scale from thaw to blizzard.

So Peters found. When he came to old Fort Retribution he left the Mackenzie and took a course that was north by west, which would lead him into the Arctic Slope range of the Rockies. That much he gained from the map on the cylinder. Jacquard had not followed the coast line but had gone into the heart of the mountains. Peters did likewise, knowing full well that his chances of hitting the little half-breed's trail were in the same category with buying tickets for a lottery.

But the lucky ticket did win, there was consolation in that. The tenth day after leaving the Mackenzie he came across the traces of a siwash camp Alcide had built. There was no sign of a trail; that had vanished weeks since. But a fire had been built and Peters was woodsman enough to know that the half-breed had built it.

He put it down as score one in his favor, pushed on and again promptly lost sight of every vestige of a sign that there was another human being in the world besides himself.

He was getting into the foot-hills now, nothing but rising ridges of snow and ice, and the rise made the going harder. Three more days of travel brought him to a blank wall and he had to retrace his steps. He struck out more to the north and pushed on, only to find his way blocked again. There was a pass through this range, for Jacquard had evidently come this way. He figured there was nothing to do but to go back over his trail and begin again. Then, quite by accident, he struck another of Alcide's camps.

There was little comfort in that with the Arctic Range towering up and never a sign of a pass that would let him through to the other side. Peters camped for the night.

Morning brought snow and he set off with the sting of it in his face. There is an exhilarating restfulness that comes with snow. The vast expanse of bleak landscape had disappeared. Peters felt that he was in a little world again. The snow made its own horizon, a close-at-hand, friendly horizon that brought companionship.

He traveled on, swinging at an easy, tireless gait behind his dogs. The going grew rougher but he gave no heed until the exertion began to tell on him. It was only then that he realized he was again going uphill. He brought his dogs to a halt.

It was the old circle, a thing he had figured out long ago in a queer way that suited his own method of thinking out things. The universe was a mighty circle; the sun had its orbit and so did the earth. Civilization was steadily marching around the earth, how many times it had gone from East to West being a matter of pure conjecture. So why shouldn't a man, once he had lost his bearings, travel in a circle? That was just what Peters had done. But it was a grim conjecture. He was lost.

He hazarded a guess at direction and pushed on again. There was a more vehement sting to the snow, it began to cut like needles of pointed steel. The wind was rising, the bitter, biting wind of the Arctic. Still he pushed on.

The trail climbed again, so he knew he was getting back into the mountains. The pace began to tell on him, breathing grew hard, a numb ache crept up from his ankles until his legs felt stiff and he trotted with an awkward, automatic gait. But the trail led upward without a halt. By dumb, blind luck he had found the pass and he intended to make the most of it. Time enough to halt when his tired limbs would take him no farther.

He put a hand to the gee-pole of the sledge and through the wind called encouragement to the dogs. Night came and still he climbed, halting finally from sheer exhaustion.

Peters awoke stiff and sore, but he broke camp and went on. Some mad, atavistic urge was driving him. Through the ache and pain of the journey he sensed a kinship with the primitive. Reason told him to go back, but reason went by him like the wind. One man was dead, another was mad, reason whispered to him as it fled. Peters laughed and added inches to his stride.

"A woman like gold!"

Not in the patois of Jacquard now, but in his own clear thought, the phrase burned itself into his brain. On he went and on. One of the dogs lagged in the traces. Peters cut him loose and dumped him into the sledge. He had found the pass and he was going to get through!

His whole body ached; the pulse at his temple beat like a trip-hammer; the wind cut him like a knife. Then another dog dropped and Peters knew that meant they could not go much farther. He was so numb with cold and fatigue that it was an effort to free the fallen dog. Somehow he managed and went on again.

But he no longer urged the team. He knew a sledge dog would keep on until he went down. He had left the Post with eleven dogs. Now he had nine. If it was folly to keep mushing like a madman, then he was mad. He admitted it with a grim smile and kept going. He had found the pass. Nothing would stop him till he got through.

He cut another dog from the traces and almost before he had started again the fourth one was down. An hour more and Peters stumbled against the sledge, lost his balance and fell. The team had stopped. Two more dogs were down and the remaining five could not budge the heavy sledge. He cut them all loose, made a clumsy pack of tent and provisions and went on alone. Then came the snow in earnest; he was heading into an Arctic blizzard.

Gradually the ache went from his legs, but with it went the relentless onward swing. He had to fight to shake off an overwhelming drowsiness. The wind lost its cutting sting and soothed rather than hurt him. Vaguely he realized that he was being lulled into the peaceful sense of security that precedes complete exhaustion. It was the sixth sense of the frontiersman that warned him then.

His only hope lay in rest. To sink down in the snow seemed like the easiest thing in the world, but even his numbed brain told him that meant death.

He stumbled and fell and as he crawled to his feet again he realized that once more he had gone in a circle. He was holding to the gee-pole of his own sledge. Blind luck had found the pass for him and the same blind luck had saved his life.

It took all his remaining strength to turn the sledge on its side, fasten his tent to it and then crawl into his sleeping bag under the shelter thus afforded.

"Blind luck," he framed the words with his lips, and fell asleep.

But was it? There came to him the vision of the golden woman even as it had come to him on the border of death at the rapids when the mad missionary had him by the throat. Peters could feel her warm breath, sense the throb of her breasts as his arms closed around her and held her fast. Then the vision passed.

As one who comes to wakefulness slowly after deep slumber, Peters gradually grew aware that he was still alive. His limbs were numb but not cold, being cramped from the close confinement of the sleeping bag and the uncomfortable tilt of the dog sledge under which he had crept from the blizzard.

His head felt strangely clear, and reflectively, as a man inured to danger and hardship places all the cards on the table, he pondered the possibilities that lay before him. He was hungry. He did not have the slightest idea how long he had been asleep. The blizzard had abated, but that told him nothing. There was no knowing how long since it had abated or whether its duration after he crawled under the sledge had been days or hours.

From where he lay, the circle of the world was marked by the curve of tent canvas above his head. Within that scant circumference his life, for some unknown number of hours, had been safe. For some other unknown number of hours it would continue safe if he remained under cover of the sledge.

In relation to that he knew exactly where he was. In the world outside he would have to take his chance like any other animal that combated Nature. But he wasn't a real animal. There were countless generations between him and the man-ancestor who could pit himself beast-like against the trials and attacks of Nature and win out. Death, in time, was a surety if he remained where he was. It seemed equally a surety if he ventured to leave this rude but adequate shelter.

His dog team, split up or pack-wise, once cut free had gone back to its forebear, the wolf. The sledge-dog could do that. Many of them showed the wolf blood in their veins. With them Nature could cope with Nature and win out. But he was a man. Too much inbreeding had robbed him of the pristine knowledge of the fundamental laws of life. The civilization his forebears had reared for him had become his master.

He could plunge into the wilds but he needed the things of civilization to keep him alive. Given nothing but a club, like one of his primitive ancestors, he would probably have starved to death in a land of plenty.

A close inspection of the radium dial of his watch informed him that it had stopped at quarter to two. Was it at night or in the day? Was it yesterday or the day before? He didn't know. He was a product of civilization and one of the toys of his heritage had failed him.

Suddenly, out of the void surrounding his makeshift shelter there came a long-drawn howl.

Peters was all action before the last note of it had gone. He might be sleepily lulled into that security which ended in the most peaceful of deaths, but so long as he had ammunition he was not going to be torn on that terrible wrack of the North.

He was out of his sleeping bag, had slipped the tent flap open and stood waiting, thumbs in belt, when the next cry, nearer than the first, curdled the still air. Its effect on him was that he gripped his belt the tighter–a great elation surged through him. That first cry had caught him unawares, but he was tense and waiting for this second one. If the first howl sent a chill through his blood the second caused it to course with redoubled energy and brought a choking catch to his throat. Here was a possibility he had not reckoned. Again the cry came, shrill but plaintive now, and with it there was a note of infinite longing.

"Fang!"

Out of the gray light of the pass the dog came. He was a gaunt spectre of the husky that had led the team from Fort Murray. But he gave vent to a full-throated bark of joy and bounded forward. Peters sprang to meet him. The Arctic void had become a living world again to them both.

VI

It was in looking for wood that Peters first grew aware of a peculiar warmth in the air. The sting of the wind had seemed to have lessened suddenly, but he gave it no heed. One of the phenomena of the North Country is the Chinook wind. After the fiercest of blizzards it will come down a valley. The snow vanishes before it.

So Peters went on in his search for firm sticks that would make a good fire. He was hungry. Food was more important than any caprice of the wind. He noted the change but that was all. It was Fang that made the discovery.

Peters stood stock still at the dog's howl. He heard no other sound. Then Fang howled again. Peters made off on a run in the direction from which the sound had come. Now, as he ran, he caught a subtle metallic odor. His hand went to his gun. He stopped short and listened.

Again the dog howled, this time close at hand, and the howl startled him. He crawled up out on a depression, not knowing what to expect. Before he came to the top of it he knew. There was a cleft in the side of the mountain! He could see it cutting like a great black gash into the wall of ice. It was from this cleft the strange odor issued. Fang stood before it bristling in every hair. Peters gripped his gun and went to the dog.

At first he thought it was a cave. But there was a steady current of air issuing from it. It was warmer than it had been down below. It must be a passage, but where in the world could it lead? Fang growled. Peters decided to make an investigation. With the dog following, he entered the passage.

As he proceeded down the narrow cleft the odor grew more pungent. The metallic scent was so strong Peters could taste it. With it there was a mocking sense of the warm, heavy fragrance that spring has, the reek of warm earth. Fang, following close at his heels, gave vent to another low, rumbling growl. But that earth smell seemed to mean food. The growl died in a whimper.

"What's the matter, old fellow?" Peters' voice had much in common with the dog's whimper. There was that queer catch again at his throat. It was all like some nightmare, with a cruel subtlety that made it seem so poignantly real. His breath came in short, quick gasps. The air in the cleft was stifling. He tried in vain to still the wild beating of his heart.

It was blacker than the blackest night. His electric torch had gone long since, he remembered, as he futilely groped in his parka, searching for it. His hand came in contact with something hard. The ivory cylinder! That tracing on the face of it was a map! What he had taken for two ranges of mountains was Alcide's mark showing this cleft. He stumbled on.

Peters could have cried for sheer joy when, feeling his way around a turn, he saw the jagged wall of the cleft standing out in bold relief not more than half a dozen yards ahead of him. There was a sullen growl from Fang.

"Quiet, boy! We've found the opening!" His voice thrilled.

The dog's growl was a warning, however, and as he climbed Peters tried once more to subdue the wild beating of his heart. He could hear it pounding against his ribs. Again he reached for his gun. The hunger pain gripped him. He had come from death through nothing short of a miracle. Ahead of him he sensed life and he was ready to go down fighting for it.

His eyes blinked in the unaccustomed glare after the long journey through the dark. He leaned down to put a restraining hand on Fang and slipping to one knee leaned anxiously against the wall of the passage. Every nerve urged him to dash ahead to the opening that must be just around the next turn.

But the light hurt his eyes. He needed breath. Too often had such disadvantages been the means of losing a fight. So Peters knelt and waited though the wait was fraught with a mad desire to spring forward recklessly and learn what was ahead of him.

He had a firm hold of Fang when he went on again, his fingers sunk deep in the scruff of the dog's neck.

"Quiet, boy, quiet."

They made the turn. Not half a dozen paces before them the passage opened to warm earth and sky. They had left a grayish-white waste when they entered the cleft. Here at the other end of it a scrub spruce was brightly green. Again Fang's growl turned to a whimper.

Peters did not hear. He had stepped forward and now stood speechless. From the dawn of history it has been the privilege of men who dared to stand on new peaks, to look out upon new vistas with the dilated eye of the man who blazes the trail. Jacquard had been here before him but still Peters swelled with the pride and elation of discovery. So he stood and gazed his fill. Like this, he thought, Balboa might have stood on his "peak in Darien" and had his first view of the Pacific.

VII

Standing at the mouth of the cleft, Fang at his side with lolling tongue, Peters could not have been more surprised if he had stepped suddenly into the Garden of Eden. He forgot his fatigue for the moment and was content just to stand and gaze at what might have been a mirage.

Worn out, deluded travelers of the open spaces had been lured deeper and deeper into trackless wastes by the spell of dream cities rising up before them, or on seeming to behold the expanse of a broad lake dancing before their eyes. They had pushed on then only to have the vision fade.

As Peters stood there he felt that this was what was likely to happen now. The moment he took a downward step to the valley below it would be gone like a wraith. He had come from tundra to paradise through the cleft in the mountain. There was snow here, plenty of it, but the change from the flat, gray waste was like being born into a new world–and it was a world of his own–he had found it!

Below him lay a valley fully two miles wide and its length was lost in the dim bluish-gray of towering cliffs that held it in on all sides. It was cold here, but not that bitter, biting cold that held sway at the other end of the long passage that burrowed its way through the mountain.

Clouds of steam rose from a lake that evidently ran the whole length of the valley. Peters had heard of the Valley of Ten Thousand Smokes. He had seen geysers and gushing torrents of boiling water, but nothing he had ever seen or heard of could compare with the valley below.

The lake was like some giant wash-tub of Nature; it was more than that. This bubbling lake, probably fed from some unknown depths, had changed the whole nature of the valley. Here above the Arctic Circle Peters stood and gazed at a Valley of Steam. There were spruce and birch growing at the foot of the cliffs and in the spaces where the snow had gone the rocks were gray with lichens.

Great drifts of snow had piled into the cliff crevices. The rising steam meeting the colder air above and attracted to the cold surfaces of the cliffs had formed huge ice-crusts that took a million different forms. It was as though a host of brooding gods looked down on the valley. At the far end a glacier crawled down the face of the cliff to meet the bubbling lake.

Here was Nature at her two extremes, ice and snow, fire and steam; for somewhere there was a seething furnace that made this giant reservoir boil. Even as he gazed he saw a huge ice block from the glacier go down into the seething water below. The spray raced upward in a thousand curves.

Man could fashion no fountain like that; nor stage such a conflict as this iron grip of ice battling with the boiling breath that came from the very bowels of the earth. Little wonder if Alcide Jacquard had gone mad before he died.

Peters leaned back against the cliff and closed his eyes. In July, and farther South, he had picked flowers at the edge of a glacier and marveled at Nature's whim. But there, when winter came, the ice was victor and the flowers vanished.

Here the battle was everlasting and there was neither victor nor vanquished. The valley was a valley of eternal youth, of eternal spring; the heights were heights of eternal age, of eternal winter.

Leaning there, eyes closed, he heard the whole valley sing, a humming, soothing drone that fell in soft cadences the way the harp of the wind plays in a forest of pines. This was the steam breaking into song as it escaped through the foaming lake from the fires down below.

It was a startled roe deer, breaking through the undergrowth that caused Peters to open his eyes and awake from his dream. Fang leaped down in full cry. He was the typical husky with a quarter strain of the wolf blood. Moreover, his stomach had shrunk. So had Peters' and he was as quick as his dog.

A shot went echoing down the cliffs. The roe gave a frightened leap, that wild spring that comes with death. Already Fang was at her throat and she came down in a quivering heap.

Peters smiled grimly as he held the smoking gun. He had shot from the hip. It was too good to be real. It was a dream, all of it. First the valley sent warmth to him. Now it sent food. All he had was his service revolver and at any other than close range the weapon would have been useless. But down below,

Fang had gone wild. His bark filled the valley. So it must be real. Already Peters could smell the venison that would soon be roasting on the spit.

With a gay halloo he leaped down to the feast. It was short work to build a fire and cut up the roe. What if there had never been a report of deer being found so far North? The caribou herds lived on the tundra, thousands of them sometimes mustering in a single herd. There was an occasional musk ox. But never a deer. Their haunt was away to the South where the big timber line ended.

But Peters was too busy to begin a debate with the God of Things As They Really Are, whether the copy-books agreed with them or not. He gave any thoughts he might have to the winds. Here was a glacier crawling to its death down the side of a mountain into a boiling lake. Beyond these very cliffs was the bleakest of winter. What hand had scooped out this valley and tucked into it the breath of spring? When venison is turning on a fire of coals of dry wood, a hungry man does not seek arguments with himself on the whichness or the whatness.

Fang gnawed a fresh bone, growling the while. If Peters did not growl, he at least made a joyful noise as he buried his teeth in the toasted, juicy meat. It was done to a beautiful brown. And when the meal was finished, man and dog curled up beside the fire and slept.

Peters grew restless in his sleep. Too much had happened to him to leave his mind wholly at ease. He passed from one troubled dream to another. Through all of them there ran the vision of the golden woman.

She was a tree that took human form only to become a tree again when he drew near. Out on the tundra he was chased by wolves. He emptied his pistol into them but still they pursued him. His dogs gave every ounce they had, but the wolf pack closed in. Then miraculously the golden omen had come between him and the pack. Another minute and the wolf pack had completely vanished. Yet, he knew that if he approached her she would vanish, too.

The cries of the pack still echoed when he awoke with a start. There was a cold, wet muzzle at his face. Fang growled low, his eyes ablaze. The dog was crouched flat against the earth, his lips lifted in a menacing snarl that bared the long, vicious teeth.

Peters reached for his gun. He, too, kept prone to the ground and waited. He could see nothing. The air was still, not even the snap of a twig to disturb the silence of the valley, save for that singing drone that came from the lake, and the rumble in Fang's throat.

For several minutes Peters lay tense, every muscle strained to sense sight or sound of some movement in the undergrowth. Finally, he relaxed and sat up. In that moment there was a sudden, swishing whir; he felt the sting of a lash against his cheek; then he was jerked to the ground. He heard Fang rage. Man and dog, they had been caught in a great net that had dropped from nowhere.

From the undergrowth now there rang howls of derision. Then from the cover, burst the men of the valley in a howling mob. Through the meshes of the net, Peters peered at them in awe. Massive men they were, clothed in skins, their great arms bare, their heavy shocks of red hair free to the wind.

But even the suddenness of the attack did not prevent Peters from making the moment one never to be forgotten, for another reason besides his awe. These men were white! It was as though a legion of Vikings had sprung forth in flesh and blood from some forgotten saga of the past. This impress on his mind was strengthened by the fact that they wore a sort of sandal, held on by leather thongs which ran cries-cross to their knees. But they were not Vikings as Peters was to learn later.

All of them carried clubs, heavy, unwieldy-looking weapons that could crush a man's skull at a blow. Some had long white spears tipped with white bone. It was the bone that caught Peters' eye. His mind now went back again to the ivory cylinder. The bone of the spears was the same grayish-tinged ivory. It was petrified ivory. Every last one of these spear points were blood brothers to that queer little block of bone Jacquard had brought out of the Arctic and which Peters now had in the pocket of his parka

Fang snarled with rage and gnashed his teeth on the meshes of the net. The giants standing around in a circle grinned.

Fang raged the more, hurtling himself against Peters and getting both of them more securely entangled in the net.

"Quiet, boy, quiet."

The dog sank to the ground at the sound of his voice, but the snarl still gave proof of his hatred for the net and this ring of men with clubs. They were only men to Fang, but a club was a club. He knew what that meant.

Peters' voice had caused his captors to break out in a fierce, guttural jargon. They had seen the dog crouch down at the sound. They gesticulated and pointed with their clubs.

It was a time for quick thinking, Peters knew that. He felt sure they had every intention of killing him. They were neither Indians nor Eskimos.

They really did look like Norsemen out of a child's picture book. From the way they squinted at him they had never seen his like before. Or had they? What of Alcide! The little half-breed had been in this valley and had gotten out of it alive.

Peters had found the real secret of the ivory cylinder. But whether or not he was ever to return to tell about it was not on his mind. He was thinking of the golden woman. Had his dream been true? Always in the dream she had vanished but not until she had done him a service.

Her dispersal of the wolf pack was nothing but a dream. Yet, there was that time at the edge of the rapids and again when he crawled, perhaps to die, under the tent lashed to the dog sledge.

Both times she had come to him. Both times she had seemed to save his life. He knew he never needed a friend more than he did now. Would she come to him?

Half a dozen of his captors had grouped themselves around the carcass of the roe. From the clamor they raised, Peters felt sure he must have killed an animal they held to be sacred. It might have been the only deer in the valley.

But now one of the men began jabbing and cutting with his spear at the wound in the roe's neck. That put an end to his conjecture as to the sacredness of the deer. The man using the spear as a probe gave a yell and the others gathered around him.

Through the net Peters saw that he had found the bullet and was showing it to the rest in the palm of his hand. They drew back and held what seemed to be a council.

It was annoying to be entangled so that he couldn't move; to have to lie there and hear a lot of gibberish that didn't mean a thing to him. If they had never seen a bullet before they certainly had never seen a gun.

It dawned on Peters why they had drawn back. No wonder they gazed at him in as much awe as, at first sight, he had gazed at them. They thought he had thrown the bullet! He would gain his freedom yet.

VIII

There was no time now for further thought on the matter. Evidently the council had come to a decision. The jabbering ceased and the valley men gathered in a ring around him and his dog. He saw that there were several lead ropes attached to the net and at a sign from a veritable giant, who seemed to be their leader, four of the men sprang to these ropes.

The working of the net was not unlike the fish-traps bank fishermen use, and Peters, despite the helplessness of his plight, wondered at the ingenuity which had invented it. The men pulled.

He braced himself but nothing happened. Then there was a snarl from Fang.

Peters saw that the ropes the men were pulling had lifted the dog from the ground still encased in the thongs of the net.

Fang's wrath sent the valley men into spasms of mocking glee. One of them poked at the husky with the butt end of a spear. Fang's jaws closed on it and the valley men howled. Peters' blood boiled at the sight and he tore at the meshes that held him.

It was no use; he only wasted his strength and drew the thongs so tight that they cut through his clothes into his flesh. The effort brought raucous shouts from the ring. He sank back to the ground in dull anger; hate gripped him and claimed him for its own. If he had been able to reach his gun he would have emptied it into that howling mob and not cared what might happen next. They were torturing his dog and he couldn't do a thing to prevent it.

The giant who was their leader gave a yell of command

and the man with the spear desisted. Now the men on the lead ropes closed in. Two others stepped forward. As if by magic the net opened and Fang rolled out of it in a raging scramble to the ground. But the last two men had slipped nooses over his legs. Now they thrust a long pole underneath the nooses and Fang, raging still, was lifted to their shoulders.

There was an expert skill about their primitive methods that made Peters marvel. He knew at once that he had no mean antagonists to contend with even if his chance for liberty should come. He saw now that two nets had dropped miraculously from nowhere in the suddenness of that first attack.

Having disposed of the dog the valley men turned their attention to him. Again the lead ropes were pulled taut. He had a sensation of flying upward. Then the net opened and he hit the ground with a thump. But the noose-throwers had been as quick as the men on the ropes. He was hog-tied.

These men took no chances; they went about their task in deadly earnest.

A pole was slipped between his ankles and wrists, then the pole was raised and he was marched off through the undergrowth like a live pig being taken to market.

A moment before he had burned at the treatment given his dog. At least these valley men had a sense of fairness. They showed no partiality. They had not poked at him with the butt end of a spear, but that was probably because they were in a hurry. He and Fang were receiving share and share alike.

From somewhere ahead of him he could hear the husky's snarls and then would come wild glee from the men carrying him. They went through the undergrowth at a dog trot. There was no path that Peters could mark. Obstructions did not deter his captors; they simply plowed through the stunted spruce forest. The released limbs came zinging against the back of his head and neck with a stinging swish.

He swore and raised his head by lifting against the thongs that bound his wrists to the pole. The thongs cut and he winced at the pain, but even that was better than having a spruce limb give you a bang on the back of the neck. The man behind him, with the pole on his shoulder, grinned.

Soon they came out of the undergrowth and Peters saw

that they had reached a sort of plateau. More valley men were gathered here and on a rock, with a mantle of black and white fur, and a head-dress of waving white-tipped tails, stood a giant who looked fully eight feet tall.

The waving head-dress accentuated his height and to Peters, hanging head downward and gazing upon a topsy-turvy world, the man seemed to tower up to the sky. The rock he was standing on was flat-topped, perfectly smooth and polished until it shone. In the center of it a fire burned.

So that was it. His captors were fire worshipers. The giant on the rock was high priest or shaman. Peters saw that the spear he carried was made entirely of the petrified bone, ornamented with rows of the white-tipped tails tied to it:

As the valley men came to the polished rock they stretched out their arms and bent low in obeisance to the giant with the headdress. He saw the two men carrying Fang simply let the pole slip from their shoulders as they bent down to pay their homage.

The dog fell to the ground with the pole on top of him. He snarled his rage, but this time there were no jeers from the valley men. All eyes were on the shaman and the fire that glowed behind him.

Peters braced himself against the fall he knew was coming. It was only a drop of a couple of feet. But the ground beneath him was solid rock and he was swung from side to side as his bearers walked. The next minute they let go of the pole and he managed to fall on his side.

It had been more than a mile through the undergrowth and his temples throbbed from the rush of blood to his head. His throat was parched, his wrists and ankles were numb from the thongs that bound them.

With his elbow he managed to feel for his gun. It was still secure, just beneath his parka If they released his bonds before the fire ceremony began he still had a chance. He would get the high-priest person first. The report of the gun was enough to cause at least a momentary panic among the valley men. He could cut Fang free and they would make a running fight of it.

There wasn't more than a chance in a thousand that he could get back to the cleft in the mountain, but once there, he could stand off a host of primitive men armed with nothing but clubs and spears. If only they untied him before their sacrifice began, they would never be able to burn him alive.

Great bundles of fagots were thrown up onto the altar rock and the tongues of fire rose higher and higher. From somewhere back on the edge of the crowd there began a weird and guttural intoning, a sort of savage chant. Peters' heart fell as he saw four large cross-pieces lifted to the altar rock, two of them on each side of the fire.

He and Fang were to be slung over the flame on the same poles to which they were now trussed. His hope for escape vanished. His head sank to his chest, he closed his eyes and gritted his teeth. He wasn't afraid to die. He had been in many a tight corner when death seemed inevitable. But this–the cross pieces were high–that damned medicine man seemed to be waiting until the fire should become a bed of hot coals–This wasn't death. It was . . .

Peters felt himself lifted, but did not open his eyes. He stiffened every muscle. Then he relaxed again. A man could bear more in a position of calm rest. Overcoming pain wasn't a matter of physical endurance. Muscles would pull and twitch at pain involuntarily. These strange captors of his, would they howl in derision at cries? Not if the sheer power of will could seal his lips.

The weird chanting had risen to a rumbling that was almost deafening. It was as if all the fiends of hell were singing some hellish hymn in unison. Of a sudden the wild anathema became a thousand bloodcurdling shrieks. Peters was hurled headlong. He held his breath. He was going out like a man. It was striking the polished surface of the rock that brought him to a startled sense that something had happened that was not in the pre-arranged order of things. He was on the alert in an instant.

He glimpsed a fleeting flash of gold and then his hands were free. He could feel the scorching breath of the fire. All about the rock was a sea of bedlam. The men of the valley had gone mad with frenzy. They were jumping around the altar rock like maniacs, howling like fiends and waving their giant dubs and spears.

Above the ungodly howls of the valley men came a piercing shriek of terror. Was there another victim? . . . He was free! Of the thousand things that surged through his brain in that brief instant the dominant one was that he was free. He had a chance to fight it out. Free! But how? There had been a fleeting flash of gold. His thongs had been cut. The piercing, terror-stricken cry! The onrushing, frenzied fiends of the valley! Peters turned and in a flash he saw just what had happened.

The golden woman had come to him! No dream vision, but a glowing vibrant creature of flesh and blood. Hers was the shriek of terror. She was the reason for the change from savage anathema to hellish rage. It was because of her the men of the valley had gone mad. It was she who had thrown herself against his captors and had severed his bonds as he fell to the altar.

Peters' hand closed on his gun and he yanked it from the holster. Then his fingers opened and the gun dropped to the polished surface of the altar. It was no mere gesture. He had dropped it intentionally. In the twinkling of an eye he had turned from death to life.

For years this moment had lain dormant within him. Passing from sleep to wakefulness he had sensed it. The locale of the scene had always been hazy in his mind. The place as he had seen it a thousand times was dark and he had thought of an empty street or a blind alley. It was the other man's life or his, just the two of them battling on the brink of Eternity. And they had no weapons but their hands. So now that uncanny understanding that had dwelt far down in his subconscious self stood revealed. And with it the golden woman of his dreams had come to life. That piercing cry was addressed to him. In the instant of a crisis a man's whole life stands before him. Peters crouched and sprang.

Before the sacrificial fire towered the medicine man. Helpless as a child against such brute strength was the woman of gold. Only a glimpse of her did Peters have as he threw himself upon the giant who held her. The glimpse told him she was the most beautiful being his eyes had ever seen. That flash of gold he sensed rather than saw when his bonds were cut was but the glint from her hair.

Her eyes, frantic, pleading eyes, as she struggled, helpless, in the hands of the priest, were like lakes of blue shot with fire, even in their fear.

Her skin was the color of dawn when the sun comes up out of the sea. The tunic of fur torn ruthlessly from her shoulders laid bare a breast of snow and coral. Glamorous, pulsating with love and life, Peters' dream of her was beggardly by comparison.

And she had set him free! All in an instant Peters had gone back centuries into the primitive. Tooth and nail were the weapons of his atavistic forebears and with tooth and nail he sprang now.

He was outweighed by fully one hundred pounds. The only advantage he had was that he made the first spring. He landed full on the giant medicine man's back, wrapped his legs about him, sunk nails and teeth in his neck and hung on with a grip of death.

He felt the golden woman slip from the giant's grasp. Just one wild pant of her breath against his face as she fell. Then he was shaken as when the wind goes through a clump of willows. He dug his nails the deeper and tore.

That vital vein in the neck was his only chalice. His teeth sank through the flesh and his breath came from him in a growl. He was thrashed about and together they went down

The giant's weight pressed back on him like a vise, crushing him to the rock. His lungs were bursting. The grip he held with his legs was broken. There was a roaring in his ears. He choked. The roaring became a cataclysm of sound. The world turned red before his eyes. It was a world of blood.

Again he could hear the men of the valley howling like fiends of hell. Again he heard the golden woman's piercing scream. His ears could bear no more. In a final explosion the world vanished in a mad red roar.

The men of the valley were chanting. They were very far away. It was the same subtle, weird note Peters had heard at the beginning of the sacrificial fire ceremony. He could measure the cadence as it rose and fell. Presently he fancied that there were words to the chant. It was still a long way off, but there was a certain repetition of word sounds.

The chant grew louder. The repetition became more distinct, a phrasing of gutturals and vowels that he could follow but could not quite pin down. There was one word in particular. Or it might be two words.... There were two words.

He could distinguish them now. They came at the highest pitch of the chant. It was probably their name for God. It was funny he should hear the men of the valley chanting. He had died when the world turned red.

They were coming to the high note again. This time he would make it out, There it was–"Thir-Keld." The chant went on while he waited breathlessly. Again the cadence swept upward. He let himself go with it.... "Thir-Keld."

The swell of it grew less and less. He was getting farther and farther away from the men of the valley. There had been a nightmare of sound. He was glad to slip back into the quiet again. When the final whisper of the chant had died he felt that it had been a dream.

The thing to know was where reality ended and the dream began. There had been a blizzard. He had found a cleft through the mountain and come upon the Valley of Steam. He had been caught in a net, bound to a pole and led up a fire altar to die. And, as always in his dreams of late, the golden woman had come to save his life. He had seen her, held fast in the arms of the giant medicine man who was bent on throwing her into the flames. He remembered the touch of her hot breath against his cheek. And the medicine man? . . .

Peters opened his eyes. The medicine man lay a scant yard from him. The sight of the giant made him shudder. The features were horrible, not a human trace left about them. It was ghastly. He prayed that he might wake up. This dream of being awake, of looking upon worse than a chambers of horrors, made him shiver.

There was something black and shiny lying on the rock. His gun! By what freak of the mind had he dropped it? He reached for it, not that he expected his hand to touch it, but rather to make sure that it was all a dream. His finger came in contact with the muzzle. It was warm.

He grabbed the gun then, broke it open and examined the

chamber. He had fired at the deer when he entered the valley. That was all–one shot. He saw two cartridges had been exploded! That accounted for the terrible features of the dead medicine man at his side! The gun had been fired point blank into the giant's face!

"The golden woman! Thir-Keld!" The words sprang to his lips.

It was she who had fired the shot!

But by what intuition? What had happened to her? Peters tried to get to his feet and sank back with a groan. Something had happened to one of his legs. From the feel of it he judged it was broken.

He managed to sit up and look about There was not a living soul in sight. He was on the fire altar alone with the dead medicine man.

IX

Painfully, Peters unlaced his boot His ankle was badly swollen but as nearly as his fingers would tell him did not seem to be broken. It had been badly wrenched and it would be several days before it would bear his weight.

He made a bandage with strips cut from his parka, refaced the boot, and with his injured leg dragging behind him crawled to the edge of the altar rock.

A whimper greeted him from below. He still had his dog! Tears came to his eyes. Fang had chewed his front feet loose but the thongs that trussed his hind legs were so twisted that he couldn't get good leeway for his jaws. Peters saw that one foot was bleeding. It was a good twelve feet to the shelf below and the steps down were cut in the rock on an angle. With his crippled leg he could never make the steps.

He gripped the edge of the rock, swung himself over, hung precariously for a moment, did his best to keep the injured leg held up at the knee and dropped.

He lit in a heap, went white at the pain and crawled to Fang. The dog went crazy and he had a hard time quieting him down so he could cut through the thongs. The injury to the dog's foot was small.

"We're a pair of cripples, old boy," Peters said to him.

Fang yelped in answer and licked his face. Suddenly the dog stiffened back and growled. Peters grasped his gun. Then out of the spruce came Thir-Keld, and on her head she wore the white-tipped tails the medicine man had worn.

For the moment Peters forgot Fang and the dog sprang forward. He yelled but Fang gave no heed. Crouched close to the ground, teeth bared, he went straight for Thir-Keld. Peters turned cold. He swallowed hard and gripped his gun.

Inch by inch Fang crouched forward. Peters cried in vain to the dog to stop. He raised his gun. The golden woman had paused. Fang's deep-throated snarl was filled with menace. The bristling arch of his neck curved upward. His teeth gleamed white. The dog had reverted to the wolf.

The sweat stood out on Peters like cold beads of ice. His whole body turned to ice. Not twenty yards away stood the golden woman of his dreams, the most beautiful being on earth. And now more than half way between crouched Fang ready to spring. He knew what that spring meant. Good God! He couldn't kill his dog! But the woman! With the muzzle of the gun resting against his shoulder Peters measured the distance.

Thir-Keld stepped forward with her hands outstretched. Her arms were bare to the shoulder, like the men of the valley. Fang sprang and Peters could feel those tearing teeth sink into the warm flesh. Quick as a flash he shot. But Fang's spring was short. His teeth snapped on empty air. He turned and sprang again and again; the menace of the spring died in mid-air and was short.

The golden woman laughed and stood still. Fang slowly circled about her. The snarl changed to a growl, which in turn became a whimper. Finally, he crawled bellywise until his head rested against her feet. Thir-Keld knelt and put her arms about him.

Peters saw it all through a daze. He still held the smoking gun. He had missed at twenty yards. Had that spring gone its full course he would have killed his dog. And there knelt the golden woman with her arms about Fang. He pulled himself up against the rock.

He felt faint. There was a mist before his eyes and through the mist the golden woman was running toward him. He put out his arms. In another moment they closed about her.

"Thir-Keld!"

"Man!"

Peters did not hear. He forgot the pain in his ankle. The nightmare on the rock passed. He was in a golden haze. The soft warmth and perfume of it was all about him. Always before it had been only a vision. Now he could feel the throb of her breast, and catch the warmth of the breath from her parted lips. It might all be a dream, but it was a dream come true; Reaching down he kissed her.

"Thir-Keld!"

"Man !"

Happy days were those spent in the Valley of Steam. With Fang at his side and Thir-Keld, the golden woman, as a guide, he explored the valley from one end to the other when his ankle was strong again.

The valley people went about their task of living, and let Peters severely alone. In the company of Thir-Keld, he followed a true explorer's bent by searching into every phenomena of this garden of Eden, and this the primitive white tribe seemed to take as the natural right of the mate of their goddess–for so they considered Thir-Keld.

One of Peters' first discoveries was that the long lake was not a lake at all, but a river that came bubbling up out of the valley at one end and lost itself in the ground at the other. He had seen hot springs before, both in cold and warm climates.

Sometimes the water bubbled up out of the ground and continued on until its course led to some above the ground stream. Other springs returned again to the bowels of the earth from which they bubbled forth. And he had discovered a hot spring that was a veritable river! But what was a boiling river, or a hundred boiling rivers, or a strange white tribe, or a hundred strange, primitive white tribes compared to the woman of gold who went by his side in the day and held him close and was held by him in the night!

And that first embrace when she had called him, "Man." He had thought nothing of it then. It came to him like a voice out of the past, a voice he had known always. It was on the day he showed her the ivory cylinder that he guessed her story.

The path led upward that day through a cave of ice in the overhanging cliffs. Peters had tried signs, had drawn pictures, but there was nothing he had said or done that could make Thir-Keld understand. Had Alcide Jacquard been in this valley? Thir-Keld shook her head and did not understand.

Then from his neglected parka he brought her the little cylinder. She looked at Peters in wonder. He saw that she knew what it was and when she pointed to the side of the cliff he resolved to find out the secret at once.

It was cold in the ice cave, bitter cold, the cold that seemed to have existed for ages. As they went along Peters sensed that frozen eyes were staring at him from behind those frozen walls. He guessed the answer to the riddle. The little cylinder was a section of a petrified tusk of a mammoth. It was probably older than the Valley of Steam. It went back to the great ice sheet in the days when the Arctic had been a country as fertile as it now was barren.

Now the cave opened out with a great room which proved his surmise was right. But the sight took his breath away. The whole place was lined with petrified tusks. And in the center there was a dais with a great seat that might have been a throne.

Two pillars were raised on either side of it like arms. As Peters gazed at them he saw that one was slightly shorter than the other. They were square but one had a round cylinder at the top. The cylinder that belonged on the other was the one he held in his hand.

Here was the ivory dream of Alcide Jacquard! Peters stepped up onto the dais and put the cylinder on the pillar. There was an ominous rumble. It seemed that the whole room would fall. He caught at Thir-Keld's arm and together they ran from the cave. The rumble grew louder. Thir-Keld crept into his arms and trembled. The rumbling ceased.

Presently she looked up at him. She had looked that way before. It was the look of a child who tries to remember, a sort of studied effort, that is, a pantomime of the process of think. Thir-Keld had looked that way on the day she had said, "Dog!"

Peters was deeply moved. Thir-Keld had not been born in the Valley of Steam. The valley men and women were white, but they were the white off-shoot of some forgotten race. Only in color of skin and hair did they show the features of the white race. In other respects they looked like giant Asiatics. The word "man" meant nothing to the valley people. Fang was the first dog any of them had ever laid eyes upon, but Thir-Keld had said, "dog."

Now she was struggling with another word. The moment before she had been wild with alarm at the rumble in the ice cave. She smiled now as she looked up at him

"Thir-Keld," he whispered.

"Ship," she answered.

The face Peters looked down into was the face of a child–and woman both. The woman did not know what a ship was, but far back the mind of the child remembered. She saw that what she said had made him glad. She smiled wistfully and snuggled against him.

"Man . . . dog . . . ship." She knew other words, for she had learned many from Peters. These three were her very own. "Man . . . dog . . . ship.'?

Peters heard her and didn't hear. His eye had stopped on something half-imbedded in the ice. He stooped down and caught hold of it. It was rotten and came away easily in his hand. But there was no mistaking what it was–a piece of heavy sail canvas. The whole story flashed through his mind.

The ship had broken up in the Arctic ice. Thir-Keld had probably been born on the ship. Those who had escaped over the ice with dog teams had found the cleft through the mountain and had come into the Valley of Steam. They had been attacked and killed. The way he, too, might have been killed.

The child had been saved. Her hair was like gold and most of the valley people had shocks of reddish-colored hair.

And she had grown up into a sort of tribal leadership until the day she had dared defy the medicine man to save his life. With the medicine man's death, Thir-Keld's power had become absolute.

That was the only story he could ever know. And Peters did not care. He knew that he possessed a woman beside whom Helen of Troy was a creature of clay. He had happiness, and he would never question the sources of it. He was content.

"Man . . . dog . . . ship." She was smiling up at him, all of her, womanly now, all of her vibrant, glowing.

Peters could feel her breast throbbing against his as he caught her close and held her.

"Love," he whispered.

She knew that word. "Love," she whispered and held up her red lips to be kissed.

"Sweet golden woman, we're going home!"

That was a new word and Thir-Keld looked up at him questioningly.

"Home, Thir-Keld. We–we're going!"

Spring was in the air. He had been happy in the valley. He had always wanted to get right to the heart of things. Maybe they would come back some day. So he mused as arm in arm they went down the path.

Presently they came to a place where the path ended in a wall of rock. It hadn't been there when they went to the cave. This was the cause of the rumble that had come when they were in the cave. A great slide had carried down a huge mass of the cliff.

They turned aside to take the path on the lower level. As they passed a stunted spruce that was torn up by the roots, a sudden catch came to Peters' throat. There was a funny little crook in the spruce about four feet above the roots. It was the tree he had seen when he first came through the cleft from the other side of the mountain. They were standing on a large flat rock. Beside it showed signs of the first fire Peters had built in the valley.

The slide had closed the passage!

Peters turned and ran, motioning to Thir-Keld to wait. He came to another open place a little higher up from where he could see the opening of the passage. The cliff was now a solid wall of rock. The Valley of Steam was a world to itself.

He stood facing the closed cleft. Rigidly his hand came to the salute. Inspector Curtot would put down the name of Constable Peters, late surgeon to His Majesty's Own Fusileers, as "missing in line of duty while on leave."

His arm came back to his side. Down on the flat rock Thir-Keld was waiting for him.

"Home," he whispered to himself as he went down. It was a new word to him, too–for it meant now, the Valley of

Steam. There he and Thir-Keld would live out the rest of their days. And–together–they would be happy.

WHITE WATER RUN

By Hugh B. Cave

Executing Northland Justice, Corporal Wayne of the Mounted battles human treachery and the fury of a hell-world plunge into mountainous waves and gleaming fangs of rock.

Even before he swung his canoe into the waist of Two-head Lake, Corporal Jim Hayme was aware of the ominous silence that lay, heavy and oppressive, over the wooded shores and over the rude cabin squatting on the point. It sprang partly from the midday heat and partly from something less tangible, more sinister.

"You think Sam Longfoot will resist arrest?" Hayme asked the man who sat in the bow of the canoe.

Hand-out Cy Cullan shrugged his craggy shoulders. He had not said much since reporting the murder of Charley Eye. Cullan was a small, bony, but powerful man whose ragged black hair grew fiercely into a month-old beard. A roving fur trader, he made his living by swapping food and supplies to the Indians for their stores of fur.

Cy Cullan knew these lakes and forests as did few other men. He knew the nomad Indian trappers who inhabited this wilderness. He was feared and respected by those with whom he did business.

"Never sure about these North Country Injuns," he muttered, shaking his shaggy head. "Better take no chances, corporal."

Hayme swung the canoe to the beach, swapped paddle for rifle, and stepped out. He did not like the look of the place. It seemed desolate, almost deserted. He advanced slowly. He had been careful to check Cullan's story of the bitter feud between Sam Longfoot and Charley Eye, and bad found witnesses to back it up. Sam Longfoot was known to have a hair-trigger temper!

A dozen yards from the cabin Hayme paused warily beside the wood pile. "Sam!" he called. "Sam Longfoot! I want to talk with you! I want you out here–with your hands empty!"

Crack! That was a prompt enough answer! The echoes of the shot went booming across the lake, and Hayme stared coldly at a long, jagged splinter ripped from a log not two feet from his head. Down on one knee, with the wood pile for a barrier, he studied the cabin's two windows.

They were not really windows, just small apertures covered with moosehide. An inch of rifle barrel protruded menacingly from a hole in. one of them.

Hayme stared at that ugly inch of snout for some time, and pictured the Indian kneeling on the cabin floor behind it, ready to kill any man who made a move to rush him. Cautiously, the Mountie reached for a chunk of wood, weighed it in his hand. Setting himself, be flung the wood with all his strength at the window. It struck the brittle skin with a mounding thud, ripped through and disappeared inside.

For an instant the rifle slewed sideways. That was all Hayme needed. Young, strong, he leaped to his feet and sped across the intervening space as though shot from a sling.

He came up under the gun and grabbed it. One savage wrench tore it from the grasp of its owner.

Next moment Hayme had flung the cabin door wide and was gaping in stunned surprise at its occupant.

"For Pete's sake!" he whispered. "A woman!"

She crouched there like a cornered animal, sullenly returning his stare. There was an ugly gash on her cheek where the chunk of wood flung by the policeman had struck her. When Hayme lowered his gun, she rose and backed away from him, defying him with her eyes.

"Are you Sam Longfoot's squaw?" Hayme demanded.

She stared in silence, giving no sign that she understood English. One thing Hayme was sure of: she was all Indian, no half-breed. About twenty years old, she had the proud, fearless bearing of a full-blooded Iroquois, and she was not hard to look at.

Cullan came in, saw her and exclaimed: "What in thunder! Was she responsible for that shootin'?"

Hayme ignored the question. "Ask her if she's Sam Longfoot's squaw," he ordered. "You're an old hand at talking to these people, Cullan."

The trader flung a question at the woman in her own tongue. "She is," he said, relaying the answer.

"Ask her where Sam is."

Cullan fired more questions and the woman replied in shrill, rapid syllables.

"She says he skipped out. Says she don't know where he went, but he knew the law was after him and he deserted her. I believe she's telling the truth, Hayme. You'll notice there's no canoe around."

"He might be touring his rat traps."

"Uh-uh." Cullan shook his head. "Look at this place. No food here. Mighty little wood. Roof needs fixing where the snow caved it. Besides, these Indians don't bother with muskrats much. They're too far from the trading posts, and the fur men that pick up their stuff–me and my competitors can't be bothered with rat skins." He launched into another barrage of questions, listening carefully to the woman's replies. "She says Sam skipped out day before yesterday We'll have a tough time overtaking him, corporal."

Hayme nodded. His gaze had swept the interior of the cabin and rested now on a basket-like contraption filled with leaves and bits of grass The basket stood in a corner beside a battered pair of snowshoes. Over one end of it hung a fisher pelt. Hayme walked over and examined it.

It was wonderfully soft and almost jet black–as beautiful a

fisher skin as Hayme had ever seen. He shot a glance at the woman. "Ask her if she'll sell this, Cullan."

The trader put the question. Sam Longfoot's squaw vigorously shook her head.

"Tell her," Hayme said, "I'll give her fifty dollars for it."

"Fifty dollars! Man, are you crazy?"

"It would make a swell present for a girl I know," Hayme mused. "See what she says."

Cullan talked to the woman. Her reply was prompt and unmistakable. She snatched the skin from Hayne's grasp and retreated with it. For a moment the corporal stood frowning at her: then with a shrug he turned away

"Forget it," he said to Cullan. "If we're going to catch Sam Longfoot, we'd better get on the move."

The Indian woman watched them from the doorway of her cabin as they paddled away. She was still watching when the cabin disappeared behind the wooded point. Jim Hayme felt sorry for her but he kept his feelings to himself.

"Seems logical," he remarked, "to suppose Sam would head straight down White Run River to White Lake. He could get to the railroad that way and skip the country. If he took any other water route out of here, he'd do a lot of aimless traveling without ever getting anywhere."

Cullan was of the same opinion. "We'll get him," he declared with confidence. "It may take time, but we'll run him down." He turned to give the younger man a thoughtful stare. "But take a word of advice, corporal. Sam Longfoot is desperate and he's a dead shot. Any man that took needless chances with him would be a fool!"

That afternoon they stopped at the fur trader's cabin on Megami, prepared something to eat and moved on again. Before dark they passed the tiny island where, yesterday they had buried the body of Charley Eye. The setting sun gleamed dully on the mound of stones they had heaped up to mark the grave.

Murder seemed out of place here. Crime belonged in cities, Jim Hayme reflected. It was sacrilege to introduce violence and bloodshed into this virgin wilderness. Yet this had been murder, and every sign pointed to as cold-blooded a kill as Hayme had ever been called on to investigate.

Cy Cullan had found the body. Stopping at the island to leave some supplies and pick up the Indian's furs, the trader had found Charley sprawled out on the floor of his cabin, with a skinning knife buried between his shoulder blades. Stabbed in the back! The knife was in Hayme s pack at this very moment. Sam Longfoot's knife.

"No one but an Indian," Cullan had declared, "would be dumb enough to leave that knife at the scene of the crime. Sam was proud of that knife, too. Made it himself. In some ways your Injun of the North Country is sly as a mink, while in others he's no more cunning than a newborn babe."

Later, under oath, the trader might have to re-identify that knife, but more likely Sam Longfoot would admit his guilt once the law caught up with him. Your North Country Indian was frequently hard to catch, but seldom hard to convict, the Mounie reflected.

Hayme gave the murder cabin a last look as they paddled past. A while later the lake was behind them and they entered the west branch of the White Run. He abandoned his meditations then. The current was too swift for comfort. Traveling the White Run was a job that called for steady nerves and lightning-fast decisions!

But as the miles rushed past, he found himself thinking more and more of Sam Longfoot's wife–her dark, flashing eyes and the proud lift of her head. He kept recalling the fisher pelt with which she had so violently refused to part.

Hayme knew, as a man somehow knows those things without the need of thinking at all, that taking Sam Longfoot alive was going to he the toughest job of his career. Longfoot had a reason for wanting to live. A big reason. The fisher pelt explained it.

They slept that night with the roar of white water in their ears, and were up again before dawn, breakfasting on steaming hot coffee and bacon and bannock. As soon as there was enough light to travel by, they took to the river again.

All that day they worked like beavers, the river a snarl of white spray bristling with rocks, full of swift, treacherous turns that would have spelled the doom of any but veteran canoeists. Parts of it were too perilous even for Hayme and Cullan, and they were forced to portage over dim trails, through tamarack bog and mosquito swamp.

But they were closing the gap. The fleeing man had come this way and was not far ahead. On some of those portages they came upon the prints of moccasined feet. On one they found the remains of a recent fire.

The afternoon ran out. Darkness stopped them. The first hint of dawn found them hard at it again. At noon the river thinned to a hissing white serpent and ran headlong into a canyon where the light of day was shut out by high, smooth walls of rock.

"Bad stretch," Cullan muttered shaking his shaggy head. "The Devil's Mouth, the Injuns call it. runs for near a mile through a gorge that would drive a snake crazy. You think we ought to try it, corporal?"

"Do you think Sam Longfoot tried it?" Hayme asked gently.

"Well . . . he maybe went through the Elbow, then climbed the cliff and portaged."

"If he did," Hayme did, "we do too."

You took the Devil's Mouth at a clip that made you dizzy, and once in, you had no ghost of a chance to change your mind about staying in. The canoe leaped forward when caught by the current. For an instant it raced along on a ribbon of blue-black water, smooth as glass. Then it lunged. Spray smashed up to smother it. Giant rocks reared their dripping heads, and others lay hidden in the white madness.

The roar of the river was a mighty thunder in Hayne's ears. He thought if he had to listen to it very long, he would go insane. It was deafening, a vast bellow made up of a thousand smaller ones, the whole great rush of sound caught up by the dark walls that slipped past in a swift black blur.

Hayme thought of Sam Longfoot, who had come down this wild river alone. Would a man capable of cold-blooded murder have the courage to do such a thing? Hayme didn't think so. Yet Sam Longfoot had done it.

Alone? Hayme wasn't so sure. "There could have been someone else in Sam's canoe," he mused. "I'll wager there was!"

But he didn't have time to do much thinking about it. Not with the river doing its seething, savage best to smash them. He had to bend all his strength to the job of paddling. He had to be alert for the bellowed shouts of warning from the veteran trader in the bow.

"Bear right! Right!" Cullan was yelling now. "Portage ahead! If we're carried past it, we're finished!"

That was a moment Hayme's strength and courage were put through the devil's own wringer in the next sixty seconds. He saw the gap in the wall ahead, on his right– a lurid strip of pebbly beach against which the white water swirled in foaming fury as it took a sharp lunge to the left. He saw what lay beyond, and it was not comforting. No canoe could live in it.

Hayme's paddle flashed. He felt the seasoned spruce straining in his grasp. He saw the muscles of Cullan's back bulging under the man's jacket. Inch by inch, they forced the canoe through the grip of the current, toward that meager patch of beach.

Then Hayme saw something else–a little moose-skin tent pitched at the high end of the beach, under the frowning rock wall. An Indian tent, without a shadow of doubt. This was the end of their journey!

They made it–by a heartbeat. Cullan sprang out, caught the bow as the river swung the stern. He hauled the canoe up and Hayme leaped out beside him. It seemed to the Mountie that for an instant the river's roar was louder and more ominous; a growl of fury that its prey had escaped.

He turned then to stare at the tent. Beyond it, a ragged trail snaked up the cliffside. Cullan's hand fell on Hayme's wrist, and the trader muttered: "Mind what I told you now! He's a dead shot, Hayme! If you take any chances with him, you're a fool!"

"Sam Longfoot isn't here," Hayme said quietly.

"Huh?"

"There's no canoe here. He must have gone up over the portage with it." Hayme lifted the rifle from his own canoe and strode forward, his gaze on the tent. It seemed strange that a man fleeing in desperation would bother to take along a tent and pitch it in a place like this, but Hayme thought he knew the reason for it.

He advanced warily, though, and his gaze shifted every few strides to the treacherous trail that curled up the cliff. The absence of a canoe probably meant that Longfoot had gone up that trail. But in all likelihood the Indian would be coming back.

There was no challenge. Hayme pulled open the tent flap, stooped, peered inside. There wasn't room for a grown man to stand up. Except for a blanket roll and an old, much-patched pack sack, the little tent was empty.

Hayme backed out and stood up. "Sam evidently got here just before we did," he declared. "He left his stuff because he couldn't safely carry everything up that trail at once. He'll be back. We'll get him." He gripped Cullan's arm. "Hide the canoe in the rocks where he won't see it. Then get out of sight and let me handle this."

"If you take any chances with him, corporal, you–"

"I'll take no chances," Hayme said grimly.

He went around the tent and stationed himself close to a jagged pyramid of rock that rose behind it. From there he could cover the whole of the trail. He set himself, his rifle ready for action. He had not forgotten the ugly welcome he had received at Sam Longfoot's cabin on Two-head Lake. Nor, for that matter, had he forgotten the fisher skin.

He watched while Cullan concealed the canoe and dropped down behind it. Time crawled. The river roared on, ceaselessly, and there was no other sound. Darkness deepened in the canyon. A moon came up.

All at once Hayme stiffened. Something had moved on the trail up there! He tightened his grip on the rifle, and watched. Suspecting nothing, the Indian descended.

It was a treacherous trail, a crooked little path that twisted up the face of the cliff in a series of angles. That the Iroquois had ever climbed it with a canoe on his shoulders was a miracle. Bits of rock fell away under him now and clattered to the beach as he descended.

At the bottom he straightened with a grunt, turned, and strode toward the tent. When Hayme stepped out to bar his way, the Iroquois halted with a strangled gasp of amazement.

"I've come a long way, Sam," Hayme said gently. "I want

to talk to you."

The Indian stared. He was a fine specimen of man, taller than most of his kind, with straight, clean features. A look of bewilderment darkened his features as he returned Hayme's stare. He spoke slowly in his own tongue, and the fragment of speech appeared to be a question of some sort.

Cullan strode up. "You want me to talk to him, corporal?"

"Ask him," Hayme said, "where he is going–and why."

Cullan put the question. Sam Longfoot gave the trader only a glance, then answered in a low, level voice, looking not at Cullan but at the policeman.

"He says," the trader translated, "he ran away from his cabin after he killed Charley Eye. He says he took this route hoping to shake off pursuit."

"Ask him why he killed Charley Eye."

There was more talk. "He says they had an argument. He says he is sorry about the whole thing, corporal. He knows he did wrong."

Hayme shrugged. "Well, that's that." He thrust a hand to his belt and tossed a knife to the ground at Sam Longfoot's feet. "Just to cinch it, Cullan, ask him if he admits the murder knife is his."

There was an odd smile at the corners of Cullan's mouth, and he scarcely looked at the Iroquois as he put the question. He was busy lighting a cigarette. The Indian picked up the knife and held it close to his eyes, peering at it in the dim light. He handed it back to Hayme and muttered his reply.

"He admits it," Cullan grunted. "He says the knife is his, all right."

Hayme drew a deep breath. Something inside him, something that been tense and tight for days, suddenly stopped hurting him.

"That's odd Cullan," he said "Mighty odd. Because the knife happens to be mine. You should have looked at it first, before adding to your string of lies!" His voice was little more than a whisper, soft against the river's thunder. "You killed Charley Eye, Cullan! Sam Longfoot had nothing at all to do with it!"

They faced each other, Hayme, grim-faced, watchful, the grizzled trader shrunk into an ugly crouch. Then Cullan backed up a step.

"You're smart, Hayme. Too smart," he snarled.

"'You killed Charley Eye!"

"Can you prove it, Hayme?"

"I'll prove it," the Mountie declared. "I'll find the motive if I have to question every Indian in the North Country! You're the lowest thing that crawls Cullan. You–"

It wasn't Hayme's fault, what happened then. He was alert. He whipped up his rifle and took a quick backward step, as the trader rushed him. The backward step was what brought disaster.

Sam Longfoot, bewildered by the talk, had moved aside. The movement put him directly behind Hayme. Cullan saw the opening and was quick as a cat to seize it.

Hayme stumbled over the Indian. Cullan crashed into him with savage force: a battering-ram of bone and muscle. The rifle flew from Hayme's hands as he tripped over the Indian's feet and went sprawling

Cullan came up with the rifle, his eyes glittering. "You're smart, corporal," he sneered. "But from now on, I'll run this show. Back up!"

Hayme slowly regained his feet. He drew a deep breath, stared at the rifle. He knew he was not to blame for the sudden turn of fate that had put the killer on top, yet his throat was dry, and bitter self-denunciation seethed in him like poison.

"You want to know why I put Charley Eye out of the way, Hayme?" the trailer asked tauntingly. "Well, he got wise that I was giving him less than market price for his furs. He got sore about it and threatened to shoot his mouth off to the rest of the Indians. So I shut him up."

"And framed Sam Longfoot!" Hayme said bitterly.

"Sure. Sam was getting independent. Talked about taking his furs to the Hudson's Bay people. I have to protect myself from smart Indians like Sam. I ought to put a bullet in him right this minute!"

Cullan growled a command at Sam Longfoot in the latter's own tongue. For an instant Sam stood rigid, staring at him. Defiance blazed in the Indian's dark eyes. But when Cullan jerked the rifle muzzle toward Sam's belly, the Iroquois retreated.

"I could shoot you down in cold blood, both of you," Cullan said then," but I won't. I'm a mild man. You and the Injun are going on a trip, Hayme. You're going down the river." His laugh was low in his throat. "That way, when they find you, there'll be no hint of blame attached to Cy Cullan. If they ever do find you. Move, now! Get in the canoe!"

Hayme wet his lips and looked at the river. There was a moon above the canyon's rim now, and the stream was a surging strip of molten silver, magnificent but deadly. A canoe could not live long in that wild madness!

But Sam Longfoot strode to the canoe and pulled it to the river's edge, turned and stood waiting. And there was something, in the Indian's magnificent calm that steadied Hayme's nerves. Sam was not unafraid. No man could face those murderous rapids without feeling a fear that twisted his throat and turned his blood cold! But there was a deadly sureness of purpose about the man that gave Hayme confidence. It was as though Sam wanted to tackle the river. As though he couldn't wait!

Hayme sent a last grim look at Cullan, then turned away. He steadied the canoe as the Iroquois stepped into the bow. One swift parting glance at the moonlit clearing, the cliff, the empty tent, and with a whispered prayer on his lips, he shoved the frail craft into the current and swung himself into the stern.

Next moment the clearing was gone. The canoe shot forward like a chip, between canyon walls that blurred past like monstrous shapes in a nightmare. With Hayme and the Iroquois paddling like madmen, the doomed craft plunged at express-train speed into a fantastic world of fury, a hell-world of mountainous waves and great geysers of spray, of dripping boulders and hurtling tons of white water.

It couldn't be done. Hayme knew it couldn't be done. Any sensible man would have thrown his paddle away and let the Devil's Mouth devour him. Yet miraculously the slender craft stayed right side up and kept going.

Deafened by the river's thunder, Hayme gripped his paddle in drenched hands and kept his gaze glued to the Iroquois' heaving shoulders. It was up to Sam Longfoot, in the bow, to spot the gleaming fangs of rock that loomed up to destroy them. Hayme could only take his cues from the Indian. Conversation in that seething inferno was impossible.

The walls swept past. The river grew wilder. More and more deafening grew the mighty voice of that tumbling torrent. But they were halfway through it! They were almost to the end of it, and still alive! As though shot from a cannon, the canoe sped into a swirling, spitting storm of spray–the river's last screaming challenge. For ten ghastly seconds a multitude of mad voices shrieked in Hayme's ears; mountains of crashing white water sought to engulf him. Then all at once, with incredible abruptness, the turmoil was behind them. The canyon walls fell away, the thunder died, the canoe shot into the moonlit calm of White Run Lake.

Hayme laid down his paddle and slumped forward, exhausted in mind and body, every tortured nerve pleading for peace. Sam Longfoot turned to stare at him, and said something in a low, soft voice.

They had done the impossible. They had ridden through death and were alive.

Hayme pointed to shore, to the end of the portage along which Cullan would have to travel to reach the lake. They paddled over the quiet water toward it, and Hayme saw Sam Longfoot's canoe there, where the Indian had cached it before returning to his camp at The Elbow.

Hayme stepped out, paced forward. He knew what he would find there, and he was right. He'd been sure of it all along. There on a nest of blankets in Sam Longfoot's canoe lay a black-eyed Iroquois baby snugly tucked into a carrying pouch fashioned of skins. Hayme noted the fine, straight features, the soft black hair. He noted the expression of pain that clung to the infant's face even in sleep.

"Sick, eh?" Hayme said gently. "And you're taking him to the white man's doctor at the Hudson's Bay post. I had a hunch that basket contraption in your cabin was a baby s crib, Sam–and when your squaw refused to sell the fisher pelt that was hanging on it, I'd have bet a year's pay I was right! You don't know what I'm talking about, but it doesn't matter. Point is, I guessed Cullan was up to something He didn't want me to know you'd taken the baby along. A killer fleeing from the law wouldn't burden himself with a papoose–and Cullan had to make me think you were a killer."

Sam Longfoot listened in respectful silence.

"All right, mister," Hayme said quietly. "I can handle the rest of this alone." Gently, so as not to disturb the baby, be slid the Indian's canoe into the lake, smiled and pointed south. "You go along, Sam. Get your son to the doctor. Good luck to you."

Hayme's meaning was clear to the Indian. Sam held out his hand, and his grip was firm. A moment later he was on his way.

Hayme sat on a windfall and waited, listening to the distant roar of the river, the soft night sounds around him. After a while he heard something else–the footsteps of a man confidently approaching along the portage. He rose, and was ready when Cy Cullan came striding into view.

Cullan stopped short, sucking breath through his teeth. Too late he reached for the rifle that was slung over his shoulder. Jim Hayme stepped into him. The Mountie's fist exploded in Cullan's face.

It took three blasting blows to lay Cullan out. One for Jim Hayme, one for Sam Longfoot, and one final blow, not quite so savage, for the little fellow. Then Hayme snapped handcuffs on the murderer's wrists, dumped him into the canoe and shoved off.

He had a long way still to go, but he was satisfied. He had his man.

RED SNOWS

By Harold F. Cruickshank

Under a Spectrum of Northern Lights, a Mountie Follows a White Trail that is Splashed with Scarlet!

Inspector Hacket shot a swift glance at the inscrutable face of Sergeant "Mac" McIlheny.

"Well, what d'you make of it, Sergeant?" he clipped.

Sergeant Mac shrugged, a gesture of impatience. He was a bit fed up with Hacket. He couldn't quite understand why the inspector had to come butting in on his special zone anyhow.

But Hacket was like that–fussy, albeit very efficient in his way.

"You've read the message as often as I have, sir," Mac grunted, referring to a message just received from Constable Keith, in charge of the old Fort Enterprise Post. "Can't you see that it's fixed–a phony?"

"But dash it, McIlheny, it's in Keith's handwriting."

"Sure enough, sir. But look at it again. Keith's a well educated man. He doesn't misplace capitals like that. Let me read it with you: 'Not A trace of Stewart so far. Held Up by Blizzard, but All's Well–'

"We don't have further, sir. Keith was forced into writing that message. It's a plant on someone's part to hold me down here, out of the way. See that capital A before 'trace'? That reads to me as though Keith had found a trace of Stewart. His mention of being held up by a blizzard is another point. 'Held Up' is spelled with caps. That isn't like Keith!"

The two great man-trackers eyed each other for a long moment in silence.

It was Hacket who finally broke the silence.

"Flimsy enough, Sergeant," he snapped. "You mean to suggest that Keith found a trace of Stewart, our missing man? And that in his effort to notify us he was captured and forced to write this note for the purpose of holding you here at the Great Slave ?"

"Exactly, sir. I'm sure of it. Then there's something else supporting my contention. You saw the native runner who brought the message. Notice anything familiar about him?"

"N-no. Can't say that I did. What?"

"Only that he was wearing those fancy bearskin mittens of Keith's," the sergeant snapped.

"What! Good God! You mean those mittens I'd twitted Keith about, the pair the little 'breed girl at Carp Lake embroidered in beadwork? You say this native was wearing them? Then why in the world didn't you hold him?" Hacket's face purpled. Here at last he had something on Sergeant McIlheny.

A thin, mirthless smile crossed the sergeant's features as he stirred his big six-foot form.

"I let him go because he's more valuable free, sir," he said. "I'm taking his trail this afternoon. There's something fishy about this note. Something's happened to Keith. If you'll be good enough to make my regular Great Slave patrol, sir, I'll–"

Inspector Hacket was breathing hard. He had been running his eyes over the cryptic message from Keith again. Now that McIlheny had made things clearer, Hacket himself was beginning to see through it. That capital B for blizzard.

He scowled.

"This suggests to me that Keith has run up against that damn crooked 'breed Baroff, Sergeant," he snapped. "Baroff! Is it possible that we can at last pin something definite on 'him?"

"I think you've hit it, Inspector," Mac agreed. "I was sure from the start Baroff had had some hand in Stewart's disappearance. Baroff has learned that Stewart has made a new rich strike down the Yellowknife. Well, nobody's seen a sign of Stewart since he came in last from the Outside. We wouldn't know he was north if I hadn't received that inquiry from his sister at Winnipeg. Easy for Baroff to get away with anything, if this note hadn't come from Keith, eh?"

"Right! Now you'll want to take the trail before dark, Sergeant," the inspector suggested. "I'll hitch your dogs and load their food aboard. Be all ready for you when you are."

Fifteen minutes later, Sergeant McIlheny. was fully equipped for the trail. He shot a glance at the inspector and nodded. Hacket smiled grimly back and nodded as Mac paid out the lash of his trail whip

Baroff, the Russian half-breed, had long been a thorn in the side of Inspector Hacket. Never had the R.C.M.P. been able to pin anything definite on the elusive renegade, who always managed to slip out from under, letting his native henchmen take the raps.

Headquarters was pressing for word of the missing prospector, Stewart, who worked in a silent, mysterious way, as he forced the grim North to reveal its host of long concealed treasures–gold and silver.

Hacket smiled thinly as Mac's dogs yelped and stretched into their collars. McIlheny made few mistakes along the white trails. Once given even the most eager clue, the big non-com followed that lead with relentless persistency.

"Hi-ye-ah! Mush!" Mac cried as he snapped the lash tip skillfully above the lead dog's dome.

As he settled down into a steady dog-trot on his rackets, Sergeant Mac was fully cognizant of the dangers which would attend his trek along the north trail, a trail that would probably be stained a dull crimson. Bull Baroff rewarded his killers well, with whiskey and the returns of this crooked trading and fur-stealing.

The man, in a perverted way, was clever. Forcing Keith to write that note to McIlheny had in its way been a clever touch. But Keith had slipped one over by inserting those superfluous capitals.

The sled runners whined in the frosty atmosphere. Sergeant Mac swung along tirelessly. He reveled in the work he did down north, albeit he had hoped for a break soon. There was a girl in the Outside, a girl whom he couldn't ask to wait much longer.

But even this thought was cast from his mind now as he shuffled along, head down, into the steady nor'easter which fanned its deathly cold breath across the Barrens.

For the next two days Sergeant McIlheny pushed his team hard along the white trail. Time and again he was convinced that the native runner ahead of him had a suspicion that he was being followed.

Suddenly Mac was aware that instead of himself being the tracker, he was being tracked. He pulled his dogs down toward the river, unhitched them, and made camp close to a clump of stunted spruces. His first act was to get fish thawed for the dogs. When they had gulped the tullabe down, they soon burrowed deep in the snow.

McIlheny climbed the river bank again, his holster flap loosened. There was a human carcajou prowling this zone the man he had tracked out of Fort Reliance. McIlheny had let none of the native's clever side-trailing and backtracking go by unnoted.

"Guess he's not quite sure who's fetchin' up on his trail," Mac soliloquized. "If he ever gets a line on me, he'll be so scared he's liable to–"

The sharp *cr-r-ang-g* of a Winchester cut Mac short. A bullet had whistled by his shoulder. He dived for the snow as another slug whined by.

Two more bullets spanged into the snow nearby; another cut through the shoulder fur of Mac's parka. He was lunging for the cover of a willow thicket when the force of the striking bullet pitched him off balance. In his headlong dive he could not prevent contact between his forehead and a knob of willow root.

A million lights danced before Mac's vision. Everything was going black. Hell! He wanted to stay awake. He quickly lowered his face to the snow and felt instant relief. His senses were clearing rapidly. There was a sudden crunching of the snow.

McIlheny froze. He knew that it would be fatal now to make one false move. The other had the drop on him, and Mac knew that the slinker must have been half crazed to shoot on sight as he had done. He decided to fake unconsciousness as the other approached stealthily.

But for all his apparent unconsciousness and prone state, Sergeant McIlheny was very much alert.

Now the attacker was muttering, faint snatches of which Mac made out. The native was babbling in half fear–fear of the police. He must now have distinguished McIlheny's equipment as police equipment. *Ayaie!* If he had killed a member of the Force.

A picture of the gallows automatically imprinted itself on his brain. And yet he had his orders from his boss. He had been instructed to hold up McIlheny–stop him at any cost.

"Ayaie!" his voice was husky, tremulous, as he gasped his expression of fear. He was playing his grim game between two deaths– death on the gallows, and death by torture at the hand of his chief if he failed.

Sergeant Mac never moved a muscle as he waited, hoping the suspense would soon be broken.

Frosted tamaracks cracked as the temperature plummeted. Mac realized that soon his face and extremities would freeze unless he could pour himself into action.

Now a willow cracked. The Indian was shuffling in from the far side of the small thicket. He was stealing in with the stealth of a prowling lynx. Mac could almost hear his breathing.

And then Mac felt a hand touch his head. He started inwardly with the knowledge that the Indian had now only a one-handed grip on his Winchester. But Mac waited a moment longer. The native was trying to turn his face upward.

Mac's nerve fibers were all bunched taut. Like a piece of spring steel he flung himself up. His right fist smashed out in a looping hook, registering squarely in that lowered, pock-marked native face. The Indian rocked back. There was the click of a carbine hammer lifting. Mac sprang. Now he had some purchase. But he was taking a chance, a grim chance as he dived.

The native's carbine almost exploded in Mac's face. But there had been no aim. Save for a powder burn, the sergeant was unharmed. And then he went to work–silently, grimly, with all the power he could force into those pummeling fists.

It was amazing how much punishment the native could absorb. McIlheny. crashed him back with a smashing hook to the face. But the man coiled up. And, as he came, a long skinning knife glinted.

Alert as he was, McIlheny was hampered by his heavy parka and the soft snow underfoot. He lunged off to one side as the knife struck down. He saved himself from the fatal stroke of that blade. As it was, he took a glancing thrust along his right thigh. The pain was terrific, but it didn't stop Mac.

Bellowing his rage now, he hurled himself into close battle and grimly went to work.

A few moments later, as he picked up the native, the man resembled a small bundle of half-cured skins. Mac half dragged him, half carried him to his campsite, where he dumped him onto the snow. Then the Mountie went to work on the knife slash in his thigh. First he plugged it with snow until all sign of bleeding had stopped. Then he flushed it with iodine and taped it securely.

A thin smile crossed his features as he rustled more wood for his almost dead fire. The smile came with the realization that he had won the first round. But it had been close. A single slip, and his prone form might now have been lying out for wolf bait.

As he munched thawed-out bannock, later, Mac watched the Indian across the fire sip from a steaming mug of black tea. The man still wore Keith's fancy bearskin mittens.

"You'll talk a lot before I'm done with you, feller," McIlheny breathed to himself. He hadn't bothered to handcuff his prisoner. It wasn't likely the man would want to get away. For one reason, the ambusher had failed, and he realized that his failure would mean death if he were picked up by any of Baroff's renegade spies.

McIlheny cast furtive glances about him. Each moment he expected to hear the telltale crunch of snowshoes about him. He had that uncanny sixth sense of experience, the feeling that he and the Indian across the fire were not alone in this section of the wilderness. He knew that if Baroc had some sinister plot in mind, he would never trust a lone native out on the trail. That man would be watched.

Now the native laid down his cup. McIlheny shifted over to him.

"Speak," he said gruffly. "Mucha Satan, what happened at Enterprise Post? Open up, else I feed you to the wolves. What happened to Constable Keith? You understand my English all right. Hurry, tell all you know, or I'll slit out your heart."

The native drew back cringingly on his seat, but Mac held him close.

"Ayaie! I dunno. No seeum Keith," the man croaked. He-"

"You lie, you carcajou. You are wearing his mitts. How came you by those? Tell me–where is Keith? Where is your boss man–Baroff?"

"Ayaie!" The native gasped. This powerful man of the Force knew something. The native's eyes almost popped from their battered, swollen sockets. Sergeant Mac had fastened a terrific hold on the nape of his neck.

"Now–you'll tell," Mac snarled. "What is Baroff up to ?"

"Uh-h. Mebbeso I tell. Bar-off, she's got heem–Keit'. I–

a-ah! I shall be keel. I–" Mac applied more pressure. He was cutting down the last of the native's reserves.

"At Lac–Provi–" The man's voice was scarcely audible. Sergeant Mac suddenly hurled himself clear. A bullet had socked hard, into the Indian's chest, followed instantly by the boom of a Winchester.

McIlheny hurled himself to cover, snatching out his Colt on the fly. As he had suspected, Baroff had not trusted this runner. The native had been closely watched. As he spoke, his words were snuffed out–with his life.

Now the sergeant snaked his way to an outcropping of wind-blown rock at the river bank. He listened, but there came no telltale sounds to disturb the grim silence of the wilds.

The red blood raced through Mac's being now. Here, at last, was something very definite to work on. The snows were red with human blood. The native had told Mac a lot as he gasped out, "Lac Provi–" The sergeant knew at once that the man could only mean Lac Providence. So that was where Baroff hid out!

McIlheny gave more than a moment's thought to Baroff. Just what had the powerful half-breed in mind? He was surely playing the game close to the rim of hell-fire when he-trapped a member of the Mounted. Hell! No crook could get away with that. And yet McIlheny shuddered as he thought back to barely more than an hour ago when he had missed death by a fraction.

Stewart, the prospector, had disappeared into thin air. Constable Keith was evidently a prisoner–most likely at Lac Providence. What in hell had come into Baroff? Had he gone utterly berserk?

McIlheny intended to learn the answer to those questions. Now he slid out along the river bank and made a wide circle of the zone

Darkness would soon drop its sable mantle over the wilderness. It was only half light now as Mac turned and shuffled along the river, cursing the pain in his right leg.

On–on. The sergeant hugged the high bank of the frozen stream. Now he stopped short in his tracks. A dark form, almost indiscernible, was climbing the bank ahead–a shadow which might even be that of some wild animal. But Sergeant Mac knew that it was a man form, a native.

"Clever trick," he breathed. "You think you're going to get the jump on me from cover, eh?" Mac turned half right. But the crunching of snowshoes in the white snow told him that the man ahead had decided not to swing round. He was heading eastward. And Sergeant Mac followed on.

The sudden faint yelp of a dog pulled Mac up short. God! Something was happening back at his camp.

He almost roared out an oath as a new situation dawned.

"By the seven-toed carcajou of hells" he boomed. "What a mug I've been!"

In the height of action, it hadn't occurred to Mac that there might be more than one spy in this immediate zone. He had been cleverly drawn way from his campsite.

Now he turned and, forgetting the pain in his leg, hit a fast clip back along the river.

A wild yelp, almost a shriek, from the campsite told him that a dog was badly hurt. He pressed forward, wheezing badly as the frost took a nip at his lungs.

He reached camp to find the last of his dogs writhing in a patch of crimsoned snow. His entire team had been knifed! His equipment, the bulk of his food supply, had been stolen.

Snows were again red. McIlheny lifted his square chin. His lips moved, but no sound came. Silently he made his vows. Somebody would pay plenty for tonight's dirty work.

A little earlier on, Mac had wished that he was traveling light, without a dog outfit. That situation had, now been forced on him. From now on he would go it alone, with just whatever grub the marauder, in his haste, had overlooked.

For the rest of the night, McIlheny kept a terrible vigil in the midst of death. As the northern lights cascaded down their riotous brilliance, festoons swept the grotesque shapes of the dead dogs, and that swiftly freezing Indian cadaver–all of which seemed to come again to life, to writhe and shudder before McIlheny's vision.

But there was no further attack during the night. Actually, the sergeant hadn't expected one. He felt sure that his attackers, the killers of the native, would be hustling back to their hideout deep in the Barrens under the protective "wing" of Bull Baroff.

With the first hesitant greys of a cold dawn, McIlheny made himself tea, then slung together a pack–his down sleeping bag, a few rations of frozen beans, bacon and a couple of hard bannocks. He would have to pull in his belt, for these were scarcely half rations for a much smaller, weaker man than he. He got to his feet and slipped off into the shadows.

A gray wolf howled dismally in the sweep of a blizzard wind as the bent form of Sergeant McIlheny approached Keith's Fort Enterprise cabin. For two days Mac had bucked this snorter on short rations. But there was every sign of a lull now. One thing the storm had brought to Mac was safety from attack along the trail.

His frosted face twitched sharply. Time and again he had been forced to halt and rub his face with snow. His nose and cheeks were peeling badly. They were raw now, and smarting.

For a long moment he scouted the area about Keith's cabin and small outbuildings. But there was no sign of life at all. Dry snow swirled into a two-foot drift against the cabin door. But still Mac was not satisfied. He loosened the flap of his holster and jerked out his gun. With great caution he moved on.

It took a moment to kick the snow from in front of the cabin door. Then Mac's fingers jerked aside the steel hasp. The door stuck as he pressed. But a hefty shove forced it inward.

The cabin was deserted. It was as he had expected. Mac swept the one-room place with a swift glance. He seemed frozen to the spot just inside the door. Something bothered him. The cabin, plainly enough, was very much deserted and, hadn't been occupied for days. Yet, there was that strange intuition, born of years of police experience, which told McIlheny. that he was not alone.

Now his glance roamed over the cabin floor. It came to halt at the cellar trapdoor. He started, for along the edges of the door's crack, there was a white powder.

A low hiss escaped him. To the Mountie's trained eye that powder suggested only one thing–frozen air–condensation, breath!

Quickly he tossed aside his mittens and dropped to his knees. He felt the fluffy frost at the door crack, then reached for the ring of the trap.

A gasp escaped McIlheny as he jerked the door up and laid it back on the cabin floor. A low moan had reached him. His hunch was right. There was someone below. Keith?

Mac didn't waste a second. He knew that the shallow cellar wasn't by any means frost-proof. Dropping to the hard clay floor he bumped against a yielding shape–a human form, huddled and bound.

In the darkness McIlheny could not identify the form. He could only hope that it was Keith's. Now he reached down and lifted the moaning shape.

"Up you–come," he grunted, hoisting the man up to the cabin floor. He clambered up and in the half light turned the trussed-up shape over.

"Stewart!" he exclaimed.

Stewart, the missing man, the man whose disappearance had brought the Mounted into grips with Bull Baroff !

The sergeant worked swiftly now. He dreaded to think of what he would see after he had stripped the mukluks from Stewart's feet. He quickly built up a fire, shuttered the lone cabin window. Snow was melting on the stove, then Mac set to work to strip Stewart of his clothing.

As he slit off the man's mukluks, he started. Those feet and lower legs were terribly swollen. He could only hope that this was the result of the taut rawhide thongs which had trussed Stewart for heaven knew how long. But no. There were at least two toes badly frosted.

McIlheny wrapped the groaning man in Keith's blankets, then fished around until he found a can of condensed milk. This he heated and poured into a tin cup. Stewart was coming out of the fog now. He stared up wildly as the sergeant approached.

"Don't bother to talk now, Stewart," McIlheny advised. "Drink this. We'll have a medicine talk after. See if you can hang on to the cup alone now, brother. I've got to rig up some grease and salve for those frostings. Great! You're doing splendidly, Stewart."

The finding of Stewart had been a lucky break for the Mountie, but it also presented a further big problem. Mac's objective was Lac Providence. He must get there quickly. But what of Stewart in the meantime?

McIlheny knew of an old Indian living a few miles to the south. He would have to mush out and tote old Payuk, or his squaw, up to the post.

He worked swiftly as he thought out his plans. Now he shifted back to the bunk and gently applied the soothing salve he had concocted.

"I think we can save those toes, Stewart," he clipped. "Will have some hot grub for you shortly. Now –feel like talking? Tell me briefly what happened. Know anything definite about Keith?"

A spot of rum from Keith's medicine case had had its effect on Stewart. He smiled gratefully at the Mountie as he passed his empty cup.

"I've been here about two days, I think, Sergeant," he breathed weakly, then winced with the pain in his frosted parts.

"He–they, Baroff's outfit, jumped my new claim. I tried to put up a fight. Got one of them. But they were too many. They trapped me and I was packed off. Cabin at some lakeshore place. Then Baroff forced me to write a note to Keith. He hates Keith's guts, Sergeant."

Mac's brows flicked up as Stewart broke off. The story was unfolding. Keith had been baited out on Stewart's trail out to the dismal white reaches of Lac Providence. Mac shuddered at the thought of what might have happened to his friend, the constable. A cut in the lake ice–then a swift push. The lake would freeze overnight, and then if it snowed, the grim, watery grave would be sealed for all time.

Stewart was talking again.

"I was tortured into writing to Keith, Sergeant," he breathed. "It was–hell. A day or so later, I found myself aboard a sled– I woke up, bound, in this cellar. Sorry–Sergeant, sorry I've got Keith into danger."

Sergeant Mac's lips had almost vanished. His eyes batted

momentarily, then he shrugged his broad shoulders.

"Never mind that, Stewart," he said`. "You did the only thing you could have done. Don't worry. Maybe I'll be in time to save Keith yet. Hell! Baroff can't get away with all this!"

He turned again to Stewart, his eyes glinting.

"Have you any idea what Baroff intended to do, Stewart?" he asked.

"I heard plenty, Sergeant. You see, about that claim-jumping: I'd foolishly made the statement. Outside, that I'd struck it rich at Campbell Lake, when all the time my new strike was further northeast along the Yellowknife River. Baroff could have got clear away with his jumping, for nobody knew I was in the vicinity of Yellowknife territory at all. My claim wasn't registered–" The man showed signs of strain and pain now and the Mountie didn't press him for further statements.

Mac could see now that if it had not been for Keith's timely insertion of those superfluous capital letters in his message, Baroff would have got clean away with a couple of major crimes, as well as Stewart's claim. But things hadn't run so smoothly for the renegade leader. Keith must have been hot on his trail. So, he had pulled Keith out of his camp at Lac Providence, a spot seldom visited by anyone.

Baroff was a clever devil. He knew that in these far, isolated reaches of God's most forgotten wilderness, men had often disappeared. Shell ice–a drop into some lake, which was sealed by the sub-zero weather and heavy snows. A natural disappearance.

Baroff evidently intended some such "natural" fate for both Stewart and Keith. Ordinarily, who could suspect? Hadn't Stewart himself stated that his new claim was supposed to be at Campbell Lake ?

Sergeant Mac breathed a low prayer of thanksgiving for Keith's clever message. Now there was a lot to work on. He would at once mush out to Lac Providence, but first he must get Payuk over to watch over Stewart.

Laying his cocked carbine on an upturned box close to Stewart's hand, the Mountie issued a few swift instructions.

"I'll lock up the cabin, brother," he said. "Don't make any sign, should anyone come. If anyone attempts to jump you, shoot on sight. I'll be back presently. Then we'll eat. So long, and good luck!"

Mac slung the kit on his dogs and soon was whirling off to the south in the last sullen greys of fading day.

Sergeant Mac crouched in the lee of an alder clump. He had, reached up with Baroff's hideout at last. The squalid old trapper's huts loomed up before him in a clear, starry night. Beyond, stretched the desolate surface of Lac Providence.

Sounds of ribaldry came from the main cabin. Evidently Baroff's native henchmen were in a state of aboriginal glee. Liquor was flowing–cheap, home-distilled rot-gut.

Prowling mongrel dogs presented an obstacle to the Mountie. He was almost afraid to step from his cover. Those snarling curs would give his presence away.

He thought of the last of his food rations. It was a clever thought. Always, Indian dogs were half starved.

Mac fished out hunks of frozen bannock, beans and small chunks of bacon. These he flung to the dogs. Instantly bedlam was let loose as the curs balled up in a snarling mass. He stepped cautiously away while the dogs fought over the food fragments.

Stealthily he crept toward the main cabin, edging round to a window, but he could see little through the dirty glass. A sputtering lantern inside bothered him.

The door opened, to disgorge a sickened native, who pitched headlong to the snow. Mac stole round the corner, edging up to the door which was open an inch. He completely ignored the spread-eagled nitchi, who was out for some time, he knew.

Voices! Baroff's voice! Mac's heart began to tear at its mooring strings. He was so close to the finish of another wilderness drama, his red blood coursed swiftly through its stream now.

"You're a damn dirty carcajou, Baroff!"

"Keith!" McIlheny breathed, quivering with sheer delight. The constable was alive, yet. But just then the sound of a fist cracking flesh and bone. Baroff had struck. McIlheny couldn't see, but he knew what had happened.

"Dat an' some more, Keit'," snarled the crook. "Tonight, we wind ever'thin' up. By god! I tol' you mont's ago not to bother my trail. Didn't I?" His words were punctuated by hard, cracking blows to Keith's face. McIlheny wanted to risk all and leap in right then.

"Go ahead, you swine," Keith muttered. "But get this, Baroff. Sergeant McIlheny's wise to you. He'll never let up until he has your neck stretched. I fixed that note you forced me to write–fixed it so that Mac would read the truth of my situation. He–"

Crack! This time it wasn't Baroff's hand which struck Keith. It was his gun barrel.

"That's mebbeso shut your trap, Keit'," the half-breed boomed. "Dat damn sergeant'll never get me. What's he got on me, huh? Tonight, you just slip peaceful into a lac'. Tomorrow, there'll be snow again. I picked out tonight special, because it's gonna be col'; den snow. Stewart'll follow youse down t'rough. By mornin', you'll bot' be sealed up. Ah-h!"

"Just about your size, you dirty Russian polecat," Keith blustered.

"Huh! Oh, hell, never mind. Guess we'll go to work. This is what'll happen. You'll be rolled in a couple uh green caribou hides an' slid into d' water. That's easy."

"Yeah! It'll be a swift end, Baroff," Keith commented. "Well, get it over."

Baroff then turned to his helpers. He was barking orders in a Yellowknife dialect which McIlheny understood. Two men were going out after Stewart, while an ax man was going out across the lake to cut the death hole.

God! How could Mac handle both situations? He could not leave Keith, and yet he knew that Stewart wouldn't stand the trip from Enterprise. It was a tough one. But he decided on one job at a time.

The natives were now coming toward the door. Mac stepped back and slid the cover as the chuckling natives came out and hurried to batter a dog team into harness. Mac waited until the heard the whine of the sled runners fade in the distance. The ax man had gone out.

But he was afraid that another contingent of renegades would be coming to hitch up a team for Keith's transportation to the hole of death. He was right. Only in the nick of time did he duck as two more Indians lurched out to stagger toward the dog compound.

Baroff was now taunting Keith again. The 'breed was evidently well primed with rot gut. Keith was taking more punishment.

McIlheny could stand no more. He kicked in the door, .45 out, ready. His second leap took him within striking distance of Baroff. Mac struck with the barrel of his Colt's, rocking the 'breed out of his seat. He swung on the remainder of the renegades.

"Not a move, dogs," he snarled. "Stand back, else I blow you apart."

Baroff was reaching for a gun, when Keith yelled a warning. Quickly the sergeant spun. The automatic in Baroff's hand exploded harmlessly, although very close. But McIlheny leaped in and caught the other's gun wrist.

He turned on all the pressure of his big, powerful frame, but Baroff was strong, too, a powerful man who was now desperate. He fought like a bull buffalo, with feet and hands. And, then he snapped in like a wolf, hoping to fasten a fang hold on his adversary.

The Mountie took a lot of punishment, but he took it silently, while he went to work on this man the Force had wanted so long.

A sudden movement from a corner of the cabin warned the trussed-up constable. A native was creeping in, knife in hand. With a yell, Keith bunched his bound form and hurtled forward, crashing the nitchi beneath him. The man rolled out from under, his knife gleaming in the lantern light. But Sergeant Mac whirled, and fired.

In that brief, split second's respite Baroff snatched at his own knife. With a booming roar of anger he lunged. But McIlheny saw the attack coming. He dived low, hooked his hands about one of the 'breed's legs and heaved. As Baroff tottered back, Mac's left shoulder hit him full in the stomach. They crashed hard to the floor.

Baroff was not quite out. McIlheny's throat was pressed close to his face. With a gurgled snarl, he struck upward with his strong teeth.

McIlheny wanted to howl with the pain, but instead he clamped on a tight scissors hold. Slowly, while he took the punishment of those teeth, he was squeezing the breath from Baroff's body. He felt the throat hold relax, then snapped up his head. Quickly he swung a looping hook to the other's jaw, another and another.

Bull Baroff slumped out, so cold he would have kept a month in the tropics.

Bleeding badly, Sergeant Mac got to his feet and swung on the natives–those who had been left in the cabin, and those who had newly stolen in.

"Dogs," he boomed "You'll get punishment for this. Now make ready a double dog outfit. We're making a forced mush to Enterprise. Move! *Awus*, you carcajous!"

The natives had lost their leader. They cringed before this powerful man of the great Force. The R.C.M.P. had at last caught up with them all. They must pay!

"Better snap a set of cuffs on that Russian, Sarge," Keith warned, weakly "He's as slippery as a damned eel. And thanks a lot for your visit. It's–been damn–nice to–have you–"

Keith almost passed out. But before giving him any attention, McIlheny. took the constable's advice. He snapped the cuffs on the still unconscious Baroff, then swung, and cut Keith's bonds. The constable sighed heavily and collapsed, and for a long moment, Sergeant McIlheny held him closely–in his powerful arms.

"Hi-ya-h-h!" Sergeant Mac paid out the long trail whip. The double string of dogs were making fast time along the trail of the native forerunners. Mac had scooped in a big string of prisoners. In the sled sat the secured form of Baroff, on his last sled ride, while on the cariole's platform clung Constable Keith.

Sergeant Mac was thinking fast as he geed the sled around a dangerous cliff curve. He was thinking of the future. Inspector Hacket wouldn't be long down North now. McIlheny would be due for a leave, for promotion.

"Inspector McIlheny. It sounded swell. So did, "Sergeant Keith!" Ah-h-h! There would be curtains at the windows of the Post cabin at Fort Reliance. There was nothing to prevent

McIlheny from marrying now! He had been promised that promotion. This job would cinch it.

As the shuddering, awesome northern lights flooded the cavalcade, McIlheny looked into Baroff's glinting eyes. His teeth clicked sharply. For a time, perhaps a long time, the North wilderness would pulse in peace again–time enough for Mac to take a long deferred spell in the Outside. But he would come back. These white trails would be calling.

He broke off his thoughts. A native runner was tearing back, gesticulating wildly. He brought news that they were in sight of the other sled outfit, the outfit sent to get Stewart.

A grim smile crossed McIlheny's weather-blasted features. That was the pay-off, the finis to the case! It had come in a blaze of glory. Hard, scrapping action that the big non-com reveled in.

On the back of the cariole, Constable Keith stared hard into the big, broad back of his sergeant.

"Swell," he breathed. That was all. It was plenty, coming from a Northman whose experiences were only second to McIlheny's in the whole of the North wilds.

THE DRIVING FORCE

By Murray Leinster

In which a Mountie knows his duty and does it.

Presently, he convinced himself that he had heard a locomotive whistle. It had sounded hoarsely just a little while before. And he had to find the railroad. That was what he was here for. He strained his ears, swaying upon his feet in the snow, listening. But he did not hear it now. The only sound was the infinitely soft tinkling as the snow fell gently, its crystals brittle and settling upon their fellows with a tiny sound that was quite indefinable. There was no wind. The tree limbs were motionless, save that they slowly bent lower and lower beneath their burden of white stuff. There was no motion anywhere. Even the snowshoe rabbits were cuddled still beneath the fleecy blanket. Only the man, in all the world, seemed an animate creature.

He was not a pretty picture. There was a mass of matted blood and hair peering out beneath the hood of his parka. What of his face could be seen was red and inflamed, bitten and scratched by icy crystals in a blinding storm. His eyes were showing blood-shot in their corners. Bundled in shapeless garments, smeared with the drifts in which he had fallen, swaying as he stood in a strange, nerve-wracked silence hoping for the sound he had imagined to be repeated, he was not a figure any artist would have chosen to paint.

He made a little sound that was close to a whimper, and then plunged forward blindly, wearily, floundering hopelessly. He was carrying a single snowshoe, and suddenly it seemed to madden him. He ripped it from its fastenings and flung it behind him. The other was gone–lost somewhere in the nebulous past. He could not remember when he had lost it.

For perhaps ten paces he went on, though he certainly took thirty steps, and then he turned and came back to it. Rocking upon his feet, he fumbled in his shapeless clothing and brought out a knife. He had to bare his hand to open it, and the cold struck home. With the glove back on, he slapped his fingers violently, yet with an effect of utter fatigue, to get the blood to circulating again. Then he tried to bend down and fell sprawling.

Laboriously, he got to his knees and cut away the rawhide thongs, and then the webbing. He made a little bundle of them with queerly clumsy movements. Then he lurched away again, wobbling upon his feet. And as he went, he listened always with a certain terrible hope, for the sound of a locomotive.

He was long past coherent thought. It seemed to him that he had been years just so, stumbling across a frozen waste. He no longer knew why he kept in movement. An overmastering fatigue weighed him down and yet his legs lifted and went forward, and lifted and went forward again, though he utterly lacked the will to command them. He watched them, after a little, with a peculiar, detached curiosity. They marched like automatons, bearing his weary body willy-nilly upon their way.

With a ludicrous precision, he saw his right foot shift to one side to avoid a sharp-pointed boulder whose tip showed as a miniature hummock amid the snow. A little later he marveled to see his left foot reach higher than usual to avoid tripping over a fallen tree limb. He felt rather inclined to laugh at them, but grew irritated instead. He wanted to rest, to stop, to fling himself down in the beautiful white soft blanket that covered the ground and sleep and sleep....

He stopped once more. Certainly he could remember hearing an engine bell. The clanging was still lingering in his ears. He listened desperately, trying to make himself hear further than his ears could reach. He almost persuaded his mind that he had heard it again, but he could not. He could convince himself that he had heard it just a short time ago, but he could not possibly delude himself that he was hearing it at the moment. With contradiction to the confusion of the rest of his thoughts, the difference came home to him. He made a little sound in his throat and went on again, wallowing through the stilly falling snow.

He had forgotten many things. It seemed as if he had been going just in this fashion for all eternity, struggling to reach the railroad line. Dimly, he remembered mushing along behind a dog team. He had been hastening even then. He could remember forcing his dogs, giving them the shortest of rests, feeding them just the precisely weighed amount to keep them at topmost speed without weakening them. He knew that somewhere in his coat, in a little bundle far beneath his outer wrappings, there were things he must not lose. They were precious and they would have to be used later. And he remembered a flash that had come out of a copse of ice-covered brushwood; that, and a blinding light and pain.

But afterwards, he remembered nothing except that he had been walking just like this.

He found himself laboring, and knew that he was struggling up a hill. It was unfair and unjust that there should be a hill here. He wanted to weep, and found no reason of self-respect why he should not. But he lost himself in the contemplation of his feet again. A little later he found his hands fumbling and discovered himself looking at a small pocket-compass. Then, in astonishment, he observed himself nodding. He was headed as he should be headed, to get to the railroad line. And he had to get there. He must make haste.

And weariness fell upon him like a breaking wave. Every muscle in his body ached dully. As he lifted each foot a cry of protest went through every nerve. He would have cried out, except that he was too tired. His eyes, too, ached unutterably. He found himself contemplating the snow with a terrible longing. It was so soft, so beautifully soft. He could lie down and let his limbs relax. In anticipation, he could almost feel the slow tide of restfulness sees slowly through his veins.

And he found his legs marching on, mechanically yet with amazing precision, carrying his aching body with them.

Suddenly, he was gathering punk from the inside of a rotten tree. He was scraping away the snow. He was making a fire. He observed himself in a certain astonishment. The flame flickered up and caught. In a little while he had a tiny blaze of unspeakably grateful warmth. He sat beside it stupidly. Slowly, it ate down to the earth beneath. He found himself gathering together small pebbles from the cleared space and putting them into the blaze. Then he was contriving a cup out of bark and scraped-up, thawed mud. He filled it with snow.

Warmth began to creep over him. He waited, dully, for sleep to come– waited dully, but in an agony of anticipation. Then he was snatching the small pebbles out and dropping them in his bark cup. They melted their way to the bottom. He grew thirsty as he saw the water. He waited anxiously to drink. And something was making him snatch out more pebbles, and yet more pebbles, to drop in with the first.

He understood vaguely when he found himself drinking the warm water. It was almost hot, and it filled his belly with a grateful feeling of utter peace. Then he slept, in utter exhaustion.

He wept openly as he found himself kicking snow over the fire again. He sniveled without shame and in a violent protest he tried to fling himself down in the soft snow again to rest and rest and rest . . . But his body had suddenly become strange to him. It wavered, and then went on with its task. He was looking at his compass again, and stumbling on, ever on, toward the railroad. He knew that he was going to the railroad, but that was all he did know. He persuaded himself that his body would let him rest, when he had reached the line. In a fretful hatred, he had come to hate this body that would not obey him, that drove him on and on, protesting, when all he wished to do was sleep.

Aeons later he found himself climbing once more. A steep hill. He must reach the top and then he might see the railroad, and then he could rest. He reached the top and wept again as he saw yet other hills before him. He must cross them. They were mountains, and he must pass them. And to reach the next hill–

His eyes were searching for a way. He could not hope to pass through the deep drifts in the valleys. He began to flounder his way along the sides of a monster hill that reached to high heaven.

Detached as he was from this alien body that would not heed his commands, his mind wandered confusedly. Sometimes he did not seem to feel fatigue. Then he thought dully of other things, while his legs marched him on. Now was a case in point. While his eyes saw the monster things before him, yet he was also seeing quite another place. It was a lecture room. He recognized it perfectly. It was at his college, years ago, and the trees were green outside and he could sleep whenever he wanted to. The professor was standing there, lecturing on psychology.

"A fixed idea may so thoroughly imbed itself in all of a

man's brain that it will color his every conscious thought and action. It may be an idea concerned with fear, or desire, or duty, but it may take possession of him until his whole being is but an expression of the possibly forgotten idea. At such times, and under the driving force of this buried concept, he may perform feats little short of the miraculous–or the insane. For example, under the stress of fear or a conception of duty, he may do things normally impossible. Without strength, without conscious courage, without even awareness of his motive, he will act under the driving force of the idea which is deeply imbedded in his mind, and often he will act in a fashion that would appall him under ordinary circumstances. This, it may be, is at the bottom of much insanity and all murder, and at the same time it may provide humanity with most of its heroes."

The professor paused, and tugged at the lobe of his ear in a slightly embarrassed manner which was a trick of his.

"Er–also," he added diffidently, "it may explain something of the results of the–ah–faith–cures and the–ah herculean strength sometimes displayed in emergencies and insanity."

With a jerk, the classroom vanished and the professor went into limbo with a little twitch, like a bubble bursting.

The man had paused, blood-smeared and utterly exhausted. Before him was a huge level space that could not actually be level. It was a valley, filled with drifted snow. And on snowshoes it might have been crossed with some ease, but a man's feet would sink with his weight. He would be mired in the powdery stuff, utterly helpless to escape.

He stood rocking upon his feet, his eyes dull, waiting for his body to let him rest. He eyed the snow with infinite longing. He hoped hungrily that he could be allowed to lie down in it and rest. He tingled all over at the thought. But he waited for permission from this new and self-willed body that caused him so much agony and possessed a determination of its own.

Dumbly, he had formed a vague association between the wandering of his mind and this present journey of his body. There was some fixed idea, some hidden motive, that was driving his body after he had forgotten it. Something, fear or desire or a conviction of duty. But it could not be desire, because he wanted nothing so much as to lie down, just to lie down....

He found himself moving toward the white expanse. He found himself wading into it as if it were the sea, until it reached his waist and beyond. And then he found his weary muscles flinging him forward. A thrill of beatific happiness swept over him. He was going to rest.

And then he was getting up again. The snow was soft. Often, in past days, he had gone on before a dog team on snowshoes, packing the trail for them, pressing down the soft stuff by his own weight until it was firm enough to bear the dog's paws. Where he had stepped the dogs could follow. Where he did not lead, they sank to their bellies, helplessly. He was doing the same thing now, flinging his body down in the stinging whiteness until the breadth of his chest and his weight had packed it hard enough for him to stand upright upon. He got up, tottering, where his chest had lain. He flung himself forward again.

Bitterly, he reproached the hands that struggled to lift him. He argued vehemently with his legs. He wept weakly as his inexorable, weary muscles tortured him. But he felt himself being lifted, being thrown forward again and lifted once more. Insanely, wasting its strength, his body was crawling and floundering and rising and falling, but nevertheless slowly progressing through the monster drift.

When he had reached the other side–and it seemed to him a hundred years, and was actually quite an hour for a hundred yards–he wept hopelessly as his legs carried him on again. He had tried cunningly to stop them. He had said that he would rise once more and throw himself down once more–and then would not get up. That was all he needed to do. Just not get up. But he had gotten up, and now he was staggering onward, and looking at his compass again, and he knew that he could not rest, that his body would not let him rest, until he had reached the railroad.

For a little space, his weariness was so great that he literally could not feel it. It was like a pain that has passed the power of the nerves to convey it to the brain. He was numbed throughout by the need for rest. He found himself speculating in hopeless misery for the reason for this mad journeying. He did not remember.

He remembered hastening frantically behind his dog-team. He was following a packed trail, then, and he remembered a flash and a shot that had struck him. There was a wound on his head somewhere, but it did not hurt him. Every smallest particle of him ached so surpassingly that he could feel no sensation he could differentiate as an injury.

And before that . . . He searched his mind dully. Why was he here? There had been a murder. He remembered that. He remembered seeing a dead man with a bullet in his head and his poke of dust ripped open. There had been a little trickle of powdered gold upon the floor, and it had been very still, there. And after that he remembered driving his dogs to their limit . . . He had been hurrying then. He was hurrying now. Why?

Laboriously, because his brain was nearly as exhausted as his body, he marshaled his facts, everything he knew. There had been a murder and he had been rushing somewhere at top speed, and someone had shot at him and he had fallen. Then he must have gotten up. The cold had stanched the bleeding in his head. He had had no dogs or food, but he had reassured himself that the precious package inside his clothing was undisturbed. And then he had plunged on.

He was gasping for breath in the effort to climb a steep hillside when he remembered the first coming of the railroad idea to his brain. The railroad was on the other side of a steep range of hills that no dog-team could cross–nor any man either, on foot and in the wintertime. At the head of the railroad line there was a mine field, cut off from civilization during the cold months. To get to it from his starting point, the normal route was to follow the hills to their ending, a good hundred miles, and round them, then follow the track back up to the railhead. And since his dogs were gone and his food likewise, he could not hope to make so long a journey. He had to go across the hills. It was necessary that he reach the railroad.

All speculations were lost as he found himself building another fire. Night was falling and he could not go on. He saw his fire blaze up and up.... Dully, he found himself gathering more and more wood. He thawed himself thoroughly, squatting down in the snow close by the fire. He managed to make hot water again, with infinite difficulty, and drank it. Then he slept fitfully, waking now and then to keep up his fire and in a state when he was ready to scream in fretful rage against the implacable force that made him wake to put more wood upon the fire. He wanted to sleep, sleep, sleep.

He dreamed, of course, little fitful dreams of huge, luxurious beds in which he sank down in utter repose, of vast mountains of cushions upon which he flung himself down. He waked, to find the sky growing faintly lighter. He put more wood upon his blaze and slept again.

Suddenly, he was in a railroad train. He was going somewhere and he was feeling an odd diffidence, a peculiar nervousness. He heard two men talking in the seat before his.

"Yep," one was saying, "they won't be wearing red coats any more, or fancy gold braid. The Royal Northwest Mounted has gone into history."

The other man puffed meditatively upon his cigar.

"It's a pity. This new force, now . . ."

"The Canadian? It isn't new. It's the same one, with the same men and the same traditions, only they've changed the color of their coats and their name. And they'll keep their boast. They've earned the right to boast, too. They always get their man. Always."

In his seat in the railroad train, the man felt a little thrill run over him. All over his body it ran. It was like fear. Every particle of his body tingled, and yet he was smiling.

Then there was snow all about him and he was heaving to his feet. Still asleep, he had built up his fire and now he was trying to contrive a way to get more hot water. He was a little less exhausted than he had been the day before, but an all-pervading emptiness made him nauseated and sick. He drank of the tepid water that was all he could manage to get and still found himself in a ravenous hunger that was terrible. He wasted precious time. The lashings of his snow-shoes were wrapped in mud and put in the blaze. He cooked them, while he fought the gathering force of the thing that was making him go onward to the railroad. He was unable even to stop to eat them. He chewed as he stumbled along, now, chewed and chewed, and chewed upon the unmasticated leather. Sometimes a little juice accumulated, which he could swallow, but it had only the effect of making him still more hungry.

All that day he floundered forward among high hills and towering mountains. Fatigue came upon him again, and terrible pangs in his stomach. Once he stopped and gathered spruce bark. It would make tea, but he could not stop, then, to make it. He tried to eat it raw, and did swallow more than a little, but it merely filled his belly for a little while. Then he knew that it was giving him no strength, not even easing the horrible craving for food.

He was doing the impossible. It is rank, sheer suicide for a man to attempt mountain travel in winter without even snowshoes. He knew it. Every step he went deeper and deeper into the crank-sided hills was a step so much nearer to oblivion. And he knew that too. He only wanted to eat and sleep, and toward nightfall even sleep came first. He was, if possible, more weary than the day before. He rocked ahead, stumbling a little, falling now and then. Even the confused thinking of the previous day was impossible. He moved in a sort of coma, from which he wakened sometimes to upbraid his body bitterly for not letting him rest.

And the day after, he rejoiced dully to see that his feet no longer possessed their machine-like precision. They were faltering. They were hesitating. His body sometimes had to stop, swaying, before it could summon strength to go forward once more. The man watched it hopefully, detached as he was from all its doings save only the agony it was suffering. Presently it would fall and be unable to rise, and then he would lie still while rest swept through him, seeping deliciously through each tiny nerve and muscle, and he would grow warm and contented and sink deeply into slumber–such beautiful, log-like slumber–from which he would never have to wake up.

And he saw depressions in the snow. The tracks of a caribou. His hunger reasserted itself. He pleaded with his body to let him go and kill the caribou. Then it, the body, would be strong . . . There was assent.

He followed the tracks, his eyes glittering, and his mouth slavering in anticipation. In that bundle inside his parka there was a revolver, among other precious things. He would kill the caribou and feast of its flesh, and maybe his body would let him rest a little, just a very little . . . He began to argue with it by anticipation.

And then it stopped. He saw that the tracks turned away. Something had frightened the animal and it had broken into a run. He could tell by the hoof-marks in the snow. And it was running in a direction that was away from the railroad track!

Weeping, he felt his legs facing him away. His body would not let him follow the tracks because they led away from the railroad, away from the direction he must go. He wept in utter desolation of soul while he was carried on, and away from the food he had visualized and almost tasted.

And he lost himself in light-headed visions. He was lying upon a huge, soft bed while someone fed him deliciously cooked food. He did not even have to lift his fingers. It melted between his lips into utterly delectable softness so that he merely swallowed as it was fed to him. And then the professor of psychology said in a staccato voice, "It may be an idea concerned with fear, or desire, or duty, but it may take possession of him until his whole being is but an expression of the possibly forgotten thing." And the bed was taken from under him and the food snatched away and he was hearing someone else say, "They're the same as the Royal Northwest Mounted. They always get their man. Always!"

And then he found himself staring down incredulously at a long, level, narrow drift of snow. A telegraph-pole was just before him, and another just beyond. He had reached the railroad.

Infinite hope filled him. Now he had reached the railroad. Now he could rest. But he found himself making yet one more fire and squatting beside it, dully. Dumbly, he remembered, now, that the railroad could not run in the winter. Short of monster snowplows before each locomotive, operation in the cold months was quite impossible. So the mines stocked up with fuel and provisions and stacked their produce in great piles, to be carried down by rail when the warm weather came.

He almost slept, though his eyes opened regularly once in every five minutes to look down the long drift of snow. He squatted before his fire in a state of semi unconsciousness. He never knew how long he stayed so. He remembered afterward that he had gathered more wood, protesting against the activity of his limbs, and he remembered contriving a bark cup and making spruce tea. But he never knew if it was an hour or a day or two days.

And then he saw dark specks far away, at the extreme limit of vision. He roused himself, in dumb resentment. He found himself getting at the precious packet inside his parka. His hands were clumsy and he was a long time getting at it. The dark specks were coming nearer and disclosed themselves as two dog teams, with a man breaking trail. The rear-most team was probably tethered to the first, and they were not pulling as they should have been, but still were making fair time over the smooth, level space between the snow-covered rails.

And something clicked abruptly in the brain of the man squatting by his fire. He had been nearly comatose from exhaustion and starvation. He had been a resentful, fretful automaton, wearied past thought or any desire but for rest and food.

But he stood up, and he was Private Baker of the force which has succeeded to the traditions if not to the name of the Royal Northwest Mounted Police, whose justified boast is that they always get their man. He was haggard and his eyes were sunk deep into his head. His cheeks were gaunt hollows and his forehead was blood-smeared from an untended wound. He was a scarecrow, but he straightened himself, standing erect and commanding, memory back with him again and knowledge of what he was after. This was his first manhunt alone.

The dog-teams came up, their driver gazing curiously at the figure standing in the snow and swaying only a very little from weakness.

"Harkness," said Private Baker, "I've been waiting for you. You're under arrest for that murder back in Skeokut."

A revolver glittered in his hand, and he moved toward the astounded, ashen man. He held a pair of handcuffs–a part of the precious package he had carried.

"G-God!" gasped the other man, staring at him. "I thought I killed you, back yonder!"

"No," said Private Baker, dryly. "You didn't. I cut across

the mountains to head you off. Now we'll go on up toward the mines and I'll get some sleep before I start to take you back. You'll continue to break trail."

And with his prisoner disarmed and handcuffed, Private Baker fell in behind the second dog-team, which had been his before he had been ambushed. He was still exhausted, still gaunt, still grim, but he began to understand some things. As he mushed on, pushing his worn-out muscles to their last possible ounce of strength, he understood many things that had been puzzling his confused brain before. "A fixed idea. . . of duty . . ."

He ate hugely and yet temperately when he allowed his prisoner to rest. And despite his leaden limbs and aching muscles he was content. He had got his man.

SNOW GHOST

By Lester Dent

A Silver Corporal Adventure

Thundering out of the storm-lashed snow kingdom came a strange herd—a reindeer herd. With it came a pretty girl—and six men who talked of murder. Also, in the wake of that reindeer herd was the Silver Corporal, a man-hunting demon of the Mounted. Weird tales had been told of this Mountie—but none so weird as the writhing white death that was a part of him.

SIX men hunkered in the snow and talked of murder. Like six shaggy devils, they were. Like devils with their horns and spike tails frozen off, who had grown a coat of thick hair for protection against an Arctic cold which had shrunk the red line in the thermometer to thirty-five below.

The giant of the crowd was growling words. In size, he was a monster among men. His sealskin parka would have housed any three of the others. He had a voice that gritted and thumped like floes of the Polar ice pack piling on a lee shore.

"C'est bien!" he rumbled. "That right! De redcoat will get here soon. An' he mus' die before he find out a t'ing about us! *Oui, M'sieu* Ferrick! Yo' bes' let Le Chinois feex heem!"

The giant lifted mittened hands nearly as large as the body of a sled dog. The mighty paws made a gesture of seizing and breaking something. "Le Chinois do heem like dat !"

The other five shivered. They shrank deeper into their parkas. Even such hardened fiends as they got jittery at the idea of killing a constable of the Royal Northwest Mounted Police. It was about the most unhealthy thing a man could do in the Northland.

And maybe they were more than little scared of the monster, Le Chinois. They didn't doubt he could break a man's back as easily as he had made that sinister gesture in thin air. They had seen him pick up a sled dog that had bitten him, and with his two hands tear it bodily apart.

The wind hooted down off the polar ice cap. It made frozen limbs of the spruce whine like tortured things. It stacked and unstacked the sand-hard snow. It shoveled snow into the fire about which the devilish six huddled, and the stuff made sickly sizzlings on the hot coals.

"Nix!" clipped the man called Ferrick. "Croakin' a Mountie is bad business, even if the Alaska border isn't far away. Them redcoats is worse'n dandruff! They've got a way of gettin' in your hair years after you thought you was rid of 'em. Lemme think!"

Ferrick had a face like a bunch of bones and some yellow hide jammed in his parka hood. He smoked a pipe. The wind from the pole kept sucking sparks out of the pipe bowl.

Two sledges stuck, curved-end-up, in the snow. A third sledge was farther from the fire. It had not been unloaded. The big bundle on it was done up in a waterproof oiled tarpaulin.

"I got it!" Ferrick rapped suddenly. He had a way of speaking as though he were always excited. "You grab this redcoat pest, Le Chinois. Bust his leg. Bust both his legs. I don't give a damn. Then let him pinch you for assaultin' him! Let him take you to his post. That'll get him away from here while we take care of the damn girl's reindeer drivel"

"Sacre Dieu!" growled Le Chinois. "Me–I no like dat idea."

"You'll like it less if you croak the redcoat and get hung for it!" sneered Ferrick. "The outfit that's hirin' me to take care of the girl's reindeer herd will hire you a lawyer. You'll only be fined for beatin' up the redcoat. They'll pay your fine. They'll pay you a bonus for your trouble–say five hundred bucks. How does that sound?"

The monster Le Chinois considered. Breath steam raced out a long, foul gray plume from his cavernous mouth, plucked by the chill wind.

"De five hun'ert buck sound dam fine," he rumbled. *"Oui!* I do heem like yo' say! Me–I don' keel heem unless I have to."

"That's bein' smart!" chuckled Ferrick. "Lookit! You can see him now–mushin' across the lake!"

Six pairs of eyes, watering in the frigid wind, peered out on the lake.

The man they saw mushed a four-dog team. It was a small team. The sledge was tiny, the grub pack on it hardly more than an armload.

The smallness extended to the corporal of the Mounted who plugged along in the sled tracks. He looked like a toy man, with a toy sledge and dogs.

"How'd a little geezer like that ever manage to get in the Mounted?" Ferrick snorted around his pipe.

Ferrick didn't know it, but he wasn't the first who had wondered about that. And some of them had damned well found out the reason. The policeman left the snow-covered lake. He mounted the slope, wending through scrub spruces. He reached the devil's half dozen about the fire. His four dogs stopped without being told to.

"Hy'ah, gents," he said, so low his words were hardly heard.

He sounded like a Yank, a former Wyoming cowhand, judging by the whang of his words. He wore dark, nearly black, snow glasses. Below them, his face looked scrawny, like the features of an old man.

The devil's half dozen greeted him jovially. They grinned at him. They couldn't keep their grins from being evil, though. But the policeman seemed not to notice.

"Seen anything of the reindeer drive?" he inquired. His voice was so low as to be almost torn away by the howling wind.

"Not a thing," Ferrick said amiably "Didn't know there was one."

"There is," whispered the policeman. "Young lady named Ida Thorne bringin' in a few thousand head from Alaska. Canadian government bought 'em to stock this part of the country. Kinda reminds me of the old cattle-trailin' days in Wyomin'. I was up in this neck of the woods, so figured I'd look the reindeer drive over en' see how they handle the critters."

He fell silent. Borne upon the booming wind came a mournful, hideous sound. It rose and fell in a yowling bedlam and finally died away as though stifled by the frigid gale.

"Wolves," grinned the undersized policeman. "Reckon the reindeer drive must be close, from the wolf tracks I've seen en' the howlin' I've heard. Guess the wolves follow a deer herd like they used to tag after a cow drive."

He seemed like a tired and homesick little man. Even his voice seemed played out.

"Might as well camp here and use our fire," Ferrick suggested.

The human monster, Le Chinois, got to his feet. The hulk of him was like a hill heaving up.

"By dam', I show yo' fine windbreak where yo' can feed de dogs," he rumbled.

"Thanky, pard," murmured the little policeman.

The two moved off. They were lost to sight in a near-by spruce thicket.

The other five of the devil's half dozen exchanged knowing leers. There was no windfall back in that spruce thicket. Le Chinois had drawn the diminutive corporal away. The others would have an alibi. They had not known Le Chinois hated policemen, they would say. And they would be very careful not to answer the constable's screams for help in time to save him from becoming a broken, helpless thing.

Le Chinois' great rumble reached their ears.

"By dam'! What yo' mean by shovin' me? *Sacre Dieu*! Me–I teach yo' not to shove Le Chinois!" Le Chinois was picking the quarrel.

A terrific blow resounded. A loud crashing of spruce boughs followed, then grunts, groans, wailings, whimperings. Over it all rose the soggy smackings of awful fists striking . Twice, distinct and ghastly crunches denoted bones breaking.

"I hope that slug-silly Le Chinois don't croak him !" Ferrick said, half delighted, half uneasy.

An ominous silence fell in the spruce clump.

A bit later, two figures appeared. One was limp, quite helpless. The features of that man leaked crimson streams which froze hard and crusty the instant they touched the snow. The second man carried the first. He carried him lightly as he would a marten fresh from a trap.

The mouths of the five watching men fell open and steaming in the frigid Arctic twilight

Surprises they must have received in their checkered past–but never such a shock as now.

The beaten, broken man was the human monster–Le Chinois. The man who carried the giant so lightly was the little policeman.

The officer looked no bigger than before. Indeed, he seemed smaller. For his parka, and the tunic he wore beneath, had been torn open. His shoulders and arms were bare to the Polar chill.

Eyeing that chest and arms, the five onlookers began to revise their opinions. The small officer's body was the faintly tanned color of a catgut fiddle string which has been used a lot. And tendons seemingly made out of those same fiddle strings stood in great bundles and knots and gullies on his torso.

More amazing even than the inhuman physical strength the little policeman obviously possessed, was his hair. There was a great shock of it. Like the plumed helmet of an ancient Roman, it waved erect. And it was the striking hue of burnished silver.

Ferrick spat his pipe and a choking oath out together. He

dived a hand for his gun. But hissed words from a breed at his left stopped him.

"Non! Non!" gulped the breed. "dat man ees de Silver Corporal."

Ferrick hastily pretended he had been reaching for the ground to shove himself onto his feet. He'd heard of the Silver Corporal somewhere. He must have heard of him over in Alaska, for that had been Ferrick's stamping grounds for years. And for the reputation of a redcoat to penetrate into Ferrick's part of Alaska, it must be a reputation indeed. Ferrick got cautious.

The little policeman dropped his burden. Steam squirmed from Le Chinois' wounds. Both the monster's arms were broken. Most of his teeth were gone. Never again would his nose be the same.

"Reckon you gents could loan me a pinch of tea?" asked the Silver Corporal. His voice was so low as to be nearly lost in the gale. "My supply has plumb played out on me."

Ferrick and the others gulped. They swallowed uneasily. They had expected the policeman to at least get tough, ask questions. But he was absolutely ignoring Le Chinois' attack, acting as though nothing out of the ordinary had occurred. He was asking for tea! It bothered Ferrick and his breeds.

"We don't know Le Chinois very well!" Ferrick began hastily to explain. "He just lately joined up with our prospectin' outfit. We didn't know he was goin' to jump you–"

"Oh, him?" The Silver Corporal's tiny voice seemed nothing but a sorrowful whisper in the wind. "There's lots of fellers like him who want to hit a policeman whenever they see one. Funny, ain't it?"

Ferrick and his men didn't think it was funny. But they laughed like it was.

"Sure, sure," cackled Ferrick hollowly. "Here–I'll loan you the tea!"

The Silver Corporal fastened his clothes. He said no word. He made tea in a little black kettle over the fire. The kettle was tiny. It might have been a utensil in a small girl's playhouse. Nor did the strange, small man speak again while he brewed his beverage.

Ferrick and his breeds looked on. They wondered where the Silver Corporal kept his gun. They hadn't seen any.

They'd have been surprised to know the truth–that the Silver Corporal didn't carry a gun. They'd have been tickled to know that. Or maybe they wouldn't have–if they had known the whole truth.

"Thanks for the tea," came the little policeman's wispy voice at last. "Reckon I'll turn in."

He faded into the spruce clump. His going was strangely soundless. But maybe that was because of the way the wind bawled down from the Pole.

"That gink gets my goat !" Ferrick shivered.

"*Sacre Dieu*! Yo' ees not firs' one whose goat hees get," muttered a breed.

"What d'you know about him?"

"Not ver' much, *M'sieu* Ferrick. De Eskimos call heem a *tongak*, a spirit from de other worl'. Dey more scared of heem den of hell. De talk t'rough de north ees that hees do many wonderful t'ings. Dey say hees run down en' catch de caribou, jus' like de *loup*–de wolf. Dey say hees whip one whole tribe of bad Indians, jus' wit' hees two bare hands. Dey say hees no can be killed. Hees man of magic!"

"A pack of damn lies!" But Ferrick shivered again, as though he had found an icicle inside his parka.

The Silver Corporal reappeared. He made no sound this time, either. It was as though a puff of furry smoke had squirted out of the spruces. He carried his rabbit-lined sleeping bag. Ferrick and the others watched him.

Near a great drift, the Silver Corporal got into his sleeping sack. He removed none of his clothing. He faced the drift. He drew the mouth of the bag shut over his head. His small form doubled low, then snapped upward from the earth.

The leap was prodigious. Fully a score of feet, he seemed to sail. Then he shot feet first into the huge drift and vanished from sight. In a trice, the booming wind had smoothed the drift and there was nothing to show where he had disappeared.

The Silver Corporal had gone to bed.

Muttering, Ferrick and the others revived the wreck of a human monster, Le Chinois. They splintered his arms and bandaged his hurts. They asked him how he had come to be so grievously injured.

"*A mon insu!*" whimpered the suffering giant. "Me I don' know. I grab heem. Den–*alors*–eet happen! De worl', she go plentee black!"

Ferrick cursed him up and down the range of an extensive fund of cusswords. Then he drew his breeds aside. They talked in low tones.

That their conversation boded no good for the Silver Corporal was evident from the furtive glances they cast at the great drift where he had vanished. But the drift surface remained undisturbed

Their sinister powwow ended. They gathered up their arms. They crept silently away in the Arctic twilight.

The Silver Corporal saw them go.

They knew little of the ways of the Silver Corporal, did Ferrick and his crew of evil thugs. If they had, they would not have spent so much time watching the drift where the strange, small policeman had vanished. They would have looked elsewhere. Perhaps they would have looked at a spot a hundred feet away, where the drift poked its tapering end into the spruce thickets.

The Silver Corporal often leaped into a drift as he had tonight. But he rarely slept at the same spot. Tonight he had tunneled, never disturbing the surface of the snow, to the spruces. He had been resting there, warm and comfortable in his rabbit-lined bag, watching Ferrick and the others.

Their sneaking departure told him they contemplated no good. He eased out of his bag. He rolled the sleeping accoutrement, silently climbed a spruce and dangled it by a strap from a limb. Wolverines had a habit of playing havoc with a man's equipment in this Arctic waste.

He was about to take up the trail when he saw movement near the spot where he had leaped into the drift. They were sharp, those pale metallic eyes of the Silver Corporal. They saw things even an old he-wolf, wily from years in this northland, might have missed.

The object he discerned resolved into a man. Crouching, the fellow worked nearer the drift. He carried a rifle, stock thrust up his parka so his body warmth would keep the mechanism of the gun from freezing. He stopped, aimed.

The man's rifle muzzle belched flame. Salvos of powder noise battled the wind. The gun was an automatic. It drove a stream of lead into the drift. With mad haste, the man clipped in fresh cartridges.

Traveling in his noiseless way, like a whorl of dark snow wafted sidewise by the frosty gale, the Silver Corporal approached the would-be killer.

He encountered bad luck–bad luck even he, the Silver Corporal, could not guard against.

A big Arctic snowshoe popped up underfoot. The rabbit was terrified. It ran wildly, flashing from one side to the other as nature had taught it best to avoid the foxes and wolves which preyed upon it. It made a racket among the spruce twigs.

The gunman heard. He whirled. He saw the Silver Corporal. His automatic rifle stuttered.

But the bullets only made zonging sounds through empty space and banged about in the spruces beyond. For the Silver Corporal was gone! Headfirst into a drift, he had vanished, so swiftly that it seemed nothing less than magic.

The gunman dropped two cartridge clips before he got a third home. He shook as from the ague. He remembered what the other breed had muttered about this strange little silver-haired man being immune from death. Terror got him. Whirling, he ran. He looked back.

The Silver Corporal had appeared like a diminutive genie, two-score feet from where he had disappeared.

"*Sacre Dieu!*" screamed the gunman. He put on more speed. Up a hill he fled, and down toward a wide stream beyond.

The Silver Corporal followed. He went warily. He might be many things, but he was not bulletproof. Besides, he wanted urgently to stay well and kicking long enough to solve this mystery. Something dirty was underfoot here. Just what it was–that question had him puzzled. And he did love to solve such puzzles. That was the reason he had taken to the Northland.

He neared the wide stream. His sharp eyes picked up a form. It was only a blur in the murk of the deep valley.

The form scudded across the ice. It vanished in stunted timber on the opposite bank of the stream.

The Silver Corporal hesitated. A man running on ice is about the best target there is, even if he doesn't slip and fall down.

Suddenly, there came a sound which decided him.

A woman's cry! It was shrill, piercing. It wasn't exactly a scream. It was more of a terrified, high-pitched shout. But the way it gargled off and ended in a stifled moan was awful.

That feminine cry sent the Silver Corporal out on the ice. With a speed almost blinding, he raced. He zigzagged, knowing shots might crash any instant.

But bullets were not his undoing.

With a deafening roar, the ice broke.

In possibly the space of time it takes to snap a finger, the Silver Corporal understood that he had been cleverly tricked. It was no man he had seen cross the ice! It must have been a dog, an animal light enough that the ice would not collapse. The canine had been decked with spruce boughs and a fur parka to give it the aspect of a man, so the policeman would follow it.

The gunman had left the dog leashed on the stream bank before putting on his shooting act. He had fled to the animal, turned it loose, and doubled back. The dog had dashed across the stream to one of the other breeds. The whole thing was a death trap to spring in case the fusillade of bullets into the drift failed to do their work.

The woman's scream? The Silver Corporal didn't know what to think about that. She must be a prisoner. Maybe they had let her scream at just the right instant to decoy him onto the ice. It didn't occur to him that the woman had lured him purposely. The Silver Corporal was a Wyoming cowpoke. To that breed, all women are good women.

Cold water hit the Silver Corporal like a sledge blow. Air was knocked screaming from his lungs.

The stream was running a mad torrent. This explained the thin sheet of ice through which he had dropped. At the freeze-up in the fall, the creek had been running high. But the cold had dried its tributaries and the level had dropped, leaving a thin, treacherous shell. The water that ran now was only that fed by great springs in the stream bed. The north country was full of such perils.

The Silver Corporal was battered about. The crushing force of the water made his struggles futile as the twistings of a limp rag. Pounding against boulders, the torrent lifted thunder in the ice-roofed cavern

Helpless, he was borne ahead. The ice roof closed down. He sucked air into his lungs. Then he was swept under.

Although the ice had now thickened to a depth of four or five feet overhead, the current was still too swift for any man to swim against. Even this mighty little silver-haired man was unable to breast it.

Farther and farther toward his doom, the Silver Corporal was tumbled.

The laboring water about him abruptly seemed to become tired. It rested. End over end, the Silver Corporal was tumbled across the bottom. His lungs already felt as though they were filling with hot sand, the result of holding his breath.

He pawed at the bottom, held himself there by grasping a waterlogged stick, and pummeled his brain. He was sure-enough jam up against it. He couldn't swim against the current. There wasn't one chance in twenty million of finding a hole. Five feet would be a conservative guess at the thickness of the ice overhead.

Well, he wouldn't drown sitting still. He loosened his grip, let the waterlogged stick slide through his hand.

An instant after he let go the stick, he stroked madly back to it. He felt the end. The stick terminated in a sharp, conical taper.

The Silver Corporal nearly lost some of the precious air in his lungs, so excited did he become. The conical end on that stick meant–

Wildly, he stroked along the bank of the now idling stream. His head cracked the ice. He had his eyes open. It was dark. He could barely see the mud he was stirring up.

He continued to paw the bank, searching furiously. His lungs were entirely full of the ghastly hot sand feel now. Each beat of his heart seemed to throw a billiard ball against either eardrum. A few seconds more, and the fish would have the Silver Corporal.

Then he found it!

A beaver burrow! It bored straight into the bank.

The Silver Corporal jammed his way into it. Many times in his life he had wished his Maker had seen fit to construct a bigger man when He came to this particular Wyoming cowhand. But now he'd have gladly been content with half his already diminutive size.

But beavers had a way of making ample-sized burrows. And the long-bladed, heavy-hilted knife the Silver Corporal hauled from inside his soaked tunic enlarged the narrow places.

The burrow turned up. His head topped the water. The air was black, nearly sickening with the castor smell of a beaver. But it was air!

The next instant, a beaver attacked him. He had never heard of a beaver assaulting a man. But then, he had never heard of a man invading a beaver's domicile in this fashion. The teeth of the animal cut into his shoulder like knives.

He flung it away. Rearing up, he saw crazily colored lights when his head hit the roof. It wasn't a yard high. Then, with a *kerflug-g!* of water, the beaver was gone.

The animal would have no trouble finding sanctuary in other burrows near by.

The Silver Corporal sagged down. The underground room wasn't large enough to stretch out in. So he curled, lay there drawing in great gulps of the musky air.

Unexpectedly, voices came to his attention!

Hauling himself up, the Silver Corporal put an ear to the frozen dirt ceiling of the tiny cell. It could not be many inches to the outside air. He heard feet thumping along the bank.

"C'est tres bon!" rasped a guttural voice. "Eet ees ver' good! Hee's feenished!"

"He sure is!" came Ferrick's clipped, excitable tones. "We've thrown rocks on that thin ice and broke it all the way down to where the water goes under thick ice. He didn't have a chance in that hell-tearing creek. He's one damn Mounted policeman we're rid of."

"*Bien!*" chuckled the breed. "Dat ees good! What do we do nex'?"

"You mean about our girl friend?"

"*Oui!*"

Ferrick swore a volley. He had a remarkable command of profanity. "To tell the truth, I ain't sure what we'll do about her," he rapped. "But it's sure her hard luck that she caught some of my boys gum-shoeing around her reindeer herd."

"Yo' mean we mus' keel her?"

"Don't make me laugh, Frenchy. Sure we gotta kill her. The point is–how? When? Where? Before we pull our big stunt, or after?"

"*Non*," muttered the breed. "Me I no like keel dat woman. She ver' pret'–"

"Horsefeathers!" snorted Ferrick. "With the money you're gettin' out of this, you can buy you a harem full of 'em like her. But if she gets loose–well, she saw us croak the policeman. They'll line us up on a board with ropes around our necks."

The pair moved out of earshot.

Cramped in the barrel of a beaver den, the Silver Corporal forked his waterproof matchbox out of his soaked clothing.

The den was floored with sticks, rushes, roots. The larger sticks were cone-shaped on the ends where the beaver's teeth had gnawed them off. Smaller twigs had been clipped through as by scissors. The match went out.

With the knife which had proved so useful in enlarging the beaver burrow, the Silver Corporal went to work on the den roof. The first inch or so was easy After that, the frozen earth got hard as a brick. But the knife had a blade like a bayonet, heavy, thick. It chipped upward.

The policeman didn't hurry too much. He cut a circle until he had sort of a lid. Opening this, he peered out cautiously. No one was in sight.

A bound, and he was outside. He landed running. He kept going at a headlong pace, but as silently as he could. He knew what would happen if he stopped. His saturated garments would freeze solid–cake him in an icy armor. He would be about as agile on the ground as an old-time knight.

He neared the camp. He saw figures about the fire. He counted. Seven of them!

That meant Ferrick had more of a gang than the five breeds who had been around the fire when the policeman arrived. The other villains must have been prowling about the reindeer herd.

Halting, the Silver Corporal lay down. He rolled in the snow. The stuff stuck to his moist garments. He gave it time to freeze there. When he stood up, he was white as a polar bear

His small form blended with the snow, now. He made for his sleeping bag.

In the darkest depth of the spruce clump, the Silver Corporal whipped his sleeping bag open. Standing beside it, with the thermometer at thirty-five below and with a howling gale from the Pole moaning like werewolves about his bare shanks, he stripped off stark naked.

His little, tendon-wrapped body was a remarkable thing. It had not changed a whit from its hue of long-used catgut, despite the terrific cold that would have turned an ordinary man blue, then the grisly white of frostbite.

Every gigantic muscle stood out as distinctly as the hamstring of a sled dog. It was as though some mysterious compound had dissolved all parts of his body except the bones and those astounding sinews.

The Silver Corporal sprang into the rabbit-lined sleeping bag. He disappeared into it completely.

His distinctive shock of silver-colored hair was literally a block of ice. He thawed it with his hands, throwing the ice lumps outside. He writhed about in the bag, drying himself. The rabbit sack was bitterly cold, but it was like a furnace after standing naked in that wailing Arctic gale.

When he was dry, he shook out his spare set of garments. They were in the bag–simply because they always served in lieu of a pillow. Without leaving the bag, he donned the clothing.

He belted on no firearm, but he did produce an object which had been the kernel of the pillow of garments. He shook this in his hand. It seemed to come alive. It crawled along his arms and over his hands. It ran out into the teeth of the gale, snapping taut with a serpentine hiss.

A white rope! It was braided of some hard stuff that looked like violin strings. It had the springy quality of a rod of whalebone.

No ordinary lass rope, this! It tapered a little, somewhat

like a bullwhip, but not as much. One end was fitted with a honda in the usual fashion. The other end, the smaller, terminated in a double-edged blade of steel, honed to a razor sharpness.

As though possessed of invisible wings, this blade sped out in the Arctic twilight. It traveled faster and faster, until the eye could no longer follow it. Fully thirty feet distant, a spruce bough thick as a man's arm parted as though by magic–and the strange white rope with its fang of steel was back and coiled around the little policeman's arm before the bough had hardly jumped away in the gale.

It smacked of wizardry. But many things about the Silver Corporal smacked of that.

He drew on gloves. They were of velvet. They had an outer casing of white silk to keep out the wind. They were warm, yet did not hamper his strangely flexible hands.

He glided toward the camp of his foes. The garments he had donned were made from the belly fur of snowshoe rabbits. They were perfectly white. He drew from a pocket a small jar. This held white grease paint which was impervious to the cold. He smeared it on his face.

He could now have dropped prone where he stood, and an unknowing wayfarer might have stepped over him without realizing it was other than a strangely shaped drift of snow underfoot.

The Silver Corporal was little less than a phantom of the white spaces.

Lost in the squirming clouds of snow which the gale shoveled about, he glided to within fifty feet of the camp.

Only two men were there now. Two breeds! They had opened the pack on the sledge. They lifted out packages.

Every package was done in a wrapping of glaring red.

These packages, they loaded into tump-line packsacks. The breeds talked as they worked, never dreaming of the phantom listener near by.

"Dis ees las' load," one said.

"*Oui*," agreed the other. "Een anot'er hour, our work here weel be done. De reindeer herd weel be destroyed."

"An' de girl, too," reminded the first.

"*Oui, oui!* She mus' die, too. Only her death weel leave us safe. *M'sieu* Ferrick ees wit' her now, ovair by de cliff. He ees try' to decide 'ow she shall be keeled."

The pair emptied the last of the sledge load into their back packs. They heaved the burden of red packages on their shoulders, adjusted the tump-lines over their greasy foreheads. They moved away.

They neither heard nor saw the white wraith which haunted their footsteps.

The first intimation they had of its presence was when a strange missile came hissing through the twilight. It was the Silver Corporal's weird rope. The heavy honda caught the rearmost breed on the temple. The man dropped without a sound.

The rope coiled backward from the man's head like a winged serpent. A hand encased in a glove of velvet and white silk arrested it in midair.

The other breed heard the squawk of snow, frozen sand-hard, as his companion fell upon it. He whirled, pawing out a revolver as he did so.

He saw the white blur that was the Silver Corporal. He lifted his gun, finger tightening in the trigger guard.

But the weapon never discharged. There came a metallic song–like a piano key touched softly. The strange white rope for an instant was taut as a rod. The steel blade on its smaller end all but passed through the breed's body. Then it sprang back out of the terrible wound it had made. The breed was dead before his form fell and steamed in the frigid twilight. There had been no sound.

The Silver Corporal bent over the packs, inspecting their contents.

His gasp of surprise at what he found shot a long plume of breath steam against the whooping Polar gale.

He concealed the packs in the snow near by. He switched the surface of the drift with his white rope so no trace of where he had hidden them would remain.

The unconscious breed seemed to lift on a weirdly distorted snow pile and rush away. A hundred yards distant, he was lowered. Hands, hard as steel because of the bone and tendon from which they were made, slapped him until pain awakened him.

"Where is the girl and Ferrick?" The breed shivered as the tiny, wispy voice of the Silver Corporal throbbed into his ears.

"*Non*!" he snarled. "Me–I don' know!"

Awful fingers seized the breed. They inflicted agony such as the villainous fellow had never felt before.

"Cough up!" said the wee voice that was like a whisper of death.

But the breed had courage, such as it was. He was fully conscious now, too. His brain was working. He pulled what seemed to him like a clever piece of brain work.

"Ferrick ees got de gal een cabin down by de lake shore." The breed pointed. "Over dat way!"

The Silver Corporal poised over him for a moment. Then he was gone!

The breed weaved upon his feet. His head whirled. The first time he tried to run, he staggered a crazy circle. Then he got lined out. He ran as though that strange little silver-haired hoodoo pursued him.

He even looked back to make sure this wasn't a fact. He saw nothing.

He should have looked to the right and a bit ahead. For the Silver Corporal was running there. He hadn't wanted to waste a half hour or so scaring the breed into telling the truth. He didn't like to torture men, anyway.

So he was letting the breed lead the way. The Silver Corporal's rope balanced easily in his hand as he raced along.

Down into a deep valley, sprinted the breed. It was almost a canyon. The opposite wall was a sheer cliff nearly half a thousand feet high!

The man veered to the left. He waded through scrub willows, up to his neck in snow. So taut were his nerves that he let out a bawl of sheer terror when a covey of ptarmigan roared out of the snow about him.

He stumbled over near the hulking cliff. So steep was the precipice that it seemed to overhang and blot out the cold-congealed gray sky with its puny flickerings of Northern Lights that were like varicolored candle flames guttering in the frigid wind.

A ramshackle cabin poked its roof out of the snow and brush. The roof had been made steep to shed the snow. It had been shingled with slabs adzed off logs. But many of the shingles were gone and the rafters shone through like the boiled ribs of a skeleton.

The cabin door gaped open. It framed a man–one of the breeds. Firelight behind the man painted the door around him with shuffling scarlet, as though it were the lurid mouth of Hades.

"What de hell ails yo'?" he shouted. He had heard his comrade squawl when the ptarmigan roared up.

"*Sacre*–" The running breed pitched into the cabin with such speed that he skidded half across it trying to stop. "De Silver Corporal! Hees keel man who ees wit' me! Hees almos' keel me!"

"Yo' ees nuts!" said the other breed expressively. But he hauled out a Webley automatic revolver. He wished Ferrick were here.

"*Non, non*! Me–I tell yo' de Silver Corporal deed not die under de ice! Hees alive an' ees hunt fo' de gal–"

No doubt the man had a lot more to say. But he had been watching the open door. He saw a blurring, tumbling mass of white seemingly fill the door. He screeched like a banshee.

He seized the Webley from his comrade. The weapon clamored at the door. Bullets blasted through the white mass outside the opening. Yet the slugs had no apparent effect. They brought no moan of agony. They drew no gushing streams of crimson as bullets should have.

The white mass before the door simply faded away. It was like nothing so much as a curtain which had fallen to the snow in front of the aperture.

The thug goggled. He might as well have shot at a ghost.

Sound came from his side. A choke, a hiss! He whirled.

His companion lay dead beside him. Like a long and thin needle, the Silver Corporal's white rope stretched upward from the body.

The breed would have fired some more. But his Webley was empty. He sprang for the door. He hated to leave that way. But he liked less the idea of remaining in this cabin of fantastic death.

He took two bounds. From over his head, a white figure flashed down. It landed with both feet astride his shoulders. A little steel club of a fist swung.

The breed was senseless before he hit the floor. He had no time to realize that flurry of white he had seen before the door was simply snow the Silver Corporal had shoved off the roof.

For, to one of the Silver Corporal's agility, it was a simple matter to leap to the roof. It was even simpler to shove off the snow, then launch the blade on his rope, spearlike, into the vitals of the first breed, and a moment later, to spring upon the last of the pair. The shingles gone from the roof had left big holes.

The Silver Corporal raced pale eyes about the cabin.

The girl lay in a corner. Ida Thorne–for she could be no one but Ida Thorne, who was bringing in the reindeer herd–was bound tightly.

The Silver Corporal retrieved his rope. He glided toward her.

Another man might have paused to drink in the ravishing beauty of the girl. Women of beauty were more scarce in the Northland than cases of heat-stroke. Women of Ida Thorne's exquisite attractiveness were scarce in any man's country. She would have been a knockout at either pole, and in between.

The Silver Corporal cut her free. He didn't say anything. And that wasn't because he was trying to be the strong, silent man, either. He didn't know what to say. He hadn't spoken to a woman in months. In truth, he was a bit scared of them.

The girl stood up. She was taller than the Silver Corporal. She rubbed her wrists and ankles– something a man other than the Silver Corporal would have done for her. She broke the conversational ice.

"Thanks," she said, and her voice had volume and music. "When I saw you break through that thin ice, I thought you were gone. I tried to scream and warn you."

The little officer grinned like a Cheshire cat. His face didn't look so thin when he grinned. The white grease paint on it made him resemble a pleasant little clown. The rope in his hand, one steel-fanged end wet and steaming with blood, took away his funny aspect, though.

"Supposin' you tell me what this is all about," his wee voice whispered through the cabin.

That was the Silver Corporal– all business.

"I don't get paid for these reindeer until I deliver them," said the girl. "Ferrick and the others were hired by an Alaskan mining company to keep me from delivering them. They don't want me to get hold of the money."

"Why?"

The answer was postponed.

Ferrick bounded in the cabin door. He discharged his pistol at the Silver Corporal's back.

The Silver Corporal heard Ferrick. He had time to turn a little. It was enough. Ferrick's bullet only goosed a tuft of rabbit fur off his white parka.

The deadly rope came alive. The steel-armed end licked hungrily through the air at Ferrick's throat.

But luck rode with Ferrick at that instant. He dodged successfully. The blade passed by him.

It spiked into the chest of a breed who came through the door behind him. The unlucky man folded down.

Five more evil-faced fellows hurdled his body on their way inside. They flourished arms. Ferrick had most of his gang along.

They closed in on the Silver Corporal, watching his deadly rope.

"Don't shoot the runt unless you gotta!" ripped Ferrick.

One threw a pistol. The little policeman dodged it. The weapon caromed off the wall and the girl pounced on it.

Ferrick ran to her, knocked her down. The blow he delivered came whistling from far behind his back. He didn't mind hitting a woman. In fact, he liked it. Their soft flesh didn't hurt his knuckles.

He liked the promptness with which the girl fell unconscious. It made him feel he packed dynamite in his fists.

The next instant Ferrick let out a screech. His dying wail wouldn't be louder, more terrible. With incredible speed, the Silver Corporal had built a loop in his white rope and snared Ferrick's arm. He jerked.

Ferrick's arm broke with a noise like a stopper coming out

of a bottle. Ligaments were rent. Only by a narrow margin did the arm stay on his body.

Ferrick sailed across the cabin. His luck still held and he got his good arm before his head. That saved his brains from being dashed out on the cabin logs.

A little white ermine of a man who moved with dazzling speed, the Silver Corporal loosed his white rope, cast the noose again. Hissing, opening widely, the loop settled over two breeds, tightened on them. The caterwauling thugs thought for an instant they were going to be merged into one messy pulp.

"Kill 'im!" Ferrick squawled.

That wasn't necessary. A rifle stock swung. It made a sound like dry wood snapping on the Silver Corporal 's head. He sagged.

A breed leaped feet-first onto the little policeman's midriff. The man struck with a pistol. He struck again.

He kept on belaboring until the Silver Corporal was only a white pile on the floor that welled steaming scarlet.

Ferrick staggered over. He was crying like a spanked baby, so great was the agony in his arm. He kicked the prostrate little form. But that wasn't very satisfactory. The tiny body was hard as iron, and hurt his toes through his flexible muck-a-lucks.

"He ain't a stiff yet," Ferrick whimpered. "But he damn soon will be! Tie 'im up! Tie the damn woman up, too!"

The breeds did the tying. They used for the fob a bundle of rawhide thongs of the type employed for filling snowshoes. They took many turns of the tough thews.

"That'll hold 'im!" Every one of Ferrick's words was a moan because of his pain. He splinted his arm after a fashion, slinging it to his chest inside his parka. He pointed at two of his hirelings. "You guys stay here!"

"*Oui*," they nodded. But they looked uneasy.

"Aw, don't be so leery," queered Ferrick. "He don't breathe fire!"

"Maybee not," mumbled a breed, "But dey say hees no can be keeled."

"The next guy who mentions that crazy story is gonna get my fist hung on his kisser!" Ferrick snarled vitriolically. "Now listen, you monks. Get this !"

They snapped to attention. Especially the two who were to stay.

"You two guys will stick right here. The rest of us will go stampede the reindeer herd. You'll be able to hear the roar of the herd comin'. That's your cue to knock the Silver Corporal en' the girl over the head. You savvy that–knock 'em over the conks!"

The pair bobbed their heads like Punch and Judy on a ventriloquist's knee.

"After you bang 'em on the bean," Ferrick continued evilly, "You cut off their bonds in a hurry. Make sure they're unconscious, first, though. When they're untied, you two beat it."

He took time out to kick the little body of the Silver Corporal. He used his heel. That didn't hurt so much.

"The reindeer herd pilin' over the cliff will smash in this cabin," he concluded. "The shack is right under the edge. These two will be crushed under a few hundred tons of reindeer meat. Then, when their bodies are found, it'll look like they was caught when the herd stampeded."

The breeds grinned in nasty appreciation. This Ferrick was a smart devil.

Their idol saw their admiration. He got a hold on himself, and worked out his pipe with one hand, filled it and lighted it. The effort put a sweat-grease on his forehead. He blew as much smoke out of the pipe bowl as he drew into his lungs. He was suffering.

He went over and picked up the white rope, using two fingers, as though it were a poisonous snake. He leered at his men.

"Any of you cookies want this for a souvenir?"

They didn't. They'd rather have packed around a couple of nice rattlesnakes.

Ferrick threw the rope on the floor. It writhed like a thing alive and became a quiet, coiled pile.

"C'mon, pals," he clipped, and weaved outside.

The breeds followed, except for the two of their number detailed to remain behind.

Ferrick's two underlings didn't like the job. When, the Silver Corporal rolled over, they both jumped on him with their feet. They kicked him. He kicked back, but feebly. He did flounce about on the floor quite a bit, though.

When the Silver Corporal lay quiet, they desisted. They could tell by his open, roving eyes that he was still conscious.

Not once had his wee, whispering voice spoken.

The girl revived. She did not speak, either.

The two breeds sauntered about and made remarks about the girl. They weren't nice remarks.

The breeds didn't know it, but the little pleasantries they were exchanging signed their death warrant. The Silver Corporal was a Wyoming cow waddy by breed. Down in his country, men died violently for making cracks like these.

The tiny policeman moved a little. His floundering scuffle with the breeds had brought him over to the rope They hadn't noticed it, but he was lying on the coils.

And while they strolled around and talked big, the razor-edged fang of steel had sliced through the rawhide thongs binding his wrists and ankles.

A breed came over to kick the little man again. And suddenly he seemed to acquire a gaping red hinge in his middle!

The only sound was a hiss, a thud. The man toppled.

The other breed bellowed and flourished his gun simultaneously.

The rope, weighted by the heavy, blade, swung once around the little Mountie's silver head. It made a shrill squeal of a sound. Then, with an accuracy that had come from years of practice, it speared through the air at the breed.

The man dodged successfully. But he had no time to fire. The Silver Corporal rushed him. The white rope looped in midair, trapped the breed's gun arm. The weapon snorted lead into the floor. The rope honda swung like a rock on a string and caught the breed's head. He went down.

Over to the girl glided the Silver Corporal. He cut her free with the red blade, then, with what seemed like a single gesture, coiled the strange white rope.

"C'mon!" he said. He didn't believe in wasting words.

She ran with him across the valley. He accommodated his pace to hers. She was a good runner, and didn't barge into deep snow often. Then she dragged back.

"My reindeer herd!" she choked. "Ferrick and the others are going to stampede the deer over the cliff! They're going to wipe out every animal. They–"

She stopped. She was talking to empty air. The Silver Corporal was gone, and she didn't quite know where.

Probably that was mean of him. He could have taken a couple of minutes and explained what he was going to do. But he wasn't used to arguing with women.

She wandered about. She didn't know what to do. She was unarmed. The Silver Corporal had not even bothered to take the guns of the thugs he had finished. That puzzled her, set her to wondering if the little silver-haired man was quite human after all.

She decided to go get those guns. She plunged for the cabin under the cliff.

Then, as suddenly as he had vanished, the Silver Corporal was with her again.

He carried the two huge packs which had been toted by the breeds he vanquished–the packs he had hidden in the snow. Under their bulk, he looked like a tiny white ant struggling with a couple of big brown crumbs.

"C'mon," he said briefly.

They found a place to climb the cliff. It took them fifteen minutes. And it was a climb that set their lungs on fire.

From the cliff top, they could see the reindeer herd. The deer were bedded down in a vast, open glade, which was buttressed around by spruce.

The Silver Corporal looked them over. An appreciative grunt shot his breath steam into the wind, There were thousands of the animals. Their antlers–both male and female had antlers–were like a thick, bare brush.

"Looks kinda like a Wyomin' dogie drive," his wee voice whispered.

"What did you say?" asked the girl. She hadn't caught his tiny tones.

He didn't answer. He was mean that way.

He could see, over to the right, the camp of the Eskimo deer drivers. They had thrown up a snow igloo. Not a man of the Inuit herdsmen was in sight. Doubtless they slept inside.

Beyond the deer herd, he thought he could see men scampering through the spruce. A match flamed.

For a long moment, the Silver Corporal hung motionless. Then he saw the match was being applied to Ferrick's pipe.

"Whew!" he murmured in his small voice. "For a minute, that had me worried."

The girl heard him this time.

"How are they going to stampede my deer?" she asked.

"I'll show you," he replied.

He raced along the cliff edge. The hooting Polar gale had swept the rocky earth free of snow here.

He lowered his packs, opened them. Red packages came to light. He tore loose the wrappings of these.

Then he asked questions.

"Why don't the gang that hired Ferrick want you to collect for the deer? "

"They own a mining company in Alaska." The girl's strong, musical voice was rapid. "They want some good placer mining leases I own. They'll have the chance to get them if I can't get the money to do the work necessary to hold them. The money I need was to come from these deer. Without it–I'm sunk! And they get the placer leases."

The Silver Corporal worked rapidly. He strung the contents of his packages along the rocky ground, very close to the edge of the resting reindeer herd.

The girl watched him. As she saw what the packages held, her attractive brown eyes widened.

"Oh!" she gasped. "So that's how they're going to stampede my deer! They were going to use–"

But the Silver Corporal had struck a match, and a deafening roar drowned out her words.

The roar came from a firecracker. The next instant, gory blobs of flame jumped from a Roman candle and raced at the peaceful reindeer.

The packs had held ordinary Fourth-of-July fireworks!

The Silver Corporal handed the girl the Roman candle. He lighted another and gave that one to her, too.

"Keep'm goin'!" he advised.

He ignited a pinwheel and hung it on a tree. The sparks set the tree on fire. But that didn't matter. There couldn't be much of a forest fire in this country.

Excitement rolled over the deer herd. Antlers tossed. The animals milled.

Eskimo herdsmen popped out of their igloo. They ogled the fireworks. Maybe they had never seen fireworks before. Or maybe they figured the big *tongak* had sent some of his pet fiends to pay them a visit.

Whatever it was, they turned tail and fled.

The deer herd heaved into motion. Panic seized the creatures. They stampeded.

Straight for Ferrick and his breeds, preparing their own fireworks in the spruces beyond the glade, the deer thundered.

Ferrick and his gang cut loose with rifles. That was useless. They lighted their fireworks, such as were in place. But they were too late with that.

The reindeer numbered thousands. They were worse than a cattle stampede to be in front of. The spruce were not tall enough to offer safe perches.

Ferrick and his gang tried a desperate plan. They made a human wedge. Rifles flaming, they tried to cut through the stampeding deer herd.

Animal after animal veered aside from them. But those behind and to the sides crowded in blindly.

Ferrick and his breeds were suddenly engulfed.

Where they had vanished, a heaving sort of a knot lasted for a time, as deer leaped their squirming bodies. But before long, the knot smoothed out as the men beneath became a gory pulp, and nothing disturbed the rushing torrent of antlers.

The Silver Corporal discovered abruptly that the girl was looking away from the ghastly sight.

He faced the other direction with her.

"The deer probably won't run far," he told her in his strange, soft voice.

"No–they probably won't." She choked on the words.

After that, her knees buckled slightly. She swayed a bit,

and felt blindly for the little form of the Silver Corporal. It was instinctive, the way his arms went about her.

But he didn't know the thing she wanted was to be held in his arms and petted and comforted and maybe kissed some.

The Silver Corporal–the sap–led her to a rock and set her down and threw cold snow in her warm, pretty, inviting face.

He was scared of women, anyway.

PHANTOM FANGS

By John Starr

Deep into the trackless Frozen Circle fear-crazed Joe Hetchy fled. But crying ever at his heels followed the phantom of the man he'd killed.

Long before Joe Hetchy reached the hermit's cabin, he heard the savage yelping of his dog. It was the guardian of Gravel Gulch, and a beast which the Crees claimed was no dog at all but the visible form of the Evil One. That was why the Indians in the vicinity did everything possible to keep in the good graces of the mysterious hermit.

Hetchy reached inside his shirt where his six-gun lay against his body. He hoped he didn't have to shoot the dog, for that would turn old Larraby against him. Just then the dog came hurtling over the snow toward him. Almost, Joe Hetchy thought, the Indians' weird tales were true, for this was the most amazing brute he'd ever seen.

The dog's long-legged, bony body was covered with short hair–hair astonishingly short for an animal which had to withstand the rigors of a Mackenzie winter. Its body was covered with scars. Life was made more miserable by the thick, brass-decorated collar around the animal's bony neck.

Joe Hetchy stopped and spoke softly to the brute. Then he tossed the dog a frozen fish brought along for that very purpose. The beast bolted it down, and looked for more. Hetchy tossed out his last fish which the dog caught and gulped down. The ugly brute didn't seem quite so savage now, but it wouldn't let the thief pass. He was wondering what excuse to offer the hermit for shooting the dog, when a weird call sounded down the gulch.

The dog's appearance underwent a startling change. Its tail drooped, its ears settled back. Its eyes seemed to be entreating Joe Hetchy for help. As a startling, carbine-like crack broke the frozen stillness the dog got down on its belly and began to whine.

The thief glanced anxiously up at the cornice of snow and ice overhanging the gulch. But it had not moved. As the crack sounded again, Joe Hetchy discovered its source. An amazing figure was coming up the gulch toward him. It was the rich hermit. In his hand he held an astonishingly long whip. As the aged man came within striking distance, the long lash writhed out and bit a piece of hide from the dog's back. With a yelp of pain, the long-legged brute turned and raced down the gulch. The hermit faced Joe Hetchy with whip raised menacingly.

"What yer comin' ter Gravel Gulch for?" he asked truculently.

"I'm lost, and played out. I'm hungry–starving!"

"Yer don't look it. Anyhow I got nothin' fer yen Hurries

me ter keep myself an' Nugget."

" Nugget?"

"Yeah. The dog, here. He's ther' only gold I got. Don't yer believe it? Yer think I got some gold, don't yer? An' yer come here ter rob me?" The hermit drew his whip back more threateningly. "Well I ain't got no gold! I ain't got nothin' but my dog, so git outer my gulch, an' git out quick!"

"But I'm starving! I–I–" Joe Hetchy wavered, then pitched forward in the snow.

"Well, since yer starvin', yer might as well freeze!" cried the old hermit and headed back down the gulch.

The thief swore softly. But he wasn't through. He was going to find out where Zeke Larraby hid his gold.

That night at dusk, Joe Hetchy stumbled through the snow toward the hermit's cabin. Nugget, the dog, came at him again, but more friendly. The thief called for help, then stretched out in the snow Presently the cabin door opened, and Zeke Larraby again appeared with his long whip. One crack from it, and the dog slunk hurriedly into the cabin. The old hermit stared at the motionless figure in the snow.

"Consarn yer hide!" he complained. "S'pose I'll have ter take yer in, er th' danged Mounted Police'll blame me fer yer death."

Catching the thief by the heels, the old man dragged him into the cabin, and barred the door.

"Lay thar by the stove," he said "an' I'll make yer some coffee. An' that's all yer'll git!"

That night Joe Hetchy and Nugget lay together on the bare floor by the stove, while Zeke Larraby crawled into his bunk with his whip. The thief and the hermit each stayed awake all night, waiting for the other to make a move. Neither did.

Early the next morning the old hermit did a peculiar thing. He went outside his cabin and made a smoke signal. That afternoon a young Cree arrived at the cabin. He didn't stay long, but when he left he took a letter from the secretive hermit. For some reason that letter worried the thief. Still the old man had a right to send out mail.

Joe Hetchy spent another night with Nugget on the cold bare floor of the cabin. But if the old hermit had any gold, he left it strictly alone. The next day, Zeke Larraby drove Joe Hetchy out. But that night the thief stole back, fed Nugget another fish, and eagerly watched the hermit through the cabin's lone window. Zeke Larraby was either unusually cunning, or he had no gold. The next night proved that it was cunning, for after the hermit had pretended to go to bed, he got up, went to the stone fireplace chimney, removed several stones, and took out bag after bag. Gold!

Joe Hetchy hurried around to the front of the cabin. Nugget didn't bark until the thief taunted him with a frozen fish. As he heard the door being unbarred, Joe Hetchy flattened himself against the cabin, and waited.

As soon as the hermit appeared with his long whip, the thief leaped out in front of him, covering him with drawn six-gun.

"Hands up, Larraby!" he rasped.

With a snarl of fury the hermit swung his whip. But the crack that answered came from a gun. But not until that moment had the thief intended to kill Zeke Larraby.

With a choking cry, Joe Hetchy dragged the hermit into the cabin, then turned to the sacks. Ten bags of raw gold! More than he had expected. More than one man could carry! But his dogsled would carry them. Cramming four bags into his pockets, the killer leaped through the open door, and headed back to his camp outside the gulch as fast as his snowshoes would carry him. And that wasn't fast enough.

Behind him, Joe Hetchy seemed to hear the explosive crack of the old hermit's whip. Feeling more and more that he was followed, the killer finally had to look back. He was followed! A ghostlike creature kept pace with him in the deep shadow of the overhanging cliff. An ominous crack came from that direction.

With a choking cry of terror, the killer plunged on. Then a familiar yelp echoed out from the shadow of the overhanging snow. It was the dog, Nugget, that followed. He hadn't expected that.

"Get back, Nugget!" he cried hoarsely.

"Get!"

But the dog wouldn't go. Joe Hetchy threw snowballs and chunks of ice at him, but Nugget thought he was only playing! The killer raised his gun. He'd have to shoot the beast after all. But a strangely startling sigh echoed above him. It came from the mammoth wall of overhanging snow.

He dare not shoot now, for fear the concussion would start the snowslide! Neither dare he let the dog follow him. Joe Hetchy cursed softly.

Everybody knew Nugget belonged to Zeke Larraby. And when the old hermit was found dead, the dog's presence with Joe Hetchy might easily be the clue that hanged him!

When the killer stumbled out of the gulch, he faced another unpleasant surprise. A little fire glowed brightly in front of his spruce lean-to. Beside that fire stood a man in a scarlet tunic. Joe Hetchy stopped in dismay. Behind came a dead man's dog-in front was a man who could arrest him for murder!

"Hello there!" suddenly called out the Mountie, advancing with drawn pistol. "Who are you ?"

The killer gasped. He hadn't thought he was visible. "I-I'm Joe Hetchy," he answered hoarsely. "This is my camp."

The Mountie, a tall, red-cheeked youngster, stared curiously at the man who joined him.

"How's things in Gravel Gulch?" he asked. "Any slides? Heard a crack like one loosening a while ago."

"I–I don't know nothing about Gravel Gulch, Constable," choked Joe Hetchy.

"Wasn't that Gravel Gulch you just came out of? Isn't that where my– where Zeke Larraby lives ?"

"Zeke–Zeke Larraby?" echoed the killer huskily. "Do you know him?"

"He's my father! Understand he's called the hermit of Gravel Gulch. I thought perhaps you could tell me something about him. That's why I waited here."

"Joe" Hetchy felt his heart thumping in his throat. "I–I'm sorry, but I never heard of him, Constable," he said. "You must be as new as I am up here, Mr. Hetchy," smiled the Mountie, buttoning up his fur jacket. "Funny my first call to duty here would come from my own father, isn't it? A Cree brought a note down to headquarters from him asking for protection against someone he thought was planning to rob him.

The corporal said dad was always getting foolish notions like that. But anyway it gives me a chance to pay him a little surprise visit. Cheerio!"

"But you can't go down there, Constable!" desperately cried the killer. "It's too dangerous. I–I just beat a snowslide out!"

Just then a furious barking broke out from the little spruce wickiup where the huskies were. The lead dog strained frantically at the rope holding him.

"Must be a wolf!" cried Larraby, searching the darkness with his gun. "There he is! See him sneaking up toward us from the gulch. Why–why it's only a dog!"

"Yes," sighed Joe Hetchy. "It–it's only a dog!"

"That Cree messenger said dad had a dog. Maybe it's his!" The Mountie started forward eagerly.

A big, bony, long-legged creature leaped out of the snow, snarled at the Mountie, then flashed past him to leap up joyously at Joe Hetchy.

"Why, the dog knows you, Hetchy!" cried Constable Larraby. "Maybe–maybe you do know dad after all?"

"No. I said I didn't! This is my dog!" The killer played with Nugget's ears, then took a frozen fish from his store and fed him.

"The ugly dog dad has surely can't be any uglier than yours," mused the Mountie. Then sharply: "What's his name?"

"Nugget!" When Joe Hetchy called the dog by name, he responded by leaping playfully up at him. The firelight gleamed on the animal's heavy, brass decorated collar.

"See? He's mine," cried the killer.

"I see," answered the Mountie thoughtfully. "And I suppose that's his name stamped on his collar?"

Even as Joe Hetchy stood dumfounded for a moment, the constable grabbed the dog and examined his collar.

"Property of Zeke Larraby," he read. Then: "So you're–"

The Mountie's speech was lost in the explosion of a six-gun. As Constable Larraby staggered back, he fired from the hip; but Nugget had crashed into him and spoiled his aim. The dog's teeth snapped viciously at the Mountie's throat. The constable and the dog went down together.

Joe Hetchy feverishly hitched his huskies. He had kept everything in readiness, his blankets, his rifle, a bag of food for himself, and a bag of frozen fish for the huskies. And now he had four bags of gold. The devil could have the other six.

Nugget could probably have killed Constable Larraby, for the Mountie had been hard hit by Joe Hetchy. But when the dog saw his only friend in full flight toward the river, he thought only of going with him. That was why bullets whined about Joe Hetchy, and a grim, bloodstained figure stumbled after him. And from the woods came the yelping of another dog-team. The killer knew he dare not shoot now. His hope lay in vanishing into the night as rapidly and as silently as possible. Before the moon became bright.

Joe Hetchy knew how to cover his trail. He had been doing it most of his life. That was why about midnight, he turned up a glassy, wind-swept creek leading away from the Liard River. He was going to travel a trail that no human being could follow.

But the killer had not gone far up the creek when the eager yelping of the dead man's dog sounded behind. That ugly brute's friendship was an appalling thing. Its yelping would certainly draw the Redcoats on his trail.

A mile or so up the creek, Joe Hetchy stopped his huskies. He was still afraid to risk the sound of shooting, so he unhitched his big yellow lead dog. Nugget howled in fear as the husky raced back at him. Somewhere in the dark shadows along the shore the two dogs came together. The sound of their combat made the remaining huskies frantic. Finally the yellow lead dog came out of the brush, and torn and bleeding, limped back to his yelping mates.

Joe Hetchy cursed fervidly. He had no idea that Nugget would put up such a fight. The lead dog whined when the harness settled on him again. But the fugitive licked the huskies on. He was going to a far country where no one knew him.

Joe Hetchy became a sick man. Either Nugget was not dead, or his ghost was on the trail–the trail that the fugitive took such pains to conceal. On two different nights now, as Joe Hetchy whipped his weary huskies through the foothills, he heard the ghostly howling of a dog behind. And if he recognized it, the Redcoats could recognize it too.

Once the fugitive looked back he saw a tall, gaunt shadow framed against the moon. Joe Hetchy emptied his gun in its direction. Whatever the thing was, it didn't reappear after that, nor did it howl any more. But the fugitive couldn't rid himself of the depressing feeling that it still stalked him.

The drifting warmth of the Japan current was bringing a quick spring to the Yukon. Deceptive mists and fogs settled in the valleys, and like thin smoke rolled down the sides of the mountains to the raging streams appearing magically in every hollow.

Joe Hetchy clung desperately to the uplands. But even there the snow and ice were rotten and spongy. Then the crippled lead dog fell dying, and before the man could prevent, the leader's hungry mates had torn him to pieces. Thinly covered sink holes opened up under them. The long sled swamped in one, and pulled the trace dog down with it. Before Joe Hetchy could get it unhitched, the dog was drowned. And again the remaining huskies had a feast. They had to eat something, for the frozen fish had played out long ago. The killer had never intended to take this treacherous route through the Cassiars, but he dare not turn back because of the thing that followed him.

Whichever way the frantic fugitive turned, he met high, green-forested and snow-capped mountains. Snowslides thudded behind him, cascades of tumbling milky water sprang up magically ahead. Even nature seemed fighting against him. But Joe Hetchy prayed and cursed, and battled on. He was fighting for his life–but he wouldn't give up his gold.

Joe Hetchy would have starved to death had it not been that birds were already coming northward by the thousands, and now and then he managed to shoot a duck and bake it in mud. But most of the man's lead went for the relentless, bullet-proof shadow which crept along behind him. And then Joe Hetchy heard echoes of shots that were not his own. There was something beside a ghost dog on his trail.

It was a man. Perhaps Constable Larraby. If so, it was because the ghost dog led the way, for only a dog's keen scent could pick up the trail that the killer took such frantic pains to conceal.

Joe Hetchy waited in ambush. He tried all kinds of mad schemes to trap his Nemesis. But to no avail.

Life became a ghastly battle of endurance between Joe Hetchy and the lone pot-bellied husky that now represented his team. Each was starving. Each looked with hungry eyes upon the other. Then came the day, when with his last bullet, Joe Hetchy killed the cannibal dog. After that life became one continuous nightmare. Several times the fugitive thought he heard a steamboat whistle. But even though flowers were peeping through the snow, and the ice had left most of the streams, Joe Hetchy knew the rivers could not be open for navigation yet. It was all a part of the sickness creeping through his blood.

In his frantic struggle to lose the thing behind him, Joe Hetchy lost himself! It was then that a new sound impressed itself on the fugitive's inner consciousness. It came from the west. An echoing, booming roar that didn't end like the steamboat whistle had. It must be a great river pounding to the sea!

Joe Hetchy tried desperately to reach that rushing western roar. But it never seemed to come any nearer until one day he stumbled into a beautiful, misty valley, filled with little rainbows, and warmed by many hot springs. Under his feet was a crush of forget-me-nots and white and purple violets. Their sweet perfume filled the man's throbbing lungs.

The valley throbbed with life. A melody of bird-life, subdued and sleepy, even though the sun was still warmly aglow in the heavens. From a nearby clump of willows came the chirping twitter of a thrush, and the sweet, sleepy, evening song of a robin. And above it all, the surge of a mighty river, nearer than Joe Hetchy had ever heard it.

The man crept toward the river on hands and knees. But he couldn't make it. He dropped exhausted beside a shining flower-circled pool. A shudder of fear went over Joe Hetchy as he saw his own reflection. Not only was his face wild and whiskered, but his jet black hair had become almost white.

With the fear of death freezing his heart, Joe Hetchy fainted beside the pool. But even as the twilight of unconsciousness stole over him, the man suddenly became aware of another presence. A trembling, furry body pressed against his. A pleading, piteous whine sounded in his ears. And then Joe

Hetchy found himself staring straight into the eyes of a dog. Nugget! Here at last was the beast which had hounded him to his death.

Joe Hetchy clutched the dog frantically by the throat. One hand closed on the heavy collar. A strand of rope was there. Someone had tied the brute, but even that had not held him back. Somehow the fugitive got to his knees, then to his feet. The dog struggled weakly to get loose. Joe Hetchy held the brute out in front of him, and kicked it. He tried to steady himself for another kick. Before he died, he was going to kill the dog. But a ghastly voice stopped him.

"You're under arrest, Hetchy!"

The fugitive dashed a trembling hand across his eyes. But the tattered, bloodstained apparition would not fade. There stood what had once been–Constable Larraby.

Around one wrist was a piece of rope, matching the one on the dog's collar. On the Mountie's other wrist was snapped one steel loop of a pair of handcuffs. He tried to get the other loop around Joe Hetchy's wrist. The fugitive lashed out weakly. Both went down. Then the constable got to his knees and flung himself on top of the killer. Both men lay there gasping for breath. Presently the Mountie reached for Joe Hetchy's wrist-again. The killer's hand closed on a round stone, not very large, but all he could lift. He began hammering on the constable's head. The Mountie struck Hetchy in the face with his steel bracelets. The fugitive shoved Constable Larraby from him, and got groggily to his feet. A moment he stood swaying, then with all his strength he threw his stone. It caught the constable on the forehead, and he lay still. The dog lay very still.

Somewhere back in Joe Hetchy's brain flashed the thought that he must live now for he was free. Free! The victor drank deeply from the pool, then lurched toward the roaring river. Time after time he fell. He was about to give up in despair when he heard voices. He shouted weakly for help, and crept forward on hands and knees. And so he was discovered by a band of Indian fishermen.

When Joe Hetchy awoke, it was with the same husky cries for help that had sent him into unconsciousness. When they ended, he lay very still in the darkness, trying to think what had startled him into wakefulness. He felt coarse blankets over him. But where were the stars? Nugget? The Redcoat? Had they all been part of his sickness ? And why was he half smothered by the sickening odor of fish?

Suddenly a crash of thunder broke over Joe Hetchy's head. The sudden glare of lightning showed him a window, and beyond that window a totem pole. And so close it seemed beside him, came the roar of the angry river. The man couldn't understand it.

The lightning came again, and after it followed a discharge of thunder that shook the earth. It rolled away, echo upon echo, through the mountains like the booming of signal guns, each more distant than the other. Through the window, Joe Hetchy saw the lightning flashing among distant, snow-capped peaks.

Soon came the patter of huge rain drops. Then the storm broke, beating upon the cabin in a mighty shock of thunder, wind, and rain. All night long the cabin shook in the mighty fury of the first spring storm. Through it all stood the leering totem pole outside the window.

With the first gray light of dawn, Joe Hetchy made a startling discovery. He was not alone. All night long from a dark corner behind him, a woman had sat watching him. She was a squat, slant eyed creature, undoubtedly belonging to a West Coast tribe. By pidgin English, and the sign language, he learned that he had been there three days. Alone. She knew nothing of a dog, or a Redcoat. And she was honest, for Joe Hetchy found his gold still hidden in the lining of his fur jacket.

About mid-morning the rain stopped. Storm had washed the air until it was like tonic. A reborn Joe Hetchy stood in the cabin door gulping the sweetness into his lungs. The miracle of change came swiftly in the next half hour. One after another the mountains dropped down out of their storm mist. The snowy crests caught the fire of the sun. Dark inundations of forest took up the shimmering gleam. Green slopes rolled out from behind veils of smoking vapor, and suddenly spring had come!

But better than spring, was the river, a leaping, foaming, tortured thing that rushed past the row of weird totem poles that decorated its northern bank. The raven, the eagle, the killer-whale, and the wolf–all were represented there. Indian women were down past them repairing fish nets. The men had already gone upstream in their dugouts for the quinnat–the spring salmon were running!

Joe Hetchy eyed the few remaining dugouts. From them his glance shifted back to the flooded river. Here was a pathway that neither man, nor dog, nor ghost could follow.

But when the friendly Indians returned that night, they declared that not until the flood left the Taku, could even the strongest dugout survive the devil-devil rapids in that roaring gorge below the village. And in addition to the devil-devil rapids there was the danger of the great Taku glacier, and the icebergs that were always breaking off to float southward to the sea.

But all that night a dog howled at Joe Hetchy's door. And that was not the worst. When the Indians who had chased the ghost dog came back, they brought with them, a tattered, redcoated figure who had a pair of handcuffs dangling from one wrist. The Indians said he was delirious with the devil-devil spirit, and must be nursed and protected. Joe Hetchy knew there was no time to lose. He must flee. Not a Siwash would accompany him as long as the river was at flood, so Joe Hetchy decided to risk it alone.

Not until Takeena, the squaw, followed him down to the swirling, milky river, did Joe Hetchy realize that she had determined to go along.

And because she was young and strong, and knew how to handle a paddle, he didn't object. And nobody else objected. Takeena had lost her first man in the devil-devil rapids, and if she went to join him with another sacrifice, it was the will of the gods. But the gods willed that the little dugout should get safely through that gorge of twisting, troubled white water.

And because she was strong and willing to work, Joe Hetchy took the Siwash squaw with him up into the Yukon.

On the bank of a little creek, Joe Hetchy, now Dapper Dan Domino, opened up his Monte Carlo, so named from Dawson's famous dance hall of the gold-rush days.

With miles and miles of dangerous water, ice, and mountains behind him, Dapper Dan Domino hoped that he was at last safe. And it seemed that he was. A year went by, and he prospered. Cheechakos, sourdoughs, and adventurers came to the Monte Carlo from all over the Yukon territory. They brought their hard-earned gold, and laid it at Dan Domino's shrine.

Dapper Dan Domino was the best dressed man in the Klondike, and as picturesque a character as the old gold rush days had ever seen. His hair was snow white now, and he had cultivated a neatly-kept Vandyke. Certainly no one would have recognized him as Joe Hetchy. But for all his prosperity, Dapper Dan Domino was a man who walked alone, brushing sleeves with those whom he scarcely seemed to notice. He was observant. He spotted a good customer as soon as he entered the door. A flick of his eye-brow was enough to direct his hirelings to the victim.

And always Dapper Dan Domino seemed to be watching that door for someone who never came. Always he seemed to be listening for something he never heard. There were those who wondered why the owner of the Monte Carlo kept the fastest string of huskies in the Yukon always hitched at his back door–for he never used them.

Not even the faithful Takeena knew his reason. She never questioned her lord and master. She did know that in spite of his prosperity and outward elegance he suffered from a strange inner sickness. She saw it in his eyes when he came to her at night. But those who worshipped at his shrine of gold never saw it. Dapper Dan Domino lived apart from them. He had no friends. He was afraid to make any. He was a man as hard and mysterious as the ice-crested mountains.

The Yukon played under the light of the midnight sun. For days and weeks that glorious orb never set. The whole world seemed a garden. A rosy, sunlit garden where green grasses grew, and amazing flowers burst forth. Birds sang at midnight. Everywhere was the song and throb of joyous life. The grassy streams and pools swarmed with fluffy, new-born ducks. For weeks at a time no lamps were lighted in the Monte Carlo. All night long the games went on with only the glow of the midnight sun to light them. The Yukon played hard. It played against time, for all too soon, the long, dark night would come.

About the middle of August the sun dipped below the horizon at midnight. After that there was no actual midnight sun, although the nights were as light as ever for a while. But by the latter part of September oil lamps were again in use at the Monte Carlo.

And, then, one evening at dusk, a tall, quick-moving stranger came to the Monte Carlo. Strangers often came there. But this man was different. He was still red-cheeked, and he seemed young. But there was a grimness about his face that hardly went with youth. Even though he was not in uniform, Dapper Dan Domino recognized the stranger as soon as he entered the door. It was the man the Siwash had saved–Constable Larraby.

For a moment Dapper Dan's eyes dulled with despair. Then he thought of his gala, and his thin lips set obstinately. He'd wait for the Redcoat to make his play.

Dapper Dan Domino never drank. But as Constable Larraby pretended to stroll casually about the room, while he covertly scrutinized the inmates, the white-haired owner of the Monte Carlo hurried behind the bar and drank several shots of raw whiskey. He was still there when the Redcoat turned his way. They stared at each other across the bar.

"So you're Dapper Dan Domino?" said the stranger softly. "I've heard a lot about you."

Dapper Dan Domino nodded grimly, and waited for the constable to make his play. The stranger eyed the white-haired old man curiously.

"Seems to me we've met before," he said. "Where'd you come from here?"

"I didn't come. I've always been here, stranger. Not just on this one spot, you understand. But never out of the Klondike. The picking's always been too good to leave."

The constable nodded thoughtfully. "Funny how a chap's memory plays him tricks, isn't it?" he said. "I could almost swear I'd met you before. But I guess I didn't."

"No. I don't think so," answered Dapper Dan Domino, with hope surging through him again. "Have a drink?"

"No, thanks." Then: "Some place you have here, Domino. They told me at Dawson that this was the crossroads of the Yukon, and that you've got acquainted with practically every inhabitant in the North country. They said that if a man were looking for someone, you could tell where he was if he was up here. How about it?"

"They were just joking with you, stranger."

"But if a man waited here long enough, he would eventually meet them all, wouldn't he Domino?"

"I–I hope you're not thinking of waiting here that long, stranger," said Dapper Dan uneasily.

The constable reached into his pocket and took out a brass-decorated dog collar. "There's one man I could wait here a long time for," he said softly, staring at the collar. "I lost track of him about a year ago."

Dapper Dan Domino gulped down another drink. "Was he a friend of yours, stranger?" he asked huskily.

"A friend of mine?" Constable Larraby laughed mirthlessly. "I couldn't be more interested in him if he were a friend. That's why I'm up here."

"You–you think he's up this way, stranger?"

The Mountie toyed with the dog collar. "If I could find the brute this collar belongs to, I'd know for sure. I lost him a year ago, too. But lately I've heard of a strange dog that answers his description being up this way. And when I find that dog, I'll find my man!"

Suddenly the door was flung open by a grizzled old sourdough who held up a bag of dust, and called for drinks for the house. As he stood there swaying in the doorway, a long-legged creature leaped past him, and stood in the middle of the room, his head poised in the air sniffing.

Constable Larraby's hand dropped into a pocket where the shape of a gun showed.

"God! There's the dog now!" he choked. "And if the man's here, he'll point him out, Domino. "

But Dapper Dan Domino wasn't there. He had hurriedly disappeared through a door behind the bar. And even then he and his squaw had started their racing huskies in a mad dash to the Arctic Circle.

Constable Larraby watched the dog with hungry eyes. The ugly brute sniffed about the room, and howled piteously. The Mountie waited for it to point his man. Finally the emaciated dog caught the scent, and with a joyous little yelp hobbled to the door behind the bar and began whining and pawing. At last young Larraby knew where he had met Dapper Dan Domino. But when he broke into that back room, he found it empty. And the days that followed were just as empty–for Dapper Dan Domino had vanished. Perhaps that was why Nugget died. But even a dog can bear only so much.

A saw-toothed range of ugly hills cast a continual shadow over the snow-bound, wind-swept tundra that rolled away to the Arctic Ocean. There was no sun, and the drifted snow that filled the crevasses seemed but little lighter than the stark black hills themselves.

A few shacks made of mud and small trees brought out from the inside, clung as closely to the black hills as safety permitted. Further out on the vast treeless tundra, a tribe of Eskimos had built their igloos. To the west was the coal mine. There Eskimos and foreigners burrowed all winter to bring out coal, which the aerial tramway dumped on the shore of the frozen inlet against the summer break-up, when the tubby, wooden coal ships would come to take it away.

Where a black arm of naked rock jutted out toward the inlet were a few more sod-patched wooden buildings that had once been used by whalers. They had been deserted a long time when Ivan Muskovich and his squaw broke through from the inside with what had once been a magnificent string of huskies, and squatted in the largest building.

There crude whale-oil lamps now feebly burned away the nights as icy darkness closed in on the top of the world. The days had grown shorter and shorter, until there was no sunrise. All was one continuous night through which moved shadowy, parka-clad figures.

Sometimes the parka wearers came by dog team. Sometimes they came out across the frozen tundra on fast reindeer sleds. The stolid, sullen-faced coal miners mostly walked for the distance was short. But regardless of how they came, all answered the same call. All trails ended at the place presided over by Ivan Muskovich. It was a sordid place, and it lured a sordid crowd who came to drink and gamble away the nights. There were several packs of greasy cards, and plenty of whalebone dice. But, best of all, there was whiskey. Whiskey which Ivan Muskovich bought from a renegade Russian who had long been smuggling it in to the coal miners.

When the mine superintendent complained, his men threatened a strike. In desperation he sent a wireless to Mounted Police headquarters at Dawson, advising of the renegade Russian who'd opened up a gambling hell and blind tiger which was demoralizing his miners and the Eskimos By wireless the superintendent was notified that Constable Larraby would be sent north to arrest the Russian.

But still, night after night, Ivan Muskovich watched his customers come, their bloodshot eyes aflame. It made no difference that he could not speak their language, even though his name was Russian. Ivan Muskovich spoke no language. And it mattered little, as long as he catered to the base desires of his customers. Sometimes he almost envied their bestial drunkenness, their sodden insensibility, for that brought temporary forgetfulness.

But Ivan Muskovich was still a man apart. Never could he overcome that hollow, inner sickness gnawing at his vitals. And as the continuous night settled down, he felt as if a tight, black cap were being pulled slowly over his head. Fear.

The faithful Takeena had made a dye of coal tar from the mine, and colored her master's hair a dirty brown. And in like manner she kept his now long and bushy mustache dyed the same color, for long ago the neat white vandyke had gone. All Dapper Dan Domino's neatness was gone. His flashy clothes had been replaced by baggy Eskimo furs. And furs were needed there in the shack where the relentless arctic wind often blew snow in the cracks, and lifted the greasy cards from the table while the men were playing.

Ivan Muskovich had little faith in his changed appearance. True, his disguise would fool any man, even as he had fooled Constable Larraby back at the Monte Carlo–fooled him until the dog had come. It would be the same again. Sooner or later that dog would come seeking its friend. Ivan Muskovich believed that with all his heart, for he had no way of knowing that Nugget was dead.

Always he felt the invisible, intangible web of the law, like a dead-man's arms reaching out for his life. The fugitive's guilty conscience lashed him into a frenzy of desperation. He had fled to the top of the world. He could flee no further. Even had there been a place to flee to, it would have been the same. If they found him here, they would find him there. There was but one chance of saving himself and his precious gold. He must kill again!

Ivan Muskovich, or Joe Hetchy, was not a killer. That was why he had fled from the Monte Carlo. It appalled him to think of taking human life again–to take it in cold blood.

Old Zeke Larraby's death was still a ghastly, ever-present nightmare, and that murder had not been premeditated as this second one would be. But the man's back was against the wall. And so Ivan Muskovich bought an old army pistol from the renegade Russian, and began shooting at an indoor target when there was no one but his squaw to see him.

Takeena lived in mortal terror now, for surely her master's strange sickness had become that deadly madness which sometimes overcomes those of the arctic. According to old superstition there was but one cure for this black delirium of the long arctic night, and that was the magic power of the Northern lights.

Perhaps there was something to the old superstition, for when the lights at last appeared, a change came over Ivan Muskovich, even as it came over the top of the world. There was little of fear or madness in the man's face now. Instead of despair, he felt only a dull and painless sort of stoicism. He felt that he had reached the depth of his suffering. And there was a certain relief in the thought that his days of frantic flight were over. Here in this shack at the top of the world he would finally face his fate. And he was not unprepared. Although the Russian army pistol was not as trustworthy or as straight-shooting as he might have wished

The thankful squaw continued to pray to the Northern lights. And as Ivan Muskovich watched their magnificent display on successive nights, he could understand why the Eskimos got out their tom-toms, and put on a great dance and potlach feast.

The lights were like a giant handful of different colored chiffon scarves being shaken across the sky. As each one changed shape and position, it changed color. It was as light as day now. The dark gray shadows had vanished from the rolling tundra, and for miles and miles the snow sparkled as if inlaid with diamonds. The sky was a dark blue, full of mystery. The moon was a great phosphorescent island in a sea of beating stars.

The hollow throbbing of the tom-toms lured even the drunken Russians out to join in the dance on the snow-bound tundra. For two days not a pound of coal was mined as the Russians and Eskimos danced, feasted, and drank the whiskey sold by Ivan Muskovich.

The fourth night found the tundra quiet and deserted. The whaling shack had no customers. Those who had danced were now at home doing penance. At each end of the crude bar a whale-oil lamp smoked and spluttered. Ivan Muskovich stood behind the bar staring at the door. His loaded pistol lay in front of him. One of the lamps flickered and went out. When Takeena attempted to re-light it, the man brushed her away. He didn't answer her plaintive little cry.

A hoarse command outside, the lonely howl of a dog, and the door of the whaling shack was flung wide open. Hardly was Constable Larraby inside when Joe Hetchy fired. A look of strange surprise flashed over the Mountie's face as he staggered back with blood gushing from his side. His gun flamed from his hip. The killer felt a burning shock in his chest. But he fired again. A cry of triumph escaped Joe Hetchy as the Mountie went down. But he cried too soon for the Mountie fired from the floor.

The second bullet spun Joe Hetchy entirely around, and even as he clutched frantically at the bar to keep from falling, the constable was up and at him with flaming six-gun. But young Larraby was not used to the icy floor. He slipped and fell headlong against the bar. His weapon bounced from his hand.

Before he could recover it, Joe Hetchy stood over him with threatening pistol. The killer took deadly aim and fired. The old army gun jammed. As the Mountie's hand closed over his own weapon, Joe Hetchy desperately pulled the trigger again. His jammed weapon exploded in his hand. Frantic with pain and fear he flung himself down at the constable. A bullet came up to meet him, tore through his lungs. He fell on top of the Mountie, and groped for his throat. He found instead a pair of handcuffs snapped on his wrists.

Constable Larraby stood over him with threatening gun.

"I'm sorry you made me do this, Muskovich," he gasped. "For I didn't come up here to kill you. I only came to–"

"And you did. You got the–the handcuffs on me at last, Larraby," choked Joe Hetchy.

"You–you know me?" cried the constable wonderingly. "You knew I was coming? That's why you were waiting for me?"

A frightful spasm of pain prevented Joe Hetchy's answer. The Mountie hurriedly poured a glass of whiskey, and held it to the fugitive's red-flecked lips. Joe Hetchy weakly brushed it aside.

"No use, Larraby," he croaked. "I'm done for. But I . . . kept ahead of you for a long time . . . didn't I? And I'd have won . . . if it hadn't been for that . . . dog."

"What dog?"

"The one that howled outside tonight."

"You're crazy, Muskovich. No dog howled outside tonight!"

"You mean that . . . wasn't Nugget your father's dog?"

"God!" choked the Mountie. "I've got you placed now. Joe Hetchy! And I'd given you up after the dog died."

A ghastly laugh escaped Joe Hetchy's foaming lips. "And so . . . Nugget had freed me," he whispered. "I–I could have fled . . . with Takeena and you never would have . . . found me."

"I may never have found you," choked Larraby. "But no man can hide from his conscience.... You know that from hearing a dog that didn't howl."

THE DANGEROUS DAN McGREW

By W. Ryerson Johnson

Corporal Thain, on the trail of three cutthroats, found instead a bush-crazy prospector who thought himself Dan McGrew. For saving Dan's life the Mountie was rewarded with the loss of his guns. It was then that he found the outlaws he hunted...

Corporal Jim Thain of the Royal Canadian Mounted skinned out of his "Yukon" sleeping bag in three seconds less than three seconds flat.

"Hey there," he blared, "hold 'em! You crazy bat-brained loony–hold 'em. Hold those guns !"

Jim was a big man and he packed a man-sized voice. His breath which came blasting out of sheet-iron lungs clouded about him in the ten-below cold like lumpy fog. But voice alone was not enough.

Without waiting to throw on a coat, without even stopping to slip into his moccasins, he tore away on the strangest fifty-yard dash of his young life.

So fast and so hard his stocking feet pounded that he did

not feel the biting cold–and there was a lot of foot space exposed to that cold! Those number thirteens of his were doing him plenty of good here. A little like snowshoes. They kept him from sinking more than ankle deep in the coarse, granular snow.

Jim's sprint was hurtling him pell-mell for a deep ice chasm. As he ran he shouted. There was both command and assurance in his roaring voice.

"Come here, Dan McGrew!" He motioned violently, as to a fractious child. "I'm Jim Thain, your friend. I won't hurt you. Come here. And hold on to those guns, big boy! Hold 'em!"

It was the sun which had awakened Jim. Over the rim of the Pelly Range it was streaming its fiery banners in a first salute to the winter morning. Here, where the glacier névé rode the broad shoulders of Big Horn Mountain, those spotlight rays were slanting off the ice fields in dazzling glints of amber and amethyst and rose.

It was the sun which had awakened him; it was *not* the sun which got him up. The "Dangerous Dan McGrew" was responsible for that.

The self-styled "Dangerous Dan" was a bush-crazed prospector whom the corporal had taken in tow the week before. Jim had found the man, wandering, lost, half starved and half frozen, "shaking hands with the willows" on Crooked Wash Creek.

Straightaway Jim had dropped his pursuit of the Meti outlaws which had brought him into this lone and frozen Yukon back-stretch, and set himself the thankless task of caring for this stray wretch. The man was in a pitiable condition. Face and hands and feet were all badly frost-bitten. For hours Jim had worked over him, thawing out the needle points of ice from his pores. More than this, Jim took clothes from his own back and forced the temporarily demented man to wear them. Then he strapped him into the six-dog komatik and made him ride.

Under Jim's conscientious care the fellow regained much of his old strength. He did not regain his mental balance. It was too soon for that. He was not vicious. Far from it. He was downright benevolent. But he was totally lacking in judgment, and gloriously irresponsible at times, as a child or a drunken man can be irresponsible.

Just now as Corporal Thain crashed through the snow in his stocking feet, shouting and gesticulating, the Dangerous Dan McGrew stood at the slick edge of a deep ice rift and calmly regarded him.

Dan McGrew had been a big man, almost as big as Jim. But now he was wasted by exposure and near-starvation. Mittened hands held out over the cliff, he stood clutching Jim's rifle and cartridge belt and service revolver. A gusty breeze roughed the fur of his dicky-hood which clung so loosely about his emaciated face. His features were twisted into a benign smile. He smiled with his whole frost-bitten face, like any child.

He waited till Jim was almost upon him, then he allowed the belt and guns to slip from his grip. Down they dropped, two hundred feet into that glacial rift. They were gone. Irretrievably lost.

Arms wildly waving, legs sprawled wide, Jim stayed his headlong rush dust in time to keep from following his weapons into that dark-shadowed chasm. He stood teetering for a second on the brink. As the clatter of the falling guns died away, he turned on the beaming prospector.

"You bush-dingy loon!" he blazed. "What'd you do that for? Why'd you throw my guns away? You dizzy bug house son-of-a-crack-brained-walrus–" He paused as the smile faded from the other's face.

Terribly blotched and garbled, that face. It had frozen and scabbed and cracked and frozen again till it hardly resembled a face.

Jim reached out his huge hand to the other's sleeve. "Why'd you throw the guns away, Dan McGrew?" His voice was surprisingly gentle.

The man responded at once to Jim's changed manner. His face beamed again. His red-rimmed eyes sparkled.

"Why Jim," he said in his deep dramatic voice, "we're friends, you and me. We don't want to maintain no show of force, Jim. I say, down with armament, Jim. That's why I took your guns out of your bedroll while you slept. I believe in disarmament."

Jim started prancing ponderously around in the snow to

warm those prize thirteens. "You believe in disarmament, huh?" he growled. "Well, looka here, you–you– Aw hell!" He grinned wryly.

Dan McGrew laid his hand on Jim's shoulder. "Old man," he asked, "did you ever hear about that time in Skagway when I took ten guns away from ten men–"

"Yeah, I've heard that one. Come on, now; we've gotta get back and slide into some duds–"

"Jim; look at me! I'm a turkey buzzard!" The prospector inched closer to the sloping brink of that glacial crevice and looked over, at the same time jerking his arms up and down. "I'm a turkey buzzard," he repeated, still smiling as he bent his knees for a leap into space. "Watch me fly."

"You poor dumb loco!" Jim rumbled.

Reaching out, he grabbed the tall, gaunt, scarecrow figure and flung it roughly backward on the snow.

Later that morning, mushing along on webs at the head of his dog team, Jim's thoughts reverted to the loss of his weapons.

Once he mused:

"If Meti Paul and his gang of hell-slinkers knew I didn't have a gun, they'd turn back and jump me so quick I couldn't see for smoke."

Sure funny how things happened sometimes Here he'd been tailing those bush-sneak breeds for six weeks, and then, just as he was closing in, he had to run across this bug-house Dan McGrew. Now, instead of bringing in three desperate criminals, he'd come dragging into headquarters–one wise-cracking loony prospector!

In spite of himself he grinned a little–grinned ruefully. Sure be a surprise for the Inspector. Good laugh for the boys, too. Yeah. After the way the Old Man had sort of set him up as an example–yeah, what a laugh.

Those coveted three stripes–where in hell were they now? Shot clear to the North Pole were his chances for that sergeantcy. And all because he had undertaken to save the life and mind of this wretched prospector. He had had to give up the outlaw trail, turn about and rush his patient out of these white hills of solitude, back to the land of men. Once outside, all the poor devil would need to make him as sound of mind as anyone, would be a few months' association with the fellow beings. A good rest-up in a hospital would do it. Even a jail. All the same –tough break for Corporal Thain of the Mounted....

Jim's thoughts were interrupted by Dan McGrew's deep voice.

"Stop!" the prospector called. He flung up his long arms dramatically. "I hear things."

Jim halted the huskies with a quick word of command.

"What do you hear, Dan McGrew ? Something like a street car, I guess?"

The prospector regarded him gravely. "Maybe," he conceded, "a very small street car. You know," he rambled on, "I got good hearin', Jim. Two years out there listenin' for somethin' to sound, all the time listenin'–But nothin' ever sounded. That's why I can hear so good. Ears had a long rest. Eyes rested, too. Nothin' to hear; nothin' to see. Just snow and quiet. That's all. Sometimes I thought I'd go crazy, Jim. And there wasn't any gold. The float signs lied. There wasn't any gold. There was a lady known as Lou. But I left her in Skagway to come and get some gold. Only there wasn't– There wasn't anything! Just snow!" His voice, which had been rising, grew tense now. "I'm tellin' you I thought I'd go crazy–"

"Sure," Jim soothed. He had learned just when to interrupt. "Lots of good men crack up in these long winters. This old devil, North–she can be bad medicine.... Well, we've had a little rest. Let's get going, Dan."

"Dan, who ?" the prospector demanded fiercely.

"Dan McGrew," Jim replied.

"That's right." The gaunt head wagged and the frost-scarred lips unbent in a contented smile. "But did you hear me when I said I heard something?" The smile broadened until the whole death's-head face was transformed. The man looked like some benevolent gargoyle. "After two years, I, the Dangerous Dan McGrew, hear something!"

"You, the who?" Jim asked, humoring him.

"I, the Dangerous Dan McGrew," he boomed, and waited expectantly.

"You, the Dippy Damn Loose Screw!" Jim filled in the gap

according to their ritual.

The prospector laughed uproariously.

"Poor loony," Jim muttered, and spoke to the dogs.

The huskies flung themselves against the traces with ludicrous suddenness. The two men shuffled on again, breaking trail for the sled. The dry snow seethed like foam around their webs.

"Poor loony," Jim repeated.

He remembered Dan McGrew as the fellow had been before he went inside two years ago–strong and broad of shoulder, with droll blue eyes that used always to be twinkling. Whooping it up with the boys, he used to recite by the hour. Kipling, Service, Knibbs. The one about the shooting of Dan McGrew was his favorite. He used to roll it out till his bass voice was heard a block away.

No wonder that now, in his temporary dementia, he thought he was Dan McGrew. Incongruous, though, in a way. He was such a good-natured, inoffensive cuss to be assuming the character of the Dangerous Dan.

"Jim," that resonant voice broke in upon the corporal's musings. Dan McGrew's voice was the only thing about him which two years in this great lone land hadn't changed. "I'm hearin' things again, Jim." Pushing back his loose dicky-hood, the prospector inclined his head and cupped his hand to a frost-blacked ear. "Maybe it's people," he added excitedly. "You know, I'm friends to everybody. Sure would like to talk to some people–"

"Forget it, Dan McGrew," Jim directed. "I've got pretty good ears myself, and I don't hear anything– Hey, wait!" Jim halted the dogs and stood silent, listening.

"By the great grizzly, you're right! There's an outfit around here somewhere. Why, Dan McGrew, you old son-of-a-gun; you've got better ears than the police force!"

Dan grinned delightedly as they stood listening for another moment. From somewhere far distant the cracking of a whip waved to them. Sound travels far in the frozen North. Jim got out his binoculars and trained them over the high-heaped glacial drift. Suddenly he held the glasses on a single point.

Slipping off an elk-skin mitten, he commenced thumbing the range adjuster. With the binoculars focused, he drew a quick breath. For a long minute he looked and when he lowered the glasses there was a chalk-white mark around his eyes where the rims had pressed into cold-reddened skin. His lips were frozen into a firm line. His face was grim.

"People–is it people you saw?" Dan McGrew was childishly excited. He clapped his mittens together and chuckled happily. "More people to talk to!"

"The only talking these people will do is with hot lead, Dan," Jim answered soberly. "That's Meti Paul out there. Meti Paul and his two pet knife-slashers, Emile and Charlie Eight-and-one-half-fingers. I was trailin' them when I found you. They're outlaws, Dan–killers. When they found I'd given up the trail, they turned around, I guess, and started back. They're headed straight for us, Dan, and we haven't got a gun!"

Five minutes later the corporal and his charge, buried almost to their eyes in snow, were snugged away at the mouth of a shallow ice rift. Farther back in the hollow, out of sight from those who would be passing by, the huskies squatted in their traces and licked at frosted jowls.

In low, tense tones Jim was hammering down the law to Dan McGrew.

"You keep still and stay hid, see?" he ordered. "Let these murderin' bush sneaks get clear past us before you do anything more'n breathe. Maybe they'll pass a short stone's throw away, huggin' the rim of the ice gorge out there. They'll be breakin' a new trail, so we can't say for sure just how close they'll pass."

"I get you, Jim. Listen: Dan McGrew Grew and the *loup garou*: That makes a rhyme, Jim. You ever hear about the time I fit the *loup garou*? I, the Dangerous–

"Yeah, I've heard that one, too. Listen, you Dippy Damn Loose Screw, keep your double-naught mind on what's happenin', see? This is plenty serious. If these ratty breeds find us here they'll kill us before you can say halellujah! Now, all I'm askin' you to do is to sit tight. This ridge hides our tracks. They'll never know we're here. They'll come on and they'll pass us, and we can swing in behind. By tonight they'll be down in the jack-pines. We can close in then and make plenty big whoopee. Old-timer, this is gonna be a real break. I mean it is. By the time you're well again you'll find Corporal Thain is Sergeant Thain."

"Oh, we'll meet these folks tonight, huh? That's nice." The pleased smile wreathed Dan's face again. "The more people I meet the quicker the better I like it, Jim. Any kind of people. I'm democratic–"

"Hey . . . listen!" Jim's voice dropped to a hoarse whisper. "Quiet now, Dan McGrew! Quiet! They're close. Wait till they get long past. Don't say anything more till I tell you."

Dan McGrew nodded vigorous acquiescence.

The cracking of the whip, the cursing commands of the drivers grew louder. Soon, mixing with these sounds, Jim could hear the groaning and creaking of a heavy wooden komatik, and the high-pitched, shivering squeak of the runners biting into dry snow.

Then the outfit swung into plain view. Jim watched tensely, holding his breath as they passed by not more than twenty yards away. First came Meti Paul, the rat-faced outlaw leader. His features were almost hidden behind the hood of his greasy drill parka.

After Meti trailed a half-starved team of huskies, bellies low, brushes drooping, long tongues lolling. Leaning on the handle-bars of the crude Indian komatik, the other two breeds shuffed along in the rear. Each of them shouted curses. One kept the long whip cracking over the dog's backs.

Jim's eyes gleamed. Sled dogs were man's best friend in the North; it made his blood boil to see the animals so cruelly treated. Well–he counciled himself grimly–after tonight these dogs would have an easier time.

As the last evil figure lurched out of sight beyond the mouth of the ice rift, the Dangerous Dan McGrew, who through it all had kept as still as a frozen ptarmigan, could contain himself no longer. He burst up suddenly from his snow covert and leaped out into the open. He started running, wabbling on his bush webs like some freakish disjointed hawk. And running, he pumped his long arms wildly up and down. Straight for the near brink of that ice gorge he headed.

"Look at me," he bellowed in his mile-carrying voice. "I'm a turkey buzzard. Watch me fly."

His huge distorted shadow jerked along behind him as he

ran, seeming at every step about to catch up.

For an instant Jim was stunned by Dan's unexpected act. Then his quick mind took command. As in a lightning flash he saw his predicament. If he acted at once he could turn back to his dogs and make a getaway before he was discovered by the outlaws. With his rangy, well-fed huskies and his light police komatik he could easily draw away from the breed's outfit. He could save his life–live to come back and fight another time.

But if he did that, Dan McGrew would dash out his poor twisted brains at the bottom of the gorge. Well, damn it, how much must he sacrifice for this crazy fool? He'd saved the fellow's life a dozen times already. There had to be a limit to this somewhere.

But even while his mind protested, his great heart was coordinating with his muscles in a bound that spumed snow ten feet in every direction. With long lunging strides he started closing up the distance between himself and the lurching lunatic.

He caught a flash picture of the three Metis standing in bludgeoned amazement. Then he fastened his attention upon that grotesque fleeing figure so rapidly nearing the precipice edge.

Hell's cinders, but that crack-brain could stretch 'em out! It wasn't human! Who would imagine that tall bag of bones could put up such a sprint ? . . . Why, confound it, if he didn't nail the fellow in about the next six steps, it would be too late.

Jim threw all his seasoned young strength into one last effort. No good! He realized that his hands could never grip the prospector before that poor sick fool had thrown himself over the cliff.

Suddenly, swerving his webs to one side, Jim hurled his bull body headlong through the air. His mittened hand closed over the beaver-tail of one of Dan McGrew's snowshoes. He held on grimly while the momentum of his dive catapulted him forward like a snow plow gone haywire. Dan toppled over backwards upon him.

Together they slid for the precipice, Jim desperately digging in with hands, head, knees, and number thirteen feet– the Dangerous Dan McGrew just coasting along on Jim's back, still weakly waving his arms and grinning his huge enjoyment of it all.

Inches away from the yawning gorge, Jim's fierce efforts brought them to a stop.

Jim had no more than dragged Dan McGrew a few yards back from the danger edge, than the two men found themselves hemmed in by the outlaw breeds. Two revolvers and a rifle threatened. The three men behind the guns were all jabbering at once and weaving about excitedly.

A cursing order from Meti Paul quieted Emile and Charlie Eight-and-one-half-fingers. Then the leader barked at Jim and Dan:

"Poot up de han's! Queek-fast, or I keel you, by gar, weeth two bullets–one for each."

Jim laughed harshly as he spread his mittened hands apart, palms outward to show that he was unarmed.

"Big talk, Paulie," he jeered at the squat, swarthy leader. 'You couldn't kill us with six bullets–twelve for each!"

"*S'pristi*, pert' soon I prove to you," the rat-faced Meti grated. Little black eyes glinted evilly from beneath his frost-rimmed parka hood. He jerked his head toward Dan. "You, too, Yellowstripe. Poot up de han's."

Dan McGrew made no move. "Yellowstripe?" he questioned in his booming voice. "You call me Yellowstripe? You think I'm an ornery Mountie? Just because I'm wearin' a few O.D. clothes of the corporal? Well, looka here; I'm no Mounted Policeman. Nol" He drew up his long disjointed form with an attempt at dignity. His eyes fixed their unwavering hypnotic stare on the shifty eyes of Meti Paul.

"I'll tell you who I am," he boomed again. "I'm the general of all the Mounted Policemen! *Kumtux?* I'm the famous Sloppy Sam McStew–" He shook his gaunt head. "I mean, the Dippy–the–" He turned with dignity to Jim. "What am I?"

"You're the Dangerous Dan McGrew," Jim pronounced emphatically.

He knew he could not shut Dan up. And if he encouraged the little play, perhaps some kind of advantage would result.

"You hear what he said?" Dan's fierce gaze swept the threatening Metis. "The Dangerous Dan McGrew–that's me."

His features relaxed; he smiled. "But don't be afraid, my friends. I won't hurt you."

"You–you weel not hurt us?" Meti Paul sputtered, his rat face darkening with anger. "*Sacre supplice*, wat thees ees? Some joke? By gar, I show you to joke!" He flourished his revolver.

"Wait!" Dan McGrew commanded. He advanced slowly toward the outlaw leader. A scant racquet's width away he stopped and reached out a mittened hand to tap gently on the black barrel of the threatening gun. "Why," he asked, in his rolling bass voice, "do you have this thing of evil? I'm fer disarmament. I am. Didn't you know I was for disarmament?"

Jim held his breath His pulse pounded in lean wrists. He knew these breeds, knew their violent elemental natures. At any second a gun might blast lethal lead. Desperately, he wanted to call out a warning, wanted to tell that poor demented fool for God's sake to step back. But the situation was taut; he feared the consequences of his own voice. Just a hair's weight more pressure on one of those gun triggers–

The deadlock broke suddenly. Before Jim's widening eyes Meti Paul started backing away! The Dangerous Dan was too big a dose for the simple, credulous-minded bushwhacker. That hypnotic stare, the death's-head face, the gangling figure, that incredible bass voice, together with Dan McGrew's boldness, made a combination which the outlaw breed could not withstand.

"You do good to back away, my friend," Dan orated. "I take guns away from people." He turned to Jim. "Don't I take guns away from people, Corporal?"

"You sure do," Jim humored him. "But let's let Paulie keep his gun for awhile yet. Let him keep it, see?" Jim strove to drive home his point. "Let him keep it."

Meti Paul started cursing, but the prospector's reverberating voice drowned him out. "I, the Dangerous Dan McGrew, am the greatest gun-taker-away-man in the Yukon. I, myself, all alone, in person, have taken away ten guns from ten men–single-handed, nobody helping me. And I have fought the *loup garou*– "

"Sh–shut oop!" Meti Paul bellowed. He waved his revolver. "I keel you, Yellowstripe; how you like dat?" He turned suddenly toward Jim. "Wha's matter weeth heem? Crazy, hein?"

Jim snorted. "Crazy? The Dangerous Dan McGrew crazy? Paulie, that's the biggest mistake you ever made in your life. Dan is the hellboilin'est, avalanche-eatin'est, grizzly-bear-chokin'est man in Canada. Why, I'm a six-horned bull moose–didn't you see him chasin' the *loup garou* over the cliff a minute ago? I had to hold him back so he wouldn't jump down there and pull the *loup garou's* tail. That's the kind of a fellow Dan McGrew is. Tough, that baby; it'd take a thousand bullets to bother him."

The uneasy breeds started muttering curses at mention of the *loup garou.* This phantom terror, this demon werewolf–as big, some said, as a winter lodge–was ever a menace to them. When things went well, the Metis, to a man, pretended not to believe in the *loup garou.* But when face to face with something which their untrained, superstitious minds could not grasp, it was easy for them to put credence in this bogy of their wilderness childhood.

Now in the light of day Meti Paul scoffed.

"Where hee's tracks, dees *loup garou*?" he demanded.

Jim laughed, shortly. "Whoever saw the tracks of the *loup garou*? You know as well as I that the *loup garou* makes no tracks."

Meti Paul grunted, batting his little eyes angrily.

Jim watched him, his own steel-gray eyes narrowing. His bronzed face was grim, his firm jaw tight set. Every rangy muscle fiber of his great body was tense. If these outlaws should give him one split-second break he would be ready to put up a life-and-death fight. It was to this end that he had abetted Dan McGrew in his tall stories. He knew the breeds would not swallow them whole. But he knew just as surely that the stories would start them worrying. If their attention could be diverted for just one instant. . . . It was his only hope.

Suddenly Emile jerked his head toward Meti Paul and commenced a savage tirade in his provincial French. Meti Paul answered him back as vehemently. Scowling, Emile left the circle and headed for the near icy hollow in which Jim's dog-team was secreted.

Jim had caught enough of their words to know what it was all about. Emile urged that they shoot their prisoners now and here. They could pitch the bodies over the cliff. Meti Paul said no. This was a too frequented pass. No use of their running any risk of being suspected of the murders

Better to take their prisoners down below timber line, leave the trail and spill their blood where the dead bodies would never be recovered.

He had sent Emile to search for the police sled and bring back any handcuffs he could find.

With the clicking of his own handcuffs over his wrists, Jim's hopes of escape from these bush killers sank to zero.

It was all Dan McGrew's fault, of course But then, he couldn't blame the poor fool. No. Dan didn't know what he was doing. It was the treacherous North–if you wanted to look at it that way–the North which had first beat Dan, and now, through Dan, was beating him. That old devil, North.

He had fought it all his life. Its demonic silences, its woolly-whippers beating down from the Polar seas. Its sixty-below cold which froze the breath before it left the mouth. Its spring torrents filled from bank to bank with tearing, grinding ice cakes. Its summer muskeg traps. And insect pests–black flies and mosquitoes, which put out the orange sun with their swarms.

Yes, he had met the North in fair fight and he had always won. But now the North had slipped up behind him. He had not thought his old enemy would take such cowardly advantage.

Dan McGrew's powerful voice sounded.

"Stand back!" he roared to Emile, who was approaching with another pair of handcuffs. "Stand back with those cussed rings. I, the Dangerous Dan McGrew, will never be handcuffed."

Emile, paused uncertainly, looking about with shifty side glances. Cursing, Meti Paul ordered the man to secure the prisoner. Emile pushed forward again, muttering to himself. He was more than a little afraid of this strange General of all the Mounties.

Dan McGrew backed away.

"What," he shrieked, "you would bind the wings of this

free-flying bird ? No! I'm not so easy as the corporal No! I'll get help from the *loup garou.*" He turned sharply about and started flopping his arms. "I'm a turkey buzzard. Watch me fly."

The crazy man took a few wabbling steps and this time he did fly! He paused not a second on the brink, but disappeared in a headlong plunge over the cliff.

The act was so unbelievable that no one moved, no one called out. But if, to Jim, Dan McGrew's suicidal action was a stunning blow, to the half-scared Metis it was like seeing a mountain or a glacier vanish. They were already near believing that Dan controlled some kind of evil power. Now they were sure of it.

As the outlaws stood rooted there in horror, the breath-catching realization came to Jim that Dan McGrew had given him a chance. Dan McGrew, dying, had given him a chance to live! Odd–the poor sick loony had got him into this fix by trying to leap from a cliff; now, the fellow's same insane urge had given him a fighting chance for freedom....

Silently, grimly, praying that Metis attention would be diverted for another split second, Jim shook off the heavy mitts from his wool-gloved hands. At the same time he wrung out of his webs. The snow lay thin over the ice here. He could move about more freely in moccasined feet. Good old number thirteens!

As he loosed himself from the encumbering racquets, his manacled hands rose high and crashed down against the head of the outlaw nearest him, the English half-breed, Charlie Eight-and-one-half-fingers. The outlaw slumped drunkenly to the snow, no sound escaping from his lips to mix with the dull thump of the steel links against his wolf-skin parka hood.

Meti Paul, who was standing closest to Charlie, wheeled at sound of the deadly thump, jerking around his revolver. Once he fired, but wildly, without aim. Before he could press trigger again, Jim's manacled hands had descended against the gun. There was a harsh metallic grating as steel scraped steel. The revolver flew out of Meti Paul's hand and tore part way through his snowshoe stringing.

The breed bent instinctively to recover his weapon, and Jim swung his steel-encased wrists upward. They connected with a sickening crunch against the side of Meti Paul's jaw. The outlaw leader, with a wolfish howl, slued heavily to one side and crashed on his back in the snow. Jim swept up the man's revolver from where it stuck in the *babiche* webbing, wheeled, and dove down behind the still form of the first outlaw he had dropped.

Two slugs from Emile's rifle fanned past his head as he dove. Other bullets sought him out as he lay there behind his human shield. But Emile, mad with excitement, was shooting raggedly. The bullets whanged past in the air or *zupped* harmlessly into the snow and ice at Jim's side.

Jim kept his head and at the first favorable second he leveled up the revolver with a steady hand. It was a short distance, and he was a sure shot. He knew that he could make his first bullet bite red.

"Dan McGrew, old fellow," his grim thoughts raced, "I'll get them all for you. This is the last–"

He pressed trigger.

A bullet bit red, all right. But it was one of Emile's rifle bullets creasing a deep furrow through the flesh of Jim's forearm. Jim's own gun lead–there wasn't any! Again and again he pressed trigger, but there was no explosion, no gun jerk, no slug hell-roaring out of that barrel.

He ducked back behind his shelter, flashing a glance at his useless gun. It was clear enough why it hadn't shot. Hammer broken clear off! He must have done it with the handcuffs when he knocked the weapon from Meti Paul's grasp. And Emile was circling around to get a better bead on him. Holy sun-dogs! Now things were bad!

Before Emile could blast away from his new position, Jim lurched up, holding his revolver above his head in a two-handed grip. With all his force he flung the weapon. It twirled through the air like a rock with an exploded dynamite charge behind it. Barrel-point first, the gun plunked into Emile's stomach. The outlaw let out an agonized groan and half doubled over. Jim cleared the space between them in a few strides.

Before Emile could straighten up, Jim clamped firm hands on the rifle barrel. He wrenched back with force enough to have uprooted a three-hundred-year-old cedar. Then, having secured the rifle, he thumped the barrel over Emile's head.

Once was enough.

Exultation swept over him. Single-handed, unarmed and handcuffed, he had cleaned up Meti Paul's cutthroat gang. Hey, man! He'd be Sergeant Thain, after all!

He turned to survey the scene of his triumph.... *Chawk*–a heavy object struck him alongside the cheek and temple. Out of the corner of his eye, as he crumpled under the blow, he caught a dizzy glimpse of a snowshoe beaver-tail, and of Meti Paul who had swung it.

So–that rat-faced leader had aroused himself at the last instant! Meti Paul –and that devil–North–had won!

Lying there on his back in the snow, Jim caught a confused picture of the leering breed as he bent over to pick up Emile's rifle. Desperately, Jim wanted to get up, but the paralyzed nerve centers would not send the impulse to his muscles. As in a horror dream he saw Meti Paul straighten with the rifle. Dimmer and dimmer grew the picture, but Jim was conscious that the gloating breed was fitting the rifle to his shoulder. Dully, he wondered if he would feel the pain.

He never knew, for before Meti Paul pressed trigger a huge shadow seemed to roll up from behind, engulfing the outlaw. Then the borders of this nightmare picture tilted dizzily and caved in from all four sides. For an instant there was blackness with swirling brilliants that came and went, came and went. And then there was nothing.

The booming voice of Dan McGrew sounded in his ears as Jim pushed himself up on shaky elbows and looked groggily around. But Dan McGrew was dead! Why–then so must he be. Well: Quick service they gave you. So this was heaven! Must be. No hot-blast heat waves fanning his face.

His vision cleared a little within the next minute and he identified his surroundings. So–same old earth, after all. Not heaven; not hell. Same old earth. He heaved a satisfied sigh. No place like home.

He flexed his wool-clad fingers. Not much colder now than before. He couldn't have been unconscious very long....

"You have a nice rest ?" he heard Dan McGrew ask pleasantly.

"Huh?–oh, yeah; I feel all refreshed, thanks." Jim waved a hand foggily before his eyes, and shook his head to clear his jumpy vision. "Hey, what happened, Dan McGrew?"

"I hit a fellow over the head and took his rifle away."

"Oh, that's how! And I thought you were crazy! Well, I'm sure much obliged. You've added years to my life. Listen, Dan McGrew: don't worry any more about that gold you didn't find. There's enough reward money up for these three carcajous to make you think you've uncovered a gold mine right here.... Hey, what you doin' here anyway? How'd you get here?"

The Dangerous Dan McGrew grinned broadly.

"First–I flew off the cliff."

"Yeah, I couldn't help but notice."

"But I didn't get far. A ledge caught me. I made a nice landing."

"Oh, I see. You'll be a good birdman some day." Jim sat up straighter. "Look here, Dan McGrew, you're not crazy; after the ledge caught you, you climbed back on top to help your partner beat up the outlaws, huh?"

"Yeah, that's substantially the thing, Jim. Y'see, I climbed back up so I could fly off again."

"Yee-ow-w," Jim groaned. He pressed tight hands to his throbbing head. "No, you're not crazy!"

The Dangerous Dan registered pleasure.

"No, I'm not crazy," he said, clapping his hands and jumping up and down.

"What I don't understand," Jim growled, "is, if you climbed back up just to jump off again, why in hell didn't you jump ? You Dippy Damn Loose Screw, how come you took time out to help me?"

"Help you, Jim ?" Dan McGrew asked, puzzled. "Were you in trouble ?" His voice vibrated with sympathy. "I'm sorry. I didn't know about that. I was delayed in flying off the cliff again because I had to take a rifle away from a man. Y'know, I believe in disarmament, Jim."

"Oh, yeah?" Jim gulped weakly. He hadn't even the strength to be sarcastic. He waved his hands feebly. "Well, hooray for disarmament!"

DEATH CACHE

By Lester Dent

A Silver Corporal Adventure

There is a legend in the Northland that those who seek to kill the Silver Corporal—that superhuman wraith of the frozen barrens—often die in traps of their own making.

A man stood spraddle-legged in the snow and shuddered again and again. The sweat of an overpowering terror steamed on his fat face. His teeth rattled.

He was stocky, well-fed, sleek, this man who stood too stricken by fright to move. He was a white man, yet native beadwork was plastered thick on his parka, on his bearskin trousers, and on his knee-high moccasins.

The man stared fixedly at a snow drift in front of him. Slowly, as if it hurt, he brought his rifle to his shoulder. No wind stirred the snow. Spruce boughs popped with the cold. The sky was gray, glazed, like the inside of an ice-cake igloo, a little smoked by clouds in the south.

He aimed his rifle at the drift–at a patch a yard across where the snow was roughened, as though recently stirred with a stick. The rifle slammed a bullet into the drift. The shot sound collided with spruce thickets, with a nearby hill, and bounced back like a hundred lesser shots. Again, the man fired, and again and again until his carbine was empty.

He drew a knife. Screaming madly, he sprang into the drift to stab and slash at the roughened snow. The blade dug deep, rasped on the frozen ground beneath.

Greater terror wracked the man as he found nothing in the snow. He reloaded his rifle and emptied it, shooting at many parts of the drift. But nothing happened–only the echoes that galloped around like roaring, unseen animals.

The man whirled and ran. He fell down in the deep snow, got up, fell again. It was as though he were living in a horrible dream, one of those nightmares in which the victim may try and try to flee, but cannot.

"He-l-p!" shrieked the man. Then he took to screaming madly at the bleak, empty wilderness about him. "Lemme alone, damn you! I ain't doin' nothin'! You keep away from me!"

The echoes mouthed the wild words faintly.

But there was no sign of the mysterious thing which had driven the fat man mad with fear.

The fellow floundered out of the snow drift. He plunged away with headlong blindness. Through a spruce thicket, boughs rasping his beaded garments, he dived. He reached a little clearing.

Seven men waited there, breeds and whites. An evil-faced, puzzled group, every man gripped a cocked rifle.

"The Silver Corporal!" bawled the running man. "I just saw him!"

Out of the grouped seven stepped their leader–gaunt Le Bouc.

Le Bouc had chin-whiskers like those of a billygoat. They looked comical. But no one ever laughed. Not at Le Bouc!

He was a fiend, this bony man with the goat whiskers. Nobody was sure how old he was. The Indians claimed he'd prowled the northland for a hundred years, and that he'd never die, because when he did, he'd be sure to take charge of hell. And since the devil reigning down there didn't want that to happen, he took pains to see that Le Bouc remained alive on earth.

Maybe the natives exaggerated. But they knew Le Bouc.

"*Sacre!*" Le Bouc raged. "What thees t'ing you say, Beautiful?"

"The Silver Corporal!" The fat, scared man called Beautiful waved his arms and steam came from his mouth with his words. "I seen 'im, I tell you! He rose right up out of a drift not forty feet from me! He looked right at me. I saw the starved face of 'im, his silver hair, and a thing coiled in his hand that looked like a white snake fifty feet long! And then he was gone!"

Beautiful flung up a pudgy hand–snapped fat fingers. "just like that, he went! Right into the snow! And I shot the drift full of holes, and jumped in and cut it to pieces with my knife. But there wasn't nobody there!"

"Wheech prove you ees crazy!" sneered Le Bouc. "You crazy wit' de cold!"

"I ain't nuts, Le Bouc! I saw him plain as I see you. A little shriveled guy. It was the Silver Corporal! Why even that infernal thing in his hand crawled around like it was alive–!"

"Shut up!" Le Bouc swiveled slowly to glower at his men, and his evil eyes widened with surprise. For on the faces of some of his men terror was stamped.

Two especially, the Tromso twins, had drawn apart. Back in their native Sweden, there was a standing reward of many thousands of kronas for these Tromso twins. They were small-faced, slender weasels of men. They looked like two slim boys. One was minus all his teeth.

"Silver Corporal bane bad medicine," muttered the one

who had no teeth. "Aye t'ank we bane go 'way."

"*Canards!* You ees start did t'ing an' you ees got to go t'rough wit' it!" snarled Le Bouc. He began to stroke his goat whiskers. The Tromso twins turned deathly pale and stumbled over themselves to get back with the others. When Le Bouc stroked his whiskers–that was a sign of death.

Who ees dis Silver Corporal?" growled Le Bouc. "He ees Mounted Policeman, *non?*"

"You ain't never heard of him?" asked Beautiful, with hanging jaw.

"*Oui!* I hear talk. But she crazy talk–talk dat not make sense. Dey say hees ghost of de snow, dat hees no can be killed, dat hees whip whole Indian tribe wit' de bare hands, dat hees no carry de gun. Such talk ees damn foolishness!"

"That's all true!" whined Beautiful. "It's a fact! Nobody knows any more'n that about the Silver Corporal, except that he's a Mountie. They say he can smell devilment, that he always turns up where there's trouble. Well, I believe it. He's found out what we're goin' to do to this Rhoda Dunsay girl. An' he's here!

"Show us where you see heem!" rapped Le Bouc.

"Listen, I don't want to go back there–!"

Beautiful choked on his whimpering objection. For Le Bouc was again pawing his whiskers. Beautiful had seen men drop dead when that happened. Trembling and sweating, he led the others back to the drift into which he had plunged his bullets and his knife.

Le Bouc was canny. First, he circled the drift, following the clearing edge, hunting tracks. Leafless limbs jutted over the snow drift, casting cold, pale shadows. Nowhere was there tracks, except those of Beautiful.

"You crazy!" sneered Le Bouc. "You no see anybody!"

"I did! I'm tellin' you the Silver Corporal has learned about this Rhoda Dunsay girl–!"

"Shut up! No dam' man can walk in de snow wit'out hees leave de tracks. You crazy an' t'ink you see somet'ing, an' you start shooting. Now let me tell you one t'ing–you act like dis again, and–!

Le Bouc fondled his beard. Beautiful shook from head to foot, but said no word. He knew he was near death.

"We go make plan, catch dis *Mam'selle* Rhoda Dunsay!" leered Le Bouc.

They wheeled, strode off. Le Bouc didn't look back. The others did. But they saw nothing, and the snowdrift was soon lost in the spruce.

A few minutes later, something happened in the clearing which they would have found of great interest. A small upheaval occurred in the snowdrift, far from the spot where Beautiful's bullets and knife had probed. And when the upheaval was over, a strange little man-figure stood there in the snow. His face looked drawn and scrawny. His hair waved erect in a great shock, the color of burnished silver.

His fur garments were unusual. Parka, trousers, both were tailored from the white fur of snowshoe rabbits. His *muck-a-lucks* were dyed white; his belt was of white leather. His clothing was thin, light. It seemed entirely insufficient to cope with the bitter cold.

He made a weird, mysterious figure there in the snow. He was almost child-like in his smallness. And a passerby would have had to look with a sharp eye to see him at all.

But by far the most remarkable thing about him was the object he carried in one hand. This was nearly forty feet long, thin and white and tough as a violin string. A heavy brass lass-rope honda weighted one end. But the thing was no ordinary lass rope, for it tapered in the fashion of a bullwhip, and the thin end terminated in a double-edged blade of steel, honed to a razor keenness on both edges.

The strange white rope seemed to come alive in the tiny man's hands. It crawled about. A loop, formed in the honda end, climbed upward and outward and settled snug on an overhanging limb.

With a bewildering agility, the mysterious little man climbed the rope. He reached the limb, ran along it with the ease of a squirrel, and with a swing across space that an onlooker would have sworn impossible, he reached another tree and was lost in the spruces.

There was left behind only a scuffed place in the snow drift to show where the Silver Corporal had departed.

Goat-whiskered Le Bouc had halted his men a couple of hundred yards distant. He was giving them orders.

"De gal weel be along soon," he said. "We mus' mak' ready grab her. Now, de firs' t'ing ees–"

He never got to say what the first thing was. The Tromso twins had drawn aside, two weasels out of the pack. Suddenly they both drew pistols.

"You men bane put hands up!" snapped the one who had teeth.

Le Bouc's face turned into a terrible thing to witness. He reached for his whiskers.

"Aye bane shoot!" warned the Tromso twin.

Le Bouc left his whiskers alone. He choked, snarled. "*Sacre!* W'at ees you t'ink you doing?"

"We t'ank we bane go away," said the Tromso twin who was toothless. "Aye bane hear plenty about dat Silver Corporal feller. Aye not like little bit. We bane go long way from here, and do him damn quick. After that aye not know where we ben go. To hell, maybe, huh?"

Both Tromso twins laughed at this wit. They backed away. The spruces received them, and they whirled and ran.

Hissing his rage, Le Bouc lunged after them, only to pull up with a disgusted snort.

"*Bien!*" he grunted. "She just as good dat we get rid of dem feller. We handle dis job alone. Den we not 'ave to divide up so many shares."

Four of Le Bouc's five remaining men, all four stolid ruffians, gave lip-smacking, greedy nods. The fifth–Beautiful–only gave a mighty shiver and wiped sweat off his face. He was thinking of the Silver Corporal.

Le Bouc scowled at Beautiful.

"You ees no damn good to 'ave aroun'!" he clipped. "*Sacre!* Dat be jus' like you to holler an' scare away de gal! So you better go down de trail t'ree mile. At dat point, de trail, she go t'rough a narrow canyon. You watch dere. De gal, should she get pas' us, you grab her!"

Beautiful quailed, pawing his beaded garments nervously. "Do I have to go alone? Maybe two of us ought to go an'–!"

"*Depechez-vous!*" hissed Le Bouc. "Hurry up!" And he touched his whiskers. Beautiful plunged away, going to wait at the point where the trail entered a narrow canyon, three miles distant.

"We weel wait 'ere!" Le Bouc grinned at the other four. "Dis place, she good as any. De gal be along soon. We grab her. Den, *bien*. Everyt'ing she rosy color."

One of the breeds smirked and fawned. "*Oui!* An' we don' have split wit' dem damn Tromso brot'ers. Good t'ing dey go!"

Le Bouc and his breeds would have changed their minds had they seen the Tromso brothers at this moment. That precious pair had circled back to the trail, reaching it at a point by which the girl should pass.

"Le Bouc, he tank he bane damn smart feller!" chuckled the Tromso brother who was without teeth. "He ain't smart as he bane tank he is."

"Yah," agreed the other. "We bane fool him. We make him tank we bane two scared fellers."

The first Tromso swept their surroundings with an involuntary glance. "Yumpin' Joe! You tank maybe Beautiful see Silver Corporal after all?"

"Naw. Beautiful bane coward. He no good for nothin' but play around with squaws. He bane go nuts."

Both twins stared along the trail, shading their eyes.

"Gal not in sight," said one. "Aye reckon it best we hurry, anyhow."

One Tromso now produced a piece of paper. He scribbled a note, using the snout of a .30-.30 cartridge for a pencil. He had a lot of trouble with the note, neither twin being able to write much English. Afterwards, he stuck the note in the split end of a stick, and stabbed the stick upright in the middle of the trail.

"It bane easiest for us to grab gal here," suggested the one without teeth.

"Yah, sure!" snorted the other. "And dot Le Bouc feller would get us. Le Bouc bane bad monkey. Our other plan bane best one."

They moved away, seeking spots where no snow lay, so as not to leave tracks. Soon, they were lost to sight.

From a boulder beside the trail stepped the tiny figure of

the Silver Corporal. His strange, springy white rope with the razor-sharp blade on one end, the heavy brass honda on the other, dangled over one arm. It seemed a living, squirming thing.

A leap took him to another rock, a second leap to a fallen log, a third to the trail. He left no tracks. He inspected the note, and read:

Miss Rhoda Dunsay,

Le Bouc and his breeds bane wait three hundred yards down trail for to grab you. Maybe it bane good idea to go around them fellers.

A friend.

The Silver Corporal replaced the note. His hands were bare to the bitter winds, yet they seemed flexible, impervious to the cold. He spoke suddenly to himself.

"This thing is gettin' to be a regular dang mystery!" His voice was strange–a wee, wispy, whispering thing, a sound as small as the man himself. But his words had a whang that smacked of the Wyoming cow country.

He glanced about. A couple of hundred feet away, a spruce tree towered. He moved to it, not once leaving a track. His weird, white rope looped upward, and a moment later he was perched in the tree, well-concealed among the evergreen boughs.

He watched the trail with eyes that were the same striking silver color as his hair.

Half an hour later, a girl swung down the trail. She was wiry, long-limbed, athletic, young. Her eyes were large, brown. They swept warily from side to side. She carried a light tumpline back pack with the manner of one accustomed to it, and she gripped a short 30-30 carbine with both hands.

She discovered the note, but looked around alertly before approaching it. Then, after she read it, she stared about even more sharply.

The girl stepped off the trail. Her going was silent, expertly swift. She circled wide of the spot where Le Bouc and his breeds were supposed to be hidden, then returned to the trail, since the spruce grew very thick and the going was rough.

But the Tromso brothers had been wildly wrong on their distance count. Le Bouc and his gang were waiting more like half a mile down the trail. When the girl returned to the path, they saw her.

"*Sacre!*" Le Bouc bellowed. "Catch dat she-fox!"

The girl heard his roaring voice. She turned and fled with long, determined strides. As she ran she tied a scarf across her face, to keep the bitterly cold air from freezing her lung tisue.

Once she stopped.

"You won't get it!" she shrieked at the men behind. "I won't give it up!"

She jerked her rifle to shoulder, aimed to the left of the five pursuers, and fired. Le Bouc and his four took to shelter, but came on, although not as swiftly. They kept hands over their mouth, breathing into cupped palms to protect their own lungs from the freezing air.

"Beautiful weel get 'er!" gritted goat-whiskered Le Bouc. "*Bien!* Dat was lucky t'ing I did, sending heem on ahead!"

The chase lend on and on. A mile, then two. Once, the fleeing girl wrenched the cloth from face, smacked it against a spruce limb to knock off the ice her breath had formed. Her features were Nordic. She had a large mouth and enough jaw to look determined. She had some freckles, but not too many.

She replaced the cloth and ran on. A ridge swelled up in her path. It was matted with spruce. Plunging into this growth, the girl was lost completely from view.

Le Bouc's men approached the thicket warily. They were excellent targets, should the girl be waiting with her Winchester. But no bullets met them, and they worked through the matted spruce.

The running figure of the girl was now not more than two hundred yards ahead. The trail angled down into a canyon.

"I 'ave tell Beautiful to wait een dat canyon!" hissed Le Bouc. "Hees damn well bettair be dere!"

"Hees dere!" shouted one of the breeds. "Look!"

The fleeing girl had passed between two large boulders.

A man was concealed behind them. He sprang out, took two lunging jumps. With both arms, he swung a clubbed rifle. The blow hit with a thud that reached Le Bouc's ears. The runner dropped like a shot rabbit, face-down in the snow.

"*Cochone!* Screamed Le Bouc. "You ees strike too hard! We don' wan' keel her until she ees tell us de t'ing we wan' to know!"

"Aw–hell! My foot slipped!" Beautiful whined back.

Le Bouc galloped up. He stared frantically at the body. Crimson was puddling about the head jammed in the snow. It steamed in grisly fashion from the scarf-swathed head.

Le Bouc dropped to his knees and grasped the hand of the fallen form, apparently with the idea of shucking off the scarf. But his hands seemed to become paralyzed, and he slowly kneaded the head under his fingers–it was horribly shapeless, like a broken egg.

"You 'ave bust her skull!" he screeched at Beautiful. He lurched to his feet. He yelled. He made mad gestures with his arms. He cursed. "You 'ave keel her! You damn fool! Dis a pret' kettle of feesh! Everyt'ing ees spoiled!"

And then Le Bouc grabbed at his goat whiskers.

Beautiful screamed like a hurt child. He knew what this meant. "Jeeze! Please don't! Please–!"

Out from under Le Bouc's beard came a nasty little black derringer. He kept it in a necklace-like sheath on his upper chest. He pointed it at Beautiful.

What came next surprised everybody. There was a strange sound, an abrupt, serpentine hiss of a sound. Le Bouc's gun arm jerked to the right. He was wrenched entirely off his feet. For an instant, he sailed through the air like a piece of paper on the end of a string. Then he slammed to the snow.

Came a low swish, and the uncanny thing which had seized Le Bouc's arm disengaged itself, slipped away through the snow. They all saw it–a thing like a thin, racing chalk line! A white rope!

"De Silver Corporal!"

Beautiful whirled and ran. Head down, breath tearing shrilly through his teeth, he plunged away. The breeds shot hateful stares in search of their phantom foe. One thought he saw something, lifted his gun. But there was a swishing sound, and a thin white snake seemed to strike from behind a boulder, a snake fanged with a razor-sharp sliver of glistening steel. The stroke ended with a *chuck!* The breed bleated in agony—for his right hand was suddenly hanging to his arm by only a hinge of hide.

"Rush heem!" bellowed Le Bouc.

His men charged the boulder, bounding around it from their side. But there was no Silver Corporal behind.

Another breed piped out in pain. Blood poured steaming from his shoulder. There had been no swish that time, no warning.

"You no can see heem!" the man wailed. Then he turned and fled, along with his fellow cohorts.

Le Bouc chased after them, howling, "*Cochons!* Cowards! Why you run away? De Silver Corporal don' even carry a gun!"

But Le Bouc showed no wish to remain and fight alone.

About the time the fugitives were lost to view in the spruce, the Silver Corporal appeared from behind a boulder. He ran to the form Beautiful had clubbed down. He wanted to see if the girl was really beyond help. He shucked off the wet red scarf.

"Hell's little tinkle-bells!" he gulped.

The dead person was not the girl, but the toothless Tromso twin.

The Silver Corporal reached up absently and finger-combed his shock of silver hair.

"Wearin' the woman's rig," he mused, the whang of a Wyoming range waddy more than ever in his wee voice. "Changed with her somewhere durin' the chase—probably in that spruce patch back a piece."

The weird white rope of a thing writhed on the Mountie's scarlet-coated arm, as if seized by rage. Wheeling, the strange little trooper ran from the spot. He did not follow the fleeing man, but went in the opposite direction, deeper into the canyon. His eyes searched alertly.

He soon found what he half expected—the end of a cord hidden beside the trail. He considered, then pulled it.

Instantly, there was a roar high up on the canyon wall. Thousands of tons of rocks, snow and gravel poured down, loosened by dynamite. Had anyone been coming along the trail, they certainly would have met death.

Many things became clear.

"The whole gang is after somethin' the girl has got," the Silver Corporal told himself in his small voice. "The Tromso twins double-crossed the others and left the note to get the girl ahead of Le Bouc. They knew he'd eventually follow her. The Tromsos grabbed her in that spruce patch, and one put on the girl's outer duds and came ahead to lead Le Bouc and his breeds into this death trap. Yeah, sure. But the Tromsos didn't know Beautiful was hidin' ahead."

The Silver Corporal knew all these men, their names and reputation. He knew most of the crooks in the north country. They, in turn, were not aware that he knew them, did not know he spent a lot of time just tagging them around. The couldn't understand the uncanny way he had of turning up just when they were in the middle of some devilment.

He was a man of mystery, this Silver Corporal. His ways were strange, the things he did even stranger. He hadn't been in the Northland long. But men who walked outside the law were beginning to curse the mention of his name, and shake in their moccasins when they heard he was in their vicinity. And sometimes they were seized with a wild madness on days when the wind went whispering across the snow and through the spruces and made sounds like the phantom Mountie's wee, small voice.

The Silver Corporal climbed over the debris blown into the canyon by the planted dynamite. He gave the dead form of the toothless Tromo twin only one glance, then went on past it and entered the spruce thicket where he was certain the Tromsos had seized the girl, Rhoda Dunsay.

In the spruces, he found the other Tromso twin, the one who had teeth. The man sat against a tree. He sat as though asleep. But it was a sleep from which only the devil's pitchfork would awaken him.

A knife stuck like a thorn from the man's heart.

The Silver Corporal did something that was rare for him—he shuddered. The eerie white rope of a weapon coiled over his arm seemed to shudder with him, as though it lived with him, exulting when he was pleased, suffering when he was pained.

The Silver Corporal was a Wyoming product. Down there, they put their women on pedestals, and all of the sex were considered sweet and good. It shocked the strange little man to think that one of them would stick a knife in a man's heart.

Of course, the girl might not have knifed the Tromso twin. The snow was too scoured by feet to tell a story. Prints made by the girl and others made by men were mingled together. Le Bouc and his breeds might even have come upon the Tromso twin and his young woman prisoner, killed the twin and taken the girl.

The Silver Corporal began to circle the spot, his metallic eyes roving alertly It would be no trouble to trail everyone who had been near this spot. But he followed no trail at the moment.

The Mountie's eyes were sharp. They missed little of what went on about him—they missed so precious little that the Indians had taken to claiming it was not human eyesight at all which he possessed, but thousands of eyes scattered all over the north so they saw everything all men did, even things done in the privacy of a cabin, tent or igloo. The Indians, however, are addicted to tall tales and legends.

The Silver Corporal saw the blue-black snout of a rifle crawl from behind a tree. He moved so quickly that he seemed to vanish momentarily and reappear a couple of yards from where he had stood. The rifle coughed a bullet that missed him.

Hunkering down, he sped to the nearest snowdrift and went into it headfirst, as a diver enters water.

Out of the surrounding spruces popped Le Bouc, Beautiful and the four breeds. Beautiful was still shaking and sweating, afraid to flee from the gang. The breed whose hand had fallen victim to the Silver Corporal's strange, deadly weapon staggered pitifully along in the rear. He had torn off his hand, thrown it away and bound up the stump. It was a wonder he was able to walk.

"After heem!" bawled Le Bouc. "Get heem!"

Le Bouc had, by curse and threat, pursued his men to come back and fight the Silver Corporal. They scattered to the far side of the drift. Shooting into the snow, stabbing with knives, they advanced.

But the Silver Corporal had expected that. He reappeared only a few feet from where he had entered the drift. None of the men saw him, for he scooted along, half buried in the snow. The spruces took him into their shelter.

He halted there to watch.

"*Sacre Dieu!*" gritted Le Bouc, right hand always on his goat-like whiskers. "We must keel heem!"

Bullets ripped through and through the snow.

Suddenly, in front of Le Bouc, there was a commotion in the snow. A figure stood up unsteadily.

"Don't shoot!" screamed Le Bouc, as his men leveled rifles.

The figure was that of the girl, Rhoda Dunsay. She was bound hand and foot with hide thongs; a wad of handkerchief silenced her jaws.

Le Bouc pounced upon the girl with a gleeful gurgle. "*Bien!* The *Bon Dieu* ees treat me swell!"

He seized her bound figure and threw her down. The others crowded around.

"What ees happen?" Le Bouc demanded of the girl, ungagging her.

"The Tromso twins seized me," she said in a voice coldly steady. "One of them stabbed the other to death, so he would not have to divide the loot. Then he took my outer garments and went off to lead you into a death trap."

The girl wore fuzzy brown woolen trousers, a woolen sweater, the garb which had been under her fur clothing.

"You fellers hunt de Silver Corporal!" Le Bouc rapped at his men.

They scattered, leaving the girl bound in the snow. They hunted fifteen minutes, but found nothing. They never even noticed where the Silver Corporal had entered the spruce–for the ghostlike lawman had a way of swishing his strange white rope over the snow behind him, smoothing it out until there remained hardly a trace that it had been disturbed.

Le Bouc came back and leered at the girl. "You mus' tell me where de cache is, *mamselle!*"

The girl looked at her scurvy captor. She shivered. "I'll tell you. I don't want to be tortured."

Le Bouc wasn't fooled. He sneered at her. "You t'ink de Silver Corporal weel help you, eh? *Non!* He weel never get you from Le Bouc!"

"I said I'd show you the cache," Rhoda Dunsay repeated .

"*Bien!* We weel keep de gun pointed at you head, an' should de Silver Corporal show heemself, de brains weel be blow' out of you pret' head!"

Le Bouc said this loudly–fairly screamed it. He wanted the Silver Corporal to hear that threat.

Taking the girl, leaving the body of the Tromso twins behind to freeze solid, they went down the trail. Two miles brought them to Le Bouc's hidden camp–to his sled and dog team.

They tied the girl on the sled, bundling her in furs. They didn't want her to die of cold before they were through with her.

Le Bouc indicated the breed who had lost a hand.

"You stay wit' sled an' guard de gal. Keep you gun press' tight to her pret' head. Should de Silver Corporal come, you shoot de gal. Savvy!"

The breed nearly fell over when he nodded. The loss of the hand had about done him in.

"Now we go take one more look fo' dat Silver Corporal!" rumbled Le Bouc.

They made a thorough job of the looking. They tramped the trail, the adjacent wilderness, hunting for tracks. They saw none.

Back to the sled they went. But the instant the sled was in sight, Le Bouc emitted a howl.

The one-handed breed was sprawled face-down in the snow.

Le Bouc sprang forward, crying, "De Silver Corporal ees get de gal!"

Then, observing a form squirming in the bundled furs on the sledge, he sucked in a sigh of relief.

"*Non!* De gal still dere." He bent over the motionless

breed, picked up the fellow's wrist, dropped it. "De dam' fool, hees pass out from dat hurt hand."

Le Bouc considered further, than announced they'd leave the breed there for the wolves. It'd be one less to share. He addressed the sled.

"Where ees de cache?"

Muffled, made barely understandable, a faint, shrill voice came out of the bundled furs. "Five miles along the trail, a cabin on the right. I'll tell you the exact spot when we get there."

"*Bien!*" said Le Bouc, much pleased. "We go to dat cabin!"

They hooked the dogs to the sledge and departed swiftly, callously leaving the wounded breed behind for the cold and the wolves.

The fat man called Beautiful brought up the rear. His beaded garments rasped together faintly as he trotted. An ugly hate burned in his eyes, flaming hottest when he looked at Le Bouc. His eyes held something else, too. Suspicion: a suspicion that the girl, Rhoda Dunsay, wasn't in that bundle of furs on the sled. Le Bouc had not looked inside them.

Beautiful, a leer on his round face, decided that the Silver Corporal had kayoed the breed guard, freed the girl from the sledge, and taken her place.

A horrible thought: It hit Beautiful like the palsy. But he said nothing about what he suspected. He, Beautiful, the white man who liked to play around with the native squaws, would hang back, let the Silver Corporal vanquish Le Bouc and the others. Then Beautiful would shoot the Silver Corporal, and have the contents of the cache for himself. He had a gun, a revolver. Le Bouc hadn't taken it. Le Bouc had apparently forgotten he had been on the point of killing Beautiful.

The cache! There should be a fortune there–wealth in furs and gold dust. Five trappers had been returning from the new gold country to the west, carrying their fur catch–and the cleanup from a rich placer gold stream they had found.

They had camped, unknowingly, in a cabin whose last occupant had died of smallpox. All five had been taken down with the dread disease. Four had died immediately. The fifth, father of the girl Rhoda Dunsay, had reached the settlement to the south. But pneumonia had seized upon him in his weak-ened condition, and he had succumbed. But before passing on, he had told Rhoda Dunsay the gold and furs were cached, and told her where the cache was.

Beautiful scowled. All this information had come to him from the squaw who had been nurse to the Dunsay man. The squaw was one of Beautiful's lady friends. But she hadn't heard exactly where the cache was.

Beautiful–he rasped his teeth at the memory–had gone to Le Bouc, told him the story–and here they were.

He plodded on, busy with his plotting. The cache belonged to him, not Le Bouc. And he'd get it. He'd let the little devil on the sled take care of Le Bouc and the others. Then he'd shoot the Silver Corporal. The girl wouldn't be hard to find. He'd kill her, too, and play safe.

Beautiful was feeling good. He even ceased to shiver and sweat.

The men came finally to a cabin and turned toward it. Very substantial, was this cabin. The logs were big, the roof of split slabs.

They pulled up before the closed door.

Le Bouc addressed the sled. "Where ees dees cache?"

"In the inner room, under the floor," came a prompt reply from the bundled furs. The voice was shrill, but very faint.

"Come!" boomed Le Bouc, and shoved open the cabin door.

Beautiful hung back, whining, "I'll stick our here and watch the dame!"

"*Bien!*" agreed Le Bouc. "Dat ver' good idea."

Le Bouc and his breeds swaggered eagerly into the cabin.

Promptly, Beautiful wheeled and ran. He'd watch this from the brush. The Silver Corporal would come out of that sledge and vanquish Le Bouc and the breeds. Then Beautiful would shoot him down–in the back, if he could.

Reaching the nearest spruce thicket, Beautiful whirled to watch.

Sure enough, the fur bundled on the sledge opened. A figure stood erect.

Beautiful nearly choked. It was the girl. The Silver Corporal hadn't taken her place!

Beautiful shook, began to sweat again. Suddenly, he seemed to hear a viperish swish of a sound–the sound of the Silver Corporal going into action. It must be his imagination, he thought in terror.

But it wasn't. There was a sharp rap as the heavy brass honda on the Silver Corporal's strange rope of a weapon hit Beautiful's temple. The fat man dropped, the beadwork on his garments grinding into the snow.

The Silver Corporal came on as silently as he had crept upon the fat dandy. He sped straight for the cabin door.

Passing the girl, he winked solemnly at her.

A volley of terror-stricken screams came out of the cabin. They were the cries of Le Bouc and his breeds. Their feet thundered for the door.

And they found something horrible in the cabin rear room.

The Silver Corporal reached the door first. He slammed it. There was a stout hasp. He clipped the leaf over the staple, thrust in a hardwood peg which, strangely enough, he had ready in his hand.

Le Bouc and his breeds hit the door. It held. They poured bullets into it. The wood was very thick; some of the bullets did not even go through.

The Silver Corporal ran to the girl, caught her arm and hauled her into the spruces. They stopped where they could see the cabin and still remain hidden. He beamed his little imp-of-mirth grin. Ordinarily, the bantam-sized Mounty was shy of women, and never spoke to a strange young lady without an introduction. But he'd been introduced to this one, back there where he had knocked the one-handed breed out and cut her bounds free and told her to bring Le Bouc and his men here.

The girl was puzzled. "What did Le Bouc find in the cabin?"

"The thing that scared him and the breeds, you mean?" the Silver Corporal queried in his tiny voice.

"Yes."

"That's the smallpox cabin. Your father left a warning sign on the door. I took it off and put it in the inside room. Le Bouc saw it when he got in there."

"You knew the sign was there–when you talked to me back

yonder?"

"Sure. I looked this cabin over weeks ago."

There was no more yelling and shooting from the cabin. The quiet was ominous.

"They'll get out!" said the girl bitterly.

The Silver Corporal's dry chuckle sounded like a wee, elfin thing in the cold silence. "I reckon they'll try!"

Rhoda Dunsay glanced at this strange little man wonderingly. She's heard talk of him. Weird tales, they were. Tales which said men who fought the Silver Corporal had a way of dying in traps of their own making.

She wondered if the cabin which held Le Bouc's gang could be such a trap.

The Silver Corporal abruptly spoke words which made her sure the cabin was indeed a trap.

"Le Bouc and them breeds have all been in jail a lot of times, and it didn't reform them," he said, speaking so low the girl could barely hear. "That sorta proves they're the kind of jaspers who don't ever reform. There's only one way to handle them kind."

The girl didn't shudder; she felt no horror at all. This mysterious little man was right. His way might be grim, terrible, but such was the way of the north.

She decided that she liked this little man, even if she hadn't known him long. She liked especially his homely, wrinkled grin.

Whur-r-room!

The cabin seemed to turn suddenly into a red-streaked monster of flame and smoke and debris, and jump a hundred feet in the air, stirring the snow, making boulders jump down slopes, making spruce boughs shuffle together. The wreckage settled slowly, in a tired way, stacking itself together with deafening crashes.

"That got 'em," said the Silver Corporal with simple certainty.

"What–what–?" The girl finished her query with a shiver.

"There was a dynamite case with two sticks, fuse and caps in it," the Silver Corporal murmured dryly. "It was on a shelf. But two more cases, plumb full of dynamite, hidden under the floor, right by the door. They tried to blow open the door, an' the boxes under the floor let loose."

The girl shut her eyes tightly. She had to ask a question.

"Did you–plant the dynamite?"

"Nope. Believe it or not, it was just where I found it when lookin' the cabin over a few weeks ago."

The girl studied him. "You're a strange person. How did you happen to get on Le Bouc's trail in the first place?

The Silver Corporal shrugged. For a moment, he thought he wouldn't answer. He had already talked more than he usually did. The girl must be the cause of that. Ordinarily, he was scared of women. But, somehow, he wasn't scared of this one.

"I just crossed their trail," he grinned. "Figured so many bad actors couldn't be together for no good reason, an' tagged along to see what devilment they were up to."

She did not speak at once.

"The furs and gold are cached behind the cabin," she said finally. "If you'll help me take them back, I'd like it–a lot."

Long ago, the Silver Corporal had made himself a rule. It was a rule to always steer clear of women–especially the pretty ones. So far, he'd stuck to it. This hadn't been hard, because he was scared of women. But here was one he wasn't scared of. He looked into her brown eyes, felt himself slipping, tried to count the freckles on her nose to get his mind on something else–and failed.

His rule was the same as broken.

DOOM ICE

By Dan O 'Rourke

Stalemate! Behind McCloud and his prisoners roared the numbing, trackless blizzard.... Ahead stretched a seething, grinding chaos of floe-ice hell.

McCloud growled out a guttural order to the dogs and pulled back on the upright to bring the fast moving sled to a quick halt. He snatched his rifle from under the tarpaulin cover of the load and whirled.

As far as he could see into the desert of snow and rocks, nothing moved. Not a tree, not even a bush of hardy willow, broke the dead monotony of Arctic landscape. Yet out of that rolling wilderness of gray and white, a rifle shot had just cracked spiteful venom.

As McCloud stood straining his eyes into the treacherous half-light of mid-forenoon, it came again. First one shot, then a salvo like the snarling of a machine gun sent the snow spurting up around him in a shower of six-inch geysers.

McCloud growled an oath into the fringe of hoar ice that rimmed his parka hood, and tossed the rifle back upon the sled. Behind the craggy rocks that thrust up jagged teeth either side of the long, shallow valley, was cover enough for an army. There was nothing to do but run for it.

As the dogs plunged off at a gallop under the urging of his twelve-foot rawhide whip, McCloud clung to the cross-piece and figured rapidly. It was early March. The iron hand of winter still gripped the northland. No Eskimo lived hereabouts. No white man had wintered within a hundred miles. And yet, out of that twilight of frozen solitude, a rifle had vomited steel menace.

Sergeant Angus McCloud of the Mounted had two errands in the Arctic. One was to bring in Stevens, the redheaded killer whose name was mentioned only in whispered curses throughout the northland. The other was to get news of the missing sealer, China Queen. Due at Barrow in September, she had last been sighted passing Point of Whales, a month later, headed the wrong way. What had become of her? Why had she deliberately run away from her winter quarters?

Some half-hour after he had been fired at, McCloud came to the end of the long valley whose bottom he had been traveling for four days. Straight ahead, the frozen surface of Christmas Bay spread a gray-white, desert flat upon the boundless circle or the Arctic Ocean. McCloud halted on a little level space above the last sharp pitch down to the ocean floe, to look around.

In front, the ice heaved up a fifty-foot ridge of jagged blocks and valleys. To right and left, the side walls of the valley ended in massive knees of lava that lurched upward, hundreds of feet at a leap, in dizzy cliffs and white-splashed jet.

McCloud's glance completed the circle, and froze in astonishment. Behind him, jammed back in a crevasse under a crag, stood a cabin. There was light enough to show it was made of driftwood, with earth heaped over it to keep out the wind. No one was in sight, outside, but light showed through the small window under the roof.

McCloud turned, crossed over to the shack, pushed open the door without knocking, and paused on the threshold. The wavering flame of a candle stuck in a potato on a table lighted the figures of five men. Three were the ordinary type of Arctic wanderer–roughly-dressed, hard-bitten customers badly in need of baths and shaves. Nearer to McCloud, tipped back in a rough chair at the table, loafed a figure that reminded him of nothing but a gorilla. He was short and thick-set, with vast' beetling shoulders, and arms reaching nearly to his knees. Above his matted black beard, a pair of eyes, red and beady as hot coals, glittered and blazed.

McCloud stepped into the hut, shutting the door behind him. His inspecting glance had showed him, among other things, rifles stacked in a corner, and a radio outfit on a wooden stand.

"I'm Sergeant McCloud of the Mounted," he stated quietly, his eyes traveling coolly around the circle of tense, hostile faces. "Last place I expected to find anybody was here. Who are you men, and what are you doing ?"

For a long instant no one spoke. Then the big man spat ten feet to the corner, and uncrossed his legs.

"Who we are, en' whet we're doin' is our own business, mister," he drawled. A mocking grin stirred the porcupine's quills around his white, snarling lips. "What you got with you that says we got to tell you something, huh ?"

A rattle of sneering laughter gritted around the cabin. McCloud felt the blood surge under his cheeks. But all his training, as well as his Scotch shrewdness, warned him to go slow. They were five to one against him, and set for murder.

McCloud shifted his gaze to the fifth man, who had sat without moving or speaking, idly puffing a huge pipe, in the far corner. He was a tall, broad-shouldered customer, with a white face, penetrating blue eyes and a shock of blood-red beard and hair. McCloud pushed his way between the others and up to him. For a moment he stood in front of the red-haired man without speaking. As their glances met, an expression of perplexity had narrowed the gray eyes of the officer. It was the red-haired man who spoke first.

"Well, what's the idea? If you've got anything to say, spit it out."

"I was wondering where I'd seen your face before," answered McCloud thoughtfully. "On the police flyers–no, that wasn't it. In a lot of places the papers, most likely. However, it doesn't matter. You're Stevens, aren't you?"

The big man nodded. "I'm Stevens," he grunted. His voice rasped jeering mockery. "What about it?"

McCloud felt in his pocket.

"I've a warrant for your arrest," he said. His voice was as gentle as if he were ordering a cup of coffee. "Murder's the charge. Hold out your hands, Stevens."

Stevens sat without stirring. Behind McCloud, the gorilla slipped silently out of his chair. A ribbon of white steel gleamed in the candle-light as his arm rose over McCloud's head.

McCloud could not see him, but he heard the giant's quick intake of breath, and his gritting step on the rough floor. The officer spun around, his hand dropping to his holster, but he did not pull the gun. Neither did the knife plunge downward.

A crackling, rasping sound, like the ripping of sail-cloth, suddenly crashed out in the cabin. It died away, and a voice not belonging to any of those present began to speak:

"This is station WGAZ with a message for any post near Fox Inlet, British Columbia. A runner from the Inlet–just arrived at Ingok–reports food supplies–supposed to be left there by sealer China Queen–never arrived. Twenty persons at Inlet– great danger of starvation. Any station receiving this–with food to spare–rush to Fox Inlet."

The voice faded in a gritting crash of static. For an instant of tight silence, nobody moved. In that split second of hesitation, McCloud had stepped sidewise so that his back was against the wall and his face to the others. The chill blue-black of the Mounted service revolver gleamed out of his furs. His voice whip-cracked authority through the cabin.

"You men there, step up one at a time. Shell your guns and knives out on the table," he directed. "All right. Now, you there, with the black beard, who was just going to stick me, how much grub have you got in this place ?"

The gorilla jerked his head toward a row of shelves over the bunks. On them were stacked a few bags of flour, a strip of bacon, and a dozen or two tin cans.

"Five of us, an' not enough fer a week," snarled the giant, his beady eyes blazing like a rat's. "Wot's th' big idea, starvin' of us so's to feed somebody else, feller? Take any of that grub, an' you'll land in hell so sudden–"

"H'm.... Enough for you for a month, but no good for the crowd at the Inlet," mused McCloud. "What's over there?"

His eyes rested on the opposite corner of the shack. A tarpaulin had been hung from the roof, screening it. None of the men answering his question, McCloud strode over threw back the canvas, and peered into the corner. The closet was filled–crammed from floor to roof–with food. Two barrels of flour, cases of bacon, stacks of tin cans–grub enough to stock a hotel.

McCloud wheeled to the gang. "Where'd all that grub come from?"

In the gripping silence that sang like high-tension current through the shack, McCloud knew he was treading close to peril. Where the grub came from was a question the rats would take a chance against his bullets with before they answered.

"Well, it don't make any difference, anyway," said McCloud, finally. "I'm taking a load of this up to the Inlet. Any funny business while I'm loading it, and I shoot to kill. Keep back where you are, and keep quiet."

McCloud's first act was to gather up the miniature arsenal on the table, also the guns stacked in the corner, and take them outside. He hid them in a rock crevice out of sight of the hut and went back. Ten minutes was enough to carry out and pile on the snow the grub he hastily selected–flour, bacon, molasses, rice, dried apples, beans. His sled was larger than he had needed traveling alone. Now the extra size was going to prove a godsend.

McCloud put the stuff on the sled, lashed it, then re-entered the hut. During all this time none of the gang had moved. Silent, tense with murderous hate, the ring of bearded faces had glared at him each time he crossed the threshold.

McCloud went up to Stevens.

"This Fox Inlet business doesn't make any difference about you," he said. "I'm taking you up there with me, first. Then we'll go back to headquarters." He pushed the blue snout of his revolver a little further out of his furs. "Coming–or want to fight about it?"

Without a word, Stevens knocked out his pipe, dropped it in his pocket, got up, pulled parka, fur, trousers, boots and mittens from a hook, and donned them.

He strode between the others to the door and through it. Not a sound came from the gang as McCloud followed him.

"You'll travel in front of the sled all the way," McCloud told Stevens when they got inside. I'll be either on the tump line, ahead, or behind at the upright. Remember, I'm carrying my gun in my hand, and the warrant only tells me to bring back the body of John Stevens–it doesn't say the body has to be alive. All ready–mush!"

The shortest distance to Fox Inlet was overland, but the easiest way was on the ice along the shore. With the heavy sled, the level going more than made up for the forty or fifty extra miles.

Once through the pressure ridge and down on the sea ice, the overloaded sled ran fairly well. Only one thing worried McCloud. The foot he had frosted a week before, when he broke through a crevasse, had started to pain and swell two days ago. Before taking the load on the sled, he had ridden all he could, to favor it. Now, after the battle of fighting the heavy load through the chaos of ice boulders and ravines at the tide crack, every step was costing agony. If it should get much worse–blood poisoning or gangrene.... McCloud put the thought out of his mind. When they had covered what he thought was eight miles, he stopped to boil tea and eat crackers and jam.

In the course of rummaging over the sled load, separating his own outfit from the supplies for the Inlet, he happened to overturn a box. On the bottom was something he had not noticed when he packed it–a square of cardboard. There was writing on the cardboard.

McCloud lit a match and held it close. He read the lines twice, turned the box over to keep Stevens from seeing, and stood pondering.

> *Sealer China Queen seized this day, December 19, by mutineers from the crew. They have killed five hands that refused to go in with them. They have disarmed me and shut me in the hold. They are going to kill me at daybreak. The leader is Tom Quirk, called the gorilla. If this comes to the eyes of any living man besides these devils, it is my last word and testimony that Quirk is the ringleader of the mutiny and murdered five with his own hands.*
>
> *JOEL SLAVIN, Master,*
> *Schr. China Queen,*
> *December 19, 1941.*

That explained everything, mused McCloud. The mutineers from the China Queen had found themselves shut in by the ice, gone ashore, and erected the cabin, furnishing it with the ship's stuff, even to the radio. Someone of them had been out hunting, seen him coming along, and tried to dust him off before he ascertained the truth.

McCloud understood now why the gang in the shack had not tried to rush him. By the same reasoning, he must travel and travel fast.

He rose, finished packing the sled, and ordered Stevens and the dogs to get going. Hours passed. As the chill March sun slanted behind the rimming mountain peaks, a drab gloom spread over the wilderness. McCloud was going badly, now. Leaden weights dragged at his limbs. The pain in his foot had grown to a throbbing ache which pulsed agony up his leg to the waist.

After what seemed an eternity of torture, a jagged barrier of inky jet loomed up out of the gray light shrouding the void. It was the shore cliffs at the opposite sides of Christmas Bay.

Following along the base of the pressure ridge, they came to where a stranded iceberg loomed, a gray mountain of colossal mystery in the star-shine. McCloud cruised along its flank till he reached an elbow, and swung around it. A hundred feet farther back he found a corner between jutting ice cliffs with a fairly level bottom.

McCloud slipped off the tump line and went about making camp. In a daze of weariness he set up the tent, served fish to the dogs, boiled tea, and warmed a can of tinned beef over the patent stove. When they had finished eating, the sergant fumbled in his duffle bag. His hand came out with two pairs of irons—one each for wrists and legs.

"I'm taking no chances, Stevens. Lie down," he ordered, briefly.

The thin white lips of the big man curled derisively.

"Sounds as though you'd been reading dime novels, McCloud," he sneered. "Pity you haven't got a tree to tie me up to."

"Now the ankles," directed McCloud.

When Stevens was shackled, arms and legs, McCloud pulled a sleeping bag off the load.

"I'm going out," he stated, briefly. "I may be some time. Liable to get cold. Better get in here."

Stevens did not answer. While McCloud held the edges of the bag, he wriggled and flopped, seal-like, down into the fur cavity. Without a backward glance, the sergeant picked up the rifle and vanished from Stevens' sight around the corner of the berg.

Hugging the base of the ice mesa, McCloud felt his way through the semi-darkness to the corner. Feeling around till he located a smooth place on the floe, he sat down and leaned back against the berg. He intended to stay awake, and watch, but he had been close to twenty hours without rest. Weariness flooded his brain with numbing poison, hung window weights of drowsiness from his eyelids. In five minutes he was asleep.

McCloud had no notion of how long he had slumbered when he awakened with a sudden start. He sat motionless an instant, trying to collect his dizzy senses. What had started him? It was an hour before midnight. The pale, pulsing streamers of the Lights drew green and purple veils across the zenith. Immeasurable silence, rigid with cold from the snow-fields of the Pole, roared in his ears. But he had heard something else.

A black form bulked between McCloud and the stars. In the chill night of the Aurora, a knife-blade gleamed like a wolf's fang.

McCloud swept out his hands, fumbling for the rifle. He could not find it. The burly mass hurled itself forward in a swift, soundless leap, like the swooping of a killer owl. It caught McCloud on the chest and crashed him back against the ice-berg. Wedged into a pocket, he felt the man's knees crushing his ribs. The white fang of steel soared overhead, and poised a thin second before the downward thrust.

McCloud shot up a hand and gripped the wrist. With the other he fumbled under his parka. His groping fingers found the butt of his revolver, and slanted the gun upward.

McCloud fired, and the steel muscled mass on top of him relaxed. With a coughing sigh, the big man slumped sidewise, and rolled off to the ice.

McCloud pushed himself up on his feet and pulled out his gun. At the sound of the shot, the white wilderness around him had suddenly grown dappled with dark figures. The crash of big-calibered revolvers echoed hoarse coughings between the ice ridges.

A slug tugged at McCloud's parka. Another crashed into the berg six inches from his head, sending a shower of ice chips into his face. Jammed back into a narrow elbow of the berg, he fired savagely at every flash and every blotch of gray-black shadow that stirred against the white background.

McCloud shot out his clip, reloaded the gun, and stood listening. Little by little the echoes thundering back and forth between the ice cliffs died away, and silence fell.

Ten feet in front of the sergeant, a black shape lay sprawled over the ice. Soundlessly, McCloud crept up and shook it. The man was dead. On hands and knees, the sergeant went on. He came to another figure, likewise limp with the weird, uncanny looseness that means the end of everything.

McCloud stopped to check up. There had been four men besides Stevens back at the cabin.

He whirled and threw up his gun. From out of the darkness at his side had come a groan. Jamming his revolver in front with his right hand, he reached an exploring left into the blot of ink. His fingers brushed the bosom of a parka. He gripped it and pulled the man up into the star-shine. It was Quirk, gorilla ringleader of the *China Queen* mutineers. He was still alive.

"Where you hurt, Quirk?" demanded McCloud shortly.

"In the leg, damn you!" Quirk snarled. "Leg an' arm, curse yuh to hell!"

The gorilla broke into a storm of luridly profane abuse. McCloud stood motionless, trying to collect his thoughts. Since discovering Captain Slavin's note, and realizing that the gang back in the shack were the mutineers of the *China Queen,* he had been intending to pick them up on the way back from Fox Inlet. Performing that errand of rescue, and carrying Stevens along at the same time, had seemed about all he could manage. Now fate had dumped into his hands a man sure to be twice as badly wanted at headquarters as the redheaded killer–and wounded, at that.

McCloud stooped down, pulled an arm of Quirk's over his shoulder and half led, half carried the fellow back to the tent There he lighted a candle and melted chunks of ice for hot water. He bathed and dressed Quirk's wounds.

The duffle bag yielded another set of ankle and leg irons. When the gorilla was shackled and laid away in the other sleeping bag, McCloud dropped on the snow and slept. Whatever was to be done later, first he must rest.

Hours passed. The sound of voices roused him. Quirk and Stevens were whispering. At his first movement of wakefulness, they started apart.

McCloud got up and went about cooking breakfast. The pain in his foot was torturing. He limped badly. The eyes of the two big men followed him through every move. McCloud knew what they had been talking about. They had been planning to wait till he got sick and weak, then jump him.

McCloud unshackled his prisoners' hands, and served tea and food. Sitting the width of the tent away from them, he likewise ate.

"When you skunks didn't rush me back at the shack, I figured you intended to trail me and do your dirty work when it was safer–while I was asleep," he told Quirk when he had finished. "You walked straight into my little trap. But you used poor judgment about one thing. You got a bullet in the leg when it ought to have been your head.

"We're going right on to the Inlet. You can't walk, so you'll have to ride. I've got a pair of spare sled runners along. You'll be lashed to them–mounted on skids, as you might say–and hitched on behind like a trailer. If you don't find it pleasant, you can put in your time thinking about the captain of the *China Queen* with a knife in his throat."

Paying no attention to the torrent of foul curses that poured from Quirk's lips, McCloud pulled the extra runners out from under the load. Dumping Quirk out of the bag, he lashed the gorilla, still in his irons, to them with rawhide. Out of more rawhide, McCloud made another tump line, some ten feet longer than the one already hitched to the sled. He fastened one end of it to the cross bar, then went and unlocked Stevens.

"From now on, you work your board, Stevens," said McCloud. "You're going to get into that and pull."

Stevens shot McCloud another of the half-amused, half-scornful glances so much more expressive than any words, and then quickly stepped forward to the tump line.

With McCloud and Stevens pulling in front with the dogs, and the huge figure of Quirk yawing from side to behind, the line moved out upon the ice. Hour after hour, the strange procession plodded northeast. The sun sank, and long drab shadows stole like ghosts over the desert. The cold tightened, gripping the men with giant's fingers, searching the joints of their clothing with needle thrusts that burned like fire.

Six hours after starting, McCloud called a halt. He boiled tea and served it with a cracker to each of the prisoners and to himself.

Quirk gulped down the tea at a swallow and hurled the cracker into McCloud's face.

"Starving us, hey?" he snarled. "Throwing us slops when you've got plenty! Let's have some grub–none of your damned pie-crust, feller! There's food on that load. Plenty of it. Unpack it."

"That's for Fox Inlet," replied McCloud. "We don't touch a crumb of it. We three will live on what I have left when I struck the shack–rations for one man for one week. We'll make it go."

Again Stevens, the silent man, smoked without speaking, but out of the black throat of Quirk rasped a growl of fury. The red, beady eyes under the beetling forehead glittered in a surge of venom. He leaned close to McCloud.

"All right fer now, yuh skunk!" he snarled. "But wait. In a couple days yuh know what's goin' to happen, huh? You're goin' fluey, cop, that's wot. You're goin' off your cock-eyed bean. An then I'll give ye a surprise. I'll give ye a party, ye damned swab–"

McCloud finished his tea, stumbled to his feet, ordered Quirk back into his handcuffs and his bag, and lashed him on the skids again. Stevens stepped into his place at the tump line without orders. McCloud shouted to the dogs, and the heavy sled commenced to creak and groan over the *sastrugi*.

The hours dragged on. McCloud moved by instinct now. Weariness flooded him like a numbing poison. The throbbing of his foot pulsed agony with every step.

Another four hours, and McCloud gave the order to make camp. Going through the load, he found that there were only four more cans of beef. Two nights, two mornings, and then–"

He looked at Quirk and Stevens. As usual, they were sitting silently watching him. He knew that when he had gone to sleep, they would slide and wriggle over, close together, and perfect some evil plan. His jaw granite, he ordered them into their bags and shackled them, hand and foot.

The next day was like the last one. Night of the second day saw the end of the tinned beef. There was nothing now but tea. Also, the fish for the dogs was all gone. McCloud shot one dog and fed its quivering flesh to its team-mates.

The sergeant's brain was getting hazy. The pain in his foot seemed to swim up in dizzy whirlings through his head. He got a piece of rawhide, pulled off his mittens, and with his left hand lashed the fingers of his right hand tightly around his revolver. He inspected the job and grunted grim satisfaction. No matter what happened, now, he could never lose the gun. Never for an instant, awake or asleep, sane or out of his head, would his finger be off the trigger.

They lay down and slept, wakened and marched on. McCloud had no idea how long they struggled before they stopped for tea. He did not try, this time, to start the stove himself. Sitting with his back to a hummock, he ordered Stevens to do it. Sevens brought him his tea first, then gave some to Quirk. Last of all he poured his own. McCloud grinned, and thought of the revolver lashed to his hand. Stevens knew it was there.

When McCloud started toward Stevens and Quirk to lock them up that night, he fell flat forward on his face. Quirk roared snarling triumph.

"What did I tell you, you swab?" he jeered. "Ye're about all done, now."

McCloud ordered Stevens to lock up Quirk. The silent man obeyed, handing the keys to McCloud when he had finished. Then the sergeant, on hands and knees, snapped the irons about Stevens' wrists and ankles, and helped him into his sleeping bag.

After breakfast the next morning, McCloud told Stevens what he had decided to do now that his foot had finally gone back on him. He had figured it out the night before. He would have Stevens take off the load of food, get on the sled himself, and then have Stevens pack the load back, around him. It would be a tough pull for Stevens, alone, McCloud realized. But a little real work wouldn't hurt him. And it probably would be the last he was ever likely to have.

The big man nodded silently as usual, and began to pull the boxes off of the sled. When he had finished, McCloud got on, leaning back against a couple of cases. Stevens packed the load again around him and between his legs, some of it even on top of him, and tied it on. As Stevens worked, McCloud's finger never left the trigger of the revolver lashed into his hand under the mitten.

The load of two men and food was hard to start. The dogs were now so worn that they pulled hardly at all. Stevens' big figure was bent into a bow, and his breath came in panting gasps before the heavy mass began to slide.

They made slow progress. At times McCloud would drift off into a haze of half-consciousness. Then would come an instant of sudden wakefulness when he would start up, drenched with cold sweat at the thought of what Stevens would do to him if he realized the truth. At such times he would note the killer's figure plodding at the tump line, feel the cold butt of the revolver between his fingers, and sink back comforted.

Noon came, but Stevens did not stop for tea. At night, McCloud sat back against a pressure ridge while the redheaded man made camp under his orders. When locking up time came, he carried the gun naked in his hand as he crawled around, putting on the irons.

In the morning, McCloud shot another dog. Stevens cut it up and distributed it. The men drank tea and pushed on. It was all Stevens could do to start the load.

The dogs were useless.

Wearily the hours dragged away. There was no longer any such thing as day or night for these three men. They marched, halted, drank tea, killed a dog to feed the others, flung down their throbbing bodies on the snow to sleep, arose, drank more tea, and marched again. Fever and pain flooding his brain with fire, McCloud crept about on hands and knees, locking and unlocking his prisoners.

Stevens never spoke. As silent as if deprived of speech,

his great furry figure labored, bent double at the tump line. Always and ceaselessly, as the grey days stretched past, Quirk cursed ribald blasphemies from the rear. Stevens' face, as he bent over McCloud with the tea, was gaunt, cadaverous, putty under red fire–the face of a walking corpse.

Dimly, McCloud realized that it was noon. There were no longer any dogs hitched to the sled. Alone, Stevens lurched and strained at the tump line.

It was noon, but it was not light. A strange, gray-yellow luminance filtered down through the clouds. The air lay inert, dead calm.

From far out on the waste, weird sounds began to drift. Deep sighs breathed through the void. A gust of wind, razor-tongued with chill, lashed into McCloud's face, and vanished. Muted with vast distance, a gigantic fiddle-string vibrated terrific resonance.

A snow-flake spat into McCloud's mouth. Another. Far to the north, a white curtain thickened.

Next instant a swirling hurricane of wind and snow swept down on them, blinding, suffocating, crushing out breath as with a gigantic hand.

In the vortex of this howling maelstrom, thought itself seemed to be numbed. No living creature, it seemed, animal or human, could stand before it. Yet out in front, Stevens' big form, bowed double, still surged, bear-like against the tump line.

For some minutes, seeming like so many hours, Stevens inched ahead. Then suddenly, McCloud saw that he had stopped. He was standing still to listen. Almost instantly, McCloud realized why. The fierce pressure of the on-shore gale against the ice had set the floe in motion.

Deep groanings issued from the frozen floor beneath them. It heaved and surged. From all around, terrific sounds like giant rifle shots whip-cracked above the screeching of the gale.

Stevens was running, now. Bent double, looking more than ever like a great furry animal, he raced on, through the lashing cataract of wind and snow. All around, the floe was moving, seething, teetering, grinding, tearing into fragments with detonations like the explosions of artillery.

Long, black fissures of open water darted at the men like snakes as the floe splintered. These were as yet narrow, and Stevens jumped them, the speed of the sled carrying it across. The fissures widened, and Stevens had to seek detours around them, twisting and doubling like a football runner. His strength amazed McCloud. For four days he had not eaten. For five days he had pulled a load of hundreds of pounds.

McCloud's thoughts were snatched off in a split second. From out the swirling haze of white had come a new, heart-chilling sound–a crunching, grinding roar, menacing as the thunder of a down-sweeping Niagara. They were now close to land, but between them and it lay a chaos of white hell where the fifty-foot thick sea ice, driven before the living gale, hurled millions of tons of momentum against the cliffs.

Stevens raced on a hundred yards more and stopped. Ahead, through openings, in the waves of billowing snow, they could get glimpses of the cliffs, with the shattered floe ice churning froth around their bottoms.

Stevens slipped off the tump line and turned to the sled. McCloud saw that he had stopped in the middle of a big cake of floe ice, surrounded by smaller pieces, and so in less immediate danger of breaking up.

Stevens bent over McCloud. He was ripping off the lashings of the grub load. He picked up a case and turned toward the shore. The snow thinned momentarily. McCloud could see his figure dashing ahead, jumping cracks, turning, doubling, the big case gripped in his arms.

A picture flashed into McCloud's fever muddled brain–a football game he had once seen, with a fullback plunging through a broken field, ducking, twisting, hurdling, falling, staggering up and going on. The howling of the gale was the roaring from the side lines–"Touchdown! Touchdown!" The writhing fissures of black water were leaping bodies, plunging for the runner's knees.

Stevens came to the churning Hades where the floe was grinding itself to flinders against the rocks. McCloud saw him leap into the air, come down in a froth of black and white, go plunging on, out of sight.

Minutes passed. Stevens was back again, grabbing another case. Against the snow curtain, the killer's face was parchment and blood, ghastly with the agony of exhaustion. Clutching the case he vanished from sight, plunging and hurdling the crevasses.

Once again he returned. Again–and again–McCloud lost count. The sled was empty. Stevens was carrying Quirk ashore. He came back again. McCloud felt himself swung upward, lifted like a child.

They were going over the broken ice–great, swaying cakes that lurched and pitched dizzily under their feet. They came to the raging tumult of the tide crack. Stevens dashed ahead, swerved at a yawning gulf of ink, crouched and leaped. He cleared the crevasse by a hair, and came down in a seething fury of crunching cakes. Fighting, slipping, staggering, waist deep in grinding froth, he battled up a jagged slope. The black shore rocks were just ahead. McCloud shut his eyes and fainted.

After a while, McCloud opened his eyes again. He was lying in a bunk in a cabin where a fire blazed in a stove. Only two other persons were there–Stevens and a woman. They sat hand in hand beside his bunk. The woman was a mere girl, pale and sunken about the face, but beautiful. In her eyes and on her lips was joy beyond telling. She stretched out her hand and touched McCloud's sleeve, timidly.

"I am Laura Stevens–John's wife," she murmured. "I've been traveling everywhere, for almost a year, trying to find him. I got in here last fall, just before it froze up, and had to stay. I was trying to find John and tell him that the man he shot didn't die, after all. The reason John ran away wasn't because he was afraid of the law, either."

Tears overflowed the girl's eyes, but she did not flinch from McCloud's gaze.

"It was all a dreadful misunderstanding. The man John shot was Price, his partner. Price cheated John in business, and John went bankrupt. Then Price taunted him about me–said that I was going away with him. I wasn't. I was visiting a friend. But John was jealous. He believed Price, and shot him. Then he went away, into the wilderness. Ever since I've been hunting–"

The girl's voice broke in a sob. McCloud raised up on an elbow and looked at Stevens.

"Did you know your wife was here when we started out from the shack with the grub?" he asked.

Stevens shook his head. "Hadn't an idea." The big, white lips under the red beard gripped savagely. "But if I hadn't come, she would have starved–because I was a coward and a fool."

McCloud nodded slowly. "Aye–that ye were," he murmured. His harsh voice was oddly hushed and gentle. "But there's more to it, man. I'm beginning to remember who ye are. Ye're Stevens of Yale–'Touchdown' Stevens who never failed to make your distance when the team needed a score. And out there on the ice when I caved in, and you knew grub had to be taken to starving folks, and a murderer brought to justice, you forgot yourself. You realized you were carrying the ball in a game a little bigger than you had ever stacked up against in the Bowl, so you went out to make another touchdown."

"And he did it!" Stevens' wife interrupted.

McCloud nodded solemnly, and extended his hand to Stevens.

"Aye," he grunted, slipping back into the burring brogue of his rare moments of emotion. "An' ye pr-r-r-ooved yoursel' a mon to do such a deed o' nerve an' br-r-avery as'll be talked aboot arround th' campfires o' th' north for twenty years. Put her there, Touchdown !"

THE VALLEY OF WANTED MEN

By Frederick Nebel

The Valley of Wanted Men—blizzard-bound sanctuary for Arctic pariahs. The long arm of Redcoat law never reached that hidden hide-out, until Sergeant Pat Quinlin mushed in on the track of a lovely, will-o'-the-wisp Delilah.

Lee, with weather like this we could make the old patrol in jig time. Then I could squat at the post, smoke the inspector's cigars and wait peacefully until my resignation papers arrive."

The speaker was Sergeant Pat Quinlin, of the Mounted, a young-old looking man, lean, blue-eyed, with a chiseled face seamed with the fine-weather lines that are the legacy of men who live in the open. The two were lounging on the sled and smoking their pipes while they "spelled" the nine dogs.

Constable Carlin, a young Englishman putting in his first term on the Force, kept twirling the thirty-foot dog whip meditatively around his mittened hand. He let off a little sigh and gave the whip a sudden snap, rising to his feet with a slight shudder.

Quinlin noticed it and asked:

"What's the matter?"

"Oh–" with a grimace.

"Come on, Lee, out with it now. What's ailing you?"

Carlin strode up and down for a short minute, then stopped in front of the sergeant and blurted out:

"I've–I've had a bad dream."

Quinlin stroked the stubble on his hard jaw and started to grin; then, throwing his hands aloft, he burst into a fit of laugher and almost toppled from the sled.

Carlin said: "Yes, go ahead and laugh, but I tell you, Pat, it was the worst dream I've ever had. I'm not by nature a dreaming man. I–hell–I feel pretty rummy over it. I dreamt we–the two of us–were set upon by a lot of cut-throats and that you were being tortured and all that sort of stuff. We were separated. Gad, it was all so vivid the whole affair still keeps dancing hazily in front of my eyes. I–"

"Lee," put in the sergeant, solemnly, "you'd better take some quinine tonight. Look out, or you'll be shaking hands with willows."

"Blast it, Pat, I'm all right otherwise; feel first rate. You may be right. The country may be getting on my nerves. My head doesn't ache; body's in fine shape. Only that bally old dream."

Quinlin mused for a moment, started to say something, then changed his mind and knocked the ashes from his pipe. Stowing the pipe away, he rocked up beside Shag, the lead-dog, and cuffed him playfully on the ear. Then he looked back at Carlin.

"All right, Lee," he said in his brisk, though not harsh, voice. "Let's mush. We should make Ben Tobin's shack before dark and after that it'll be a long, tough trail to

To-oot-aw-nek. Ready! Let's go!"

At three in the afternoon they left level country behind and began to work up a tortuous trail toward the summit of a hogback. Heavy bush was here, overgrowing what little trail there was, and in places matted windfalls lay twisted in all manner of curious shapes.

It took them just two hours to make three miles and the summit, and dusk was beginning to fling out rapidly over the land.

At the top Quinlin brought the hard breathing dogs to a stop and pointed into the valley below.

"Down there," he explained to Carlin, "is where old Ben Tobin lives. Ben's a funny old duck, Lee. Good as gold, but–well, odd. He's been trapping for about twenty years. And instead of trading hereabouts for grub and the like he drives his furs all the way to The Pas, gets good Dominion dollars and brings 'em back to this God-forsaken hole.

"He's been saving that money for twenty years; hides it some place, though only the Lord knows where. We've warned him about it. A lot of fellows know he hides it, and some day someone is going to get nosey–if–if you know what I mean."

"Yes, I understand," nodded Carlin, interested.

"He makes the statement sometimes that he's looking for someone dear to him," went on Quinlin. "Don't know whether it's a man, woman or dog, for he never says much. Just that he's looking for someone dear to him. And maybe that's why he's saving the money. Little daffy, poor old fellow, I suppose, so don't be astonished at anything he says."

Carlin nodded understandingly and twirled the whip in the air. But before he cracked it Quinlin laid a restraining hand on his arm and pointed to the valley floor. Black dots were moving on the snow; a dog team and a driver. Quinlin reached for his glasses, adjusted the focus and swept the distant outfit.

Still looking, he spoke to Carlin:

"Six dogs–toboggan–small man–"

A pause; then, suddenly:

"Hell, no, Lee, it's a woman. Her capote hood's thrown back and I can see a white face. Now what the–"

He stared at the constable with wide, popping eyes, astonishment written all over his face. He took another look through the glasses, then lowered them abruptly and whistled softly.

"Yes, she *is* white, Lee!" he clipped with a snap of his fingers. "A white woman way up this way. It's–by God, man, it's enough to make me believe I'm seeing things! Whip those dogs up. She came from the direction of Tobin's cabin. Ben ought to know something about her."

Carlin cracked the whip and the dogs went off with Quinlin half-a-dozen leaps ahead of the leader. By this time the mysterious woman was out of sight, swallowed up by the vast sweep of snow and tall timber and many lakes that sprawled all over this remote fringe of the world.

II

Quinlin led the way down to the valley floor and proceeded at a lively gait in the direction of Tobin's trapping shack. Dusk was full upon them by this time and the stars were beginning to show faintly.

Rounding a sharp bluff, the sergeant espied, a quarter of a mile ahead, a dark blot against the snow. He explained that was the cabin, as they drew nearer.

Carlin said:

"This would make any man daffy."

The sergeant chuckled as he drew up the dogs before the split-log shack and rubbed his hands together with pleasant anticipation.

"Lee, you might feed the dogs while I have a preliminary chat with Ben," he told the constable.

Then he pushed open the door softly, intending to surprise the old hermit as he had done many times before on his long patrol. The room was bathed in shadows. Only the rosy glow from the sheet iron stove made objects faintly distinguishable. The sergeant closed the door behind him softly and pulled off his mittens, bending his brows quizzically. No one greeted him. Nothing stirred.

He took a few steps forward, paused at the table and drummed thoughtfully on it for a moment with his fingers. As his eyes became accustomed to the gloom he could make out objects more clearly; the book-shelf, piled with ancient papers and magazines and worn old books; the roughly constructed cupboard; in the rear, the bunk....

The bunk ! *And something in the bunk!*

With quick steps he flung across the room and stopped before the bunk, and his body stiffened, held taut for a moment, and then relaxed. He leaned over the twisted body that lay there, ran his hand over the face, shuddered, then fumbled inside the rough woolen shirt. He brought his hand out slowly, reverently.

"Dear Heaven!" he jerked under his breath. "Poor old Ben. Somebody got you at last–and you didn't find 'the dear one,' did you ? Pretty tough, Ben."

The body of Ben Tobin was cold. With a prayer on his lips the sergeant turned away, went to the table and lit a candle. He stood by the stove and ran a studious eye about the little room. A stool, overturned, lay in a corner near the door. He picked up the candle and bent down to examine the floor. Blood spots.

"H-m-m," he mused, and stood erect.

He went over to the bunk, looked for a wound in the chest, found none, and turned the body over. The wound–an ugly knife gash–was in the back! Simultaneously with his discovery of this the sergeant's moccasined foot touched something on the floor that moved. Bending, he picked up a long, thin knife covered with blood–thinner than the hunting knife usually comes and constructed with a faun's hoof for a handle.

"Exhibit A," he said, grimly, as he placed the knife on the table.

Then he turned the dead man over again and folded the arms across the chest. In doing so his fingers became entwined with some silky substance and, reaching down, he pulled from the lifeless hand a long strand of golden hair–undeniably from a woman's head! A little shocked, he held it aloft.

After a moment he said half aloud, "A woman's hair, and that knife looks suspiciously like one a woman would carry if she carried one at all. So help me, if she's guilty, whoever she is, she'll swing!"

He half-turned, to call Carlin. An explosion boomed in his ears, his brain seemed to snap, and he crumbled to the floor like a deflated balloon. Consciousness was not completely gone, but almost.

He was in a fog, unable to rise, unable to exert any muscle at all, not even those that controlled his eyelids. All the cords at the back of his neck seemed to have contracted and were now burning.

It seemed an eternity before his eyes began to clear and he gained some control over his nervous system. The throbbing in his brain eased away and finally he fought to a sitting position.

He felt the back of his neck. Not much blood there. Merely a flesh wound. But the faintest flick of a bullet at that point is quite strong enough to numb the whole nervous system temporarily.

The sergeant got to his feet tentatively, found they served him fairly well, and discovered at the same moment that he still held the strand of golden hair in his hand. This gave birth to another thought and he gave a quick start toward the table, brought up sharply and clipped off an oath.

The knife was gone!

This in turn made him think of Carlin, and of a sudden he wondered why the constable had not come to his aid. Instantly he whipped out his service pistol and threw open the door– stepped out into the clear, frigid night which now seemed unreal and ghostly under the pale radiance of the Aurora

No Carlin. No sled. No dogs.

He cupped his hands at his mouth and called:

"Lee! Oh, Lee!"

Only echoes mocked him. He went a little farther and studied the snow. To the south the trail was all mixed up– marked by the mysterious woman's outfit and by his own. It would be difficult, therefore, to pick out a new trail in that direction.

But to the north! There he found a new trail; the marks of a sled, of a dog team, and of a man on snowshoes. He bent down and studied these last marks– suddenly shot erect and sucked in his breath.

"By Lord," he muttered, "they're Carlin's tracks. He bought those snowshoes from a trapper who'd come over from the Labrador. Yes, sir, a snowshoe shaped like an egg–an Ungava Indian shoe–and I'll bet there's not another pair like 'em over this way. But–but, why?"

That night he slept at the cabin on robes spread in front of the stove, while on the bunk old Ben Tobin slept the eternal sleep. He was up before dawn next morning. He tied the corpse in several wolf skins, carried it outside and hoisted it up into a tree by means of a rawhide line swung over a limb. He climbed the tree himself then and fastened the body to the trunk.

"No wolves'll get you here, Ben," murmured the sergeant. "I'll get back in the spring and bury you."

III

"But I must follow the woman," he told himself, as he made a makeshift pack of a caribou-hide robe and stuffed it with the last of Tobin's provisions. "Carlin can wait for a while. Tobin has been killed. It's the murderer of Tobin I'm wanting–and the evidence hangs on a wisp of golden hair. It's a distasteful job all around, damn it!"

So he struck out southward, bending under the pack and the dead man's blankets, came to the spot where the woman's trail swerved to the eastward, and headed into a rugged, battered country unknown to himself, where in places the sullen ridges rose to the dignity of minor mountain ranges, and all about there was a tomb-like silence.

All that day he followed the trail made by her rackets and her dogs. At night he made a camp in the lee of a balsam grove and wrote at length in his journal. Finished, he braced himself against a stump and meditated over his pipe.

The sharp snap of a twig or branch in the gloom brought him out of his thoughts without a start but with a sudden concentration of the eyes on the brush directly opposite. He listened intently. Heard a crunching sound that was patently made by a falling foot.

Involuntarily, as was his habit in such situations, he began to hum a merry little ditty of the voyageurs; then arose, casually, and began gathering more wood for the fire. Little by little he worked toward the source of the noise. Presently he heard more crunching sounds, as if the feet were moving away.

Of a sudden he dropped the wood he had gathered and made a flying leap into the bush, landing flat on the snow. A gun cracked and lead whined just above him, but he was out of sight. At the same time, however, he saw not six feet away a veritable giant of a man, a mighty Cree Indian with smoking rifle.

"Don't make a move," lashed out the sergeant. "I've got you covered and by all that's holy I'll blow you up if you so much as move a finger. Drop that rifle!"

The Indian hesitated, guttural sounds issuing from his throat. Quinlin laid his revolver across his arm and shot at the stock of the Indian's rifle. The slug hit its mark and with a grunt of surprise the big fellow fell back and dropped the gun. Quinlin stood up and went forward.

"Get over to my camp," he said tersely. "And lively!"

With a black look delivered from under craggy brows the Indian moved out of the bush and stood by the fire.

"Sit down," Quinlin told him.

Hesitantly he obeyed.

Quinlin proceeded with: "Now what's the idea of poking around my camp, eh? And don't you know it's bad business to go shooting at a redcoat? Talk. Let me in on the why and wherefore, old boy."

Not a muscle in the carven face of the Indian moved. Even his lips seemed scarcely to move.

But he was saying, in a deep voice:

"Make no talk."

For a long minute Quinlin eyed him coldly; then:

"You won't, eh?"

The Indian moved his head in slow, determined negation. Then he leaned back, with one foot half outstretched toward the fire, and calmly began cramming tobacco into a greasy old pipe.

After a few moments the hard expression on Quinlin's face became whimsical. He chuckled.

"Well, you're a determined devil, aren't you?" he said. "So be it. I'll have to arrest you for firing at an officer of the law. Consider yourself my prisoner. That plain?"

Without any expression whatever the Indian nodded his head. Then, with a sudden movement, his half-bent leg shot out and crashed into the fire. The hot coals flew into the air and drove the sergeant stumbling backward. With amazing agility for a man of his immense bulk the Indian vaulted over the fire and landed full upon the sergeant, and the next moment they were up on their feet and rocking back and forth in silent, grim combat.

Quinlin was no little man. He measured perhaps an inch over six feet, and his lean, tough body weighed something like a hundred and ninety. As men go, he was big, but alongside of the Indian he was small.

For this son of the woods towered up to nothing under six-feet-five, with a gorilla-like body that weighed at least two-hundred-and-fifty. In less time than you can tell it he wrenched the revolver from the sergeant's hand, threw it away, and locked him in his mighty arms.

Quinlin gritted his teeth and fought with the strength of a strong heart and a steel body. It was his courage, his spirit, that made up the difference in weight and size. Thus he found himself holding his own, but with nothing to spare, as they rocked, strained against each other under the cold stars. And only hard breathing and the muffled footsteps on the snow broke the stillness of the night which, though bitter cold, was without wind.

The breaks of the game don't always fall to the righteous. Quinlin knew he was licked, when carrying the fight away from the fire, he broke through an air pocket in the crusted snow and one leg went down almost to the hip. The Indian gave a satisfied grunt and, as if in payment for the trouble he'd had, cracked the sergeant on the jaw.

"You'll pay for this," Quinlin chuckled grimly.

"Make no talk!"

"I'll talk as much as I damn well please. And, as I said, you'll pay for this."

The Indian was dragging him from the hole in the snow and toward the fire. He picked up the sergeant's pistol and quite unceremoniously pressed it against his back.

"Down," he ordered.

Quinlin sat down and stuffed his pipe.

"Well, you're top-dog right now, so what's your pleasure?" he sighed off philosophically.

After a moment the Indian asked:

"What do over this way?"

"I'm looking for–for my partner, Constable Carlin," Quinlin lied. "We got separated back there."

He jerked his head toward the west.

The Indian shot him a quick, searching look, then shook his head.

"Lie," he muttered.

"How do you know?" plied the sergeant with a sidelong glance.

"I know," was the only response.

"Then why ask me ?"

For a long moment the Indian eyed him stolidly. Then– "Turn back."

"Who says so?"

"Me."

And he touched his chest.

The sergeant gave a short, harsh laugh.

"If that's what you want to talk about, old boy, save your breath. To that kind of talk I'm deaf, dumb and blind. When you talk that way I can't understand a word you're saying. So dry up and blow away. I'm in no great hurry. Keep me prisoner if you want. Do what you damn please. But–remember–in the end I'll get you. Take that in your pipe and smoke it, Sitting Bull."

A dark cloud swept over the Indian's face. Here indeed, he might have thought, was a hard man to deal with. He rose solemnly.

"We go on," he said. "We talk with Master. Maybe he kill. Don't know."

"And who is the Master?"

"A mighty man. Him live 'Defiance Valley.'"

Quinlin scratched his chin.

"Never heard of the place."

"No," said the Indian. "No one outside know. No law ever reach Defiance Valley. The Master, law."

"Thanks for the information," put in the sergeant crisply. "And, mind, if the law has never reached Defiance Valley, be advised that it's on its way now in the person of Pat Quinlin, the same being myself, if you don't know. So let's get going.

"Oh, no, I haven't forgot I'm your prisoner, only, such little trifles don't worry me. Every dog has its day. But don't think I'm classing myself with dogs, though if I had the choice between their company and some men's, I'd choose the dogs."

The Indian scowled and mumbled deep in his throat. Then he said:

"Sleep here. Start dawn. Me watch."

"Suits me," Quinlin acquiesced nonchalantly. "I've got all the time in the world."

IV

The dawn dusk was heavy upon the land when they struck out next morning. Quinlin led the way, while behind him the Indian strode with a ready rifle in the crook of his arm.

At noon Quinlin, rounding a bend in a narrow waterway, saw up ahead smoke, a sled and six lounging dogs. He slowed down and looked over his shoulder at the Indian. The Indian nodded understandingly and indicated with a gesture of his hand for the sergeant to keep moving. When they drew up by the campfire Quinlin looked around for signs of a human being.

After a moment there were sounds in the bush and a girl came out with an armful of sticks. She looked quizzically at the sergeant, then turned to the Indian as she threw the wood down beside the fire. Here there was acknowledgment in her gaze but no hint of greeting.

The Indian nodded, drew her aside and spoke in undertone. Quinlin watched her face out of the corners of his eyes. She kept looking obliquely into space as the Indian spoke, frowned now and then, then shook her head and shrugged her shoulders.

The Indian paused, spoke some more, and again she shook her head negatively. Finally she turned away from him with an impatient gesture and went about replenishing the fire.

It was when she threw back her capote hood that Quinlin snapped his teeth together and sucked in his breath. Her hair was gold, all shimmering gold, tied in a simple knot at the back.

In the glow from the fire her face was radiant and more beautiful than he at first had perceived. He felt his breast, where was concealed his journal containing the single strand of golden hair that he had taken from Ben Tobin's lifeless hand!

They ate in silence. No one spoke. Qulinlin realized that, although the girl seemed unfriendly to the Indian, she would join forces against himself if he tried to make a break for freedom. She did not cross gazes with Quinlin–gave him no attention at all. She ate, like the Indian and himself, in silence. The red coat he wore beneath his opened furs might just as well have been a rag for all she seemed to care.

With a sudden toss of the head she rose and went over to her sled, rumaging aimlessly in the equipage. The sergeant thought he saw tremor after tremor pass over her small, well-knit body. The Indian leaned forward and bared his teeth

"You make no talk," he hissed.,

Flint was in the sergeant's eyes as he said:

"Put on a new record, Long Jim. That gets monotonous after a while. I have a habit of talking when, where, and how I please."

A sinister note came into Long Jim's tone.

"The Master will see you make no talk."

"Well, leave that to the Master, and you go shut your face for a while."

With an ugly rumble in his throat the Indian heaved over and made a vicious pass with a clenched fist at the sergeant's face. Quinlin, quick as a flash, caught the flying hand by the wrist and with a deft jerk twisted the arm with such savageness that Long Jim was momentarily unbalanced.

Taking prompt advantage of this sudden whim of chance and most unexpected opening, Quinlin's free hand dived for the Indian's revolver, yanked it out, and as Long Jim tried to close the sergeant spun backward and shot out his feet.

They caught the Indian in the middle in time to ward him off, and Quinlin then completed the backward somersault with the ease of an acrobat and landed square on his feet just as the Indian was lunging in a second attack.

"As–you–are!" commanded Quinlin, biting off each word sharply. "The breaks are against you just now."

At the same time he saw the woman flying toward a gun belt that lay near the fire.

"Madam!" he lashed out. "Not another step."

With which order he leaped back a pace and sent a fast shot at the revolver in the belt and smashed it. The woman stopped in her tracks with a sob of anguish. Long Jim had heaved forward with a vicious snarl, but in the twinkling of an eye the sergeant had him covered, his gun jammed against the big fellow's abdomen.

"Keep your hands up or I'll let daylight into you," he jerked out; then– "And back up! Lively! Show some speed. Madam, not another move out of you. As you are, there. Never mind backing toward that tree. I see the rifle leaning against it. The two of you, now, side by side."

He reached inside his fur coat and threw them a pair of manacles.

"Snap 'em on. One bracelet on your wrist, madam, and the other on Long Jim's."

His voice bore such a quality of command that the manacles were snapped on as soon as he had finished speaking. He relaxed a bit then and chuckled in his grim, harsh way. But in the woman's eyes was a defiant light.

Her chin was upflung. her usually full lips drawn in a thin line of determination. Her bosom heaved tumultuously and her hands clenched and unclenched continuously. Quinlin thought he had never seen a woman so ravishingly beautiful.

Presently he said:

"Now I have an idea that we all shall turn back–the three of us. We shall stop at a certain cabin, go over certain things, and then continue going back to The Pas where a magistrate may ask you what you know about the death of one Benjamin Tobin. I am *positive* that *one* of you knows something about it."

Here his eyes were hard upon the woman; then they moved to the Indian.

"And I'm pretty sure the other has something up his sleeve. Now the both of you sit down."

When they were seated he took out his journal, kneeled, placed it on his knee and with pencil in one hand and gun in the other he spoke:

"Long Jim, eh?" to the Indian, and he wrote down the name and general description of the Indian, inquiring his age, which was forty.

Then to the woman–"And your name, madam ?"

"Rose."

"Rose what ?"

"Just Rose."

"You will have to give your full name eventually."

He tapped his pencil on the book, eyeing her frankly. He saw her own eyes were moist.

She was saying–"Just Rose."

"Age?" he asked at last.

"Twenty-three."

" Married ?"

"No."

He wrote a few more notes, closed the book and stowed it away.

"Very well," he clipped in a matter-of-fact tone. "We'll start immediately. The two of you line up the dogs."

Reluctantly Rose called the dogs and she and the Indian, bound to each other by the handcuffs, lined them up. Meanwhile, Quinlin gathered up the girl's and the Indian's guns, unloaded them and placed them on the sledge and stood by while the Indian and Rose threw their robes and blankets on. This done, they stood by for further orders.

The sergeant stood at some distance from the sled, pondering over the situation. Finally:

"You'll ride–on the sled, Miss Rose. You, Long Jim, will walk ahead of the dogs."

He threw the Indian the key. "Unlock the cuffs, take the one from Miss Rose's wrist and lock both your own wrists together."

"I don't have to ride. I'll walk," spoke up Rose.

"It happens, please, that I want you to ride," was the sergeant's peremptory reply. "Unlock those, Long Jim."

The Indian, muttering behind his teeth, unlocked the manacles and placed both bracelets on his own wrists. At an order from Quinlin he sullenly threw back the key.

"Very well, now," spoke up the sergeant. "Up in front of the team, and you, Miss Rose, on the sled."

V

Instead of obeying she turned her face up toward him.

"Please–please don't take me out?" she faltered.

"I wonder if you do not know better than ask such a question. Will you please get–"

"Oh, but you mustn't take me out! You mustn't! It–someone–I– Oh, you mustn't! Please! They'll–"

She broke off in a sob and grasped the sergeant's fur with shaking hands, pressed close to him and looked up at him with the most wonderful eyes he'd ever seen. Her whole soul–a soul crying out in anguish–was in those eyes.

"Not–not for my sake, but for someone else's," she pleaded.

"For the Indian's ?"

"No. For–oh, for someone I love. Please, Sergeant."

Held under a spell by her unfaltering eyes, possessed of a sudden, wild desire to break the Oath, he nevertheless said:

"You ask this. You ask me for pity–you, who murdered Ben Tobin. Your hair–a piece of your golden hair was in his cold hand when I found him!"

She did not move. Only her soul seemed to shrink back in her liquid eyes, but they did not move from his. They held him–almost hypnotized him.

And then the thing happened. The Indian was upon him in a mad leap. While the woman had held him under her spell the Indian had edged around and taken one flying leap. He bore the outraged sergeant to the snow and at the same time drove his manacled fists against his jaw.

Quinlin went limp and lay huddled on the snow. Vaguely he could see the giant bend over him, remove his pistol. Heard his deep voice calling the dogs to action.

And then–again vaguely–the woman was bending over him. He tried to raise his hands but all power seemed to have deserted him. Everything seemed like a nightmare. She bent closer, touched his forehead with a soft hand, then suddenly kissed him on the lips.

And the next moment she was gone and he was trying vainly to struggle up.

Then he heard Rose and the Indian arguing. He didn't know if he were dreaming or if they actually were speaking But he heard:

"We take him Master."

And from Rose:

"No, Jim. You were wrong in the first place–bringing him this far. He mentioned a partner–and the partner may be following this trail."

Then she knew nothing about Carlin! They had not crossed trails yet!

Consciousness faded a little more from Quinlin and he heard no more of the wrangle.

VI

When he awoke it was nearly twilight. A wind was rattling in the spruces. But otherwise there was no sound. The place was deserted. Near him lay his guns and his improvised pack. Doubtless the girl had seen to their being left. She would not want him to starve, possibly.

He sat up, rubbing his head; then arose shakily and went about building a fire.

It snowed that night and was still snowing when he took up the trail in the morning. He had to work for the most part by his compass, until, in the afternoon, he began to recognize the country ahead and knew he was nearing the borders of his patrol.

He had hard going, for, due to a sudden rise in the temperature, the new snow lay soft and powdery, and he kept sinking through, even though he wore long, wide rackets.

At four he was on his patrol line. As night was near, he went off his proposed route in the direction of the late Ben Tobin's cabin. It would be his last warm shelter for many days, and perhaps he could find some clothing and food that he might have overlooked on his previous visit.

Dusk was gathering in rapidly, but even through the gloom he could see wisps of smoke rising from the chimney. He slowed down, a little perplexed; instinctively felt for his revolver. He pushed on after a minute, a bit cautiously, leaving the open trail and taking to the bush, with intentions of approaching the cabin from the other side, where there was no window.

He circled the cabin in the rear and began approaching it from the other side. He drew his service pistol as he reached the wall and began creeping around to the door. Here he listened. There was a light within but no sounds. He raised his hand to the door and began to ease it open a crack. Then suddenly he whipped it open and swung up his pistol.

The place was empty. But there was a fire in the stove, and a bundle of blankets was on the floor, and the floor was wet from a recent visitor's dripping furs and moccasins. Quinlin took a step outside, scanned the murk, looked down at the virgin snow.

Yes, there were tracks! Tracks made by a long and narrow snowshoe about four feet long. Quinlin put a hand to his ear. Sounds were in the forest nearby. After a moment he nodded his head in comprehension.

"The stranger's gathering wood," he murmured and re-entered the cabin.

He took off his furs and hung them up. He stood over the nondescript pack on the floor, wondering whether the man would be white or Indian, good or had. He pushed the pack over with his foot.

"May be just an honest trapper," he meditated.

He let the pack fall to its original position, and the slight jolt caused the blade of a knife to fall through an opening. It chinked against the floor.

Quinlin bent down, intending to thrust it back. But the shape of the blade caused him to hesitate. Then he abruptly yanked it out and shot to his feet as if propelled by a spring.

It was a knife that had killed Ben Tobin! The knife with the faun's hoof for a handle!

The sergeant, his jaw suddenly hard and his eyes glinting like chips of blue steel, flung to the center of the room and trained his revolver on the door.

His hand tightened on his revolver as he heard sounds just outside the door. Then the door rattled, swung open, and a furred figure rocked in with his arms full of wood. He kicked the door shut with his heel looked up, gasped and dropped the wood where he stood.

The sergeant had half-risen, and now he shot erect, and the corners of his wide mouth drooped sardonically. He gave a short, harsh laugh and eyed the man coldly.

VII

The man was–Constable Lee Carlin. "Pat! Lord, is it you?" Carlin's voice was choked with emotion.

He stumbled forward and grasped the sergeant by the shoulders, but felt the hard muzzle of his partner's revolver against his chest, and saw no hint of greeting in those steely eyes. He took his hands off and fell back a pace.

"Why, Pat! Why–"

Words failed him.

The sergeant said in a colorless voice:

"Until you can explain certain mysterious happenings to my satisfaction, Constable, to you I am Sergeant Quinlin. Sit down."

Awed, speechless, Carlin felt his way upon a stool and stared with unseeing eyes at the table.

Quinlin, grim and unbending, sat down opposite him and

with slow precision drew out the knife and laid it on the table.

"Can you explain how this came into your possession?" he asked.

"I stole it from the man who waylaid me."

Quinlin's eyes dilated.

"You what ?"

"I–Lord! I see what's the trouble now. You think I played you false."

"With every good reason," was the sergeant's prompt rejoinder.

"But I didn't, Pat. How could you believe it?"

"I was knocked over with a bullet while examining the dead body of Ben Tobin in here. When I came to, the knife I found beside him was gone. I saw no tracks except those made by your own rackets– and they led north."

"Now let me explain," put in Carlin eagerly. "While I was feeding the dogs I was put out–or nearly so–from behind. Dimly I heard the shot, and I thought later that you were killed. When I came to I was riding on our sled and my abductor was mushing behind on my snowshoes and his own were on the sled.

"I started to brawl with him and he knocked me out for my pains. Then I asked him where he was taking me, and why. He said no place in particular–just to lead you on with suspicion against me. I mentioned the shot and he said he hadn't killed you–just put you out for a while. And why all these mysterious moves?

"'Why,' he said, 'to prevent a woman from being suspected.'

"And when I asked of what he just laughed. The next day while crossing a lake the ice broke. We lost the sled and all the dogs. In the confusion he dropped the knife and I picked it up. He didn't know it. Then he said, 'Well, I guess we part now.'

"'This is far enough.' And then he left me. I stumbled on a trapper's shack, but he had a touch of rheumatism and could only give me aid in the way of advice and a few blankets and provisions. I just got back here a little while ago."

Quinlin asked "That all of it?"

"Yes, Pat. And so help me, God, it's true."

The sergeant extended his hand. "I believe you, Lee. I've

been a blasted fool. Shake!"

Then Quinlin explained his own side of the story, and between them they tried to put two and two together. The upshot of it was, they became more entangled in the meshes of mystery than before. What connection had Carlin's abductor with the case, and with the woman, and where did the Indian fit in? And still further, who was The Master?–the super-power behind it all ?

"Do you think he was killed for the money he was supposed to have concealed ?" ventured Carlin referring to Tobin.

Quinlin's idea was: "If a man committed it, yes; if the woman, no. Woman very seldom kill for money. Remember that, Lee, in your dealings with criminals. We'll have to make tracks for Defiance Valley. The solution, if there is any, lies there. The fellow who got you mentioned no names, eh?–not even his own?"

"No, Pat. But he was concerned over the woman. An oldish fellow, not a bad sort taken by and large; regular sourdough. Medium sized, grizzled and rough."

"Well, I'm glad we two are straightened out, Lee. In the morning we'll start out for an independent trading post thirty miles west, draft an outfit and double back."

It took them just two days to make the thirty miles. After much haggling with the canny Scotch trader Quinlin succeeded in getting a nondescript of seven dogs and a worn old Mackenzie toboggan. By a mere stroke of luck, Jerry Plate, a hard bitten old crossbreed and old friend of Quinlin's, offered his aid as guide and general handy man.

"No, Pat, Defiance Valley ain't in my ken," he rolled off, "but just gimme a lay o' the land, an' I'll smell m' way, I will. I'm just ripe f'r a tough trail, an' if I c'n help yer out, Pat, let's know."

He was a short, broad man, more white than Indian, with button eyes and piratical mustache. He spoke out of the side of his mouth, spat often and copiously, and looked what he was; a hard boiled sourdough and a good man to have beside you in a pinch.

The three of them pulled out of the post with a mountainous load on the sled. Fine weather. Good going. And the dogs showed up better than Quinlin had thought they would.

On the morning of the second day they passed the death cabin and by nightfall they were twenty miles beyond. Quinlin had a general idea of the trail up to the waterway where Rose and the Indian had tricked him, and for two days he led the way.

After that he and Jerry exchanged ideas as they pressed on through a wild, raw country; up steep ridges, down through tortuous, yawning ravines where the snow lay in great windrows.

"Somebody's been through here," explained Jerry. "See that dead stump stickin' up outer the snow. See where it's been hacked wit' an ax? 'Course the campfire's buried under the snow some place."

Another day passed, and still another. Jerry, scouting up ahead, brought down a moose with one shot.

"I never like t' waste bullets," he said dully, when Quinlin commended him.

On the tenth day after passing Tobin's cabin Carlin, taking his turn at breaking trail ahead of the dogs, caught sight of a moving shape in the forest ahead. He called out. The form stopped, looked around, and the constable called to Quinlin:

"A woman!"

Quinlin came up from the rear in long strides. As he did the woman dodged in the bush and began running away. Without a word to his companions, the sergeant set off after her.

He was a fast man on snowshoes, and in short time he caught up with the fugitive and grabbed her. But when he turned her about she was not, as he had supposed, Rose of the golden hair. She was dark and undeniably pretty and frightened stiff, at the moment.

"Pardon me," he offered. "Thought you were someone else. You live here?" He swept his hand about vaguely.

"Yes," she replied in an awed whisper.

After a pause he said, "Defiance Valley?"

She gave a start–clasped her mittened hands to her breast. By this time Jerry and Carlin came trotting up with the dogs.

Quinlin was saying to the girl, "You will please show us the way to Defiance Valley."

Carlin, looking at her, could not suppress a smile. And the

girl–she looked no more than twenty–smiled back wistfully with her dark, haunting eyes.

Jerry offered: "Pa'don, miss, but a little birdie tells me Defiance Valley ain't many miles from here. Be I right?"

Without a word the girl dropped her head in resignation, and with a gesture to Quinlin started off. The sergeant strode along beside her.

"What do you know about the Valley, Miss ?" he asked off-handedly.

She gave him a quick look but made no reply.

"You must know something," he plied.

After a pause she said: "I only know that if I am caught showing you the way, well–"

She shrugged her shoulders meaningly.

VIII

The sergeant stopped her abruptly. "You mean your life is in danger?"

"Anybody's life is in danger–who brings the law to Defiance Valley. Once you enter the Valley, you take your life in your own hands."

Carlin spoke up: "I say, Pat, it's kind of rummy to place the lady in a bad way."

Her eyes went soft on the young constable.

Quinlin was saying, "I was thinking the same."

But the girl said, "It's no use now. The thing is done. There is Defiance Valley!"

Through a rift in the trees she pointed to a column of smoke rising clear cut on tile frigid air. As he looked intently, Quinlin could make out a cluster of buildings–possibly ten–deep in the center of the valley. And on all sides towered sheer walls of snow and timber.

The girl was saying:

"And now let me go."

With that she struck out, giving Carlin a last, blood-warming smile.

The constable shot at Quinlin:

"They'll do her harm, Pat. We'd better hold her."

"Lee, they haven't seen us yet. If we held her we'd ball up

the whole shooting match. Take it easy."

A moment later the girl was lost in the bush.

Jerry crammed a wad of tobacco into his mouth and said, "Now that we've found the Valley, let's eat. I'm so hungry m,' stomach thinks m' throat's cut."

"But they'll see our smoke," put in Carlin.

"Naw. We'll just back-trail a mile. The timber'll hide us."

After supper they exchanged ideas on the method of entering the Valley. Carlin was a bit moody and Jerry began poking fun at him.

"Kinder stuck on the gal, hey, Lee," he chuckled. "Look out, boy. Women has made many a bloke sorry he took t' wearin' the Scarlet." Carlin laughed away his discomfort. Quinlin looked into the fire. Of late Rose was always in his memory–her eyes, the kiss,and–yes!–the golden hair. He hated to think of her as a killer.

He hated to consider that she had enchanted him with her charms merely to give Long Jim a chance to strike him. He had never thought he was susceptible to such charms. He had considered himself case-hardened and callous to sentiment if that sentiment interfered with his duties as a policeman.

When darkness came he led Carlin away toward the valley, leaving Jerry with the dogs. At the brink he stopped.

"You'll stay here, Lee, unless I need you," he said. "I'm just going to scout around to get a lay of the land. If I don't return use your judgment. But I'll return. So long, for a while."

There was no moon, and this in some measure aided him. It took him an hour to make the descent. Once on the valley floor he proceeded with the utmost caution, advancing by degrees through the dark forest. At last he was on the border of the little settlement.

Lights blinked here and there. Faintly he heard the mingled sounds of a fiddle and a feminine voice raised in song. In a clearing to one side half a dozen tents were pitched, and he could see dogs lounging about.

"Regular village," he mused. "Looks like the hangout for traders. Those are trail tents over there. And that big cabin in the center, there; that's where the music is coming from. H-m-m. Got the earmarks of a trading post. Funny we never got wind of this place at headquarters."

Dodging from one tree to another, he worked nearer the large building. Presently the music stopped. Then the door opened and for a brief moment he saw Rose pause there, then close the door with a bang and walk off toward a cabin on the outskirts of the settlement.

The door opened again and a man, his face dark with anger, rocked out and strode after her in a businesslike manner. He caught up to her as she opened the door to her apparent dwelling and forced his way in.

Quinlin drew his pistol and hastened toward that cabin, keeping in the shelter of the trees. When directly in front of it he went out into the open and crossed to the cabin. The one window was frozen and afforded no view of the interior. But he heard scuffling sounds. He hesitated for a moment, then gripped his revolver tightly and went over to the door.

He swung it in and with a quick movement stepped inside and kicked it shut behind him.

"Cut it!" he rasped out.

The man had Rose by the wrists in a savage hold, and his eyes blazed as he whirled on the intruder. Rose's eyes went wide and a stifled cry came to her lips.

"You deaf?" the sergeant called to the man. "I said cut it–let go the lady's hand!"

The fellow was big, powerful and handsome in a reckless way. He released Rose's wrists and hooked his thumbs in his wide belt. His mouth sagged at one corner and his cleft jaw went hard.

"Who the hell are you?" he dragged out.

"Quinlin's my name, of the Mounted, and I'm telling you to lay off the rough stuff," was the crisp response.

The man shot to his full height as the sergeant threw back his furs and revealed his scarlet tunic

"How did you get here ?" he exploded.

"Walked. But never mind so many questions," Quinlin advised. "I want the lady there–not you, though if you give me any lip I'll make you join us."

The man gasped.

"Lord, stranger, don't you know where you are? Ha! You're talking through your hat. You're lucky if you get out alive. With one yell I can bring a whole gang on you."

"If–I don't blow your head off before you yell," clipped Quinlin. "Are you the fellow they call The Master?"

"And what if I am–or not?"

"Nothing. But never mind the palaver. Miss, get your trail garb on as fast as you know how and take a pair of snowshoes. Lively, if you please!"

Again those wide, pleading eyes were upon him, and the lips began to quiver. Her hands started out in a gesture of anguished entreaty. But the sergeant, with an effort, remained cold and unbending.

And then–quite suddenly–her face froze and she went a little limp. The young fellow started forward. Quinlin felt a draft against his back and ducked sidewise against the wall.

The door closed and a tall, elderly man in the garb of a Jesuit missionary stood there with a restraining hand raised above his head. Rose disappeared behind a curtain. Her recent attacker stopped in his rush for Quinlin and fell back. Quinlin nodded to the Jesuit and lowered his gun.

IX

The missionary spoke: "Welcome, Sergeant. It is indeed a surprise to see His Majesty's police. I am Pere La Bau. I minister to all creeds here in this sanctuary of the wilderness. But, I pray, Monsieur Bellamy"–here he turned to the other–"why all the disturbance?"

Bellamy, without answering, clapped on his beaver cap and strode out with averted eyes. Pere La Bau followed his hasty exit with mildly amused eyes, then returned his gaze to Quinlin.

"You are after–that man?" he asked in his low, unhurried voice.

"No, Father," returned the sergeant. "The lady–in there. For certain reasons, because of certain evidence I have, she must come with me."

The missionary evinced no surprise. He drew an immaculate finger tip across his lower lip meditatively, then glanced up at the sergeant obliquely.

"It is too bad. We shall miss her. But–I say, Sergeant, while she is getting ready let us sit down and have a smoke. I am eager for news of the outer world."

He waved the sergeant to a chair and sat down himself, drawing a pouch from his black robe and extending it. Quinlin stuffed his pipe with the proferred tobacco, lighted up and inhaled luxuriously. Then the missionary began loading his own, smiling and explaining his work in this remote section.

Gradually Quinlin began to sense a peculiar sensation, as if his head were floating up and away from his body. He felt sick at his stomach, and a mist seemed to be drifting in front of his eyes. He heaved up to his feet, and the room seemed to spin around.

He started for the door, but somehow or other he couldn't prevent his legs from taking him in circles. The last thing he remembered was the hazy, indistinct picture of the missionary still idly cramming tobacco into a little black pipe. He crumpled to the floor.

He had wild dreams, fantastic nightmares, in which he fought with dragons and fanged giants and all forms of weirdly contorted creatures. When he awoke from the unnatural sleep he was shaking in every limb and dripping with perspiration.

He was in a small, ramshackle trapping shack, he guessed. It was pitch dark. There was no fire, and he shivered even under the mass of robes and blankets that covered him. He mopped the cold sweat from his face and fought to his feet, leaning against the cold wall.

He felt his way around the shack. His gun was gone. The mysterious knife was gone. The little hovel was bare of any furnishings whatever; not even a stool upon which to sit, not even a stove. The door was barred from the outside. There was no window.

After a while Quinlin sat down, suddenly shoved his hand into an inner pocket then exhaled a sigh of relief. They had not taken his journal. He took it out, flicked back the pages and felt the strand of golden hair. Yes, it was still there– the lone piece of golden evidence.

He drew the robes closer about his body. He hoped Carlin had not, like himself, made any rash moves. He was glad he had brought along Jerry Plate. Jerry and Carlin ought to be able to help him. But would the girl who had led them to the Valley tell there were three? If she did, the game was well-nigh up.

The sergeant's ruminations, were interrupted by the sudden opening of the door. A man came in, closed the door and lighted a candle that he held in his hand. He was not above medium height. His beard was scraggly; his eyes pale and whimsical. He grinned at the sergeant and set the candle on the mantelpiece.

"Greetin's Serge. Kind o' chilly in here, eh?"

"No chance of me sweating at all, stranger."

The fellow was saying, "I been sent here t' make you an offer."

"All right. Shoot!"

"You mayn't know it, Serge, but you're about a mile away from the settlement. I been sent here to offer you–no t' *ask* you t' make believe you never saw Defiance Valley. In other words, t' clear out before somethin' happens t' you."

"Who sent you ?"

"A lady–as fine a lady as ever wore a pair of moccasins."

"The lady called Rose?"

The man eyed him sharply. "Yeah–the same. She's took an oncommon int'rest in you, an' she's takin' an orful risk. Me, I'd guide you out, Serge, because she asked me to. I'd do anything for Rose."

"Rather a gallant, eh?" Quinlin said. "No–hell, no. She nursed me through the scurvy once. I ain't f'rgot. She's all gold–like her hair–God bless her."

Quinlin thought over this for a minute. Then:

"Send Rose my heartfelt gratitude, but tell her I refuse aid. I am here for a purpose. And I shan't leave Defiance Valley until that purpose is realized. That's all."

The man shrugged his heavy shoulders. "Well you're fixin' f'r your own funeral, Serge. But–lemme tell you somethin': You'll never take Rose out. If there was any chance o' you doin' it, me, I'd be the first one t' cook your goose. Get that, Serge, an' don't think your red coat worries me any."

"H-m-m," mused Quinlin. "And who are you?"

"Well, there's some folks as call me 'Hell-bent' Jackson. I'll be givin' Rose your message. S'long."

And with that he was gone.

An hour later there was movement of some sort outside the door. Quinlin got to his feet and clenched his fists. It seemed to him now that the only way to win free was by a reckless move, trusting the rest to luck.

He made ready to spring, his muscles taut, as the door opened. He even sprang forward, but brought up suddenly when he saw his visitor, Father La Bau, accompanied by Long Jim.

"Ah, Sergeant, 'tis only I," he murmured in his low, gentle voice. "Let us go in. The Indian, I presume, has orders to guard the cabin while we talk."

X

Quinlin retreated into the cabin in perplexed indecision. The missionary was already lighting a candle.

After a moment he said, "First, sergeant, I'm sorry it was my fault that threw you into this predicament. I smoke unusually strong tobacco, and when one is fresh from the trail–and a hard trail–it is liable to make him groggy if he is not used to it. It was indeed thoughtless of me. And it is possible you thought I drugged it. Hence my amends, which you may or may not believe."

"It struck me as a drugged mixture," was the sergeant's frank but courteous reply. "However, supposing it wasn't, what is the object of your visit here?"

The Jesuit Father drew a thoughtful finger along his lower lip. In the flickering candle light his eyes were opaque– seemingly transparent, now a pale blue, now gray, forever changing in color under light and shadow.

"My visit!" he echoed. "In the cause of humanity, I assure you, Sergeant. This Valley contains some Godless men, and to them the law means nothing. The most of them have killed a man sometime.

"Wherefore they are reckless, and some of them would be particularly pleased at the opportunity of shooting a redcoat. They would brag about it. And they have sworn allegiance to one man, and his word is law."

"The Master?"

"Some call him by that name," nodded the priest. "He has but to say, 'Kill that man.' And *that* man, whoever he may be, will be killed. I am merely explaining this to show you how futile it is for one man–or two or three–to come here in the name of the law."

"And why do you remain here, Father?"

"Oh, I have my little flock," smiled the missionary. "And I live in hopes of some day converting the bad ones. And then I comfort those who die."

"My dear Father," put in the sergeant, "you have professed yourself a disciple of humanity. The law is a disciple of humanity, too. Why not unite? Why not divulge to me the methods, or what you know, of this clique?"

"I have given my word of honor to speak nothing of that sort, monsieur," replied Pere La Bau. "I have revealed too much as it is, I fear. I have been allowed to speak with you and ask you to swear you will leave this Valley and forget you ever saw it–to swear by the Book."

The sergeant's face went grim.

"Father, I appreciate your kind indulgence, but my answer is–no! The fools! Do they think they can do away with me and remain untouched.

"Are they blind to the Force's record? Do they forget that in the dead of winter two years back Corporal Tyson tracked a murderer from Fort Resolution to Coronation Gulf–a thousand miles of the worst country this side of hell–do they?"

The missionary recommended silence with raised hand. "Very well, Sergeant. I am sorry. I have only tried to help you to the best of my ability. Good-night."

"Good-night, Father."

The priest moved toward the door, opened it and started to go out. But he paused on the threshold and his hands started to rise slowly above his head.

Just outside the door stood Constable Carlin with his revolver trained on the black-robed missionary. To one side lounged Jerry Plate, covering Long Jim.

"Pat, that you?" Called Carlin in an anxious voice.

"The same, Lee, God bless you," sang out the sergeant. "Hello, there, Jerry." And to the missionary–"Please step outside, Father."

Jerry handed the sergeant the rifle he had taken from Long Jim.

Quinlin was saying:

"Father, you may return to the settlement. I am keeping the Indian as material witness."

The missionary nodded and then said, "I think it unwise of you, Sergeant, to hold the Indian. You will bring all the dangerous element of Defiance Valley upon you. Merely my personal opinion, of course."

"Thanks, Father, but we must take him," answered Quinlin. "You may go."

Pere La Bau bowed, turned and strode off into the darkness.

Carlin had manacled the Indian by this time.

Jerry said:

"Let's mosey along, Pat. We better hide up in the hills. Soon as they get wind o' this hell'll pop. Lee an' me have been shot at more times 'n I c'n count. But we gave 'em the slip right along, eh, Lee?"

"Yes," spoke up the constable as they moved off with their sullen captive. "When you didn't come back, Pat, I started down into the Valley and soon found Jerry after me. We kept sneaking about until this Indian pounced upon us with a half-a-dozen other rascals.

"We were locked in a cabin, where we learned that you, too, had been captured. In the night that girl–Marie trapped on the window and when I opened it she passed me a loaded revolver and I–I–"

"Go ahead, Lee, tell the truth," chided Jerry.

"I–I–"

Jerry cut in:

"He took the revolver, leaned out and kissed her, and the danged fools kept huggin' each other till I yanked him away. Haw! Haw!"

Carlin flushed.

"We–Jerry and I–attacked attacked the guard when he brought us food. Jerry got his gun and we broke away, and ever since we've been looking for you. When we saw the Indian and the missionary heading this way we trailed 'em."

Long Jim's eyes darkened ominously as he heard Carlin's story and his breath hissed in his throat.

XI

At daybreak they were two miles up in the spruce-covered hills. It was snowing lightly, but enough to cover up their trail.

"The luck seems to be coming our way for once," observed Quinlin. "They'll have some time finding us."

They had no food. Their dogs and provisions had been gathered in by The Master henchmen. Food was a necessary item, so Jerry sacrificed one of his snowshoes by using the lacing for a rabbit snare.

"We can't afford to give our position by shootin'," was his comment.

They snared four rabbits and drank raw spruce tea. The site of their camp was on a sharp eminence that commanded a view of the country for miles about. As the day broadened they could see far away to the southward the cabins of Defiance Valley.

"With plenty of food and ammunition we could hold this hill till the cows came home," remarked Quinlin.

"But with on'y twenty slugs between us," supplemented Jerry, "it ain't so easy."

Carlin was trying to pierce the thin cloud of snow with his glasses.

"There's a lot of hustle and bustle down there," he said. "Groups starting out in several directions, and all armed. And it looks as though four are coming up this way. It's pretty far, but I think they're heading this way–four or five."

With the passing of another hour Carlin was positive that four men were heading toward their lofty retreat.

Quinlin said:

"We must trick them. Avoid any shooting. We'll waylay them, tie 'em up and take their guns and ammunition. We need ammunition."

For the time being they bound the Indian hand and foot and secured him to a tree. Then the three of them started down the incline and waited in a thicket. Hours passed before the men came toiling, up the rugged slope; four of them in single file and carrying rifles.

Quinlin was whispering:

"You fellows pounce on the first two. Leave the last two for me. Work fast, now. Club your revolvers and hit hard. Ready!"

The first of the four came rocking by the thicket. Jerry shot out and brought his gun butt down on the man's head even as Carlin bore the second fellow down with his clubbed revolver.

Quinlin caught the first of his two on the forehead and sent him reeling back against the other. In a flash he had the last man covered, while the other pitched unconscious to the snow.

"That gun!" he rasped out. "The revolver, too. Now open your coat!"

Black with rage the only conscious one of the quartet threw down his guns and pulled open his coat.

"That's the stuff," bit off Quinlin "Take that knife from your belt. That's all. You may close your coat."

Carlin and Jerry were already hauling their men up the slope. Quinlin followed while the man he had disarmed was forced to carry his unconscious companion. Once at the spot where they had left the Indian, Quinlin and his companions bound the prisoners securely with strips cut from the prisoner's own caribou-hide garments. Then Jerry built a roaring fire, so that their hands and feet, thus bound and preventing free circulation, would not freeze.

"Now," spoke up Quinlin. "There's a rifle for each of us and an extra revolver. Come here a moment, boys."

He drew Jerry and Carlin aside.

"Two of us are going down into the Valley. Lee, I think you'd better come along. Jerry, you know you're not officially in the service. If you got banged up I'd have to explain a lot.

"So the best thing for you to do is remain here and guard these roughnecks. I'm going to clear this thing up now or be eternally damned. I've been made as ass of. I'll make 'em talk, the whole bloody lot of them!"

XII

Side by side Quinlin and Carlin swung down the slope. The sergeant's blood was up now. He had been rubbed the wrong way once too often, and his reckless gait and the hard, bitter set of his face made it patent that he was ripe for anything short of murder.

He was in no mood for words, as Carlin found out after a few unsuccessful attempts to start a conversation. The sergeant's replies were nothing more than clipped phrases and chopped off words.

As they reached lower country the snowfall increased, with a sharp wind at its back that whirled it in circles and corkscrew twists. The flakes doubled in size and evolved into pellets that slashed and cut like the tip of a rawhide whip.

"This will conceal our approach," ventured Carlin.

"Yup, Lee. 'S right," shot back the sergeant.

It took them just three hours to fight through storm and bush to the first cabin of the little outpost. They drew up on the lee side of a tree for a hurried consultation.

Quinlin said, "Farther on there's a sort of store. Suppose it's the general hangout. Heard singing and dancing there when I first hit the Valley. It's likely that those who aren't searching for us are in there. Let's go!"

"Right-o, Pat," spoke up the constable.

They sank their heads in their furs and plodded on side by side. There was no need for a cautious approach now. The white cloud of the storm concealed them. A man passed within six feet of them and did not recognize them.

Quinlin led the way up to the trade store and they stood beside the window for a moment. It was so frozen that even by placing the heel of his hand against it Quinlin could not clear a space through which to look.

"Well, Lee, we'll have to walk right in," he explained. "For maybe a minute they won't recognize us, we're so covered with snow. We're the last people in the world they'll expect. Come on."

Quinlin pushed open the door and kept his head lowered

as he went in. Carlin was at his heels. As he closed the door Quinlin, with a deft movement, threw down the heavy bar that locked it against intrusion from the outside. Out of the corner of his eye he saw six men gambling at a table near the great sheet-iron stove.

One leaned against the counter in the rear eyeing the card players in a detached superior manner. This man was Bellamy, the big, handsome fellow he had caught attacking Rose that night in the cabin where later he had smoked the fatal tobacco. None of the players looked up. Even Bellamy, who appeared deep in thought, did not stir.

Quinlin caught Carlin's eye and motioned to the men at the table. Then they strode forward. Both pulled their guns at the same time.

Carlin said:

"Every man keep his hands right where they are–on the table!"

Quinlin stood in front of Bellamy and eyed him coolly. The whole thing had been done in such a smooth, unhurried manner that Bellamy could not quite believe his eyes. His hand involuntarily slid toward the revolver at his hip.

"Cut it!" barked Quinlin. "Don't you recognize me, Bellamy?"

Bellamy suddenly exploded: "Crise-mighty! Where did *you* drop from?"

Quinlin laughed his short, harsh laugh.

"Kind of surprising, eh? From now on you and your bunch of roughnecks are going to get the surprises of your life. The law has come to Defiance Valley. I've met tough ones before like you. Now do what I tell you. Unbuckle your gun belt and let it drop. Now reach under your arm and pluck out that knife. I see the strap under your shirt. Come on. I've not got all night. Now keep your hands high and move over there with your playmates."

There was steel in the sergeant's voice and a bad light in his eyes. Bellamy, almost crying with baffled rage, rocked over by the others. His big chest rose and fell slowly, and the cords in his powerful neck bulged, and his face flamed red with uprising passion.

By this time Carlin had the others disarmed. Six guns and

six knives lay on the table. Quinlin lined them all against the wall and then spoke to Carlin.

"There must be a storeroom here, Lee. Find it, will you?"

Carlin tried several doors in the rear and soon found the one that opened into the storeroom. It was a cubby-hole of a place, dark, unlighted and without a single window.

"Just the place," chuckled Quinlin. "All right, boys, file into that room. Go ahead, Bellamy; you're the leader."

"By cripes, I'll–" started Bellamy.

But Quinlin cut him off with:

"You'll go right into that room, that's what you'll do. And no lip! Get along!"

Fuming with sullen rage, his eyes venomous, Bellamy moved reluctantly into the room and the others, four whites and two Indians, followed with black looks, curses and guttural snarls.

Quinlin saw the last man through the door, then shot home the bolt. He made the prison more secure by driving several spikes in the floor and bracing between these and the door a stout length of timber which he found leaning against the wall.

"That'll hold 'em for a while, Lee," he said.

Then there were sounds at the front door. Somebody was knocking. Quinlin went over quickly, threw up the bar and stood aside with drawn pistol. The door swung in and a fur-swathed man heaved in, rubbing the snow from his eyes and cursing the weather. When he looked tip and beheld Quinlin he gulped and gave a cracked chuckle.

"Oh, hello, Serge. Where'n 'ell you blow from ?"

"Hello, Jackson."

Hell-bent Jackson flung an eye around the room and frowned.

"Where's the crowd?" He caught his breath at sight of Carlin. "Oh, glad t' see you, cons'able. Too bad we lost that team."

"Team?" put in Quinlin.

Carlin leaped forward and his steely fingers caught Jackson by the shoulder.

"This, Pat–this is the fellow that waylaid me. *This is the fellow that stole our outfit. This is the fellow that shot at you and stole the knife?"*

XIII

"So-o!" breathed out Quinlin. "So you're the sharpshooter that creased my neck back there in Ben Tobin's cabin!"

Jackson was unmoved.

"You must admit, Serge, I'm some shot. I could 'a' killed you dead, but I just wanted t' keel y' over f'r a while."

Quinlin eyed him searchingly.

"You're a cool devil, Jackson, aren't you? I'll bet you know more about this case than any other person."

"Think so, Serge? What if I was t' tell you I knew less'n you about it?"

"I'd say you were a liar."

"Yeah–I s'pose you would, so it's no use me sayin' it. I wish t' hell I *did* know somet'in' about it. Then I'd know where I stand. But his way– What the hell's all the noise about back there?" he asked abruptly, indicating the storeroom.

"A few citizens of Defiance Valley caged up," answered the sergeant. "I'll have to hog-tie you in another room."

"Who's all in there, Serge?" Jackson hastened on.

"I don't know 'em. Only one; Bellamy they call him."

Jackson spat out of the side of his mouth with sudden gusto.

"He is, eh? Thats the guy I'm lookin' f'r. He's gotta talk cold turkey t' me or, by cripes, I'll riddle him clean as a whistle."

With that Jackson clamped his jaw and started for the storeroom. But Quinlin stayed him.

"Say, Jackson, hold on here. Give me that gun. Come on. Hand it over. You're under arrest, too."

Jackson whirled, his crooked mouth agape and his pale eyes wide.

"I tell you, Serge, I want that lousy pup of a Bellamy. He's *gotta* talk."

"Never mind. Personal grievances don't cut any ice with me. I'm in a hurry, so hand over your gun and we'll tie you up."

"You're in a hurry, eh? Well, God 'Lmighty, me, I'm in a hurry, too. What are you here for? You're lookin' f'r Rose, ain'tcha? Well, so'm I. But she ain't t' be found. There's some dirty work goin' on an' if this pup Bellamy don't know a thing 'r two about it I'll be a cock-eyed liar. You can't hog-tie me, Serge. I'm the on'y friend that gal has."

Carlin put in–

"Marie–how about her?"

"Gone, too. That room, Serge. Bellamy . . ."

For a while Quinlin was in a dilemma. Was Jackson lying? Or was he on the square? But time was precious, and he could not afford to consider it at length.

"Well, Jackson," he said, "we'll see Bellamy. But give me your gun."

Jackson handed over the revolver reluctantly.

"Just now you're top-dog, Serge."

Quinlin stood by the door with ready gun while Carlin threw open the bolt and kicked away the improvised jamb.

The sergeant called:

"Only you, Bellamy. And come out with your hands up. The rest stay in there."

Sullen, with hands raised, Bellamy came out. Carlin put home the bolt and then went over and dropped the bar across the front door, thus obviating a surprise attack.

Jackson was saying, "Bellamy, what's goin' on? Where are the gals?"

Bellamy's lips curved into a sneer. "Go on, you traitor!" he snarled.

"I'm no traitor, you damn pup! I'm no friend o' these Mounties by a long shot, but they got the jump on me. I been huntin' high an' low f'r the gals an' can't find 'em. Now where the hell are they, hey?"

"I don't know."

"Liar! You'll never get that gal, Bellamy. She hates you. I'd rather see her dead than wit' you. You'll never get Marie. Rose won't let you an' I won't. I'd cut out your heart. Where are they, dammit? Where's Rose? Where's Marie? Speak, you big bum!"

"Don't call me a bum!" snapped Bellamy.

"Go t' hell. You're twenty-six kinds of a bum an' a couple o' pups besides."

Bellamy strained under this scathing tirade like a dog on a

leash.

Quinlin put in:

"Easy, Jackson. Take it slow. That kind of talk's not getting you anywhere."

He turned to Bellamy.

"Are you going to speak? Tell what you know about the disappearance of the women?"

"I'll say one thing," bit off Bellamy. "I didn't know they had disappeared!"

Jackson lunged forward with–

"Liar!"

But Quinlin pushed him aside.

"Jackson, easy, I say."

"I'll–"

"You'll keep your mouth shut!" Quinlin cut in. "We'll have to take Bellamy's word for it. Haven't time to argue. All right, Bellamy. Back into the storeroom."

Carlin opened the door and said, as Bellamy backed in:

"If you've harmed that girl, Bellamy, Heaven help you!"

And he slammed the door against the big fellow's smirking face.

Quinlin stood pondering over the situation. Finally:

"Jackson, as man to man, who killed Ben Tobin?"

"I don't know, Serge."

"Rose?"

"If she did, d'you think I'd tell you?"

"No; I suppose not."

"But she didn't" Jackson flung at him.

"Then who did?"

"Don't know."

"Trying to shield her, eh? I admire you for that. Then if you believe she didn't, Jackson, can I place you on your honor until we find her? You seem to think she and the girl called Marie are in jeopardy. If you know she's not guilty–"

"Maybe she can't prove it, Serge."

"Can you?"

"No. But I believe her. Stake m' life on her. She knows a lot but she don't talk. But I say she's innocent. An' until we find her, Serge, I'll play square. After that I'm for her an' against you, even t' the point o' killin'."

"Jackson, you're a strange man. No wonder they've named you 'Hell-bent.' But I'll take a chance on you."

They muffled themselves against the storm, buckled on their rackets and stepped out into the swirling clouds of snow. Great windrows were piling up against the cabins. The wind, pounding down from Hudson's Bay, was at the height of all its mad, chaotic fury; whistling, screaming, booming in the big timber with maniacal abandon.

It caught Carlin and bowled him over, and Quinlin, reaching to help him up, felt it cut his face like a cat-o'-nine-tails. Jackson, tough old sourdough, fought for his balance while he drew his parka hood closer about his face and cursed in his throat.

It was a blizzard such as neither he nor Quinlin had seen in all their years of trail pounding. The wind looped and dived downward, drove horizontally, crosswise, up an down, so that no matter how the men tried to hide their faces it found them out and tried to crush them. Holding on to each other, they struggled up against one of the cabins and leaned there.

"S tough!" gasped Jackson.

"Damned tough!" supplemented Quinlin.

Carlin was struggling for his breath.

"If–if she's out in this hell . . ." He choked.

And at the same time Quinlin was thinking of Rose. She could never exist in a storm like this. It would crush a man–a strong man–before very long. He prayed for her–hoped she was safe until they could reach her, if ever they would.

It would be difficult to suppose what was going on inside the rough, tough, hard-bitten old soul who called himself Hell-bent Jackson.

Quinlin was yelling in his ear–

"You've been through all the cabins?"

"Yep. Both gals are gone."

Quinlin hugged the wall, wondering how on God's earth he could find them, when he hadn't the remotest idea of their whereabouts. Here was a blizzard so furious, so destructive, that it cut and battered him even while he stood by the cabin; so dense that he could see scarce six feet into the white cloud. In desperation he called out to Jackson:

"Any cabin in the hills where they might find shelter?"

Jackson's voice came in snatches, tossed about by the wind: "One t' the north . . . three miles east . . . two miles"

And Quinlin yelled back:

"We've got to take a chance. They couldn't travel far in this. They didn't go north, because we had a camp up there and I didn't pass anybody on the way in. We'll take a chance on the one to the east."

XIV

A minute later they were pressing on, fighting up through a country thick with bush and jackpine, so steep in places that they had to haul themselves up by grasping the bushes.

It seemed hours before they won to the summit, and by this time night was full upon them and the storm still in mid-career. They struggled desperately along the backbone of the ridge until suddenly there loomed up before them the squat form of a cabin. They stopped, the three of them, and huddled

together.

They could see near the cabin two sleds almost buried, and here and there were groups of dogs burrowing in the snow.

Jackson said, "Me, Serge, I'll rap on the door. When they see it's me all alone they'll let me in. I'll take a long time gettin' in, an' you an' your pardner, who are gonna hide at the corner, 'll rush around an' break in behind me."

"You're double-crossing 'em, Jackson," Quinlin barked.

"Serge, I'd double-cross any one o' them in a second if I thought it'd save those gals. Let's go."

Jackson zigzagged ahead and Quinlin and the constable hid around the corner of the cabin. Jackson worked up to the door and let his hand thump against it. He waited a moment and struck it again, after the manner of a man who is too feeble to knock vigorously. When the door opened he swayed on his feet, tried to remove his rackets and purposely slumped down. Rough hands reached down and hauled him inside.

At that moment Quinlin and Carlin, having removed their snowshoes, bounded for the door and burst in. In a flash Jackson was on his feet. The man who had let him in snarled out a string of curses in French and English and hacked at him with a knife. Jackson ducked the thrust and cracked the fellow on the jaw with his revolver.

Carlin and the sergeant, covered with snow and ice, charged three men who had risen from comfortable seats by the stove and were now yanking at their weapons.

"In the name of the law–" began Quinlin.

But one fellow had his gun out and was swinging it in a line for the sergeant's chest when Carlin lunged over and cracked the man's wrist with the barrel of his own revolver.

Quinlin ducked a wild shot and from an awkward position put a neat shot through the fellow's forearm, while Carlin rushed the other and bore him crashing against the wall with such force that the man sank down senseless from the impact.

At that instant the door that led into the rear room opened and Pere La Bau, clothed in his somber black robes, stood framed in the doorway with a shocked expression on his face.

"Children!" he exclaimed. "Shooting! Knives! What's the meaning of all this?"

Quinlin was in no mood for gentle words, though he tried his best to be civil.

"Who's in that room, Father?" he asked, crisply.

"Why, no one, Sergeant. I pray, be seated there."

"Father, the law will respect you so long as you respect the law," snapped Quinlin. "Personally, I think you have not aided justice. You have thwarted it several times. It is my wish that you remain quiet and do not take too much advantage of your station. This is time for action–not idle talk. What do you know about the women called Rose and Marie?"

"I know nothing, Sergeant."

"What are you doing up here away from the village with two sleds and two sets of dogs ?"

"I pray, Sergeant, am I answerable to such questions?"

"If your interest is with humanity and justice, yes. I am treating you with as much partiality as I am able. You are wearing my patience rather severely, Father."

Jackson, with an oath, started for the next room.

"There's only one way, Serge, an' that's t' go right in."

Pere La Bau drew himself up to his full height and looked down at Jackson with a cold, agate stare. Jackson made to shove him out of the way, but Quinlin stayed him.

"*Jackson*" he rasped out. "Lay off. I'm handling this. Lay off, I tell you."

Jackson retreated slowly, his hands clenched.

Quinlin said:

"Father, I shall have to look through that room. Please step aside."

The missionary raised a hand.

"Sergeant–"

"Pardon, Father," Quinlin cut in. "I must see that room."

With that he strode forward and Father La Bau, his lips taut and his eyes narrowed, stepped aside.

Quinlin struck a match as he went in with ready revolver. In one corner, clasped in each other's arms, Rose and Marie crouched.

"Thank Heaven!" breathed Quinlin.

Then his mouth went hard and he whirled about and confronted the missionary.

"Again you have tried to thwart the law, Father," he ground out. "Why are these women here?"

Pere La Bau smiled and drew a finger tip across his lower lip.

"I brought them here because there was a disturbance in the Valley," he answered easily.

They locked eyes for a long moment.

Then Quinlin said:

"It would be proper for me to say I believe you," and

turned on his heel.

"Lee," he addressed the constable, "go outside and see what you can do with the dogs. Line up one team. That's all we'll take."

Then to the missionary:

"We are taking one outfit, Father, and we are taking the two women–in the name of the law. Some of these fellows are banged up, so you'd better look after them."

Pere La Bau bowed stiffly, his face an expressionless mask.

Carlin was pulling on his mittens as he moved toward the door, but before he reached it, it whipped open and half-a-dozen men surged in with roaring guns. Carlin hurled himself backward.

Jackson made a leap for the rear room, and Quinlin grabbed the constable by the collar and swung him in behind Jackson. Then he sent three fast shots at the attackers, knocked one over and retreated into the back room, slamming shut the door against an Indian's face and shooting home the bolt.

"Jackson . . . Carlin!" he called.

"Here, Serge," jerked Jackson.

And Carlin was at his side in an instant.

The sergeant said:

"No door in here, eh? But there's one parchment window. Cut it away. Take the women. Clear out. Hurry! They're breaking the door. I'll hold 'em back . . . give you a chance to get a start."

"But–" began Carlin.

And Quinlin rasped:

"No talk. Quick! The window–break it open while there's a chance."

He found a table and put it against the door, adding to this his own braced weight. Jackson was opening the window. Carlin was bundling up the women. The sergeant had both guns out and his shoulder jammed against the table.

Of a sudden he felt warm, dry fur against his face, then two soft, white hands. He looked around and found Rose looking up at him.

"My dear, go–go with Jackson and the constable," he jerked out. "I'll hold them off–"

"But you come, too. They–they'll–"

"Rose, dear, please go. The door is breaking. Get a head start."

"But you–you, Pat," she cried, in a choked voice. Then she clutched him tightly and kissed him many times on the lips.

"Rose, for Lord's sake, go!" broke forth Quinlin. "Jackson–I say, Jackson, will you take Rose here. Hurry, Jackson."

Jackson came over and by sheer force tore her from the sergeant. She screamed. She cried. And as Jackson put her through the window she called:

"Pat, come to me. I love you, Pat. Oh, how I love you!"

XV

And then she was gone, swallowed up by the storm. But the words still rang in the sergeant's ear and kept echoing through his brain. They thrilled him to that point where he felt he could kick any man under the sun.

He realized that he was fighting a losing game at the door. He knew that eventually the door would break down and it would be a case of one man against many. But the women had to have a start, and by keeping the split-log table braced against the door he would hold the attackers back long enough to make that head start possible.

When the door finally broke in he leaped back in the shadows with his shoulders hunched and his guns clapped to his hips. Daggers of flame slashed through the gloom, the explosions indistinguishable from the mad noises of the storm. One of the attackers pitched head-first across the upturned table and another recoiled from the room into the arms of those behind him, his face frozen in a twisted grimace.

The sergeant stood with his back to the wall, a motionless, grim figure with death in each hand.

Presently he heard a voice yelling:

"We want those women, Sergeant, an' we want 'em now. If you don't give 'em up they're gonna get hurt."

For answer Quinlin sent a shot through the doorway. Then he moved toward the window, firing at intervals to keep the doorway clear. He won to the opening, put a leg over the sill and swung out into the storm-tossed night. For a moment he stood by the window and emptied his one gun at the doorway.

At last he turned, crept to the corner of the house and found his snowshoes as he had left them. He strapped them on with difficulty, reloaded his empty revolver and rocked off into the blizzard

XVI

Quinlin kept to the timber, avoiding the open trail. The day was becoming crystal clear and he might be seen by the enemy. Too many lives were in danger for him to take a chance. He passed the little shack where first he had been held prisoner, and some inner instinct prompted him to turn off and look it over. He found it locked from the outside.

But a voice called:

"Dam' yer t' 'ell, if yer don't open the door an' unhook me I'll do murder when I do get free! An' I will, mind!"

Quinlin's heart beat faster. It was the familiar voice of Jerry Plate.

"Jerry! God bless you, Jerry, it's Pat here!" the sergeant yelled.

"Pat! You, Pat! Well, blow that lousy lock off an' onhook me."

It took four shots to shatter the lock, and the sergeant rushed in and found Jerry tied hand and foot and almost freezing to death.

Jerry was saying:

"I feel ashamed, Pat. The beggars tricked me. That big Injun, Long Jim– a sly fox. I'm squattin' b' the fire an' he's squattin' on t' other side an' all of a once he shoots out his foot an' it rains hot coals on me."

"An old trick of his, Jerry," said Quinlin as he helped the old sourdough up. "Played it on me too. And they brought you here and skint out, eh? H-m-m. And then they went to the tradehouse and freed Bellamy and his bunch. Yep. It works out that way."

"What?" asked Jerry.

"No time to explain. Here, chew on this chunk of bannock and limber up your muscles at the same time. No time to lose."

Ten minutes later Jerry was strapping on a pair of dilapidated snowshoes he found in the shack. Side by side he and the sergeant struck out, with Jerry packing the latter's extra revolver. Steadily they worked up into higher country, and toward evening they heard shots somewhere in the uncharted wilderness before them.

"The parties have met," remarked Quinlin. "As I figure, Jerry, there are about twenty-five or thirty cut-throats against two men and two women." With this he gave a brief explanation of the case of Hell-bent Jackson. Then–"The outlook is pretty rotten. Stretch your legs, old boy!"

Reaching the summit, they found the timber stunted but thick, with all about matted windfalls that hindered their progress. They heard more shots–nearer this time. They began going down hill, and then in the growing dusk Quinlin spotted a cabin way down in the bottom of the ravine. Jets of flame were spurting from the window. Men were moving about in the bush down there and shooting at the window.

"The whole gang is there," observed Quinlin.

Jerry spat out tobacco juice and flipped his revolver in the air.

"The show is on, Pat. I'm ripe for anything. Let's horn in."

While the sergeant was intently watching the maneuvers, Jerry lay down on the snow, laid the barrel of his long revolver across his left arm and fired the first shot One of the dark figures seemed to sit down peacefully enough, but the next moment he rolled over sidewise. There was a stir in the ranks of the outlaws.

At that instant a burst of flame came from the cabin and another figure pitched to the snow. Jerry spat, took careful aim and let go another slug. It hit its mark and put another fellow out of business.

"Hate t' go wastin' shots," the old sourdough drawled.

A volley was returned but all the shots went wild.

"Now," suggested Quinlin, "let's change our position."

Cautiously, on hands and knees, they continued working in an arc until they reached a point on the outlaw's flank. This main party was again creeping up on the cabin and for a few minutes there was a warm exchange of shots between it and the defenders of the cabin.

Quinlin and Jerry joined in and the attack from this new quarter was so unexpected that three of the outlaws went down before the others realized the situation and flung themselves back in mad haste.

The group that had started out in search of Jerry and the sergeant found them out by the gun flashes and swooped down in that direction. Quinlin heard them coming, crouched lower in the bush and picked the leader off as he leaped over a fallen tree. Jerry followed up with two fast shots that caught the next fellow in the same act and dropped him like a log.

Some in the main party were now directing shots in the sergeant's direction, and this volley drove him and Jerry farther down into the ravine while they still kept picking off the fellows in the other group, until but two remained out of six. These two gave up the cause and dashed back to the main attack.

"Hit?" Quinlin flung over his shoulder at Jerry as he reloaded his rifle.

"One bounced off m' head an' I feel a stingin' in m' left calf. On'y flesh cuts though. You hit?"

"Scratched on the right thigh; that's all."

The next move showed that neither of them was lacking in nerve. Side by side they began forcing the fight, advancing on the outlaws and keeping up a steady fire as they crawled ahead under the bushes, with lead whining past their ears and kicking up the snow in their faces. Those in the cabin increased their fire, too, and the night was wild with gunfire and yells.

The outlaws began to break and scatter, and in their mad confusion they afforded easy targets. Through a rift in the foliage Quinlin caught sight of a tall man in a long fur coat. He paused with his finger on the trigger, for under the white moonlight he recognized Pere La Bau, and the missionary had a smoking rifle in his hands. The next instant he was lost to sight.

Then the cabin door opened and Carlin and Hell-bent Jackson burst out in pursuit. Quinlin and Jerry straightened up and went along with great leaps. The four joined, shouted greetings and proceeded after the fleeing outlaws.

Jerry was the first to catch up with the rear guard and Hell-bent Jackson was a few steps behind him. Quinlin and Carlin came up on either side and for a moment there was some fast and furious gun talk. Jackson went down, cursed at the top of his voice and heaved up to his feet again.

Carlin and Bellamy were at each other with clubbed rifles, and Jerry and the Indian Long Jim had thrown aside their guns and were doing some clever knife work. Quinlin had caught sight of Pere La Bau again and was running him down. The missionary suddenly stopped, whirled and fired point-blank. The slug whanged by the sergeant's face and clipped off part of his beard. The next moment he was upon the missionary and knocked aside his gun as it boomed a second time.

XVII

"Drop that gun!" snarled the sergeant.

Quinlin ducked a hard-driven right and drove two fast jolts to the man's abdomen. He received a glancing blow on the cheek that almost snapped his head off, caught a follow-up square on the other cheek and ground his teeth in pain. For a moment he lashed out wildly until his head cleared then lurched back, stopped abruptly and met the next rush without moving an inch.

He broke under the man's guard and beat a tattoo on his ribs until the latter clinched and then hurled himself away. Quinlin went after him and knocked his head back and forth with two lefts and two rights that hit square on all tries. Then they closed, crashed to the snow and rolled down the incline to where Carlin was telling Bellamy to get up so that he could knock him down again. By some trick of his trade as an all-around brawler, Jerry had disarmed the Indian and was backing him against a tree. Jackson sat on a stump, doubled up and groaning.

Quinlin and La Bau brought up with a thud against a tree and as they struggled to their feet the sergeant freed his right and whipped it to La Bau's jaw with such steam behind it that the latter's head snapped back, cracked against the tree and the man dropped without a sound;

Bellamy was out. Carlin was snapping handcuffs on Long

Jim's wrists.

"Pat, I just knew you'd come," he cried. "We were in a rummy situation down there. The rest of the gang cleared out, but we'd better get down to the cabin. Jerry's cut up a bit and Jackson says he's passing out. Lord, that man is a fighter and a reckless devil."

"How are the women?" Quinlin asked.

"Shaken up, Pat. Rose has been calling us all kinds of cowards for letting you stay to give us a start. And Marie–"

"I can guess the rest, Lee," cut in Quinlin jocularly. "But let's trot these birds down there."

Carlin walked Long Jim down at the point of his gun and Jerry unceremoniously grabbed La Bau and Bellamy by the feet and hauled them along sled-fashion. Quinlin picked up the broken, shattered man who called himself Hell-bent Jackson.

"Pretty bad, Jackson?" he asked as he carried him down.

"Yeah, S-serge. Bound out, I reck- reckon. Can't get . . . m' dam breath. Figure I'm carryin' eight slugs now, not– not countin' 'em as went clean t'rough. Purty–purty tough f'r a man t' carry eight slugs, Serge . . . not countin' 'em as went clean t'rough. y'understand."

"You'll be all right," Quinlin said, and he knew in his own heart he was lying.

"No, Serge, M' innards is gittin' all mixed up wit' each other. C'n feel it. An', Serge, Rose loves you, she does. You . . . must believe her . . . Serge."

When they reached the cabin Quinlin laid Jackson tenderly on a bed of wolf skins. Rose was at his elbow, her eyes big and moist.

"Pat, you–you won through," she half whispered.

Bellamy and La Bau had come back to consciousness. Carlin stood over them with his gun while Jerry made life miserable for the Indian Long Jim. Quinlin left Rose and confronted the two white men.

"One of you two is the ringleader–the Master," he said crisply. "Which one?"

Bellamy moistened his lips and looked at La Bau. The latter drew a finger tip across his lower lip meditatively and regarded the sergeant obliquely.

"Well," he began, "I am called The Master."

"You–a missionary–a Jesuit!" exclaimed Quinlin.

La Bau chuckled cynically.

"Merely for effect–the robes and that stuff. I never dealt directly with my men. Bellamy, here, was my lieutenant. He gave out orders and said they were from The Master. None of the men really knew who The Master was, except Bellamy, Long Jim and the women. And the role of missionary? Merely a whim–and then it brought in contributions from transient trappers for a proposed mission house– which never was to be built."

"You cur!" rasped out the sergeant; then leaned closer and asked, "And what do you know about the killing of Ben Tobin?"

La Bau gave a hollow chuckle and shook his head negatively.

"He lies!" cut in Rose.

"Eh?" jerked Quinlin.

"He lies!" she repeated. "He engineered the whole thing. One night a man came in from the outside to escape the law. He was a professional killer and he told a story about a man named Mr. Tobin who kept a lot of money in his cabin. Said he was going to get Mr. Tobin after a while.

Bellamy pumped him, found out where the old man lived and then a few nights later one of the Indians put the informer out of the way.

"La Bau wanted me to go and find out just where Mr. Tobin hid the money. I refused, even though he called himself my foster father. Then he said he'd give Marie to Bellamy if I didn't do as he told me.

"Marie is the daughter of a Doctor Wallace who came through here twelve years back with his wife in an effort to teach the Indians sanitary conditions. They died themselves during that same winter and Marie was left with an Indian woman who later became La Bau's servant.

"I love Marie with all my heart, so to save her from Bellamy, whom she despised, I set out with Long Jim. La Bau never let me go far alone, for fear I'd run away, and he always kept Marie under watch, for he must have known I wouldn't leave her. Hence Long Jim's company.

"I had no plans. But I was bound to save Marie at all costs. I found the old man home, and when he saw me I thought he'd gone mad. He got a picture from a wallet and studied it and me. He asked me who I was. I said just Rose. Then he threw his arms around me and cried, 'Oh, God, I've found my dear one!' I had found my father! He said La Bau had run off with my mother when she was eighteen and I was two. I never knew. Mother died young. La Bau never told me.

"I wanted to stay with my father. He wanted me to stay. But there was Marie to think of. I said I had to go back. I told him why they had sent me and he told me where the money was hidden, and I swore I'd never tell.

"Then Long Jim, who had been waiting outside, came in and I told him to get out. He laughed and came forward toward father and I drew my knife–the only weapon I had at the moment–and threatened him with it. He wrested it from me, and as father ran to the wall for his rifle Long Jim flung the knife and it caught father in the back."

The sergeant raised his hand and turned to the Indian.

"Do you hear that, Long Jim?"

An animal snarl grated in the Indian's throat and his eyes stared hard at the floor.

Rose went on–

"I can't understand how I ever pulled the knife out, but I did and dragged father to the bunk. He died feeling my hair, which he said is like my mother's. Long Jim was hunting high and low for the money. He couldn't find it and he attacked me. I hit him with a stool and ran out.

"I ran back with a gun, but he had barred the door. Then I drove off and left him probably hunting for the money. I wanted to kill him, but after thinking a while I knew it would put La Bau in a rage and he would give Marie to Bellamy. I resolved not to let on that I had found my father."

Hell-bent Jackson was struggling for words.

"Serge, she didn't even–even tell me . . . best friend. I'd tagged behind Rose an' Jim. Didn't trust that Injun. But I busted. . . snowshoe . . . stopped t' fix it . . . they got away ahead. Met Rose comin' back alone all skeered . . . asked her . . . wouldn't tell. So I goes an' looks f 'r m'self. An' I finds a Mounty feedin' his dogs an' hears noise in the cabin.

"I scrapes a bit o' snow off the winder an' sees another Mounty an' he's holdin' up a knife I knew belonged to–to Rose . . . there. So I sneaks around, leans over an' cracks Carlin on the bean wit' m' rifle, takes a careful shot at the serge an' puts him t' sleep.... Knife on the table.... Oh, Serge, I can't talk no more. S'long, Serge. S'long, Rose . . . like yer hair . . . all gold...."

XVIII

Lee," said Quinlin to the constable, "it fits in with your story. Hard man, Jackson, and he's just died hard. Twelve wounds."

He turned back to Rose.

"But, dear girl, why didn't you reveal all this at first?"

"I couldn't. I didn't dare. Long Jim warned me on the trail when he brought you into my camp. He said I was to say nothing–said I should remember Marie was a pawn in The Master's hand and her fate rested on my silence.

"It was hard to give in to the killer of my father. But there was Marie. I tried to be patient, resolving that some day he and La Bau would pay. And I knew that some day La Bau would want me. He was just holding off, playing with me like a cat. You–you can't imagine . . .!"

"I can," murmured Quinlin in a hushed voice; and then he turned on La Bau. "You heard all of that. La Bau. God help you at the hands of a jury! And Long Jim didn't find the money–eh?–after killing old Tobin."

"Evidently, no," purred La Bau. "There is, Sergeant, no blood on my hands. I did not order Long Jim to kill Tobin. I–"

A horrible snarl rattled from the Indian's throat. He whirled on The Master, and, though manacled, clamped his grotesque hands around La Bau's throat and bore him back against the floor.

"Liar!" he roared. "You tell me kill Tobin if him show fight."

Quinlin and Carlin flung themselves upon the Indian and tried to tear him loose. But Long Jim was raving mad, and the blows they struck seemed only to increase his fury. Finally his effort slowed down and at last he sank down on The Master with a chilling rattle in his throat.

Quinlin rolled him off and found a knife sticking in his chest. The hilt was still grasped in La Bau's dead hand. He had pressed it up into the Indian even while the latter was choking him to death.

"Well," mused Quinlin, "so Long Jim killed Tobin. It took us an awful long time to find it out."

"It was kinder roundabout," put in Jerry. "But then it led t' the findin' o' Defiance Valley. Pat, they ought t' make you 'n inspector f'r this haul. Bellamy, here, is still alive, an' we'll see he stays that way. It'll make a better case in court if you got at least one o' the ringleaders."

When they drove back into Defiance Valley a day later the place was deserted. The cabin doors swung open in the wind and the cabins themselves were empty and bare. The big trade house had been cleaned of everything but the stove and the rough furniture.

Trails led away in all directions, made by those who had fled the country and taken with them as much as they could carry. Not even a dog remained.

Defiance Valley was dead. The Master was dead. Long Jim and many others were dead. And so was Hell-bent Jackson, who died fighting for a woman who once had nursed him through the scurvy.

Quinlin and Rose were standing in front of the trade house.

Quinlin was saying, "And not even Jackson knew that La Bau was not a Jesuit missionary but in reality The Master?"

"No, Pat. Jackson often told me he hailed from the States, where he had done a bit of killing. And he had been in the Klondike. He served under Bellamy and the unknown Master like the rest of them, but he always took it upon himself to watch over me. Bellamy used to plead with me to get Marie to live with him, and that night you came be actually attacked me because I refused, as usual."

"Yes, Rose, under the rough Jackson was a knight. He believed you in spite of all the evidence against you. And I–I didn't, Rose."

"It's the way of the Scarlet, Pat. You would have broken

all its grand traditions by doing otherwise. And I love you for it–and for your courage and for you, Pat."

"I loved you, my Rose, from the first. Was always thinking about you–your eyes–your kiss–your golden hair."

"Oh, Pat–!"

"And, Rose darling, when my term is up this year we'll go down into the Shamattawa country and establish a trading post. 'Tis a great country, Rose; strong woods, much trade, and not so far from God's Lake, where each year there is the greatest Christmas celebration on the frontier. And, Rose, you'll be loving me always?"

"Always, Pat," she whispered and nestled in his arms

Had they looked around the corner they would have seen Carlin and Marie in each other's arms.

While inside the trade house the redoubtable Jerry Plate chewed tobacco and spat copiously into the wood-box, explaining to the morose Bellamy the danger of playing with dynamite, fire, and men who wear scarlet coats.

"'S bad business, mister. Them fellers is harder t' kill 'an anyt'ing I know. O' course, if you do kill one, why, your goose is cooked f'r sure. Might just as well walk t' the nearest post an' give up. Me, I'd a sight ruther fool around wit' dynamite 'an a Mounty."

"Oh, go t' hell!" exploded Bellamy.

"Not yet. I'm goin' right wit' Sergeant Pat. I'm goin' t' start buildin' his tradin' post in the Shamattawa country, so's him an' the wife–which she'll be 'fore long–c'n move right in when Patrick leaves the Force."

He got up, went to the door and looked out.

"H'm. Looks like snow. Well, let 'er come. We're all through here, and a damn fine job it is, too."

His gaze rested a moment on Quinlin and Rose, and he turned back into the trading house with a broad grin on his seamed face.

"Yessir," he addressed the scowling Bellamy. "It sure do look like a wedding."

On the way out the sergeant stopped at the cabin in which old Ben Tobin had died. He lowered the frozen body from the tree and placed it on the sled. Rose wanted to be near her father's grave. And while Quinlin did this, Rose pried out one of the great stones that formed the fireplace and from the hole pulled a moosehide pouch packed with her father's hoarded wealth. It was his dying wish that she should take it.

Today, if you will go to the end of steel on the Hudson's Bay Road, and from there work southeastward by river, lake and portage, you will come to a river that the Indians call Shamattawa. It is a country of majestic pine and spruce, where in the summer the flowers bloom in great profusion and the star-gemmed nights are cool and haunting.

Near the river you may come upon a large trading station and on the main building see a sign bearing the legend:

SHAMATTAWA TRADING
COMPANY, LTD,
QUINLIN, CARLIN & PLATE